Tevye's Daughters

SHOLOM ALEICHEM

Tevye's Daughters

Translated by

FRANCES BUTWIN

CROWN PUBLISHERS, INC., NEW YORK

PRINTED IN THE UNITED STATES OF AMERICA
D E F G H

For My Parents

Gershon and Sonia Mazo

Contents

CONTENTS

Introduction

"The Holy One, blessed be He," quotes Tevye the Dairyman, *"wished to grant merit to Israel"*; and in his own fashion he interprets this to mean: The Lord wanted to be good to Tevye, so He blessed him with seven daughters. And what kind of daughters? Meek, ugly, sickly creatures? No! Beauties—everyone of them—fine, well-grown girls, charming and good-tempered, healthy and high-spirited—like young pine trees! But that was as far as the Lord went in His bounty. He granted to Tevye neither money nor luck. And what good are beautiful and gifted daughters if you have neither money nor luck to go along with them? "If they had been ill-tempered and ugly as scarecrows," remarks Tevye ruefully, "it would have been better for them and certainly healthier for me." But then there would have been no Tevye the Dairyman as we know him, no chronicle of Tevye's daughters, as Sholom Aleichem planned and developed it, for the honor and enrichment of Yiddish literature.

That Sholom Aleichem planned the stories of Tevye's daughters as a single chronicle, there can be no doubt. A single theme runs through them all, and the style is identical. But he wrote each one as a separate narrative, with Tevye himself doing the narrating, addressing himself to Sholom Aleichem whom he meets from time to time over a period of fifteen to twenty years—sometimes in the woods near Boiberik, sometimes in Boiberik or on a train to Yehupetz. Each story has the same form; it is enclosed in a capsule, very much like a typical

Yiddish letter. Tevye usually begins by greeting his old friend Sholom Aleichem, whom he has not seen for a long time; he goes on to recapitulate something of what went on before, picks up his story from there, and ends finally with farewells and good wishes, and a promise of more to come at some future meeting. This form is peculiarly suited to Tevye's rambling and informal style of narrative, and because we wished to preserve it and also to indicate the lapse of time between the stories, or chapters, we scattered them through the book instead of presenting them in a solid block. And to make the book complete we have reprinted "Modern Children" and "Hodel" from *The Old Country.*

In spite of the fact that these stories are separated by intervals of time and that each one presents a complete incident with its own climax and denouement, taken together they have the unity of a novel. On the surface, this novel is a family chronicle whose theme is the timeless and never-resolved conflict between the younger and older generations. Examined more closely, *Tevye's Daughters* is something more than a family saga. It is a story of social conflict laid at a precise turn of history—the last days of Tsarist Russia. With the accession of Nicholas II, the government of the Tsars had reached its final peak of intrigue and corruption. This was the last stage in its battle for survival. There was wide political unrest throughout the country, culminating in the revolutionary struggle of 1905-6, whose failure was followed by counter-revolution and a general disillusionment among the masses of people.

The political events of those years are reflected both directly and indirectly in the tragedies of Tevye's daughters. And we must also remember that along with the political conflict, which made its direct impact on the Jews in the form of economic and civic oppression and bloody pogroms, went the ferment within Jewry itself—the breaking up of old paternalistic molds, the influx of new movements: Zionism, the *Haskalah,* the Bund, the spread of secular learning and the revolt against narrow religious sectarianism. In the midst of this vortex, Tevye and his wife Golde represent the comparatively peaceful, patriarchal way of life; while their daughters are acted upon by, and in turn react violently to, the sweeping new currents.

But Tevye himself is not a static figure either. He is deeply religious, but he is no fanatic. He is aware of the changes taking place about him and unconsciously absorbs the spirit of those changes. For Tevye the Dairyman, whose fame as a dealer in milk and butter and cheese has spread like the sound of the *shofar* over the world, can't avoid rubbing elbows with the world. On his rounds with his horse and wagon he has met and had dealings (much to his sorrow) with Menachem-Mendel the *luftmensch,* the entrepreneur, who "deals in things you can't put your hands on," and makes and loses fortunes in less time than it takes Tevye to recite *Shma Yisroel.* He has met and talked with the young students, the sons of shoemakers and tailors, who have turned their backs on the study of the *Torah* and live six in a garret and feast on black bread and herring in order to attend the university. He has had dealings with the pompous *negidim* of Yehupetz who spend their summers in their *datchas* in Boiberik, and whose wives have expensive stomach ailments and travel abroad for cures. He has talked with men who understand a *medresh* and with men who don't know the difference between a *medresh* and a piece of horseflesh.

Tevye has been shaken from his moorings. He is a man in conflict with himself, he is not too sure that his way is always the best; and so we find him aiding and abetting his daughters in spite of his better, that is, more instinctive, judgment.

In "Modern Children," Tevye's oldest daughter Tzeitl defies the convention of "arranged marriages." Her mother wants her to marry the rich widower, Lazer-Wolf the Butcher. Tevye's wife Golde is, after all, nothing but a woman. Woman-like she is a realist; she sees only what's in front of her and what she sees she doesn't like. Poverty, illness, and struggle have always been her lot. She wants something better for her daughters. To her "something better" means a pantry full of good food, a fur-lined cloak for weekdays and a cloak with a ruffle for Saturdays, shoes and stockings, linen and bedding—in short, a rich husband like Lazer-Wolf the Butcher. Tevye has no objection to these things either. He doesn't hold with the newfangled notion of romantic love; but when he is confronted with it, he weakens. We find him, against his better judgment, helping

Tzeitl marry the poor tailor Motel Kamzoil from Anatevka. "That's modern children for you," says Tevye. "You sacrifice yourself for them, you slave for them day and night—and what do you get out of it?" But in his heart he is proud of his modern children, he is even proud of their defiance of him.

Hodel, the second of Tevye's daughters, has been infected with revolution. She is in love with Pertschik, the revolutionary young student, the son of the cigarette-maker. Again Tevye helps his daughter against his better judgment. He goes so far as to fabricate a story about a rich aunt and an inheritance to explain to Golde why Pertschik has to leave right after the hasty marriage ceremony. Driving Hodel and her brand-new husband to the station in his wagon, Tevye marvels at the young couple's apparent lack of emotion. But he reserves judgment. Tevye is not an old woman, he can wait and see. He waits, and he sees Hodel follow her husband to his prison in exile. Though his heart is broken at parting from her, and though he lays no claim to understanding her motives, in a curious way he is proud of her too.

But with his third daughter, Chava, Tevye comes to real grief. Chava is in love with a gentile, the peasant Fyedka Galagan, who is "another Gorky." Now Tevye might condone modern love, he might even shrug his shoulders at revolution with its crazy nonsense of "what's yours is mine and what's mine is yours," but he will never condone apostasy. When Chava marries her Fyedka and goes over to the gentiles, she severs herself completely from her family. She forfeits all the "mercy" that Tevye might have for the weaknesses of his children. For the essence of Tevye is his religion, it is his chief *raison d'être,* the condition of his survival; and if he condoned his daughter's apostasy, he would become something very much less than Tevye. . . .

The tragedy of Schprintze is of a different sort. Schprintze has fallen in love with a rich young man, she has tried to step out of her class. Or rather she has tried to ignore the division of class. Aarontchik is a good man, she tells her father, and he is surrounded by vulgar people who know nothing but money and money and money. But Tevye is not one to scorn "vulgar money." For the first time since he lost his fortune in the deal with Menachem-Mendel he permits himself to spin a dream of wealth. . . . "Perhaps God has willed it that through this quiet little Schprintze you should be rewarded for all the pain and suffering you have undergone until now and enjoy a pleasant and restful old age? Why not? Won't the honor sit well on you?" But he knows all along that he is deceiving himself, and he tries his best to talk Schprintze out of her infatuation. For in spite of Kishinevs and Constitutions, pogroms and revolutions, in spite of all the edicts of the Tsar's ministers to whom a *Zhyd* is a *Zhyd* whether he resides in a palace in Odessa or is squeezed with a family of ten into a hut in Kasrilevka—in spite of all this, the Jews themselves are as rigidly as ever divided into the rich and poor, the haves and have-nots, "those who walk on foot and those who ride on horseback." As the widow's brother, he of the barrel shape and the thick gold chain puts it, "You are an intelligent person, how could you permit this, that Tevye the Dairyman, who brings us cheese and butter, should try to marry into *our* family?"

In the story of Beilke, the youngest and most beautiful of Tevye's daughters, the circle swings around again. Here it is Beilke herself, unlike her older sisters, who insists on marrying the rich Padhatzur, who made his pile in the Russo-Japanese war. When Tevye in revulsion against the pretensions and vulgarity of his rich son-in-law tells Beilke that "your sister Hodel would have done differently," she answers him, "I've told you before not to compare me to Hodel. Hodel lived in Hodel's time and Beilke is living in Beilke's time. The distance between the two is as great as from here to Japan." Beilke is the product of disillusionment. She knows very well that Hodel's husband will die in prison unless her Padhatzur, stuffed with money he has made at the expense of the government, will bribe that same government to have Pertschik's sentence lifted. Tevye bows to the inevitable and accepts from his son-in-law a ticket to the Holy Land.

But Tevye never starts out for the Holy Land. More disasters intervene. Even the self-assured Padhatzur who "might have entertained a Rothschild in his home" meets with financial failure, and has to flee to America "where all unhappy souls go." And the wave of pogroms which has engulfed the big cities finally overtakes Tevye who was sure "they would never reach him." Tevye's family from time immemorial had lived in a village, and when the May Laws of 1882 drove the Jews out of the villages, denied them the right to own land, and herded them together in the little towns of the Jewish Pale, Tevye's family was left untouched. But now in the days of Mendel Beiliss, when the whole world "went backwards," in the days just preceding the First World War, Tevye was finally "reached." He was politely told to "Get thee out." He was ordered to leave his "fatherland," as he ironically calls it. But even in this extremity, Tevye savored a small triumph, more bitter than sweet, but still a triumph. His daughter Chava, whom he had chosen to count as dead, repents and comes back to her father and to her God. And so at the last Tevye stands vindicated. The religion he clung to so tenaciously through all his reversals of fortune is all that is left to him. "Tell our friends not to worry," he tells Sholom Aleichem at the final parting. "Our ancient God still lives."

To understand Tevye at all we must first understand his peculiar relation to God. To Tevye, God is not a remote Deity to whom one prays on Sabbaths and High Holy Days or in times of great trouble. He is not the Lawgiver to whom Moses spoke amidst thunder and lightning on Mt. Sinai. Tevye is on much more intimate terms with God. He speaks to Him on weekdays, as well as on the Sabbath, indoors and outdoors and in all kinds of weather, just as surely as his forefathers, Abraham, Isaac and Jacob, spoke with God indoors and outdoors and in all kinds of weather. "You do not ask questions of God," says Tevye, but he persists in asking questions at all times. He never lets God alone. What are we and what is our life? What is this world and what is the next world? Why do you always pick on Tevye to do Thy will? Why don't you play with someone else for a change, a Brodsky or a Rothschild? What is the meaning of Jew and non-Jew? What and why and once more why and wherefore? If Tevye's daughters are at war with society, Tevye himself wages his own war against God and man, and since he believes men's actions to be chiefly inspired by God, God is the chief Adversary.

Tevye gives battle with the only weapon he has at his disposal—the Holy Word. He fights God with God's own weapons and on God's own ground. For Tevye considers himself a man of learning, and in his time and place learning meant one thing—the knowledge of the *Torah* and its application to daily life. He would sooner quote Scriptures than eat, and every mouthful he eats is accompanied by a quotation. As Golde says bitterly, "You drum my head full of quotations and you've done your duty by your children." Says Tevye, "I have to answer even this with a quotation." To Tevye, talk is not a substitute for action. It is the only wholly satisfying action he knows.

Though Sholom Aleichem was a humorist and Tevye is his most famous character, Tevye is not funny. Nearly everything that happens to him and his daughters is tragic. His humor lies in his evaluation of what happens to him, in what he says and the way he says it. In the fact that he misquotes more often than he quotes, and that usually his interpretation of what he is quoting is completely cockeyed, lies his all-pervading charm to the Yiddish reader. No wonder Sholom Aleichem's audiences used to roll in the aisles with laughter. The juxtaposition of a lofty phrase in Hebrew or Aramaic with a homely Yiddish phrase which is supposed to explain it but has no bearing on it whatever—that is the gist of Tevye's humor. Tevye, of course, has no idea that he is funny. He continues to quote in Hebrew, in Russian, in whatever comes in handy. It is this play on language that is so difficult to convey successfully in translation. Whenever possible I used the archaic or Biblical phraseology for the Hebrew quotations and simple idiomatic English for the Yiddish; and to indicate the former I used italics—separated by a dash from the latter.

For example: When Tevye goes to see the priest and the priest's dogs jump on him, he says, "I gave them this quotation to chew on—*'Lo yechratz ḳelev l'shonoh.'*" Which means literally, "Not a dog shall bark," and comes from Exodus, Chapter 11, Verse 7: "But against any of the children of Israel not a dog shall bark." Tevye follows this with the Russian proverb: *"Nehai sobaḳa daram nie breshe,"* and interprets the whole thing to mean, "Don't let a dog bark for nothing."

Tevye likes to use the same quotation over and over, putting it to a different use each time. Speaking of the Jews who start running from town to town when there is a rumor of a pogrom, he says,

"They journeyed and they encamped, they encamped and they journeyed" (referring of course to the Israelites wandering in the desert), and interprets this to mean, "You come to me and I will come to you." Again he assures Beilke that he will come back from Palestine. *"They journeyed and they encamped—Tuda i nazad*—I will go and I will return."

A number of times when Tevye wants to indicate that he is through and no more need be said on the subject he says impressively, *"Here ends the lesson for the Sabbath before Passover."* He is simply repeating a phrase in the prayerbook which is the same as saying The End or Period.

Tevye is never at a loss for a quotation. When nothing apt occurs to him he reaches into his memory and snatches at the first thing that he can lay his hands on. Describing a guest of Padhatzur's who ate an enormous amount of food he says, *"Sh'loshaw she'ochlu,"* which means literally, "Three who have eaten," and comes from the passage in *Perek:* ". . . the three who have eaten and not a word of *Torah* passed between them are as those who have eaten an idolatrous sacrifice." He blithely interprets this to mean, "He ate enough for three."

Tevye is unique among Sholom Aleichem's characters. No other character displays his peculiar blend of innocence and shrewdness, kindliness and irony, weakness and toughness. He is less of a type and more of a personality than any of the others, but Tevye did not spring full-grown from a desert, he was not "God's only son." Though he lived in the country, and not in one of the little towns where the Jews were packed together "as tightly as herring in a barrel," Tevye was brother and uncle and cousin to the people of Kasrilevka and Anatevka and Mazapevka and even of Yehupetz and Odessa. He was related to Menachem-Mendel by marriage and no doubt to half of Kasrilevka as well. He knew the Benjamin Lastechkys, the Samuel Fingerhuts, the fish peddlers and tinmen, the poultrywomen and traveling salesmen, the Zaidels and the Reb Yozifels. It isn't stretching the point too far to consider them all as minor characters in the drama of Tevye and his daughters, and their stories as a background for the central action.

This background is as rich and varied as Sholom Aleichem's

genius. There is the robust comedy of the Railway Stories, the puckish humor of Motel the Orphan in "What Will Become of Me," the lyric mood of "Another Page from the Song of Songs." Though they are in no sense "proletarian" stories, there is a social awareness in "The Passover Expropriation," "The Littlest of Kings," and "An Easy Fast," which illustrates and further extends the social conflict in *Tevye's Daughters*. Taken together, all of these stories are a part of the life, forever vanished, which Sholom Aleichem reproduced so faithfully, with tenderness, with humor and with sharp penetration, but never with malice or bitterness.

The nearest we come to bitterness in Tevye himself is when he reflects on the ways of the world: "I wasn't worried about God so much. I could come to terms with Him one way or another. What bothered me was people. Why should people be so cruel when they could be so kind? Why should human beings bring suffering to others and to themselves when they could all live together in peace and goodwill?" Tevye contents himself with asking questions. His daughters went a step farther. They challenged the conventions of "cruelty and suffering," they "strained after a new life" and took desperate chances to attain it. Sometimes they won, more often they lost. Their story is as pertinent today as it was when they lived it.

I wish to express thanks to Mike Baker and Dr. David Aelony who helped me over the rough spots of the translation, and especially to Rabbi Norman Frimer who so patiently traced Tevye's quotations and misquotations to their sources.

F. B.

St. Paul, August, 1948

The Bubble Bursts

"THERE are many thoughts in a man's heart." So I believe it is written in the Holy *Torah.* I don't have to translate the passage for you, Mr. Sholom Aleichem. But, speaking in plain Yiddish, there is a saying: "The most obedient horse needs a whip; the cleverest man can use advice." In regard to whom do I say this? I say it in regard to myself, for if I had once had the good sense to go to a friend and tell him such and such, thus and so, this calamity would never have taken place. But how is it said? *"Life and death issue from thine own lips.*—When God sees fit to punish a man he first takes away his good sense."

How many times have I thought to myself: Look, Tevye, you dolt, you are not supposed to be a complete fool. How could you have allowed yourself to be taken in so completely and in such a foolish way? Wouldn't it have been better for you if you had been content with your little dairy business whose fame has spread far and wide, everywhere from Boiberik to Yehupetz? How sweet and pleasant it would have been if your little hoard still lay in its box, buried deep where not a soul could see or know. For whose business is it whether Tevye has money or not? Was anyone concerned with Tevye when he lay buried nine feet deep, wrapped in his poverty like a dead man in his shroud? Did the world care when he starved three times a day together with his wife and children?

But lo and behold! When God turned his countenance on Tevye and caused him to prosper all at once, so that at last he was beginning to arrive somewhere, beginning to save up a *ruble* now and then, the world suddenly became aware of his presence, and overnight, mind you, plain Tevye became Reb Tevye, nothing less. Suddenly out of nowhere a multitude of friends sprang up. As it is written: *"He is beloved by everyone."* Or, as we put it: "When God gives a dot, the world adds a lot."

Everyone came to me with a different suggestion. This one tells me to open a drygoods store, that one a grocery. Another one says to buy a building—property is a sound investment, it lasts forever. One tells me to invest in wheat, another in timber. Still another suggests auctioneering. "Friends!" I cry. "Brothers! Leave me alone. You've got the wrong man. You must think I'm Brodsky, but I am still very far from being a Brodsky. It is easy to estimate another's wealth. You see something that glitters like gold at a distance. You come close and it's only a brass button."

May no good come to them—I mean those friends of mine, those well-wishers—they cast an evil eye on me. God sent me a relative from somewhere, a distant kinsman of some kind whom I had never seen before. Menachem-Mendel is his name—a gadabout, a wastrel, a faker, a worthless vagabond, may he never stand still in one place. He got hold of me and filled my head with dreams and fantasies, things that had never been on land or sea. You will ask me: *"Wherefore did it come to pass?"* How did I ever get together with Menachem-Mendel? And I will answer in the words of the *Hagadah: "For we were slaves."* It was fated, that's all. Listen to my story.

I arrived in Yehupetz in early winter, with my choicest merchandise —over twenty pounds of butter fresh from Butterland and several pails of cheese. I had salted away everything I had, you understand, didn't leave a smidgen for myself, not as much as a medicine spoon would hold. I didn't even have the time to visit all of my regular customers, the summer people of Boiberik, who await my coming as a good Jew waits for the coming of the Messiah. For say what you will, there isn't a merchant in Yehupetz who can produce a piece of goods that comes up to mine. I don't have to tell you this. As the prophet says: *"Let another praise thee.*—Good merchandise speaks for itself."

Well, I sold out everything to the last crumb, threw a bundle of hay to my horse and went for a walk around the town. *"Man is born of dust and to dust he returneth."* After all, I am only human. I want to see something of the world, breathe some fresh air, take a look at the wonders Yehupetz displays behind glass windows, as though to say: "Use your eyes all you want, but with your hands—away!"

Standing in front of a large window filled with seven and a half *ruble* gold pieces, with piles of silver *rubles,* and stacks of paper money of all kinds, I think to myself: God in Heaven! If I had only a tenth of what all of this is worth! What more could I ask of God and who would be my equal? First of all, I would marry off my oldest daughter, give her a suitable dowry and still have enough left over for wedding expenses, gifts, and clothing for the bride. Then I would sell my horse and wagon and my cows and move into town. I would buy myself a Synagogue seat by the Eastern Wall, hang strings of pearls around my wife's neck, and hand out charity like the richest householders. I would see to it that the Synagogue got a new roof instead of standing as it does now, practically roofless, ready to cave in any minute. I would open a school for the children and build a hospital such as they have in other towns so that the town's poor and sick wouldn't have to lie underfoot in the Synagogue. And I would get rid of Yankel Sheigetz, as president of the Burial Society. There's been enough guzzling of brandy and chicken livers at public expense!

"Sholom aleichem, Reb Tevye," I hear a voice right in back of me. I turn around and take a look. I could swear I have seen this man somewhere before.

"Aleichem sholom," I answer. "And where do you hail from?"

"Where do I hail from? From Kasrilevka," he says. "I am a relative of yours. That is, your wife Golde is my second cousin once removed."

"Hold on!" I say. "Aren't you Boruch-Hersh Leah-Dvoshe's son-in-law?"

"You've hit the nail right on the head," he says. "I am Boruch-Hersh Leah-Dvoshe's son-in-law and my wife is Sheina Sheindel Boruch-Hersh Leah-Dvoshe's daughter. Now do you know who I am?"

"Wait," I say. "Your mother-in-law's grandmother Sarah-Yenta and my wife's aunt, Fruma-Zlata, were, I believe, first cousins, and if I am not mistaken you are the middle son-in-law of Boruch-Hersh Leah-

Dvoshe's. But I forget what they call you. Your name has flown right out of my head. Tell me, what is your name?"

"My name," he says, "is Menachem-Mendel Boruch-Hersh Leah-Dvoshe's. That's what they call me at home, in Kasrilevka."

"If that's the case," I say, "my dear Menachem-Mendel, I really owe you a *sholom aleichem* and a hearty one! Now, tell me, my friend, what are you doing here, and how is your mother-in-law, and your father-in-law? How is your health, and how is business with you?"

"As far as my health," he says, "God be thanked. I am still alive. But business is not so gay."

"It will get better, with God's help," I tell him, stealing a look meanwhile at his shabby coat and the holes in his shoes. "Don't despair, God will come to your aid. Business will get better, no doubt. As the proverb says: *'All is vanity.*—Money is round, it is here today, gone tomorrow.' The main thing is to stay alive and keep hoping. A Jew must never stop hoping. Do we wear ourselves down to a shadow in the meanwhile? That's why we are Jews. How is it said? If you're a soldier you have to smell gunpowder. *'Man is likened to a broken pot.* —The world is nothing but a dream.' Tell me, Menachem-Mendel, how do you happen to be in Yehupetz all of a sudden?"

"What do you mean how do I happen to be in Yehupetz all of a sudden? I've been here no less than a year and a half."

"Oh," said I, "then you belong here. You are living in Yehupetz."

"Sshh" he whispers, looking all about him. "Don't talk so loud, Reb Tevye. I *am* living in Yehupetz, but that's just between you and me."

I stare at him as though he were out of his mind. "You are a fugitive," I ask, "and you hide in the middle of the public square?"

"Don't ask, Reb Tevye. You are apparently not acquainted with the laws and customs of Yehupetz. Listen and I'll explain to you how a man can live here and still not live here." And he began telling me a long tale of woe, of all the trials and tribulations of life in the city of Yehupetz.

When he finished I said to him, "Take my advice, Menachem-Mendel, come along with me to the country for a day and rest your tired bones. You will be a guest at our house, a very welcome guest. My wife will be overjoyed to have you."

Well, I talked him into it. He went with me. We arrive at home. What rejoicing! A guest! And such a guest! A second-cousin-once-removed. After all, blood is thicker than water. My wife starts right in, "What is new in Kasrilevka? How is Uncle Boruch-Hersh? And Aunt Leah-Dvoshe? And Uncle Yossel-Menashe? And Aunt Dobrish? And how are their children? Who has died recently? Who has been married? Who is divorced? Who has given birth? And who is expecting?"

"What do you care about strange weddings and strange circumcisions?" I tell my wife. "Better see to it that we get something to eat. As it is written, *'All who are hungry enter and be fed.*—Nobody likes to dance on an empty stomach.' If you give us a *borsht,* fine. If not, I'll take *knishes* or *kreplach,* pudding or dumplings. *Blintzes* with cheese will suit me too. Make anything you like and the more the better, but do it quickly."

Well, we washed, said grace, and had our meal. *"They ate,"* as Rashi says. "Eat, Menachem-Mendel, eat," I urged him. *"'Forget the world,'* as King David once said. It's a stupid world, and a deceitful one, and health and happiness, as my grandmother Nechama of blessed memory used to say—she was a clever woman and a wise one—health and happiness are only to be found at the table."

Our guest—his hands trembled as he reached for the food, poor fellow—couldn't find enough words in praise of my wife's cooking. He swore by everything holy that he couldn't remember when he had eaten such a dairy supper, such perfect *knishes,* such delicious *vertutin.*

"Stuff and nonsense," I tell him. "You should taste her noodle pudding. Then you would know what heaven on earth can be."

After we had eaten and said our benedictions, we began talking, each one naturally talking of what concerned him most. I talk about my business, he of his. I babble of this, that, and the other, important and unimportant. He tells me stories of Yehupetz and Odessa, of how he had been ten times over, as they say, "on horseback and thrown off the horse." A rich man today, a beggar tomorrow, again a rich man, and once more a pauper. He dealt in something I had never heard of in my life—crazy-sounding things—stocks, bonds, shares-shmares, Maltzev-shmaltzev. The devil alone knew what it was. The sums that he reeled off his tongue were fantastic—ten thousand, twenty thousand, thirty thousand—he threw money around like matches.

"I'll tell you the truth, Menachem-Mendel," I say to him. "Your business sounds very involved, you need brains to understand all of that. But what puzzles me most is this: from what I know of your better half it's a wonder to me that she lets you go traipsing around the world and doesn't come riding after you on a broomstick."

"Don't remind me of that," he says with a deep sigh. "I get enough from her as it is, both hot and cold. If you could see the letters she writes me you would admit that I am a saint to put up with it. But that's a small matter. That's what a wife is for—to bury her husband alive. There are worse things than that. I have also, as you know, a mother-in-law. I don't have to go into detail. You have met her."

"It is with you as it is written: '*The flocks were speckled and streaked and spotted.*—You have a boil on top of a boil and a blister on top of that.' "

"Yes," he says. "You put it very well, Reb Tevye. The boil is bad enough in itself, but the blister—ah, that blister is worse than the boil."

Well, we kept up this palaver until late into the night. My head whirled with his tales of fantastic transactions, of thousands that rose and fell, fabulous fortunes that were won and lost and won again. I tossed all night long dreaming in snatches of Yehupetz and Brodsky, of millions of *rubles,* of Menachem-Mendel and his mother-in-law.

Early the next morning he begins hemming and hawing and finally comes out with it. Here is what he says. "Since the stock market has for a long time been in such a state that money is held in high esteem and goods are held very low, you Tevye have a chance to make yourself a pretty penny. And while you are getting rich you will at the same time be saving my life, you will actually raise me from the dead."

"You talk like a child," I say to him. "You must think I have a big sum of money to invest. Fool, may we both earn before next Passover what I lack to make me a Brodsky."

"I know," he says, "without your telling me. But what makes you think we need big money? If you give me a hundred *rubles* now, I can turn it in three or four days into two hundred or three hundred or six hundred or maybe even into a thousand *rubles.*"

"It may be as it is written: *'The profit is great, but it's far from my pocket.'* Who says I have anything to invest at all? And if there is no hundred *rubles,* it's as Rashi says: *'You came in alone and you go out by yourself.'* Or, as I put it, 'If you plant a stone, up comes a boulder.' "

"Come now," he says to me, "you know you can dig up a hundred *rubles.* With all the money you are earning and with your name . . ."

"A good name is an excellent thing," I tell him. "But what comes of it? I keep my name and Brodsky has the money. If you want to know the truth, my savings come all in all close to a hundred *rubles.* And I have two dozen uses for it. First of all, to marry off my daughter . . ."

"Just what I've been trying to tell you," he breaks in. "When will you have the opportunity to put in a hundred *rubles* and to take out, with God's help, enough to marry off your daughter and to do all the other things besides?"

And he went on with this chant for the next three hours, explaining how he could make three *rubles* out of one and ten out of three. First you bring in one hundred *rubles* somewhere, and you tell them to buy ten pieces of I-forget-what-you-call-it, then you wait a few days until they go up. You send a telegram somewhere else to sell the ten pieces and buy twice as many for the money. Then you wait and they rise again. You shoot off another telegram. You keep doing this until the hundred *rubles* become two hundred, then four hundred, then eight hundred, then sixteen hundred. It's no less than a miracle from God. There are people in Yehupetz, he tells me, who until recently went barefoot—they didn't have a pair of shoes to their names. They worked as errand boys and messengers. Now they own palatial homes, their wives have expensive stomach ailments, they go abroad for cures. They themselves fly all over Yehupetz on rubber wheels, they don't recognize old friends any more.

Well, why should I drag out the story? I caught the fever from him. Who knows, I think to myself, maybe he was sent by my good angel? He tells me that people win fortunes in Yehupetz, ordinary people with not more than five fingers to each hand. Am I any worse than they? I don't believe he is a liar, he couldn't make all these things up out of his own head. Who knows, suppose the wheel turns, and Tevye becomes a somebody in his old age? How much longer can I keep on toiling and moiling from dawn until dark? Day in and day out—the same horse and wagon, night and day the same butter and cheese? It's time, Tevye, that you took a little rest, became a man among men, went into the Synagogue once in a while, turned the pages of a holy book. Why not? And on the other hand, if I lose out, if it should fall buttered side down? But better not think of that.

"What do you say?" I ask my wife. "What do you think of his proposition?"

"What do you want me to say?" she asks. "I know that Menachem-Mendel isn't a nobody who would want to swindle you. He doesn't come from a family of nobodies. He has a very respectable father, and as for his grandfather, he was a real jewel. All his life, even after he became blind, he studied the *Torah*. And Grandmother Tzeitl, may she rest in peace, was no ordinary woman either."

"A fitting parable," I said. "It's like bringing *Hannukah* candles to a *Purim* Feast. We talk about investments and she drags in her Grandmother Tzeitl who used to bake honeycake, and her grandfather who died of drink. That's a woman for you. No wonder King Solomon traveled the world over and didn't find a female with an ounce of brains in her head."

To make a long story short, we decided to form a partnership. I put in my money and Menachem-Mendel, his wits. Whatever God gives, we will divide in half. "Believe me, Reb Tevye," he says, "you won't regret doing business with me. With God's help the money will come pouring in."

"Amen and the same to you," I say. "From your lips into God's ears. There is just one thing I want to know. How does the mountain come to the prophet? You are over there in Yehupetz and I am here in the country; and money, as you know, is a delicate substance. It isn't that I don't trust you, but as Father Abraham says, '*If you sow with tears you shall reap with joy.*—It's better to be safe than sorry.'"

"Oh," he says, "would you rather we drew up a paper? Most willingly."

"Listen," I say to him, "if you want to ruin me, what good will a piece of paper do me? '*The mouse is not the thief.*—It isn't the note that pays, but the man.' If I am hung by one foot I might as well be hung by both."

"Believe me, Reb Tevye," he says to me, "I swear to you on my word of honor, may God be my witness, that I have no tricks up my sleeve. I won't swindle you, but I will deal with you honestly. I will divide our earnings equally with you, share and share alike—a hundred to you, a hundred to me, two hundred to you, two hundred to me, four hundred to you, four hundred to me, a thousand to you, a thousand to me."

So I dug out my little hoard, counted the money over three times, my hands shaking the whole time, called over my wife as a witness, and explained to him again that this was blood-money I was giving him, and sewed it carefully inside his shirt so that no one would rob him of it on the way. He promised that he would write me not later than a week from Saturday and tell me everything in detail. Then we said good-bye with much feeling, embraced like close friends, and he went on his way.

When I was left alone there began to pass in front of my eyes all sorts of visions—visions so sweet that I wished they would never end. I saw a large house with a tin roof right in the middle of town, and inside the house were big rooms and little rooms and pantries full of good things, and around it a yard full of chickens and ducks and geese. I saw the mistress of the house walking around jingling her keys. That was my wife Golde, but what a different Golde from the one I knew. This one had the face and manner of a rich man's wife, with a double chin and a neck hung with pearls. She strutted around like a peacock giving herself airs, and yelling at the servant girls. And here were my daughters dressed in their Sabbath best, lolling around, not lifting a finger for themselves. The house was full of brightness and cheer. Supper was cooking in the oven. The samovar boiled merrily on the table. And at the head of the table sat the master of the house, Tevye himself, in a robe and skullcap, and around him sat the foremost householders of the town, fawning on him. "If you please, Reb Tevye. Pardon me, Reb Tevye."—And so on.

"What fiendish power money has!" I exclaimed.

"Whom are you cursing?" asked Golde.

"Nobody. I was just thinking," I told her. "Daydreams and moonshine . . . Tell me Golde, my love, do you know what sort of merchandise he deals in, that cousin of yours, Menachem-Mendel?"

"What's that?" she said. "Bad luck to my enemies! Here he has spent a day and a night talking with the man, and in the end he comes and asks me, 'What does he deal in?' For God's sake, you made up a contract with him. You are partners."

"Yes," I said. "We made up something, but I don't know what we made up. If my life depended on it, I wouldn't know. There is nothing, you see, that I can get hold of. But one thing has nothing to do with the other. Don't worry, my dear wife. My heart tells me that it is all for the best. We are going to make a lot of money. Say amen to that and go cook supper."

Well, a week goes by and two and three. There is no news from my partner. I am beside myself with worry. It can't be that he has just forgotten to write. He knows quite well how anxiously we are waiting to hear from him. A thought flits through my head. What shall I do if he skims off the cream for himself and tells me that there is no profit? But that, I tell myself, can't be. It just isn't possible. I treat the man like one of my own, so how can he turn around and play a trick like that on me? Then something worse occurs to me. Profit be hanged. Who cares about profit? *"Deliverance and protection will come from the Lord."* May God only keep the capital from harm. I feel a chill go up and down my back. "You old fool," I tell myself. "You idiot. You made your bed, now lie on it. For the hundred *rubles* you could have bought yourself a pair of horses such as your forefathers never had, or exchanged your old wagon for a carriage with springs."

"Tevye, why don't you think of something?" my wife pleads with me.

"What do you mean why don't I think of something? My head is splitting into little pieces from thinking and she asks why don't I think."

"Something must have happened to him on the road," says my wife. "He was attacked by robbers, or else he got sick on the way. Or he may even be dead."

"What will you dream up next, my love?" I ask. "All of a sudden she has to start pulling robbers out of thin air." But to myself I think: "No telling what can happen to a man alone on the road."

"You always imagine the worst," I tell my wife.

"He comes of such a good family," she says. "His mother, may she intercede for us in Heaven, died not long ago, she was still a young woman. He had three sisters. One died as a girl; the other one lived to get married but caught cold coming from the bath and died; and the third one lost her mind after her first child was born, ailed for a long time, and died too."

"To live until we die is our lot," I tell her. "We must all die sometime. A man is compared to a carpenter. A carpenter lives and lives until he dies, and a man lives and lives until he dies."

Well, we decided that I should go to Yehupetz. Quite a bit of merchandise had accumulated in the meanwhile—cheese and butter and cream, all of the best. My wife harnessed the horse and wagon, and *"they journeyed from Sukos"*—as Rashi says. On to Yehupetz!

Naturally my heart was heavy and my thoughts gloomy as I rode through the woods. I began to imagine the worst. Suppose, I think to myself, I arrive and begin to inquire about my man and they tell me, "Menachem-Mendel? Oh, that one? He has done well by himself. He has feathered his own nest. He owns a mansion, rides in his own carriage, you wouldn't recognize him." But just the same I gather up courage and go to his house. "Get out!" they tell me at the door, and shove me aside with their elbows. "Don't push your way, Uncle. We don't allow that."

"I am his relative," I tell them. "He is my wife's second cousin once removed."

"Mazl-tov," they tell me. "We are overjoyed to hear it. But just the same it won't hurt you to wait a little at the door."

It occurs to me that I should slip the doorman a bribe. As it is said: *"What goes up must come down"*; or, "If you don't grease the axle the wheels won't turn." And so I get in.

"Good morning to you, Reb Menachem-Mendel," I say.

Who? What? *"There is no speech. There are no words."* He looks at me as though he has never seen me before. "What do you want?" he says.

I am ready to faint. "What do you mean?" I say. "Don't you recognize your own cousin? My name is Tevye."

"Tevye . . ." he says slowly. "The name sounds familiar."

"So the name sounds familiar to you. Maybe my wife's *blintzes* sound familiar too? You may even remember the taste of her *knishes* and *kreplach?*"

Then I imagine exactly the opposite. I come in to see Menachem-Mendel and he meets me at the door with outstretched arms. "Welcome, Reb Tevye. Welcome. Be seated. How are you? And how is your wife? I've been waiting for you. I want to settle my account with you." And he takes my cap and pours it full of gold pieces. "This," he tells me, "is what we earned on our investment. The capital we shall leave where it is. Whatever we make we shall divide equally, share and share alike, half to me, half to you, a hundred to me, a hundred to you, two hundred to you, two hundred to me, five hundred to you, five hundred to me. . . ."

While I am lost in this dream, my horse strays from the path, the wagon gets caught against a tree, and I am jolted from behind so suddenly that sparks fly in front of my eyes. "This is all for the best," I comfort myself. "Thank God the axle didn't break."

I arrive in Yehupetz, dispose of my wares quickly and, as usual, without any trouble, and set out to look for my partner. I wander around for an hour, I wander around for two hours. It's no use. It's as Jacob said about Benjamin: *"The lad is gone."* I can't find him anywhere. I stop people in the street and ask them, "Have you seen or have you heard of a man who goes by the elegant name of Menachem-Mendel?"

"Well, well," they tell me, "if his name is Menachem-Mendel, you can look for him with a candle. But that isn't enough. There is more than one Menachem-Mendel in the world."

"I see, you want to know his family name. At home in Kasrilevka he is known by his mother-in-law's name—Menachem-Mendel Leah-Dvoshe's. What more do you want? Even his father-in-law, who is a very old man, is known by his wife's name, Boruch-Hersh Leah-Dvoshe's. Now do you understand?"

"We understand very well," they say. "But that isn't enough. What does this Menachem-Mendel do? What is his business?"

"His business? He deals in seven and a half *ruble* gold pieces, in Putilov shares, in stocks and bonds. He shoots telegrams here, there, and everywhere—to St. Petersburg, Odessa, Warsaw."

They roll with laughter. "Oh you mean Menachem-Mendel-who-deals-in-all-and-sundry? Turn left and follow this street and you will see many hares running around. Yours will be among them."

"Live and learn," I say to myself. "Now I am told to look for hares." I follow the street they pointed out to me. It's as crowded as our town square on market day. I can barely push my way through. People are running around like crazy—shouting, waving their hands, quarreling. It's a regular bedlam. I hear shouts of *Putilov,* "shares," "stocks . . ." "he gave me his word . . ." "here is a down payment . . ." "buy on margin . . ." "he owes me a fee . . ." "you are a sucker . . ." "spit in his face . . ." "look at that speculator." Any minute they will start fighting in earnest, dealing out blows. *"Jacob fled,"* I mutter to myself. "Get out, Tevye, before you get knocked down. God is our Father, Tevye the Dairyman is a sinner, Yehupetz is a city, and Menachem-Mendel is a breadwinner. So this is where people make fortunes? This is how they do their business? May God have mercy on you, Tevye, and on such business."

I stopped in front of a large window with a display of clothing in it and whom should I see reflected in it but my partner Menachem-Mendel. My heart was squeezed with pity at the sight. . . . *I became faint.* . . . May our worst enemies look the way Menachem-Mendel looked. You should have seen his coat. And his shoes. Or what was left of them. And his face! A corpse laid out for burial looks cheerful by comparison. "Well, Tevye," I said to myself as Esther had once said to Mordecai, "'*if I perish, I perish.*—I am done for.' You may as well kiss your savings good-bye. '*There is no bear and no woods.*—No merchandise and no money.' Nothing but a pack of troubles."

He looked pretty crestfallen on his part. We both stood there, rooted to the ground, unable to speak. There seemed to be nothing left to say, nothing left to do. We might as well pick up our sacks and go over the city begging.

"Reb Tevye," he says to me softly, barely able to utter the words, the tears are choking him so, "Reb Tevye, without luck, it's better never to have been born at all. Rather than live like this, it is better to hang from a tree or rot in the ground."

"For such a deed," I burst out, "for what you've done to me, you deserve to be stretched out right here in the middle of Yehupetz and flogged so hard that you lose consciousness. Consider for yourself what you've done. You've taken a houseful of innocent people who never did you a speck of harm, and without a knife you slit their throats clear through. How can I face my wife and children now? Tell me, you robber, you murderer, you—"

"It is all true, Reb Tevye," he says, leaning against the wall. "All true. May God have mercy on me."

"The fires of hell," I tell him, "the tortures of *Gehenna* are too good for you."

"All true," he says. "May God have pity on me. All true. Rather than to live like this, Reb Tevye, rather than to live—" And he hangs his head.

I look at him standing there, the poor *shlimazl,* leaning against the wall, his head bent, his cap awry. He sighs and he groans and my heart turns over with pity.

"And yet," I say, "if you want to look at it another way, you may not be to blame either. When I think it over, I realize that you couldn't have done it out of plain knavery. After all, you were my partner, you had a share in the business. I put in my money and you put in your brains. Woe unto us both. I am sure you meant it for the best. It must have been fate. How is it said? '*Don't rejoice today, because tomorrow—*' Or, 'Man proposes and God disposes.'

"If you want proof, just look at my business. It seems to be completely foolproof, a guaranteed thing. And yet when it came to pass last fall that one of my cows lay down and died and right after her a young calf—was there anything I could do about it? When luck turns against you, you are lost.

"I don't even want to ask you where my money is. I understand only too well. My blood money went up in smoke, it sank into the grave. . . . And whose fault is it if not mine? I let myself be talked into it. I went chasing after rainbows. If you want money, my friend, you have to work and slave for it, you have to wear your fingers to the bone. I deserve a good thrashing for it. But crying about it won't help. How is it written? *'If the maiden screamed*—You can shout until you burst a blood vessel.' Hindsight, as they say . . . It wasn't fated that Tevye should be a rich man. As Ivan says, 'Mikita never had anything and never will.' God willed it so. *'The Lord giveth and the Lord taketh away.'* Come, brother, let's go get a drink."

And that, Mr. Sholom Aleichem, is how my beautiful dream burst like a bubble and vanished into thin air. Do you think I took it to heart? Do you think I grieved over the loss of my money? Not at all. We know what the proverb says: *"The silver and the gold are mine.*—Money is worthless." Only man is important, that is, if he is really a man, a human being. For what did I grieve then? I grieved for the dream I had lost, the dream of wealth that was gone forever. For I had longed, how I had longed, to be a rich man, if only for a short while. But what did it avail me? The proverb says, *"Perforce you live and perforce you die.*—You live in spite of yourself and you wear out your shoes in spite of yourself."

"You, Tevye," says God, "stick to your cheese and butter and forget your dreams." But what about hope? Naturally, the harder life is the more you must hope. The poorer you are the more cheerful you must be.

Do you want proof? But I think I have talked too long already. I have to be on my way, I have to tend to business. As it is said: *"Every man is a liar.*—Everyone has his affliction." Farewell, be healthy and happy always. . . .

If I Were Rothschild

IF I WERE ROTHSCHILD, ah, if I were only Rothschild—a Kasrilevka *melamed* let himself go once upon a Thursday while his wife was demanding money for the Sabbath and he had none to give her. If I were only Rothschild, guess what I would do. First of all I would pass a law that a wife must always have a three-*ruble* piece on her so that she wouldn't have to start nagging me when the good Thursday comes and there is nothing in the house for the Sabbath. In the second place I would take my Sabbath gabardine out of pawn—or better still, my wife's squirrel-skin coat. Let her stop whining that she's cold. Then I would buy the whole house outright, from foundation to chimney, all three rooms, with the alcove and the pantry, the cellar and the attic. Let her stop grumbling that she hasn't enough room. "Here," I would say to her, "take two whole rooms for yourself—cook, bake, wash, chop, make, and leave me in peace so that I can teach my pupils with a free mind."

This is the life! No more worries about making a living. No more headaches about where the money for the Sabbath is coming from. My daughters are all married off—a load is gone from my shoulders. What more do I need for myself? Now I can begin to look around the town a little. First of all I am going to provide a new roof for the old Synagogue so the rain won't drip on the heads of the men who come to pray. After that I shall build a new bathhouse, for if not today, then tomorrow—but surely soon—there is bound to be a catastrophe—the roof is going to cave in while the women are inside bathing. And while we are putting up a new bathhouse we might as well throw down the old poorhouse too and put up a hospital in its place, a real hospital such as they have in big towns, with beds and bedding, with a doctor and attendants, with hot broths for the sick every day. . . . And I shall build a home for the aged so that old men, scholars who have fallen upon hard times, shouldn't have to spend their last days on the hearth in the Synagogue. And I shall establish a Society for Clothing the Poor so that poor children won't have to run around in rags with—I beg your pardon for mentioning it—their navels showing. Then I shall institute a Loan Society so that anyone at all—whether he be a teacher or a workman, or even a merchant—could get money without having to pay interest and without pawning the shirt off his back. And a Society for Outfitting Brides so that any girl old enough to marry and without means should be outfitted properly and married off as befits a Jewish girl. I would organize all these and many other such societies in Kasrilevka.

But why only here in Kasrilevka? I would organize such societies everywhere, all over the world, wherever our brethren the Sons of Israel are to be found. And in order that they should all be run properly, with a system, guess what I would do. I would appoint a Society to head them all, a Board of Charity that would watch over all the societies under it. This Board of Charity would keep watch over all of Israel and see to it that Jews everywhere had enough to live on, and that they lived together in unity. It would see to it that all Jews sit in *yeshivas* and study the Bible, the *Talmud,* the *Gamorah,* and the various Commentaries and learn all the seven wisdoms and the seventy-seven languages. And over all these *yeshivas* there would be one great *yeshiva* or Jewish Academy which would naturally be located in Vilno. And from there would come the greatest scholars and wise men in the world. And all of this education would be free to everyone, all paid for out of my pocket. And I would see to it that it was all run in orderly fashion, according to plan, so that there should be none of this grab-and-run, hit-and-miss, catch-as-catch-can business. Instead, everything would be run with a view to the common welfare.

But in order to have everyone think only of the common welfare, you have to provide one thing. And what is that? Naturally, security. For, take it from me, security from want is the most important thing in the world. Without it there can be no harmony anywhere. For alas, one man will impoverish another over a piece of bread, he will kill, poison, hang his fellow-man. Even the enemies of Israel, the Hamans of the world—what do you think they have against us? Nothing at all. They don't persecute us out of plain meanness, but because of their lack of security. It's lack of money, I tell you, that brings envy and envy brings hatred, and out of hatred come all the troubles in the world, all the sorrows, persecutions, killings, all the horrors and all the wars. . . .

Ah, the wars, the wars. The terrible slaughters. If I were Rothschild I would do away with war altogether. I would wipe it off completely from the face of the earth.

You will ask how? With money, of course. Let me explain it to you. For instance, two countries are having a disagreement over some foolishness, a piece of land that's worth a pinch of snuff. "Territory" they call it. One country says this "territory" is hers and the other one says, "No, this territory is mine." You might think that on the First Day, God created this piece of land in her honor. . . . Then a third country enters and says, "You are both asses. This is everybody's 'territory,' in other words, it's a public domain." Meanwhile the argument goes on. "Territory" here, "territory" there. They "territory" each other so long that they begin shooting with guns and cannon and people start dying like sheep and blood runs everywhere like water. . . .

But if I come to them at the very beginning and say, "Listen to me, little brothers. Actually, what is your whole argument about? Do you think that I don't understand? I understand perfectly. At this feast you are concerned less with the ceremonial than with the dumplings. 'Territory' is only a pretext. What you are after is something else—something you can get your hands on—money, levies. And while we are on the subject of money, to whom does one come for a loan if not to me, that is, to Rothschild? I'll tell you what. Here, you Englishmen with the long legs and checkered trousers, take a billion. Here, you stupid Turks with the scarlet caps, take a billion also. And you, Aunt Reisel, that is Russia, take another billion. With God's help you will pay me back with interest, not a large rate of interest, God forbid, four or five percent at the most—I don't want to get rich off you."

Do you understand what I've done? I have not only put over a business deal, but people have stopped killing each other in vain, like oxen. And since there will be no more war, what do we need weapons for? What do we need armies and cannons and military bands for, and all the other trappings of war? The answer is that we don't. And if there are no more weapons and armies and bands and other trappings of war, there will be no more envy, no more hatred, no Turks, no Englishmen, no Frenchmen, no Gypsies and no Jews. The face of the earth will be changed. As it is written: "Deliverance will come—" The Messiah will have arrived.

And perhaps, even—if I were Rothschild—I might do away with money altogether. For let us not deceive ourselves, what is money anyway? It is nothing but a delusion, a made-up thing. Men have taken a piece of paper, decorated it with a pretty picture and written on it, *Three Silver Rubles*. Money, I tell you, is nothing but a temptation, a piece of lust, one of the greatest lusts. It is something that everyone wants and nobody has. But if there were no more money in the world there would be no more temptation, no more lust. Do you understand me or not? But then the problem is, without money how would we Jews be able to provide for the Sabbath? The answer to that is—How will I provide for the Sabbath now?

Modern Children

MODERN children, did you say? Ah, you bring them into the world, sacrifice yourself for them, you slave for them day and night—and what do you get out of it? You think that one way or another it would work out according to your ideas or station. After all, I don't expect to marry them off to millionaires, but then I don't have to be satisfied with just anyone, either. So I figured I'd have at least a little luck with my daughters. Why not? In the first place, didn't the Lord bless me with handsome girls; and a pretty face, as you yourself have said, is half a dowry. And besides, with God's help, I'm not the same Tevye I used to be. Now the best match, even in Yehupetz, is not beyond my reach. Don't you agree with me?

But there is a God in heaven who looks after everything. *"A Lord merciful and compassionate,"* who has His way with me summer and winter, in season and out. And He says to me, "Tevye, don't talk like a fool. Leave the management of the world to Me."

So listen to what can happen in this great world of ours. And to whom does it have to happen? To Tevye, *shlimazl.*

To make a long story short, I had just lost everything I had in a stockmarket investment I had gotten involved in through that relative of mine, Menachem-Mendel (may his name and memory be forever blotted out), and I was very low. It looked as if it was all over with me. No more Tevye, no more dairy business.

"Fool," my wife says to me. "You have worried enough. You'll get nowhere worrying. You'll just eat your heart out. Pretend that robbers had broken in and taken everything away. . . . I'll tell you what," she says to me. "Go out for a while. Go see Lazer-Wolf, the butcher, at Anatevka. He wants to see you about something very important."

"What's the matter?" I asked. "What is he so anxious to see me about? If he is thinking of that milch cow of ours, let him take a stick and knock that idea out of his head."

"What are you so anxious about her for?" she says to me. "The milk that we get out of her, or the cheese or butter?"

"I'm not thinking about that," I answer. "It's just the idea. It would be a sin to give the poor thing away to be slaughtered. You can't do that to a living creature. It is written in the Bible. . . ."

"Oh, enough of that!" she comes back at me. "The whole world knows already that you're a man of learning! You do what I tell you. You go over and see Lazer-Wolf. Every Thursday when our Tzeitl goes there for meat, he won't leave her alone. 'You tell your father,' he keeps saying, 'to come and see me. It's important.' "

Well, once in a while you have to obey your wife. So I let her talk me into it, and I go over to Anatevka, about three miles away. He wasn't home. "Where can he be?" I ask a snub-nosed woman who is bustling around the place.

"They're slaughtering today," says the woman, "and he went down to bring an ox. He'll be coming back pretty soon."

So I wait. And while I'm waiting I look around the house a little. And from what I see, it looks as if Lazer-Wolf has been a good provider. There is a cupboard filled with copperware—at least a hundred and fifty *rubles'* worth; a couple of samovars, some brass trays, silver candlesticks and gilded goblets. And a fancy *Hannukah* lamp and some trinkets made of porcelain and silver and everything.

"Lord Almighty!" I think to myself. "If I can only live to see things like that at my children's homes. . . . What a lucky fellow he is—such wealth, and nobody to support! Both his children are married, and he himself is a widower. . . ."

Well, at last the door opens and in stamps Lazer-Wolf.

"Well, Reb Tevye," he says. "What's the matter? Why is it so hard to get hold of you? How goes it?"

"How should it go?" I say to him. "I go and I go, and I get nowhere. *'Neither gold nor health nor life itself,'* as the *Torah* says."

"Don't complain, Reb Tevye," he answers me. "Compared with what you were when I first knew you, you're a rich man today."

"May we both have what I still need to make me a rich man," I say. "But I am satisfied, thank God. *'Abracadabra askakudra,'* as the *Talmud* says."

"You're always there with a line of *Talmud,"* he comes back. "What a lucky man you are, Reb Tevye, to know all these things. But what does all that wisdom and knowledge have to do with us? We have other things to talk about. Sit down, Tevye." He lets out a yell, "Let's have some tea!" And as if by magic the snub-nosed woman appears, snatches the samovar, and is off to the kitchen.

"Now that we are alone," he says to me, "we can talk business. Here is the story. I've been wanting to talk to you for a long time. I tried to reach you through your daughter. How many times have I begged you to come? You understand, I've been casting an eye . . ."

"I know," I say, "that you have been casting an eye on her, but it's no use. Your pains are wasted, Reb Lazer-Wolf. There is no use talking about it."

"Why not?" he asks, with a frightened look.

"Why yes?" says I. "I can wait. I'm in no hurry. My house isn't on fire."

"But why should you wait, if you can arrange it now?"

"Oh, that's not important," I say. "Besides, I feel sorry for the poor thing."

"Look at him," says Lazer-Wolf with a laugh. "He feels sorry for her. . . . If somebody heard you, Reb Tevye, he'd have sworn that she was the only one you had. It seems to me that you have a few more without her."

"Does it bother you if I keep them?" I say. "If anvone is jealous . . ."

"Jealous? Who is talking of jealousy?" he cries. "On the contrary, I know they're superior, and that is exactly why—you understand? And don't forget, Reb Tevye, that you can get something out of it too!"

"Of course . . . I know all a person can get from you. . . . A piece of ice—in winter. We've known that from way back."

"Forget it," he says to me, sweet as sugar. "That was a long time ago. But now—after all—you and I—we're practically in one family, aren't we?"

"Family? What kind of family? What are you talking about, Reb Lazer-Wolf?"

"You tell me, Reb Tevye. I'm beginning to wonder. . . ."

"What are you wondering about? We're talking about my milch cow. The one you want to buy from me."

Lazer-Wolf throws back his head and lets out a roar. "That's a good one!" he howls at me. "A cow! And a milch cow at that!"

"If not the cow," I say, "then what *were* we talking about? You tell me so I can laugh too."

"Why, about your daughter. We were talking about your daughter Tzeitl the whole time. You know, Reb Tevye, that I have been a widower for quite a while now. So I thought, why do I have to go looking all over the world—get mixed up with matchmakers, those sons of Satan? Here we both are. I know you, you know me. It's not like running after a stranger. I see her in my shop every Thursday. She's made a good impression on me. I've talked with her a few times. She looks like a nice, quiet girl. And as for me—as you see for yourself—I'm pretty well off. I have my own house. A couple of stores, some hides in the attic, a little money in the chest. I live pretty well. . . . Look, Tevye, why do we have to do a lot of bargaining, try to impress each other, bluff each other? Listen to me. Let's shake hands on it and call it a match."

Well, when I heard that I just sat and stared. I couldn't say a word. All I could think was: Lazer-Wolf . . . Tzeitl. . . . He had children as old as she was. But then I reminded myself: what a lucky thing for her. She'll have everything she wants. And if he is not so good looking? There were other things besides looks. There was only one thing I really had against him: he could barely read his prayers. But then, can everybody be a scholar? There are plenty of wealthy men in Anatevka, in Mazapevka, and even in Yehupetz who don't know one letter from another. Just the same, if it's their luck to have a little money they get all the respect and honor a man could want. As the saying goes, *"There's learning in a strong-box, and wisdom in a purse. . . ."*

"Well, Reb Tevye," he says. "Why don't you say something?"

"What do you want me to do? Yell out loud?" I ask mildly, as if not wanting to look anxious. "You understand, don't you, that this is something a person has to think over. It's no trifle. She's my eldest child."

"All the better," he says. "Just because she is your eldest . . . That will give you a chance to marry off your second daughter, too, and then, in time with God's help, the third. Don't you see?"

"Amen. The same to you," I tell him. "Marrying them off is no trick at all. Just let the Almighty send each one her predestined husband."

"No," he says. "That isn't what I mean. I mean something altogether different. I mean the dowry. That you won't need for her. And her clothes I'll take care of too. And maybe you'll find something in your own purse besides. . . ."

"Shame on you!" I shout at him. "You're talking just as if you were in the butcher shop. What do you mean—my purse? Shame! My Tzeitl is not the sort that I'd have to sell for money!"

"Just as you say," he answers. "I meant it all for the best. If you don't like it, let's forget it. If you're happy without that, I'm happy too. The main thing is, let's get it done with. And I mean right away. A house must have a mistress. You know what I mean. . . ."

"Just as you say," I agree. "I won't stand in your way. But I have to talk it over with my wife. In affairs like this she has her say. It's no trifle. As Rashi says: *'A mother is not a dust rag.'* Besides, there's Tzeitl herself to be asked. How does the saying go? 'All the kinsmen were brought to the wedding—and the bride was left home'. . . ."

"What foolishness!" says Lazer-Wolf. "Is this something to *ask* her about? *Tell* her, Reb Tevye! Go home. Tell her what is what, and get the wedding canopy ready."

"No, Reb Lazer-Wolf," I say. "That's not the way you treat a young girl."

"All right," he says. "Go home and talk it over. But first, Reb Tevye, let's have a little drink. How about it?"

"Just as you say," I agree. "Why not? How does the saying go? *'Man is human*—and a drink is a drink.' There is," I tell him, "a passage in the *Talmud*. . . ." And I give him a passage. I don't know myself what I said. Something from the *Song of Songs* or the *Hagadah*. . . .

Well, we took a drop or two—as it was ordained. In the meantime the woman had brought in the samovar and we made ourselves a glass or two of punch, had a very good time together, exchanged a few toasts—talked—made plans for the wedding—discussed this and that—and then back to the wedding.

"Do you realize, Reb Lazer-Wolf, what a treasure she is?"

"I know. . . . Believe me, I know. . . . If I didn't I would never have suggested anything. . . ."

And we both go on shouting. I: "A jewel! A diamond! I hope you'll know how to treat her! Not like a butcher . . ."

And he: "Don't worry, Reb Tevye. What she'll eat in my house on weekdays she never had in your house on holidays."

"Tut, tut," I said. "Feeding a woman isn't everything. The richest man in the world doesn't eat five-*ruble* gold pieces, and a pauper doesn't eat stones. You're a coarse fellow, Lazer-Wolf. You don't even know how to value her talents—her baking—her cooking! Ah, Lazer-Wolf! The fish she makes! You'll have to learn to appreciate her!"

And he: "Tevye, pardon me for saying it, but you're somewhat befuddled. You don't know your man. You don't know me at all. . . ."

And I: "Put gold on one scale and Tzeitl on the other. . . . Do you hear, Reb Lazer-Wolf, if you had a million *rubles,* you wouldn't be worth her little finger."

And he again: "Believe me, Tevye, you're a big fool, even if you are older than I am."

We yelled away at each other that way for a long time, stopping only for a drink or two, and when I came home, it was late at night and my feet felt as if they had been shackled. And my wife, seeing right away that I was tipsy, gave me a proper welcome.

"Sh . . . Golde, control yourself," I say to her cheerfully, almost ready to start dancing. "Don't screech like that, my soul. We have congratulations coming."

"Congratulations? For what? For having sold that poor cow to Lazer-Wolf?"

"Worse than that," I say.

"Traded her for another one? And outsmarted Lazer-Wolf—poor fellow?"

"Still worse."

"Talk sense," she pleads. "Look, I have to haggle with him for every word."

"Congratulations, Golde," I say once more. "Congratulations to both of us. Our Tzeitl is engaged to be married."

"If you talk like that then I know you're drunk," she says. "And not slightly, either. You're out of your head. You must have found a real glassful somewhere."

"Yes. I had a glass of whiskey with Lazer-Wolf, and I had some punch with Lazer-Wolf, but I'm still in my right senses. Lo and behold, Golde darling, our Tzeitl has really and truly and officially become betrothed to Lazer-Wolf himself."

And I tell her the whole story from start to finish, how and what and when and why. Everything we discussed, word for word.

"Do you hear, Tevye," my wife finally says, "my heart told me all along that when Lazer-Wolf wanted to see you it was for something. Only I was afraid to think about it. Maybe nothing would come of it. Oh, dear God, I thank Thee, I thank Thee, Heavenly Father. . . . May it all be for the best. May she grow old with him in riches and honor—not like that first wife of his, Fruma-Sarah, whose life with him was none too happy. She was, may she forgive me for saying it, an embittered woman. She couldn't get along with anybody. Not at all like our Tzeitl. . . . Oh, dear God, I thank Thee, dear God . . . Well, Tevye, didn't I tell you, you simpleton. . . . Did you have to worry? If a thing has to happen it will happen. . . ."

"I agree with you," said I. "There is a passage in the *Talmud* that covers that very point. . . ."

"Don't bother me with your passages," she said. "We've got to get ready for the wedding. First of all, make out a list for Lazer-Wolf of all the things Tzeitl will need. She doesn't have a stitch of underwear, not even a pair of stockings. And as for clothes, she'll need a silk dress for the wedding, and a cotton one for summer, a woolen one for winter, and petticoats, and cloaks—she should have at least two—one, a fur-lined cloak for weekdays and a good one with a ruffle for Saturdays. And how about a pair of button-shoes and a corset, gloves, handkerchiefs, a parasol, and all the other things that a girl nowadays has to have?"

"Where, Golde, darling, did you get acquainted with all these riggings?" I ask her.

"Why not?" says she. "Haven't I ever lived among civilized people? And didn't I see, back in Kasrilevka, how ladies dressed themselves? You let me do all the talking with him myself. Lazer-Wolf is, after all, a man of substance. He won't want everybody in the family to come bothering him. Let's do it properly. If a person has to eat pork, let him eat a bellyful. . . ."

So we talked and we talked till it was beginning to get light. "My wife," I said, "it's time to get the cheese and butter together so I can start for Boiberik. It is all very wonderful indeed, but you still have to work for a living."

And so, when it was still barely light I harnessed my little old horse and went off to Boiberik. When I got to the Boiberik marketplace—Oho! Can a person ever keep a secret? Everybody knew about it already, and I was congratulated from all sides. "Congratulations, congratulations! Reb Tevye, when does the wedding come off?"

"The same to you, the same to you," I tell them. "It looks as if the saying is right: 'The father isn't born yet and the son is dancing on the rooftops'. . . ."

"Forget about that!" they cry out. "You can't get away with that! What we want is treats. Why, how lucky you are, Reb Tevye! An oil well! A gold mine!"

"The well runs dry," I tell them, "and all that's left is a hole in the ground."

Still, you can't be a hog and leave your friends in the lurch. "As soon as I'm through delivering I'll be back," I tell them. "There'll be drinks and a bite to eat. Let's enjoy ourselves. As the Good Book says, *'Even a beggar can celebrate.'* "

So I got through with my work as fast as I could and joined the crowd in a drink or two. We wished each other good luck as people do, and then I got back into my cart and started for home again, happy as could be. It was a beautiful summer day, the sun was hot, but on both sides of the road there was shade, and the odor of the pines was wonderful. Like a prince I stretched myself out in the wagon and eased up on the reins. "Go along," I said to the little old horse, "go your own way. You ought to know it by now." And myself, I clear my throat and start off on some of the old tunes. I am in a holiday mood, and the songs I sing are those of *Rosh Hashono* and *Yom Kippur*. As I sing I look up at the sky but my thoughts are concerned with things below. The heavens are the Lord's but the earth He gave to the Children of Adam, for them to brawl around in, to live in such luxury that they have time to tear each other apart for this little honor or that. . . . They don't even understand how one ought to praise the Lord for the good things that He gives them. . . . But we, the poor people, who do not live in idleness and luxury, give us but one good day and we thank the Lord and praise Him; we say, *"Ohavti, I love Him"*—the Highest One—*"for He hears my voice and my prayer, He inclines His ear to me . . . For the waves of death compassed me, the floods of Belial assailed me. . . ."* Here a cow falls down and is injured, there an ill wind brings a kinsman of mine, a good-for-nothing, a Menachem-Mendel from Yehupetz who takes away my last penny; and I am sure that the world has come to an end—there is no truth or justice left anywhere on earth. . . . But what does the Lord do? He moves Lazer-Wolf with the idea of taking my daughter Tzeitl without even a dowry. . . . And therefore I give thanks to Thee, dear God, again and again, for having looked upon Tevye and come to his aid. . . . I shall yet have joy. I shall know what it is to visit my child and find her a mistress of a well-stocked home, with chests full of linens, pantries full of chicken fat and preserves, coops full of chickens, geese and ducks. . . .

Suddenly my horse dashes off downhill, and before I can lift my head to look around I find myself on the ground with all my empty pots and crocks and my cart on top of me! With the greatest difficulty I drag myself out from under and pull myself up, bruised and half-dead, and I vent my wrath on the poor little horse. "Sink into the earth!" I shout. "Who asked you to show that you know how to run? You almost ruined me altogether, you devil!" And I gave him as much as he could take. You could see that he realized he had gone a little too far. He stood there with his head down, humble, ready to be milked. . . . Still cursing him, I turn the cart upright, gather up my pots, and off I go. A bad omen, I tell myself, and I wonder what new misfortunes might be awaiting me. . . .

That's just how it was. About a mile farther on, when I'm getting close to home, I see someone coming toward me. I drive up closer, look, and see that it's Tzeitl. At the sight of her my heart sinks, I don't know why. I jump down from the wagon.

"Tzeitl, is that you? What are you doing here?"

She falls on my neck with a sob. "My daughter, what are you crying about?" I ask her.

"Oh," she cries, "father, father!" And she is choked with tears.

"What is it, daughter? What's happened to you?" I say, putting my arm around her, patting and kissing her.

"Father, father, have pity on me. Help me. . . ."

"What are you crying for?" I ask, stroking her head. "Little fool, what do you have to cry for? For heaven's sake," I say, "if you say *no* it's *no*. Nobody is going to force you. We meant it for the best, we did it for your own sake. But if it doesn't appeal to you, what are we going to do? Apparently it was not ordained. . . ."

"Oh, thank you, father, thank you," she cries, and falls on my neck again and dissolves in tears.

"Look," I say, "you've cried enough for one day. . . . Even eating pastry becomes tiresome. . . . Climb into the wagon and let's go home. Lord knows what your mother will be thinking."

So we both get into the cart and I try to calm her down. I tell her that we had not meant any harm to her. God knows the truth: all we wanted was to shield our daughter from poverty. "So it was not meant," I said, "that you should have riches, all the comforts of life; or that we should have a little joy in our old age after all our hard work, harnessed, you might say, day and night to a wheelbarrow—no happiness, only poverty and misery and bad luck over and over. . . ."

"Oh, father," she cries, bursting into tears again. "I'll hire myself out as a servant. I'll carry rocks. I'll dig ditches. . . ."

"What are you crying for, silly child?" I say. "Am I forcing you? Am I complaining? It's just that I feel so wretched that I have to get it off my chest; so I talk it over with Him, with the Almighty, about the way He deals with me. He is, I say, a merciful Father, He has pity on me, but He shows me what He can do, too; and what can I say? Maybe it has to be that way. He is high in heaven, high up, and we are here below, sunk in the earth, deep in the earth. So we must say that He is right and His judgment is right; because if we want to look at it the other way round, who am I? A worm that crawls on the face of the earth, whom the slightest breeze—if God only willed it—could annihilate in the blink of an eye. So who am I to stand up against Him with my little brain and give Him advice on how to run this little world of His? Apparently if He ordains it this way, it has to be this way. What good are complaints? Forty days before you were conceived, the Holy Book tells us, an angel appeared and decreed: 'Let Tevye's daughter Tzeitl take Getzel, the son of Zorach, as her husband; and let Lazer-Wolf the Butcher go elsewhere to seek his mate.' And to you, my child, I say this: May God send you your predestined one, one worthy of you, and may he come soon, Amen. And I hope your mother doesn't yell too much. I'll get enough from her as it is."

Well, we came home at last. I unharnessed the little horse and sat down on the grass near the house to think things over, think up some fantastic tale to tell my wife. It was late, the sun was setting; in the distance frogs were croaking; the old horse, tied to a tree, was nibbling at the grass; the cows, just come from pasture, waited in the stalls to be milked. All around me was the heavenly smell of the fresh grass—like the Garden of Eden. I sat there thinking it all over. . . . How cleverly the Eternal One has created this little world of His, so that every living thing, from man to a simple cow, must earn its food. Nothing is free. If you, little cow, wish to eat—then go, let yourself be milked, be the means of livelihood for a man and his wife and children. If you, little horse, wish to chew—then run back and forth every day with the milk to Boiberik. And you, Man, if you want a piece of bread—go labor, milk the cows, carry the pitchers, churn the butter, make the cheese, harness your horse, drag yourself every dawn to the *datchas* of Boiberik, scrape and bow to the rich ones of Yehupetz, smile at them, cater to them, ingratiate yourself with them, see to it that they are satisfied, don't do anything to hurt their pride. . . . Ah, but there still remains the question: *'Mah nishtano?'* Where is it written that Tevye must labor in their behalf, must get up before daybreak when God Himself is still asleep, just so that they can have a fresh piece of cheese, and butter for their breakfast? Where is it written that I must rupture myself for a pot of thin gruel, a loaf of barley bread, while they—the rich ones of Yehupetz—loll around in their summer homes without so much as lifting a hand, and are served roast ducks and the best of *knishes, blintzes* and *vertutin?* Am I not a man as they are? Would it be a sin, for instance, if Tevye could spend one summer himself in a *datcha* somewhere? But then—where would people get cheese and butter? Who would milk the cows? The Yehupetz aristocrats, maybe? And at the very thought of it I burst out laughing. It's like the old saying: "If God listened to every fool what a different world it would be!"

And then I heard someone call out, "Good evening, Reb Tevye." I looked up and saw a familiar face—Motel Kamzoil, a young tailor from Anatevka.

"Well, well," I say, "you speak of the Messiah and look who's here! Sit down, Motel, on God's green earth. And what brings you here all of a sudden?"

"What brings me here?" he answers. "My two feet."

And he sits down on the grass near me and looks off toward the barn where the girls are moving about with their pots and pitchers. "I have been wanting to come here for a long time, Reb Tevye," he says at last, "only I never seem to have the time. You finish one piece of work and you start the next. I work for myself now, you know, and there is plenty to do, praise the Lord. All of us tailors have as much as we can do right now. It's been a summer of weddings. Everybody is marrying off his children—everybody, even the widow Trihubecha."

"Everybody," I say. "Everybody except Tevye. Maybe I am not worthy in the eyes of the Lord."

"No," he answers quickly, still looking off where the girls are. "You're mistaken, Reb Tevye. If you only wanted to you could marry off one of your children, too. It all depends on you. . . ."

"So?" I ask. "Maybe you have a match for Tzeitl?"

"A perfect fit!" the tailor answers.

"And," I ask, "is it a good match at least?"

"Like a glove!" he cries in his tailor's language, still looking off at the girls.

I ask, "In whose behalf is it then that you come? If he smells of a butcher shop I don't want to hear another word!"

"God forbid!" he says. "He doesn't begin to smell of a butcher shop!"

"And you really think he's a good match?"

"There never was such a match!" he answers promptly. "There are matches and matches, but this one, I want you to know, was made exactly to measure!"

"And who, may I ask, is the man? Tell me!"

"Who is it?" he says, still looking over yonder. "Who is it? Why, me—myself!"

When he said that I jumped up from the ground as if I had been scalded, and he jumped too, and there we stood facing each other like bristling roosters. "Either you're crazy," I say to him, "or you're simply out of your mind! What are you—everything? The matchmaker, the bridegroom, the ushers all rolled into one? I suppose you'll play the wedding march too! I've never heard of such a thing—arranging a match for oneself!"

But he doesn't seem to listen. He goes right on talking.

"Anyone who thinks I'm crazy is crazy himself! No, Reb Tevye, I have all my wits about me. A person doesn't have to be crazy in order to want to marry your Tzeitl. For example, the richest man in our town—Lazer-Wolf, the Butcher—wanted her too. Do you think it's a secret? The whole town knows it. And as for being my own matchmaker, I'm surprised at you! After all, Reb Tevye, you're a man of the world. If a person sticks his finger in your mouth you know what to do! So what are we arguing about? Here is the whole story: your daughter Tzeitl and I gave each other our pledge more than a year ago now that we would marry. . . ."

If someone had stuck a knife into my heart it would have been easier to endure than these words. In the first place, how does a stitcher like Motel fit into the picture as my son-in-law? And in the second place, what kind of words are these, "We gave each other our pledge that we would marry"? And where do I come in? . . . I ask him bluntly, "Do I still have the right to say something about my daughter, or doesn't anyone have to ask a father any more?"

"On the contrary," says Motel, "that's exactly why I came to talk with you. I heard that Lazer-Wolf has been discussing a match, and I have loved her now for over a year. More than once I have wanted to come and talk it over with you, but every time I put it off a little. First till I had saved up a few *rubles* for a sewing machine, and then till I got some decent clothes. Nowadays almost everybody has to have two suits and a few good shirts. . . ."

"You and your shirts!" I yell at him. "What childish nonsense is this? And what do you intend to do after you're married? Support your wife with shirts?"

"Why," he says, "why, I'm surprised at you, Reb Tevye! From what I hear, when you got married you didn't have your own brick mansion either, and nevertheless here you are. . . . In any case, if the whole world gets along, I'll get along, too. Besides, I have a trade, haven't I?"

To make a long story short, he talked me into it. For after all—why should we fool ourselves?—how do all Jewish children get married? If we began to be too particular, then no one in our class would ever get married at all. . . . There was only one thing still bothering me, and that I still couldn't understand. What did they mean—pledging their troth? What kind of world has this become? A boy meets a girl and says to her, "Let us pledge our troth." Why, it's just too free-and-easy, that's all!

But when I looked at this Motel standing there with his head bent like a sinner, I saw that he was not trying to get the best of anybody, and I thought: "Now, what am I becoming so alarmed about? What am I putting on such airs for? What is my own pedigree? Reb Tzotzel's grandchild! And what huge dowry can I give my daughter —and what fine clothes? So maybe Motel Kamzoil is only a tailor, but at the same time he is a good man, a worker; he'll be able to make a living. And besides, he's honest too. So what have I got against him?

"Tevye," I said to myself, "don't think up any childish arguments. Let them have their way." Yes . . . but what am I going to do about my Golde? I'll have plenty on my hands there. She'll be hard to handle. How can I make her think it's all right? . . .

"You know what, Motel," I said to the young suitor. "You go home. I'll straighten everything out here. I'll talk it over with this one and that one. Everything has to be done right. And tomorrow morning, if you haven't changed your mind by that time, maybe we'll see each other."

"Change my mind!" he yells at me. "You expect me to change my mind? If I do, I hope I never live to go away from here! May I become a stone, a bone, right here in front of you!"

"What's the use of swearing?" I ask him. "I believe you without the oath. Go along, Motel. Good night. And may you have pleasant dreams."

And I myself go to bed, too. But I can't sleep. My head is splitting. I think of one plan and then another, till at last I come upon the right one. And what is that? Listen, I'll tell you. . . .

It's past midnight. All over the house we're sound asleep. This one is snoring, that one is whistling. And suddenly I sit up and let out a horrible yell, as loud as I can: "Help! Help! Help!" It stands to reason that when I let out this yell everybody wakes up, and first of all—Golde.

"May God be with you, Tevye," she gasps, and shakes me. "Wake up! What's the matter with you? What are you howling like this for?"

I open my eyes, look around to see where I am, and call out in terror, "Where is she? Where is she?"

"Where is who?" asks Golde. "What are you talking about?"

I can hardly answer. "Fruma-Sarah. Fruma-Sarah, Lazer-Wolf's first wife . . . She was standing here a minute ago."

"You're out of your head," my wife says to me. "May God save you, Tevye. Do you know how long Fruma-Sarah has been dead?"

"I know that she's dead," I say, "but just the same she was here just a minute ago, right here by the bed, talking to me. Then she grabbed me by the windpipe and started to choke me. . . ."

"What on earth is the matter with you, Tevye?" says my wife. "What are you babbling about? You must have been dreaming. Spit three times and tell me what you dreamt, and I'll tell you what it meant."

"Long may you live, Golde," I tell her. "It's lucky you woke me up or I'd have died of fright right on the spot. Get me a drink of water and I'll tell you my dream. Only I beg you, Golde, don't become frightened: the Holy Books tell us that sometimes only three parts of a dream come true, and the rest means nothing. Absolutely nothing. Well, here is my dream. . . .

"In the beginning I dreamt that we were having a celebration of some kind, I don't know what. Either an engagement or a wedding. The house was crowded. All the men and women we knew were there—the *rov* and the *shochet* and everybody. And musicians, too. . . . In the midst of the celebration the door opens, and in comes your grandmother Tzeitl, may her soul rest in peace. . . ."

"Grandmother Tzeitl!" my wife shouts, turning pale as a sheet. "How did she look? How was she dressed?"

"How did she look?" I say. "May our enemies look the way she looked. Yellow. A waxen yellow. And she was dressed—how do you expect?—in white. A shroud. She came up to me. 'Congratulations,' she said, 'I am so happy that you picked such a fine young man for your Tzeitl who bears my name. He's a fine, upstanding lad—this Motel Kamzoil. . . . He was named after my uncle Mordecai, and even if he is a tailor he's still an honest boy. . . .'"

"A tailor!" gasps Golde. "Where does a tailor come into our family? In our family we have had teachers, cantors, *shamosim,* undertakers' assistants, and other kinds of poor people. But a tailor—never!"

"Don't interrupt me, Golde," I tell her. "Maybe your grandmother Tzeitl knows better. . . . When I heard her congratulate me like that, I said to her, 'What is that you said, Grandmother? About Tzeitl's betrothed being a tailor? Did you say Motel? . . . You mean a butcher, don't you? A butcher named Lazer-Wolf?'

" 'No,' says your grandmother again. 'No, Tevye. Your daughter is engaged to Motel, and he's a tailor, and she'll grow old with him—if the Lord wills—in comfort and honor.'

" 'But Grandmother,' I say again, 'what can we do about Lazer-Wolf? Just yesterday I gave him my word. . . .'

"I had barely finished saying this when I looked up, and your grandmother Tzeitl is gone. In her place is Fruma-Sarah—Lazer-Wolf's first wife—and this is what she says: 'Reb Tevye, I have always considered you an honest man, a man of learning and virtue. But how does it happen that you should do a thing like this—let your daughter take my place, live in my house, carry my keys, wear my clothes, my jewelry, my pearls?'

" 'Is it my fault,' I ask her, 'if Lazer-Wolf wanted it that way?'

" 'Lazer-Wolf!' she cries. 'Lazer-Wolf will have a terrible fate, and your Tzeitl too, if she marries him. It's a pity, Reb Tevye. I feel sorry for your daughter. She'll live with him no more than three weeks, and when the three weeks are up I'll come to her by night and I'll take her by the throat like this. . . .' And with these words Fruma-Sarah grabs me by the windpipe and begins choking me—so hard that if you hadn't waked me up, by now I'd have been—far, far away. . . ."

"Ptu, ptu, ptu," spits my wife three times. "It's an evil spirit! May it fall into the river; may it sink into the earth; may it climb into attics; may it lie in the forest—but may it never harm us or our children! May that butcher have a dream like that! A dark and horrible dream! Motel Kamzoil's smallest finger is worth more than all of him, even if Motel is only a tailor; for if he was named after my uncle Mordecai he couldn't possibly have been a tailor by birth. And if my grandmother—may she rest in peace—took the trouble to come all the way from the other world to congratulate us, why, all we can do is say that this is all for the best, and it couldn't possibly be any better. Amen. Selah. . . ."

Well, why should I go on and on?

The next day they were engaged, and not long after were married. And the two of them, praise the Lord, are happy. He does his own tailoring, goes around in Boiberik from one *datcha* to another picking up work; and she is busy day and night, cooking and baking and washing and tidying and bringing water from the well. . . . They barely make enough for food. If I didn't bring her some of our cheese and butter once in a while—or a few *groschen* sometimes—they would never be able to get by. But if you ask her—my Tzeitl, I mean—she says everything is as good as it could be. Just let Motel stay in good health.

So go complain about modern children. You slave for them, do everything for them! And they tell you that they know better.

And . . . maybe they do. . . .

Competitors

ALWAYS, right in the midst of what some of us call the Reign of Terror—when everyone is pushing and shoving, this one getting in, that one getting out; when people are fighting for a seat in the carriage, as though they were vying for honors in the Synagogue—then you see both of them appear. There they are—the two of them—he and she.

He—swarthy, stout, hairy, with a cataract over one eye. She—red-faced, bony, pock-marked. Both of them in rags and tatters, both in patched shoes, both with identical baggage—he with a basket, and she with a basket; his filled with twisted white rolls, hard-boiled eggs, oranges, bottles of seltzer water; and hers, also with twisted white rolls, hard-boiled eggs, oranges, and bottles of seltzer water.

Sometimes it happens that he has in his basket small bags of purple grapes, black cherries, or green grapes as sour as vinegar. Then she also comes in with the same purple grapes, black cherries, or green grapes as sour as vinegar.

And always the two of them come at the same time, push their way through the same door of the carriage, and cry out their wares together, in the very same words. Only their accents are different. He speaks in a slightly asthmatic voice, slurring the r's, mumbling his words as though he had no tongue. She speaks out clearly, in a loud sharp voice, all tongue.

Maybe you think that they cut prices, try to compete with each other, engage in unfair trade practices? Not at all. Their prices are identical. Their competition consists only of this: which of them can arouse the greatest sympathy. Both of them implore you to take pity on their five orphaned children (he has five orphans and she has five orphans). Both of them peer right into your eyes, push their wares under your nose and argue so persistently that whether you need it or not, you are forced to buy something.

Only they talk so much, cry and beg and plead with you so much, that you become confused. Which one should you buy from—him or her? You decide to solve the problem by buying a little from each, but they won't let you do this.

No, my friend. If you're going to buy something, you'll have to but it from one or the other. You can't dance at two weddings with one pair of shoes.

So, wanting to be fair, you think you'll buy from one of them one time and from the other next time. But if you try it you'll find yourself abused by both sides.

"Look here, mister, anything wrong with the way I look to you today?"

Or, "My good man, it seems to me that last week you bought some food from me and you didn't become poisoned or choke on it."

You decide to make a moral issue of it. You read them a lecture on ethics. After all, you say, the other party has a soul too, he or she has to keep body and soul together. You know what they say in German: "*Leben und leben lassen*—Live and let live." To this you get an answer not in German, but in plain Yiddish, a trifle disguised, but quite easy to understand.

"Uncle! You can't sit on two horses with one behind."

Yes, dear friend, that's the way it is. Never try to please the whole world, you won't succeed. And think twice before you try to become a peacemaker—it doesn't work. I know from sad experience. I could tell you a good story of the time I made a fool of myself trying to make peace between a husband and wife. And what was the upshot? I caught the devil from my own wife. But I don't want to confuse one story with another. Though it sometimes happens in business that you show a person a piece of goods—let's say cowhides—and you start talking about silks from China. However, let's get back to our story.

It happened one time in the fall, on a rainy day when the sky was overcast and down below everything was dark and gloomy and wet. The station was packed with travelers both coming and going. They were all in a hurry, all of them running and pushing and crawling over each other with suitcases, with bundles of different shapes and sizes, pillows, quilts, featherbeds. You should have heard the clatter and rattle, the shouting and scolding. And right in the thick of it, the two of them have to appear—he and she. Both loaded with things to eat, as always. Both pushing through one door, as always. Suddenly—how did it happen? Both baskets are on the ground. The rolls and the eggs, the oranges and the bottles of seltzer water, are scattered in the mud; and our ears are filled with cries and shrieks and sobs and curses that mingle with the laughter of the train crews and the noise and tumult of the passengers. The whistle blows, the bell rings. Another minute and we'll be on our way.

Inside the carriage there is a hubbub too. The passengers are talking it over, airing their views on the subject—and, naturally, all together, like women in the Synagogue, or geese in the marketplace. It is hard to follow their conversation, to get the gist of it, except for a phrase here and there.

"A bumper crop in rolls this year."

"A massacre of eggs."

"What did anybody have against the oranges?"

"What did you expect from him—an Esau, a nonbeliever."

"Just offhand—at how much would you estimate the loss?"

"Serves them right. Do they have to push their way where they are not wanted?"

"But what else can they do? It's their livelihood."

"Ha-ha-ha," booms a deep bass voice. "A fine livelihood. A Jewish livelihood."

"A fine livelihood, you say," pipes up a young, thin, squeaking voice. "Do you know of a better way a poor Jew can make his livelihood? If so, let's hear it."

"Young man!" thunders the bass. "I wasn't talking to you."

"Not talking to me? But *I* am talking to you. Do you know of a better way of making a living? So. You are silent. You have nothing to say."

"How do you like that leech? He won't let me go."

"Quiet, everybody. Be still. Here she comes."

"Who?"

"She herself, the woman with the basket."

"Where is she, the beauty? Where?"

"Here, here she is."

Pock-marked, red-faced, her eyes swollen with weeping, she pushed her way through the crowd with her empty basket, looking for a vacant place, and finally she sat down on the floor on her upturned basket, hid her swollen eyes in her torn shawl and wept quietly.

A strange silence descended on the carriage. Not a word was uttered, not a sound was heard. We were all tongue-tied until a deep bass voice called out, "Why is everybody so quiet?"

"What do you want us to do—shout?"

"Come, let's take up a collection."

Do you know who is talking? Just guess. The same man who only a few minutes ago was laughing at a poor Jew's livelihood. He is a strange-looking creature with an odd cap on his head, a cap with a broad shiny visor in front. Besides this he is wearing smoked glasses so that you can't see his eyes. He has no eyes, only a nose, a broad, fleshy, bulbous nose.

Without any more ado he pulls his cap off his head, throws in a couple of silver coins and begins going from one person to another, all the while thundering in his deep bass voice: "Come, everybody. Give what you can. A little or a lot, whatever you can afford. You know what the *Talmud* says, 'Never look a gift horse in the mouth.' "

We all reached into our pockets, opened our wallets, and the change began to ring out—all kinds of change, silver and copper, large and small. There was a Russian peasant in the crowd, with high boots and a silver chain around his neck. He yawned, crossed himself, and threw in a coin too. Only one passenger refused, he wouldn't give a thing. And who do you suppose he was? The same fellow who a few minutes ago had taken it upon himself to defend a poor Jew's means of livelihood. A young intellectual with well-nourished plump cheeks, a small yellow pointed beard, and golden pince-nez. One of these fellows with rich parents, rich parents-in-law and plenty in his own pocket, who travels third-class to save money.

"Young man, put something into the cap," says the personage with the smoked glasses and the bulbous nose.

"I am not giving anything," says the young intellectual.

"Why not?"

"Just because. It's a matter of principle with me."

"I knew before I came to you that you wouldn't give anything."

"And how did you know?"

"I could tell by your looks. Your secret was divulged by the way your cheeks bulged. As the *Talmud* says, 'You can spot a gentleman by his boots.'"

The young intellectual went into such a rage that his pince-nez almost fell off. He began screaming, "You are an ignorant lout, a low vulgarian, an impudent ass."

"Thank heavens," answered the bulbous nose calmly. "Thank heavens I am not also a robber and a highwayman." He went up to the weeping woman. "Aunty, haven't you cried enough for one time? You'll spoil your pretty eyes. Here, hold out both your hands and I'll pour the money into them."

A strange woman. I thought that when she saw all the money he had collected she would overwhelm us with thanks, melt with gratitude. But instead of thanks, she overwhelmed us with curses. A fountain, a torrent of abuse began pouring from her lips.

"It's all his fault, may he fall by the wayside and break his neck and bones and skull, dear Father in Heaven. He is to blame for everything. It all comes from him, may no good come to him. May he sink into the ground, sweet Father. May he never live to come home again, but meet with violent death instead, from cholera or fire or plague or pestilence. May he dry up and his flesh shrink from his bones."

Dear Lord, where does a person find so many maledictions? Luckily the man with the smoked glasses interrupted her. "Enough, my woman, enough. Enough of your blessings and benedictions. Tell us instead what the conductor and the guards had against you?"

The woman lifted her swollen eyes to him.

"It's all on account of him, curse him. He was afraid I'd grab all the customers away from him, so he tried to push into the carriage ahead of me. So I squeezed past him, so he caught my basket from behind, and then I let out a yell; and the guard winked at the conductor and both of them together heaved our baskets and scattered everything in the mud—may *his* bones be scattered like that. Believe me, I am telling the truth, when I say that as long as I've traveled on this route with my merchandise no one has ever before as much as touched a hair on my head. Why do you think they left me alone? Because of their kind hearts? May *he* have a boil for every egg I've had to give away, for every roll I've handed out at the station. Everyone, from the lowest to the highest, has to have his gullet stuffed with something. From early morning I have to be handing it out—if I could only hand out chills and fever to them. The head conductor takes his share first, anything he wants. Then I have to start dividing it up among the other conductors, this one gets a loaf, that one some eggs, a third gets an orange. What more do you want? Even the fellow who fires the ovens, do you think he doesn't demand his share? A plague on him! He threatens to report me to the guard if I don't give him something. He doesn't know that the guard has been taken care of long ago. Every Sunday I bring him a bag of oranges. He always picks the biggest, the finest, the best oranges. . . ."

"Aunty, from the looks of things," says the man with the smoked glasses, "you must be rolling in wealth."

"What are you saying?" She looks at him quickly, as though offering an apology. "I barely, barely come out even. And I sometimes lose and have to take it out of my own hide. I am getting poorer all the time."

"Then what's the use of doing business at all?"

"What else do you want me to do—become a thief? I have five little children to support—may *he* have five different kinds of pains in his bowels. And I myself am a sick woman—may *he* lie sick in the hospital, dear God, from now until the fall. The way he has ruined my business, run it into the ground. May he rot in the ground. It was such a good business, such a fine thriving business."

"A good business, did you say?"

"A wonderful business. With a steady income. How do you say it —a gilt-edged investment."

"But just a minute ago you were saying that you are getting poorer all the time."

"Of course. How can I make a living if I have to give away more than half of my merchandise to the head conductor and the rest of them? What do you think I have there? A well, a bottomless spring? A stolen fortune?"

Our friend with the bulbous nose and smoked glasses begins to lose patience. "Aunty, you are pulling my leg now."

"Me, pulling your leg?" She is indignant. "May *his* legs fester and drop off. He has wrecked my life, may God wreck his. Actually he is only a tailor, a pants-patcher. He spent most of his life jabbing a needle through cloth, and he was lucky to make enough for water for his *kasha.* Then he got jealous of me. He saw me eating a slice of bread, may the worms eat him. He saw—may his eyes drop out of his head—how with this basket I kept five little orphans alive. So he goes and buys himself a basket too. One of these days I will buy him a shroud, dear Lord. So I ask him, 'What's this?' And he says, 'A basket.' 'And what are you going to do with this basket?' I ask. And he says, 'The same as you are doing.' 'And what's that?' And he says, 'You should know. I have five children too, and they also have to eat once in a while. You won't raise them on dry bread.' And ever since then he's been following me around everywhere with his basket. He drags the customers away from me, may his teeth be dragged out of him one by one. He tears the bread right out of my mouth, may he be torn into bits, sweet Father, dear loving Father."

Our friend with the smoked glasses hits upon an idea, an idea that has already occurred to most of us.

"But why do you both have to pound the same piece of earth? Why do you both follow the same route?"

The woman stares at him with her red swollen eyes. "What else do you want us to do?"

"Find yourself another route. The railway line is a long one."

"And what about him?"

"Who?"

"My husband."

"Which husband?"

"My second husband."

"Which second husband?"

The woman's red pock-marked face gets redder still. "What do you mean, which second husband? That's him over there, the *shlimazl* I've been talking about."

All of us leap out of our seats.

"That man, that competitor of yours, that's your second husband?"

"What did you think he was? My first husband? Oh-ho. If my first husband were only still alive . . ."

There is a lilt in her voice as she draws out the words, a strange light in her eyes as she gets ready to tell us who her first husband was and what sort of man *he* was. But who wants to listen to her? We are all busy talking, laughing, making wisecracks. We laugh and laugh and can't stop laughing.

Perhaps you can guess what we are laughing about.

Another Page from the Song of Songs

"FASTER, Buzie, faster," I tell Buzie and take her hand in mine and together we race up the hill. It is the day before *Shevuos* and we are setting out to pick greens. "We haven't all day," I tell her. "We have a big mountain to climb and after the mountain there is a river. Over the river there is a trestle made of boards, that's the 'bridge.' The water runs under the bridge, the frogs croak, the boards creak and shake—and there, over there on the other side of the bridge, that's where the real Garden of Eden is, Buzie. That's where my Estates begin."

"Your Estates?"

"I mean the big meadow. It's a great field that stretches far and wide without any end. It has a green blanket over it, sprinkled with yellow dots and covered with tiny red shoots. Wait till you smell it. It has the most wonderful smells in the world. And wait till you see my trees. I have many, many trees—tall, spreading trees. And I have a little hill all my own to sit on. I can sit on top of my hill, or I can say the Magic Word and fly off like an eagle straight above the clouds. I can fly over forest and field, over sea and desert, till I come to the other side of the mountain of darkness."

"And from there," Buzie interrupts me, "you walk seven miles on foot until you come to a lake."

"No, to a deep wood. First I walk through this wood, then through another wood, then I come to the lake."

"And you swim across the lake and count seven times seven."

"And there springs up in front of me a tiny gnome with a long beard."

"And he asks you, 'What is your heart's desire?'"

"And I tell him, 'Lead me to the Queen's daughter.'"

Buzie snatches her hand out of mine and starts running downhill. I run after her. "Buzie, why are you running away?"

Buzie does not answer. I've offended her. She doesn't like to have me talk about the Queen's daughter. She likes all my stories except the one about the Queen's daughter.

You probably remember who Buzie is. I have told you about her once before. But in case you've forgotten I shall tell you again.

I had an older brother named Benny who was drowned. He left behind him a mill, a young widow, two horses and a child. The mill was abandoned. The horses were sold. The widow remarried and moved to some distant place and the child was brought to us. That child was Buzie.

Do you want to hear something funny? Everybody thinks that Buzie and I are sister and brother. She calls my father "Father" and my mother "Mother." We live together just like sister and brother and love each other just like a sister and a brother.

Like a sister and a brother? Then why is Buzie so shy with me? Why does she act so strange sometimes?

Let me tell you something that happened once. We had been left alone, she and I, all by ourselves in the house. My father had gone to the Synagogue to say *kaddish* for my brother Benny, and my mother had gone out to buy matches. Buzie and I sat huddled together in a corner and I was telling her stories. Buzie loves to hear me tell stories, stories from *cheder* or else fairy tales I make up for her. She moved quite close to me. Her hand was clasped in mine.

"Go on, Shimek. Go on, tell me more."

Silently, night descends. Slowly the shadows cover the walls, quiver in the half-light, then creep to the ground and melt. We can barely make each other out. I can only feel her little hand trembling in mine. I can hear her heart beating and see her eyes gleaming in the dark.

Suddenly she snatches her hand away. "What is it?" I ask, surprised.

"We mustn't do it," she says.

"Mustn't do what?"

"Hold hands like this."

"Why not? Who told you we mustn't?"

"Nobody. I know it myself."

"But we aren't strangers. Aren't we brother and sister?"

"If we were only brother and sister," says Buzie softly, and it seems to me that she is speaking in the words of the *Song of Songs: "O that thou wert as my brother . . ."*

It is always like this. Whenever I speak of Buzie, I think of the *Song of Songs. . . .*

Where were we? It is the day before *Shevuos.* We are running down the hill. Buzie runs ahead and I run after her. Buzie is offended because of the Queen's daughter. She likes all my stories except the one about the Queen's daughter. But Buzie can't hold a grudge very long. She has forgotten about it in less time than it takes me to tell it. She is looking at me once more with her big lovely eyes. She tosses her hair back and calls out to me, "Shimek! Look, Shimek, can you see what I see?"

"Of course I see, silly. Why shouldn't I see? I can see the blue sky, I can feel the warm breeze. I can hear the birds chirping and see them sailing over our heads. It is our sky, our breeze, our birds. Everything is ours, ours, ours. Give me your hand, Buzie."

"No," she says. She won't give me her hand. She is suddenly shy. Why should Buzie be shy with me? Why should she blush?

"Over there," calls Buzie, running ahead. "Over there, on the other side of the bridge." And it seems to me that she speaks in the words of the Shulamite. *"Come, my beloved, let us go forth into the fields. Let us lodge in the villages. Let us get up early to the vineyards. Let us see whether the vine has budded, whether the vine blossom be opened."*

And here we are, at the bridge.

The river runs under the bridge, the frogs croak, the boards creak and shake, and Buzie trembles. "Oh, Buzie, you are . . . What are you afraid of, silly? Hold on to me or, better still, let me put my arm around you and you put your arm around me. See? Like this."

We have crossed the bridge.

And now we walk ahead, still with our arms tightly around each other, she and I, all by ourselves in the holy stillness of the first morning of Creation. Buzie holds on tightly to me, very tightly. She is silent, but it seems to me that she is speaking in the words of the *Song of Songs: "I am my beloved's and my beloved is mine."*

The meadow stretches far and wide without end. It is like a green blanket sprinkled with yellow dots, covered with red shoots. And the smells that rise from it—they are the most wonderful smells in the world. We walk along, the two of us, arm in arm, over the Garden of Eden, in the morning of the world.

"Shimek," says Buzie, looking into my eyes and moving closer to me, "when are we going to start picking greens for *Shevuos?*"

"The day is long, silly," I tell her. I am burning with excitement. I don't know where to look first, whether up at the blue cup of the sky, or down at the green blanket of the fields. Or over there, toward the end of the world, where the sky melts into the earth. Or should I look into Buzie's lovely face? Into her big thoughtful eyes, as deep as the sky, as pensive as the night? Her eyes are always pensive, always troubled. A deep sorrow lies hidden in them. I am familiar with her sorrow, I know what is troubling her. She grieves for her mother who married a stranger and went off far away, never to return.

At our house, Buzie's mother is never mentioned. It's as though Buzie never had a mother. My parents have become her parents. They love her as though she were their own child; they watch over her anxiously, let her have anything her heart desires. This morning Buzie said she wanted to go with me to pick greens for *Shevuos* (I had put her up to it). At once my father turned to my mother. "What do you think?" As he spoke, he looked at her over the tops of his silver-rimmed spectacles and with his fingers he combed the silver strands of his beard. A conversation took place between my father and mother that went something like this:

Father: What do you say?
Mother: What do *you* say?
Father: Should we let them go?
Mother: Why shouldn't we let them go?
Father: Am I saying no?
Mother: What are you saying then?
Father: I'm only saying, should they go?
Mother: Why shouldn't they go?

And so on. I know on which foot the shoe pinches. My father has told me twenty times over, and after him my mother has warned me that over there is a bridge and under the bridge there is water. A river . . . a river . . . a river . . .

Buzie and I have long ago forgotten the bridge and the river. We are wandering over the wide, open field, under the wide, open sky. We run and we fall down and roll over and over in the sweet-smelling grass. Then we get up and run, and fall down again. We haven't even started to pick greens for *Shevuos*. I lead Buzie over the broad meadow and boast to her about my possessions.

"Do you see these trees? Do you see the sand? Do you see this hill?"

"And is all of it yours?"

Buzie looks at me as she says this and her eyes laugh at me. She is always laughing at me. I can't bear to have her laughing at me. I sulk and turn away from her. Buzie sees that I am offended. She runs in front of me, looks into my eyes earnestly, takes my hand and says, "Shimek." My anger disappears and I feel good again. I take her hand and lead her to my little hill, the little hill on which I sit every year. If I want to I can sit on my hill and look over my Estates. Or else I can utter the Magic Word and be borne aloft like an eagle. I can fly above the clouds, over forest and field, over sea and desert. . . .

We sit on my hill (we still haven't picked any greens for *Shevuos*) and tell stories, that is I tell stories and Buzie listens. I tell her about how it is going to be some far-off day when we are both grown up and marry each other. We will rise up by magic and fly above the clouds, and travel over the whole world. First we will travel over the countries that Alexander of Macedonia had traveled over. Then we will take a trip to the Holy Land. There we will visit all the mountains and the vineyards, and we will fill our pockets with figs and dates and olives. Then we will get up and fly further. And everywhere we go we will play different tricks on people, because no one will be able to see us.

"No one will see us?" asks Buzie, and catches me by the hand.

"No one, no one at all. We will be able to see everybody and nobody will be able to see us."

"If so, Shimek, I want to ask a favor of you."

"A favor?"

"A tiny favor."

I know beforehand what this favor is. She wants us to fly over there where her mother is living with her new husband. She wants me to play a trick on her stepfather.

"Why not?" I tell her. "With the greatest pleasure. You can depend on me. I will play them a trick that they will remember me by."

"Not them, just him, just him," Buzie pleads with me. But I don't consent right away. When someone has made me angry, I am terrible in my wrath. How can I forgive her so easily? The insolence of a woman—marrying a perfect stranger and going off somewhere, the devil knows where, and deserting her own child, never even writing her a letter. . . . Whoever heard of such an outrage?

I got all wrought up for nothing and now I am sorry. But it's too late. Buzie has covered her face with her hands. Is she weeping? I would gladly tear myself into little pieces for making her weep. Why did I have to wound her tenderest feelings so? In my own mind I call myself all sorts of harsh names: "You ox, you ass, you idiot, you blabber-mouth." I come close to her, take her hand in mine. "Buzie. Buzie!" I want to speak to her in the words of the *Song of Songs: "Let me see thy countenance. Let me hear thy voice."*

Suddenly I look up. Where did my father and mother come from? My father's silver-rimmed spectacles gleam at a distance. The silver strands of his beard are whipped by the breeze. My mother beckons to us from afar, waving her shawl. Buzie and I sit there as though we were turned to clay. What can our parents be doing here?

They have come to see where we are. They want to make sure that no harm has come to us. Who can tell—a bridge, a river . . . a river . . .

What queer people our parents are.

"And where are the greens?" they ask.

"The greens?"

"Yes, the greens you were going to pick for *Shevuos.*

Buzie and I look at each other. I understand the look in her eyes. It seems to me that she is saying, *"O that thou wert as my brother."*

"Well, as for the greens, I am sure we will find some," says my father, smiling, and the silver strands of his beard shine in the rays of the noonday sun. "God be thanked that the children are well and that no harm has come to them."

"God be thanked," echoes my mother, wiping her red perspiring face with her shawl. They both look at us tenderly, beaming with unconcealed pride. . . .

What queer, queer people our parents are. . . .

Hodel

YOU LOOK, Mr. Sholom Aleichem, as though you were surprised that you hadn't seen me for such a long time. . . . You're thinking that Tevye has aged all at once, his hair has turned gray. . . .

Ah, well, if you only knew the troubles and heartaches he has endured of late! How is it written in our Holy Books? *"Man comes from dust, and to dust he returns.*—Man is weaker than a fly, and stronger than iron." Whatever plague there is, whatever trouble, whatever misfortune—it never misses me. Why does it happen that way? Maybe because I am a simple soul who believes everything that everyone says. Tevye forgets that our wise men have told us a thousand times: "Beware of dogs. . . ."

But I ask you, what can I do if that's my nature? I am, as you know, a trusting person, and I never question God's ways. Whatever He ordains is good. Besides, if you do complain, will it do you any good? That's what I always tell my wife. "Golde," I say, "you're sinning. We have a *medresh*. . . ."

"What do I care about a *medresh?"* she says. "We have a daughter to marry off. And after her are two more almost ready. And after these two—three more—may the Evil Eye spare them!"

"Tut," I say. "What's that? Don't you know, Golde, that our sages have thought of that also? There is a *medresh* for that, too. . . ."

But she doesn't let me finish. "Daughters to be married off," she says, "are a stiff *medresh* in themselves."

So try to explain something to a woman!

Where does that leave us? Oh, yes, with a houseful of daughters, bless the Lord. Each one prettier than the next. It may not be proper for me to praise my own children, but I can't help hearing what the whole world calls them, can I? Beauties, every one of them! And especially Hodel, the one that comes after Tzeitl who, you remember, fell in love with the tailor. And is this Hodel beautiful. . . . How can I describe her to you? Like Esther in the Bible, *"of beautiful form and fair to look upon."* And as if that weren't bad enough, she has to have brains, too. She can write and she can read—Yiddish and Russian both. And books—she swallows like dumplings. You may be wondering how a daughter of Tevye happens to be reading books, when her father deals in butter and cheese? That's what I'd like to know myself. . . .

But that's the way it is these days. Look at these lads who haven't got a pair of pants to their name, and still they want to study! Ask them, "What are you studying? Why are you studying?" They can't tell you. It's their nature, just as it's a goat's nature to jump into gardens. Especially since they aren't even allowed in the schools. "Keep off the grass!" read all the signs as far as they're concerned. And yet you ought to see how they go after it! And who are they? Workers' children. Tailors' and cobblers', so help me God! They go away to Yehupetz or to Odessa, sleep in garrets, eat what Pharaoh ate during the plagues—frogs and vermin—and for months on end do not see a piece of meat before their eyes. Six of them can make a banquet on a loaf of bread and a herring. Eat, drink and be merry! That's the life!

Well, so one of that band had to lose himself in our corner of the world. I used to know his father—he was a cigarette-maker, and as poor as a man could be. But that is nothing against the young fellow. For if Rabbi Jochanan wasn't too proud to mend boots, what is wrong with having a father who makes cigarettes? There is only one thing I can't understand: why should a pauper like that be so anxious to study? True, to give the devil his due, the boy has a good head on his shoulders, an excellent head. Pertschik, his name was, but we called him "Feferel"—"Peppercorn." And he looked like a peppercorn, little, dark, dried up and homely, but full of confidence and with a quick, sharp tongue.

Well, one day I was driving home from Boiberik where I had got rid of my load of milk and butter and cheese, and as usual I sat lost in thought, dreaming of many things, of this and that, and of the rich people of Yehupetz who had everything their own way while Tevye, the *shlimazl,* and his wretched little horse slaved and hungered all their days. It was summer, the sun was hot, the flies were biting, on all sides the world stretched endlessly. I felt like spreading out my arms and flying!

I lift up my eyes, and there on the road ahead of me I see a young man trudging along with a package under his arm, sweating and panting. "*'Rise, O Yokel the son of Flekel,'* as we say in the synagogue," I called out to him. "Climb into my wagon and I'll give you a ride. I have plenty of room. How is it written? *'If you see the ass of him that hateth thee lying under its burden, thou shalt forbear to pass it by.'* Then how about a human being?"

At this the *shlimazl* laughs, and climbs into the wagon.

"Where might the young gentleman be coming from?" I ask.

"From Yehupetz."

"And what might a young gentleman like you be doing in Yehupetz?" I ask.

"A young gentleman like me is getting ready for his examinations."

"And what might a young gentleman like you be studying?"

"I only wish I knew!"

"Then why does a young gentleman like you bother his head for nothing?"

"Don't worry, Reb Tevye. A young gentleman like me knows what he's doing."

"So—if you know who *I* am, tell me who *you* are!"

"Who am I? I'm a man."

"I can see that you're not a horse. I mean, as we Jews say, *whose* are you?"

"Whose should I be but God's?"

"I know that you're God's. It is written: *'All living things are*

His.' I mean, whom are you descended from? Are you from around here, or from Lithuania?"

"I am *descended,"* he says, "from Adam, our father. I *come* from right around here. You know who we are."

"Well then, who is your father? Come, tell me."

"My father," he says, "was called Pertschik."

I spat with disgust. "Did you have to torture me like this all that time? Then you must be Pertschik the Cigarette-maker's son!"

"Yes, that's who I am. Pertschik the Cigarette-maker's son."

"And you go to the university?"

"Yes—the university."

"Well," I said, "I'm glad to hear it. Man and fish and fowl—you're all trying to better yourselves! But tell me, my lad, what do you live on, for instance?"

"I live on what I eat."

"That's good," I say. "And what do you eat?"

"I eat anything I can get."

"I understand," I say. "You're not particular. If there is something to eat, you eat. If not, you bite your lip and go to bed hungry. But it's all worth while as long as you can attend the university. You're comparing yourself to those rich people of Yehupetz. . . ."

At these words Pertschik bursts out, "Don't you dare compare me to them! They can go to hell as far as I care!"

"You seem to be somewhat prejudiced against the rich," I say. "Did they divide your father's inheritance among themselves?"

"Let me tell you," says he, "it may well be that you and I and all the rest of us have no small share in *their* inheritance."

"Listen to me," I answer. "Let your enemies talk like that. But one thing I can see: you're not a bashful lad. You know what a tongue is for. If you have the time, stop at my house tonight and we'll talk a little more. And if you come early, you can have supper with us, too."

Our young friend didn't have to be asked twice. He arrived at the right moment—when the *borsht* was on the table and the *knishes* were baking in the oven. "Just in time!" I said. "Sit down. You can say grace or not, just as you please. I'm not God's watchman; I won't be punished for your sins." And as I talk to him I feel myself drawn to the fellow somehow; I don't know why. Maybe it's because I like a person one can talk to, a person who can understand a quotation and follow an argument about philosophy or this or that or something else. . . . That's the kind of person I am.

And from that evening on our young friend began coming to our house almost every day. He had a few private students and when he was through giving his lessons he'd come to our house to rest up and visit for a while. What the poor fellow got for his lessons you can imagine for yourself, if I tell you that the very richest people used to pay their tutors three *rubles* a month; and besides their regular duties they were expected to read telegrams for them, write out addresses, and even run errands at times. Why not? As the passage says, *"If you eat bread you have to earn it."* It was lucky for him that most of the time he used to eat with us. For this he used to give my daughters lessons, too. One good turn deserves another. And in this way he became almost a member of the family. The girls saw to it that he had enough to eat and my wife kept his shirts clean and his socks mended. And it was at this time that we changed his Russian name of Pertschik to Feferel. And it can truthfully be said that we all came to love him as though he were one of us, for by nature he was a likable young man, simple, straightforward, generous. Whatever he had he shared with us.

There was only one thing I didn't like about him, and that was the way he had of suddenly disappearing. Without warning he would get up and go off; we looked around, and there was no Feferel. When he came back I would ask, "Where were you, my fine-feathered friend?" And he wouldn't say a word. I don't know how you are, but as for me, I dislike a person with secrets. I like a person to be willing to tell what he's been up to. But you can say this for him: when he did start talking, you couldn't stop him. He poured out everything. What a tongue he had! *"Against the Lord and against His anointed; let us break their bands asunder."* And the main thing was to break the bands. . . . He had the wildest notions, the most peculiar ideas. Everything was upside down, topsy-turvy. For instance, according to his way of thinking, a poor man was far more important than a rich one, and if he happened to be a worker too, then he was really the brightest jewel in the diadem! He who toiled with his hands stood first in his estimation.

"That's good," I say, "but will that get you any money?"

At this he becomes very angry and tries to tell me that money is the root of all evil. Money, he says, is the source of all falsehood, and as long as money amounts to something, nothing will ever be done in this world in the spirit of justice. And he gives me thousands of examples and illustrations that make no sense whatever.

"According to your crazy notions," I tell him, "there is no justice in the fact that my cow gives milk and my horse draws a load." I didn't let him get away with anything. That's the kind of man Tevye is. . . .

But my Feferel can argue too. And how he can argue! If there is something on his mind, he comes right out with it. One evening we were sitting on my stoop talking things over—discussing philosophic matters—when he suddenly said, "Do you know, Reb Tevye, you have very fine daughters."

"Is that so?" said I. "Thanks for telling me. After all, they have someone to take after."

"The oldest one especially is a very bright girl," said he. "She's all there!"

"I know without your telling me," said I. "The apple never falls very far from the tree."

And I glowed with pride. What father isn't happy when his children are praised? How should I have known that from such an innocent remark would grow such fiery love?

Well, one summer twilight I was driving through Boiberik, going from *datcha* to *datcha* with my goods, when someone stopped me. I looked up and saw that it was Ephraim the Matchmaker. And Ephraim, like all matchmakers, was concerned with only one thing—arranging marriages. So when he sees me here in Boiberik he stops me and says, "Excuse me, Reb Tevye, I'd like to tell you something."

"Go ahead," I say, stopping my horse, "as long as it's good news."

"You have," says he, "a daughter."

"I have," I answer, "seven daughters."

"I know," says he. "I have seven, too."

"Then together," I tell him, "we have fourteen."

"But joking aside," he says, "here is what I have to tell you. As you know, I am a matchmaker; and I have a young man for you to consider, the very best there is, a regular prince. There's not another like him anywhere."

"Well," I say, "that sounds good enough to me. But what do you consider a prince? If he's a tailor or a shoemaker or a teacher, you can keep him. I'll find my equal or I won't have anything. As the *medresh* says . . ."

"Ah, Reb Tevye," says he, "you're beginning with your quotations already! If a person wants to talk to you he has to study up first. . . . But better listen to the sort of match Ephraim has to offer you. Just listen and be quiet."

And then he begins to rattle off all his client's virtues. And it really sounds like something. . . . First of all, he comes from a very fine family. And that is very important to me, for I am not just a nobody either. In our family you will find all sorts of people, spotted, striped and speckled, as the Bible says. There are plain, ordinary people, there are workers, and there are property owners. . . . Secondly, he is a learned man who can read small print as well as large; he knows all the Commentaries by heart. And that is certainly not a small thing, either, for an ignorant man I hate even worse than pork itself. To me an unlettered man is worse—a thousand times worse—than a hoodlum. You can go around bareheaded, you can even walk on your head if you like, but if you know what Rashi and the others have said, you are a man after my own heart. . . . And on top of everything, Ephraim tells me, this man of his is rich as can be. He has his own carriage drawn by two horses so spirited that you can see a vapor rising from them. And that I don't object to, either. Better a rich man than a poor one! God Himself must hate a poor man, for if He did not, would He have made him poor?

"Well," I ask, "what more do you have to say?"

"What more can I say? He wants me to arrange a match with you. He is dying, he's so eager. Not for you, naturally, but for your daughter. He wants a pretty girl."

"He is dying?" I say. "Then let him keep dying. . . . And who is this treasure of yours? What is he? A bachelor? A widower? Is he divorced? What's wrong with him?"

"He is a bachelor," says Ephraim. "Not so young any more, but he's never been married."

"And what is his name, may I ask?"

But this he wouldn't tell me. "Bring the girl to Boiberik," he says, "and then I'll tell you."

"Bring her?" says I. "That's the way one talks about a horse or a cow that's being brought to market. Not a girl!"

Well, you know what these matchmakers are. They can talk a stone wall into moving. So we agreed that early next week I would bring my daughter to Boiberik. And driving home, all sorts of wonderful thoughts came to me, and I imagined my Hodel riding in a carriage drawn by spirited horses. The whole world envied me, not so much for the carriage and horses as for the good deeds I accomplished through my wealthy daughter. I helped the needy with money—let this one have twenty-five *rubles,* that one fifty, another a hundred. How do we say it? "Other people have to live too. . . ." That's what I think to myself as I ride home in the evening, and I whip my horse and talk to him in his own language.

"Hurry, my little horse," I say, "move your legs a little faster and you'll get your oats that much sooner. As the Bible says, *'If you don't work, you don't eat.'* . . ."

Suddenly I see two people coming out of the woods—a man and a woman. Their heads are close together and they are whispering to each other. Who could they be, I wonder, and I look as them through the dazzling rays of the setting sun. I could swear the man was Feferel. But whom was he walking with so late in the day? I put my hand up and shield my eyes and look closely. Who was the damsel? Could it be Hodel? Yes, that's who it was! Hodel! So? So that's how they'd been studying their grammar and reading their books together? Oh, Tevye, what a fool you are. . . .

I stop the horse and call out: "Good evening! And what's the latest news of the war? How do you happen to be out here this time of the day? What are you looking for—the day before yesterday?"

At this the couple stops, not knowing what to do or say. They stand there, awkward and blushing, with their eyes lowered. Then they look up at me, I look at them, and they look at each other. . . .

"Well," I say, "you look as if you hadn't seen me in a long time. I am the same Tevye as ever, I haven't changed by a hair."

I speak to them half angrily, half jokingly. Then my daughter, blushing harder than ever, speaks up: "Father, you can congratulate us."

"Congratulate you?" I say. "What's happened? Did you find a treasure buried in the woods? Or were you just saved from some terrible danger?"

"Congratulate us," says Feferel this time. "We're engaged."

"What do you mean—engaged?"

"Don't you know what engaged means?" says Feferel, looking me straight in the eye. "It means that I'm going to marry her and she's going to marry me."

I look him back in the eye and say, "When was the contract signed? And why didn't you invite me to the ceremony? Don't you think I have a slight interest in the matter?" I joke with them and yet my heart is breaking. But Tevye is not a weakling. He wants to hear everything out. "Getting married," I say, "without matchmakers, without an engagement feast?"

"What do we need matchmakers for?" says Feferel. "We arranged it between ourselves."

"So?" I say. "That's one of God's wonders! But why were you so silent about it?"

"What was there to shout about?" says he. "We wouldn't have told you now, either, but since we have to part soon, we decided to have the wedding first."

This really hurt. How do they say it? It hurt to the quick. Becoming engaged without my knowledge—that was bad enough, but I could stand it. He loves her; she loves him—that I'm glad to hear. But getting married? That was too much for me. . . .

The young man seemed to realize that I wasn't too well pleased with the news. "You see, Reb Tevye," he offered, "this is the reason: I am about to go away."

"When are you going?"

"Very soon."

"And where are you going?"

"That I can't tell you. It's a secret."

What do you think of that? A secret! A young man named Feferel comes into our lives—small, dark, homely, disguises himself as a bridegroom, wants to marry my daughter and then leave her—and he won't even say where he's going! Isn't that enough to drive you crazy?

"All right," I say. "A secret is a secret. Everything you do seems to be a secret. But explain this to me, my friend. You are a man of such —what do you call it?—integrity; you wallow in justice. So tell me, how does it happen that you suddenly marry Tevye's daughter and then leave her? Is that integrity? Is that justice? It's lucky that you didn't decide to rob me or burn my house down!"

"Father," says Hodel, "you don't know how happy we are now that we've told you our secret. It's like a weight off our chests. Come, father, kiss me."

And they both grab hold of me, she on one side, he on the other, and they begin to kiss and embrace me, and I to kiss them in return. And in their great excitement they begin to kiss each other. It was like going to a play. "Well," I say at last, "maybe you've done enough kissing already? It's time to talk about practical things."

"What, for instance?" they ask.

"For instance," I say, "the dowry, clothes, wedding expenses, this, that and the other. . . ."

"We don't need a thing," they tell me. "We don't need anything. No this, no that, no other."

"Well then, what do you need?" I ask.

"Only the wedding ceremony," they tell me.

What do you think of that! . . . Well, to make a long story short, nothing I said did any good. They went ahead and had their wedding, if you want to call it a wedding. Naturally it wasn't the sort that I would have liked. A quiet little wedding—no fun at all. And besides there was a wife I had to do something about. She kept plaguing me: what were they in such a hurry about? Go try to explain their haste to a woman. But don't worry. I invented a story—*"great, powerful and marvelous,"* as the Bible says—about a rich aunt in Yehupetz, an inheritance, all sorts of foolishness.

And a couple of hours after this wonderful wedding I hitched up my horse and wagon and the three of us got in, that is, my daughter, my son-in-law and I, and off we went to the station at Boiberik. Sitting in the wagon, I steal a look at the young couple, and I think to myself: what a great and powerful Lord we have and how cleverly He rules the world. What strange and fantastic beings He has created. Here you have a new young couple, just hatched; he is going off, the Good Lord alone knows where, and is leaving her behind—and do you see either one of them shed a tear, even for appearance's sake? But never mind—Tevye is not a curious old woman. He can wait. He can watch and see. . . .

At the station I see a couple of young fellows, shabbily dressed, down-at-the-heels, coming to see my happy bridegroom off. One of them is dressed like a peasant with his blouse worn like a smock over his trousers. The two whisper together mysteriously for several minutes. "Look out, Tevye," I say to myself. "You have fallen among a band of horse thieves, pickpockets, housebreakers or counterfeiters."

Coming home from Boiberik I can't keep still any longer and tell Hodel what I suspect. She bursts out laughing and tries to assure me that they were very honest young men, honorable men, whose whole life was devoted to the welfare of humanity; their own private welfare meant nothing to them. For instance, the one with his blouse over his trousers was a rich man's son. He had left his parents in Yehupetz and wouldn't take a penny from them.

"Oh," said I, "that's just wonderful. An excellent young man! All he needs, now that he has his blouse over his trousers and wears his hair long, is a harmonica, or a dog to follow him, and then he would really be a beautiful sight!" I thought I was getting even with her for the pain she and this new husband of hers had caused me; but did she care? Not at all! She pretended not to understand what I was saying. I talked to her about Feferel and she answered me with "the cause of humanity" and "workers" and other such talk.

"What good is your humanity and your workers," I say, "if it's all a secret? There is a proverb: 'Where there are secrets, there is knavery.' But tell me the truth now. Where did he go, and why?"

"I'll tell you anything," she says, "but not that. Better don't ask. Believe me, you'll find out yourself in good time. You'll hear the news—and maybe very soon—and good news at that."

"Amen," I say. "From your mouth into God's ears! But may our enemies understand as little about it as I do."

"That," says she, "is the whole trouble. You'll never understand."

"Why not?" say I. "Is it so complicated? It seems to me that I can understand even more difficult things."

"These things you can't understand with your brain alone," she says. "You have to feel them, you have to feel them in your heart."

And when she said this to me, you should have seen how her face shone and her eyes burned. Ah, those daughters of mine! They don't do anything halfway. When they become involved in anything it's with their hearts and minds, their bodies and souls.

Well, a week passed, then two weeks—five—six—seven . . . and we heard nothing. There was no letter, no news of any kind. "Feferel is gone for good," I said, and glanced over at Hodel. There wasn't a trace of color in her face. And at the same time she didn't rest at all; she found something to do every minute of the day, as though trying to forget her troubles. And she never once mentioned his name, as if there never had been a Feferel in the world!

But one day when I came home from work I found Hodel going about with her eyes swollen from weeping. I made a few inquiries and found out that someone had been to see her, a long-haired young man who had taken her aside and talked to her for some time. Ah! That must have been the young fellow who had disowned his rich parents and pulled his blouse down over his trousers. Without further delay I called Hodel out into the yard and bluntly asked her: "Tell me, daughter, have you heard from him?"

"Yes."

"Where is he—your predestined one?"

"He is far away."

"What is he doing there?"

"He is serving time."

"Serving time?"

"Yes."

"Why? What did he do?"

She doesn't answer me. She looks me straight in the eyes and doesn't say a word.

"Tell me, my dear daughter," I say, "according to what I can understand, he is not serving for a theft. So if he is neither a thief nor a swindler, why is he serving? For what good deeds?"

She doesn't answer. So I think to myself, "If you don't want to, you don't have to. He is your headache, not mine." But my heart aches for her. No matter what you say, I'm still her father. . . .

Well, it was the evening of *Hashono Rabo*. On a holiday I'm in the habit of resting and my horse rests too. As it is written in the Bible: *"Thou shalt rest from thy labors and so shall thy wife and thine ass. . . ."* Besides, by that time of the year there is very little for me to do in Boiberik. As soon as the holidays come and the *shofar* sounds, all the summer *datchas* close down and Boiberik becomes a desert. At that season I like to sit at home on my own stoop. To me it is the finest time of the year. Each day is a gift from heaven. The sun no longer bakes like an oven, but caresses with a heavenly softness. The woods are still green, the pines give out a pungent smell. In my yard stands the *succah*—the booth I have built for the holiday, covered with branches, and around me the forest looks like a huge *succah* designed for God Himself. Here, I think, God celebrates His *Succos,* here and not in town, in the noise and tumult where people run this way and that panting for breath as they chase after a small crust of bread and all you hear is money, money, money. . . .

As I said, it is the evening of *Hashono Rabo*. The sky is a deep blue and myriads of stars twinkle and shine and blink. From time to time a star falls through the sky, leaving behind it a long green band of light. This means that someone's luck has fallen . . . I hope it isn't my star that is falling, and somehow Hodel comes to mind. She has changed in the last few days, has come to life again. Someone, it seems, has brought her a letter from him, from over there. I wish I knew what he had written, but I won't ask. If she won't speak, I won't either. Tevye is not a curious old woman. Tevye can wait.

And as I sit thinking of Hodel, she comes out of the house and sits down near me on the stoop. She looks cautiously around and then whispers, "I have something to tell you, father. I have to say good-bye to you, and I think it's for always."

She spoke so softly that I could barely hear her, and she looked at me in a way that I shall never forget.

"What do you mean—good-bye for always?" I say to her, and turn my face aside.

"I mean I am going away early tomorrow morning, and we shall possibly never see each other again."

"Where are you going, if I may be so bold as to ask?"

"I am going to him."

"To him? And where is he?"

"He is still serving, but soon they'll be sending him away."

"And you're going there to say good-bye to him?" I ask, pretending not to understand.

"No. I am going to follow him," she says. "Over there."

"There? Where is that? What do they call the place?"

"We don't know the exact name of the place, but we know that it's far—terribly, terribly far."

And she speaks, it seems to me, with great joy and pride, as though he had done something for which he deserved a medal. What can I say to her? Most fathers would scold a child for such talk, punish her, even beat her maybe. But Tevye is not a fool. To my way of thinking anger doesn't get you anywhere. So I tell her a story.

"I see, my daughter, as the Bible says, '*Therefore shalt thou leave thy father and mother*'—for a Feferel you are ready to forsake your parents and go off to a strange land, to some desert across the frozen wastes, where Alexander of Macedon, as I once read in a story book, once found himself stranded among savages. . . ."

I speak to her half in fun and half in anger, and all the time my heart weeps. But Tevye is no weakling; I control myself. And Hodel doesn't lose her dignity either; she answers me word for word, speaking quietly and thoughtfully. And Tevye's daughters can talk.

And though my head is lowered and my eyes are shut, still I seem to see her—her face is pale and lifeless like the moon, but her voice trembles. . . . Shall I fall on her neck and plead with her not to go? I know it won't help. Those daughters of mine—when they fall in love with somebody, it is with their heads and hearts, their bodies and souls.

Well, we sat on the doorstep a long time—maybe all night. Most of the time we were silent, and when we did speak it was in snatches, a word here, a word there. I said to her, "I want to ask you only one thing: did you ever hear of a girl marrying a man so that she could follow him to the ends of the earth?" And she answered, "With him I'd go anywhere." I pointed out how foolish that was. And she said, "Father, you will never understand." So I told her a little fable—about a hen that hatched some ducklings. As soon as the ducklings could move they took to the water and swam, and the poor hen stood on shore, clucking and clucking.

"What do you say to that, my daughter?"

"What can I say?" she answered. "I am sorry for the poor hen; but just because she stood there clucking, should the ducklings have stopped swimming?"

There is an answer for you. She's not stupid, that daughter of mine.

But time does not stand still. It was beginning to get light already, and from within the house my old woman was muttering. More than once she had called out that it was time to go to bed, but seeing that it didn't help she stuck her head out of the window and said to me, with her usual benediction, "Tevye, what's keeping you?"

"Be quiet, Golde," I answered. "Remember what the Psalm says, '*Why are the nations in an uproar, and why do the peoples mutter in vain?* Have you forgotten that it's *Hashono Rabo* tonight? Tonight all our fates are decided and the verdict is sealed. We stay up tonight . . . Listen to me, Golde, you light the samovar and make some tea while I go to get the horse and wagon ready. I am taking Hodel to the station in the morning." And once more I make up a story about how she has to go to Yehupetz, and from there farther on, because of that same old inheritance. It is possible, I say, that she may have to stay there through the winter and maybe the summer too, and maybe even another winter; and so we ought to give her something to take along—some linen, a dress, a couple of pillows, some pillow slips, and things like that.

And as I give these orders I tell her not to cry. "It's *Hashono Rabo* and on *Hashono Rabo* one mustn't weep. It's a law." But naturally they don't pay any attention to me, and when the time comes to say good-bye they all start weeping—their mother, the children and even Hodel herself. And when she came to say good-bye to her older sister Tzeitl (Tzeitl and her husband spend their holidays with us) they fell on each other's necks and you could hardly tear them apart.

I was the only one who did not break down. I was firm as steel —though inside I was more like a boiling samovar. All the way to Boiberik we were silent, and when we came near the station I asked her for the last time to tell me what it was that Feferel had really done. If they were sending him away, there must have been a reason. At this she became angry and swore by all that was holy that he was innocent. He was a man, she insisted, who cared nothing about himself. Everything he did was for humanity at large, especially for those who toiled with their hands—that is, the workers. That made no sense to me. "So he worries about the world," I told her. "Why doesn't the world worry a little about him? Nevertheless, give him my regards, that Alexander of Macedon of yours, and tell him I rely on his honor—for he is a man of honor, isn't he?—to treat my daughter well. And write to your old father some times."

When I finish talking she falls on my neck and begins to weep. "Good-bye, father," she cries. "Good-bye! God alone knows when we shall see each other again."

Well, that was too much for me. I remembered this Hodel when she was still a baby and I carried her in my arms, I carried her in my arms. . . . Forgive me, Mr. Sholom Aleichem, for acting like an old woman. If you only knew what a daughter she is. If you could only see the letters she writes. Oh, what a daughter. . . .

And now, let's talk about more cheerful things. Tell me, what news is there about the cholera in Odessa?

The Happiest Man in Kodno

THE BEST TIME of the year to travel is in the autumn, right after the High Holidays. It is neither too hot nor too cold and you are not obliged to look at the dripping sky or at the dark dismal earth. Drops of rain beat against the windows and roll down the sweating windowpanes, like tears. You sit in the third-class carriage like a Lord in his castle, surrounded by other nobles just like yourself. You take a look outside and you see at a distance a wagon creeping along, the wheels sloshing in the mud. On the wagon sits one of God's creatures, bent over double, with a sack on his shoulders, and whips along his poor little horse who is also one of God's creatures. You lean back and thank God that you are sitting under a dry roof in company with others. I don't know about you, but for me autumn is the best time of the year to travel.

The first thing I do is grab a seat. If I am lucky enough to get a seat by a window, then I am really a king. I take out my tobacco pouch and begin smoking cigarette after cigarette. I look around to see who my fellow-passengers are, to see if there is anyone worth talking to. The car is packed tight with people, row upon row of beards, noses, caps, protruding stomachs—all in the image of man. But wait! Off in a corner by himself sits an odd creature, different from the others. My eyes are sharp. I can spot an odd character among a hundred others.

At first glance he seems to be an ordinary fellow—a Jew like the rest, the kind we call an "everyday Jew." But he is dressed strangely.

His coat is not quite a coat and yet not a gabardine. He has something on his head that is not quite a hat and yet not a skullcap. In his hands he holds something that might be either an umbrella or a broomstick. An odd-looking character.

But it isn't his clothes that attract me so much as his manner. He can't seem to sit still in one spot. He keeps moving about restlessly from place to place. And his face isn't still either. His eyes shoot sparks, his face is glowing, it has a rapt joyous look on it, as though he had just won a fortune in the lottery, or married off a daughter to a millionaire, or entered his son in a gymnasium. Every few minutes he jumps up, and runs to the window and mutters to himself, "A station? Not yet?" And he sits down again, each time a little closer to where I am sitting. And his face continues to shine. . . .

You must know that by nature I am not the sort of person who likes to worm secrets out of people. I never pry into other people's affairs. I go according to this theory, that if a man has something on his chest he will unburden himself of his own accord.

And I am not wrong this time either. At the very next station the restless passenger moved closer to me, so close this time that his mouth almost touched my nose.

"And where are you going?" he asked me.

I could tell from the way he asked the question, from the eager look in his eyes and the restless motion of his hands, that he was not so eager to know where I was going, as to tell me where *he* was going. And so I humored him, I didn't answer his question, but asked instead, "And where are you going?" This started him off.

"Where am I going? To Kodno. Have you ever heard of Kodno? That's where I'm from. It isn't far, just three stations away. That is, you get off at the third station from here and then you still have to ride an hour and a half by wagon to get to Kodno. I say an hour and half. It's closer to two hours, two solid hours and a little bit over. And that only if the road is clear and you're riding in a carriage. I am going to have a carriage meet me today. I sent a telegram ahead to have a carriage meet me at the station. Do you think it's for myself? Don't worry—for my part I can squeeze into a wagon with six others, and if not, I can take my umbrella in one hand, my bundle in the other and make the trip on foot too. I can't afford to hire carriages every day. Business being what it is, I can sit at home altogether."

Here he paused, sighed, looked all around him first to make sure that no one was listening, then began to speak softly right into my ear:

"I am not traveling alone. I am traveling with a Professor—a famous doctor. How do I happen to be traveling with a Professor? I'll tell you. Have you ever heard of Kashavarevka? That's a town near here. A certain very rich man lives there—maybe you have heard of him—his name is Borodenko, Itzik Borodenko. How do you like his name? An odd name, isn't it? But he's a rich man, rolling in wealth. In Kodno we value him at half a million. For my part, I will allow him a whole million. And seeing how stingy he is, I will even make it two million. For example, you must have traveled widely in these parts—have you ever heard of a man named Borodenko giving great sums to charity? So far we've never heard of it in Kodno either. But let that go. I am not—how do you say it—God's deputy. I am not collecting charity. Everybody is too generous with other people's money.

"It isn't charity I speak of now, but plain ordinary human decency. If God has blessed you with so much money that you can afford to send for a famous specialist for your sick child, will it hurt you if another benefits from your good fortune? Nobody is asking you for money. All we want is a kind word. But wait till you hear this.

"We heard in Kodno that a daughter of this same Borodenko that I am telling you about had suddenly become ill. (In Kodno we hear about everything.) What sort of illness do you think it was? Not an illness, but an unhappy love affair. She fell in love with a gentile and he jilted her, so she took poison. (In Kodno we hear about everything.) This happened only yesterday. Well, they made haste and sent off for a doctor, a famous Professor from the big city. A rich man can afford to get the best. So I got an idea. Since this doctor, this Professor, won't be staying very long, he will be leaving today or tomorrow and on his way back he has to pass our station anyway —why can't he get off and run over to Kodno between trains and see my son?

"I have a son who is sick, at home. You ask what's wrong with him? I don't know myself. It's something they call internal. He has no pains of any kind, and he doesn't cough either, thank God. But he has no strength—he is weak, as weak as a fly. That's because he won't touch any food, he won't eat a thing. Sometimes he will drink a glass of milk, and that only by force. You have to weep and plead with him to take it. Aside from that he won't take a spoonful of soup or a bite of bread. And meat? He won't look at meat. He turns his head away.

"He has been this way since he had a hemorrhage last summer. He hasn't had any since then, thank God. But he is so weak, you can't imagine how weak he is. He can't move a limb. But what can you expect when the boy has been running a fever since before *Shevuos*. There is no remedy for it. We've taken him to the doctor more than once. But what do our doctors know? Give him a lot of food, he says, give him fresh air. But he won't touch any food, and as for fresh air—where would we get that? Fresh air—in Kodno? Kodno is a fine little town, we have a good number of Jews living there. We have a Synagogue, two Synagogues in fact. We have a Rabbi, we have everything. But from two things God has delivered us—from fresh air and a livelihood.

"Still we scrape up a living somehow. We live off each other. But fresh air? If we want fresh air, we have to go outside the town to the Landowners' Estate. There you will find fresh air. When Kodno belonged to the Polish Squire we were not allowed on the estate. The Squire didn't permit it, and not so much the Squire as the Squire's dogs. But now the estate belongs to Jewish landowners and we are allowed to go in. When I say Jewish landowners, I don't mean they are Jews like us. They don't go to our Synagogue and certainly not to our Baths. And they don't mind eating chicken with butter. Naturally they are clean-shaven and go without hats, that's taken for granted. Even in Kodno there are certain young men nowadays who find a hat too weighty for their heads.

"But we have nothing to complain about. The landowners are good to us. In autumn they send down a hundred sacks of potatoes for the poor. In winter they give us straw for fuel. For Passover they provide us with *matzos*. Recently, they donated some bricks for the Synagogue. If it wasn't for that chicken cooked in butter, I wouldn't find fault. Mind you, I don't want to slander them. They think very highly of me. They wouldn't exchange me for a barrel of *borsht*. Whenever something comes up, they call on Reb Alter—my name is Alter. Whether it's a calendar for the new year or *matzos* for Passover—anything to do with Jewish customs—they send for me. And they give my wife a good bit of business too—my wife has a shop—they buy salt and pepper and matches from her. I can't complain about our landowners.

"And their sons—the young students—are wild about my boy. In summer when they all come home from St. Petersburg they gather at my house and read with him. They spend days reading books with him. And books, you must know, are my son's first love. They are dearer to him than his father and his mother. I hate to say it, but I'm afraid that it's these books that have ruined his health, though my wife insists that it's his military service. That's nonsense. He's forgotten his military service long ago. But whatever it is, books or military service, there he is—sick, sick to death, wasting away like a candle. . . ."

For a moment something like a cloud passed over the shining face of my acquaintance. But only for a moment. The sun came out quickly again and drove away the cloud. His face began to glow once more, his eyes lit up, and a smile appeared on his lips. He went on talking:

"Well, where were we? Oh, yes, I decided to run over to Kashavarevka. Naturally I didn't set out just so, how do you say it—empty-handed? I took along a letter from the Rabbi of Kodno. (The Rabbi of Kodno is known all over.) A very handsomely written letter, addressed to Itzik Borodenko: 'Whereas, God has blessed you to such an extent that you are in a position to summon a Professor to your home when you need his services, and since our Alter has a son who is lying on his deathbed, perhaps a spark of pity will awaken in your breast and warm your heart so that you will enter into his need, and prevail upon the Professor to stop off in Kodno between trains and visit the sick boy.' And so on and so on. A very handsome letter."

Suddenly a whistle sounds, the train stops.

"Aha. A station. I'll just run over to the first-class carriage for a second. I want to take a peek at my Professor. When I get back I'll finish my story."

In a few minutes he came back, looking even happier and more exalted than before. If I might express myself thus, he looked as though he had "beheld the divine Presence." Moving up close to me he whispered into my ear as though he was afraid he might wake up someone. "He is asleep. The Professor is sleeping. May he rest well with God's help, so that when he comes to us, it will be with a clear head. Where were we? Oh, yes, in Kashavarevka. I arrived in Kashavarevka and went straight to Itzik Borodenko's house. I rang the bell once, twice, three times. Out came a big fellow with a red face, licking his chops like a cat, and he says to me in Russian, '*Chto nada?*'—What do you need? And I say in Yiddish, 'It must be *nada*. If I didn't need anything I wouldn't have traveled here all the way from Kodno.'

"He listens to me, keeps on chewing and licking his chops, and finally shakes his head and says, 'You can't get in today. The Professor is sitting in consultation.'

" 'That's just why I came here,' I tell him. 'On account of the Professor.'

"And he says in an insulting tone, 'What business can you have with a Professor?'

"Instead of explaining, I handed him the Rabbi's letter. 'It's easy for you to stand there talking,' I said. 'You are snug and dry inside, and I am standing here with the rain pouring on me. Here, take this document and be so kind as to give it to your employer, put it right into his hands.'

"He went in, and I remained standing there, waiting for them to send for me. I wait half an hour. I wait an hour. I wait two hours. The rain keeps coming down on me in a torrent and still nobody sends for me. I was beginning to feel offended, not so much for my sake as for the Rabbi's. Imagine them ignoring a letter from the Rabbi of Kodno! So I rang the bell again, several times. The same red-faced lout jumps out and shouts at me furiously, 'What's the idea of ringing that bell? Who do you think you are?' And I answer, 'And who do you think you are, letting me stand out here in the rain for two hours?' I try to push my way in, but he quickly slams the door in my face. What's to be done? It looks bad. I am ashamed to go home empty-handed. After all, I am a leading citizen of Kodno, not some tramp that can be chased away from the door. And above all, my heart aches for my son.

"But there is a merciful God in heaven. I look up—a carriage pulled by four horses drives up and stops right at the door. I ask the coachman whose carriage and horses these are, and I learn that they are Borodenko's carriage and horses and they have come to take the Professor to the station. If so, I think to myself, very good. In fact, excellent.

"Before I am through asking, the door opens and out comes the Professor himself, a tiny, shrunken little old man with a face—how shall I describe it—the face of an angel. An angel from heaven. Behind him comes Borodenko himself, and behind him the red-faced lout carrying the Professor's suitcase. I wish you could have seen this Borodenko, this millionaire, homely and cross-eyed and dressed in a jacket of ordinary cloth, the kind we wear in Kodno, standing there with his hands in his pockets. I look at him and think to myself, 'Dear God in Heaven, so this is the creature you blessed with millions.' But you can't argue with God. The millionaire looks at me sideways, with his cross-eyes and says, 'What do you want here?'

"I go up to him and tell him why I came. 'I brought you a letter from the Rabbi,' I say.

"And he says, 'Which Rabbi?'

"How do you like that? He wants to know which Rabbi. 'From the Rabbi of Kodno,' I tell him. 'I came from Kodno especially to see the Professor and to ask if he wouldn't be so kind as to do me the favor of stopping at my house for a quarter of an hour between trains to see my sick son.'

"I was thinking to myself, 'The man has just suffered a misfortune, his daughter took poison, maybe he will have some pity in his heart for a poor father's plight.'

"But there wasn't a sign of pity on his face. He didn't even answer me. He turned to the red-faced lout as though to say, 'How about clearing this beggar out of the way?'

"Meanwhile the Professor had stepped into the carriage with his suitcase. A moment more and he would be gone. What should I do? Seeing that the game was as good as lost anyway, I had no choice. I said to myself, 'What will happen will happen! I must save my child.' I took a deep breath and jumped in front of the horses. What would you like to know? Shall I tell you how it felt to be trampled by the horses' hooves? I am not sure whether I was trampled under their hooves or not. I am not sure just what happened or how long I lay there, or if I lay there at all. I only know that in less time than it takes to tell this, the little Professor was standing by me and saying, *'Chto takoie?'*—What's the matter? And calling me *'golubtchik,'* dear one, and asking me to tell him my request, not to be afraid, to tell him everything.

"So I began talking while the millionaire stood by looking at me with his cross-eyes. You must know that I don't speak Russian fluently, but this time God gave me extra strength and I talked! I poured out everything there was in my heart. 'Herr Professor,' I said, 'God himself must have sent you as His messenger to save my son's life. He is my only son, the only one left to me of six. And if it has to cost money, I have twenty-five *rubles*. It isn't my own money—where would I get so much money? It's my wife's money that she has been saving up to buy merchandise for her shop. But I will give you the twenty-five *rubles* and the devil take my wife's shop. I must save my son.'

"I unbuttoned my coat and was about to take out the money. But the Professor put his hand on my shoulder and said, *'Nitchevo.'*—It doesn't matter. And he told me to get into the carriage with him. Do you think that I am inventing this? I swear to you by everything holy, by my hope of seeing my son well, that I am telling the truth. So I ask you, isn't the millionaire Borodenko worth less than the least little fingernail of the Professor? He almost ruined me, this Borodenko; he was ready to kill me, without a knife. Luckily my trick worked. But suppose it hadn't? Eh? What do you say?"

Suddenly there was a stir in the carriage. My friend ran up to the conductor.

"Is this Kodno?" he asked.

"This is Kodno."

He turned to me. "Good-bye, and have a good trip and don't tell anyone whom I am traveling with. I don't want them to know in Kodno that I am bringing a Professor. The whole town will come running."

He whispered this hurriedly, pressed my hand, and was gone.

A few minutes later when we were ready to start again I looked out of the window and saw a rickety old carriage with a couple of broken-down nags hitched to it. Inside sat a tiny old man wearing glasses, with youthful pink cheeks, and a short gray beard. Opposite him in the carriage sat my friend, barely hanging on to the edge of his seat. He was looking into the old man's eyes and you could see him quivering all over with emotion—his face was glowing and his eyes almost popped out of his head with excitement.

I was sorry that I didn't have a camera with me. I would have liked to take a picture of him, to let the whole world see what a really happy man looked like, the happiest man in Kodno.

A Wedding without Musicians

THE LAST TIME I told you about our Straggler Special, I described the miracle of *Hashono Rabo*. This time I shall tell you about another miracle in which the Straggler Special figured, how thanks to the Straggler Special the town of Heissin was saved from a terrible fate.

This took place during the days of the Constitution when reprisals against the Jews were going on everywhere. Though I must tell you that we Jews of Heissin have never been afraid of pogroms. Why? Simply because there is no one in our town who can carry out a pogrom. Of course you can imagine that if we looked very hard we could find one or two volunteers who wouldn't deny themselves the pleasure of ventilating us a little, that is, breaking our bones or burning down our houses. For example, when reports of pogroms began drifting in, the few Squires, who are enemies of our people, wrote confidential letters to the proper authorities, saying it might be a good idea if "something were done" in Heissin also; but since there was no one here to do it, would they be so kind as to send help, in other words, would they dispatch some "people" as quickly as possible.

And before another twenty-four hours had passed a reply came, also confidentially, that "people" were being sent. From where? From Zhmerinko, from Kazatin, Razdilno, Popelno and other such places that had distinguished themselves in beating up Jews. Do you want to know how we learned of this deep secret? We found it out through our regular source of news, Noah Tonkonoy. Noah Tonkonoy is a man whom God has endowed with a pair of extra-long legs and he uses them to good purpose. He never rests and he is seldom to be found at home. He is always busy with a thousand things and most of these things have to do with other people's business rather than his own. By trade he is a printer, and because he is the only printer in Heissin he knows all the squires and the police and has dealings with officialdom and is in on all their secrets.

Noah Tonkonoy spread the good news all over town. He told the secret to one person at a time, in strictest confidence, of course, saying, "I am telling this only to you. I wouldn't tell it to anyone else." And that was how the whole town became aware of the fact that a mob of hooligans was on the way, and that a plan for beating up Jews had been worked out. The plan told exactly when they would start, on which day, at which hour, and from which point, and by what means —everything to the last detail.

You can imagine what terror this struck in our hearts. Panic spread quickly. And among whom do you think it spread first? Among the poor, of course. It's a peculiar thing about poor people. When a rich man is afraid of a pogrom, you can understand why. He is afraid, poor fellow, that he will be turned into a pauper. But those of you who are already paupers, what are you afraid of? What have you got to lose? But you should have seen how they bundled up their children and packed up their belongings and began running hither and yon, looking for a place to hide. Where can a person hide? This one hides in a friendly peasant's cellar, another in the Notary's attic, a third in the Director's office at the factory. Everyone finds a spot for himself.

I was the only one in town who wasn't anxious to hide. I am not boasting about my bravery. But this is the way I see it: what's the sense of being afraid of a pogrom? I don't say that I am a hero. I might have been willing to hide too, when the hour of reckoning came. But I asked myself first, "How can I be sure that during the slaughter the friendly peasant in whose cellar I was hiding, or the Notary, or the Director of the factory himself, wouldn't . . ." You understand? And all that aside, how can you leave a town wide open like that? It's no trick to run away. You have to see about doing something. But, alas, what can a Jew do? He appeals to a friendly official. And that is just what we did.

In every town there is at least one friendly official you can appeal to. We had one too, the Inspector of Police, a jewel of a fellow, willing to listen to us and willing to accept a gift on occasion. We went to the Inspector with the proper gifts and asked for his protection. He reassured us at once. He told us to go home and sleep in peace. Nothing would happen. Sounds good, doesn't it? But we still had our walking newspaper, Noah, who was broadcasting another secret through the length and breadth of the town. The secret was that a telegram had just arrived. He swore by everything holy that he had seen it himself. What was in that telegram? Only one word—*Yediem*. An ugly word. It means simply, "We are coming." We ran back to the Inspector. "Your honor," we told him, "it looks bad." "What looks bad?" he asked, and we told him, "A telegram has just arrived." "From where?" We told him. "And what does it say?" We told him, *"Yediem."* At this he burst out laughing. "You are big fools," he said. "Only yesterday I ordered a regiment of Cossacks from Tolchin."

When we heard this we breathed more easily. When a Jew hears that a Cossack is coming, he takes courage, he can face the world again. The question remained: who would arrive first, the Cossacks from Tolchin, or the hooligans from Zhmerinko? Common sense told us that the hooligans would arrive first, because they were coming by train, while the Cossacks were coming on horseback. But we pinned all our hopes on the Straggler Special. God is merciful. He would surely perform a miracle and the Straggler would be at least a few hours late. This wasn't too much to hope for, since it happened nearly every day. But this one time it looked as though the miracle wouldn't take place. The Straggler kept going from station to station as regular as a clock. You can imagine how we felt when we learned, confidentially of course, through Noah Tonkonoy, that a telegram had arrived from the last station, from Krishtopovka. *Yediem* it said, and not just *yediem*—but *yediem* with a *hurrah!* in front of it.

Naturally we took this last bit of news straight to the Inspector. We begged him not to rely on the Cossacks who might or might not arrive from Tolchin sometime, but to send police to the station, at least for the sake of appearances, so that our enemies wouldn't think that we were completely at their mercy. The Inspector listened to our pleas. He did what we asked, and more. He got himself up in full uniform, with all his orders and medals, and took the whole police force, that is the gendarme and his assistant, to the station with him to meet the train.

But our enemies weren't asleep either. They also put on their full-dress uniforms, complete with ribbons and medals, took a couple of priests along, and also came to meet the train. The Inspector asked them sternly, "What are you doing here?" And they asked him the same question, "What are you doing here?" They bandied words back and forth, and the Inspector let them know in no uncertain terms that their trouble was for nothing. As long as he was in charge, there would be no pogrom in Heissin. They listened, smiled knowingly, and answered with insolence, "We shall see."

Just then a train whistle was heard from the distance. The sound struck terror to our hearts. We waited for another whistle to blow and after that for the shouts of *"Hurrah!"* What would happen after the *"Hurrah!"* we knew only too well from hearsay. We waited, but heard nothing more. What had happened? The sort of thing that could only happen to our Straggler Special.

When the Straggler Special drew into the station, the engineer stopped the locomotive, stepped out calmly and made his way toward the buffet. We met him halfway. "Well, my good fellow, and where are the cars?" "Which cars?" "Can't you see that you are here with the locomotive and without cars?"

He stared at us. "What do I care about the cars? They are the business of the crew." "Where is the crew?" "How should I know where the crew is? The conductor blows the whistle when he is ready and I whistle back to let him know that I am starting, and off we go. I don't have an extra pair of eyes in back of my head to see what's going on behind me." That was his story and according to that he was right. But right or wrong, there stood the Straggler Special without cars and without passengers. In other words, it was a wedding without musicians.

Later we learned that a band of hooligans had been on the way to

Heissin, all of them handpicked youths, armed to the teeth with clubs and knives and other weapons. Their spirits were high and liquor flowed freely. At the last station, Krishtopovka, they invited the crew to join them and treated everybody to drinks—the conductor, the fireman, the gendarme. But in the midst of this revelry they forgot one little detail, to couple the cars back to the locomotive. And so the locomotive went off at the usual time to Heissin and the rest of the Straggler Special remained standing in Krishtopovka.

Neither the hooligans nor the other passengers nor the crew noticed that they were standing still. They continued to empty bottle after bottle and to make merry, until the station master suddenly noticed that the locomotive had gone off and left the cars behind. He spread the alarm, the crew came tumbling out. A hue and cry was raised. The hooligans blamed the crew, the crew blamed the hooligans, but what good did it do? The cars couldn't budge without the locomotive. At last they decided that the only thing to do was to set out for Heissin on foot. They took heart and began marching toward Heissin, singing and shouting as they went.

And so they arrived in their usual good form, singing and yelling and brandishing their clubs. But it was already too late. In the streets of Heissin the Cossacks from Tolchin were riding up and down on horseback with whips in their hands. Within half an hour not one of the hooligans remained in town. They ran off like rats in a famine, they melted like ice in the summer.

Now I ask you, didn't the Straggler Special deserve to be showered with gold, or at least written up?

What Will Become of Me?

SUPPOSE you try to guess where the Garden of Eden is. You will never guess. Do you know why? Because it's different for everybody. For instance, for my mother the Garden of Eden or the true Paradise is where my father, Peissi the Cantor, is now. There, she says, dwell all the pure souls who suffered on this earth. Because they have lost this world they have gained the next. That is as plain as day. The best example is my father. For where else should he be but in the Garden of Eden? Didn't he suffer enough in this world? And my mother wipes her eyes, as she always does when she speaks of my father.

But ask my friends and they will tell you something else. For them Paradise is somewhere on a mountain of pure crystal that reaches up to the sky. There boys run and jump and play all day long as free as birds. They have no lessons to do. They bathe in rivers of milk and eat honey by the fistfuls. Is that good enough for you? Then along comes a bookbinder and tells me that the only true paradise is to be found Friday in the bath. I swear by all that is holy that this is what I heard from our neighbor Pessie's husband, Moses the Bookbinder. Now try to figure out who is right. If you asked me, for instance, I would tell you that the Garden of Eden is in Menashe the Doctor's orchard. In all your life you have never seen such an orchard. Neither on our street, nor in our whole town, nor in the whole wide world has there ever been such an orchard. There never has been and never will be. Everybody knows that.

Now what shall I tell you about first? Shall I tell you about

Menashe the Doctor and his wife, or about their paradise, I mean their orchard? I think that first of all I should tell you about Menashe and his wife. They are the owners of the orchard and they should have the honor of being first.

Menashe the Doctor wears a cape both summer and winter, in imitation of the "black doctor." One of his eyes is smaller than the other and his mouth is twisted to one side. It became twisted once when he was sitting in a draft. I don't understand how a mouth can become twisted from a draft. Think of all the winds and hurricanes I've been through in my short life. My head should have been turned around on my shoulders by now. I think it's only a habit with him. For instance, there is my friend Berel who blinks his eyes. Another boy Velvel lisps. Everything in the world is a habit. But in spite of his twisted mouth, Menashe makes out better than any of the other doctors. In the first place, he isn't as proud as the others. When you call him, he drops everything and comes at a run, sweating and out of breath. In the second place, he doesn't bother writing prescriptions. He makes his own medicines.

It happened one time that I suddenly came down with chills and fever and sharp pains in my chest. (I must have been playing in the river too long.) My mother rushed off to get Menashe the Doctor. He looked me over and said to my mother out of his crooked mouth, "You have nothing to worry about. It's a joke. The rascal caught a cold in his lungs."

And he took a blue bottle out of his pocket and poured something white out of the bottle into six pieces of white paper. He called these "powders." He wanted me to take one of those "powders" at once. I twisted and squirmed and tried to get out of taking it, for my heart told me that it would taste as bitter as gall. I had guessed right. There are bitter things and bitter things. Have you ever tasted the bark of a young tree? That was how this "powder" tasted. I took it and saw the Angel of Death face to face. He left the other five powders with my mother and told her to give me a powder every two hours until they were all gone.

But they didn't reckon with me. My mother had barely turned her back on me—she had gone to tell my brother Elihu that I was sick—

when I poured the five powders into the washbasin and filled the five papers with flour. My mother had taken a chore on herself that day. Every two hours she had to run to our neighbor Pessie's to look at the clock. After each powder that I took she noticed that I looked a little better. After the sixth one I got out of bed, completely cured.

"That's what I call a doctor," my mother said joyfully. She kept me home from *cheder* all day and gave me sweet tea and white rolls to eat. "Menashe is the best doctor of them all, may God grant him health and a long life. His powders work miracles, they make the dead come to life again," my mother boasted to the neighbors, wiping her eyes, as usual.

Menashe the Doctor's wife is known as Menashacha. She is a terrible woman, a regular witch. She wears men's boots and she has a deep gruff voice like a man. Whenever she talks, she seems to be scolding. She has a wonderful reputation in town. They say that in all her life she has never given a beggar a crust of bread to eat. And her house and pantry are filled with the best of everything. In her cellar you will find preserves from last year and the year before last and the year before that and from ten years ago. What does she do with all these preserves? She herself won't be able to tell you. She only knows that when summer comes she has to start making jams and preserves. Do you think that she cooks them over a coal fire? Not on your life. A fire made of thistles and pine cones and even of last year's leaves is good enough for her. This fire gives off such an acrid smoke that a person can choke to death. If you happen to stray into our neighborhood during the summer and smell something scorching, don't be frightened. There is no fire. It's only Menashacha cooking preserves. She makes them herself out of the fruits that grow in her own orchard. And now, at last, we have come to the orchard itself.

What fruits won't you find in this orchard? Apples and pears and cherries, plums and gooseberries and currants, peaches, raspberries, rough cherries, blackberries. What more can you ask for? Even grapes for *Rosh Hashono* grow in Menashe the Doctor's orchard. It's true that when you taste these grapes you behold Krakov and Lvov in front of you, they are that sour. But she gets good money for them.

She gets money for everything, even for her sunflowers. God help you if you ask her to let you pick a sunflower. She would sooner pull a tooth out of her head than a sunflower from her garden. So you can imagine what it's like asking for an apple or a pear or a plum. You take your life into your hands if you try.

I know the orchard by heart, inside and out, the way a good Jew knows his Psalms. I know where every tree grows, and what fruit it bears and whether it produced a good crop this year or not. How do I know all that? Don't get excited, I've never been inside the orchard. How could I when it's surrounded by a tall fence which is covered with sharp barbs? And do you think this is all? Inside the orchard there is a dog tied to a rope. Did I say a dog? He is more like a wolf. Just let anyone go by, or let him think he heard someone go by, and he begins tearing at the rope and jumping in the air and barking as though the devil had him by the throat. Then how did I become so familiar with the inside of the orchard? Listen, and I will tell you.

Do you know Mendel the *Shochet?* You don't? Then you certainly don't know Mendel's house. It's right next door to Menashe the Doctor's house and it faces the orchard. When you are on the roof of Mendel's house you can see everything that's going on in Menashe the Doctor's orchard. The problem is how to get up on Mendel's roof. To me that's no problem. Do you know why? Because Mendel's house is right next door to ours and it's much lower than our house. When you climb up into our attic (I do it without a ladder, some day I may tell you how) and put your foot out of the little window, you are on Mendel's roof. Once on the roof you can stretch out on its slope, either with your face down or your face up, but you have to stretch out flat, or someone will see you and ask, "What are you doing on Mendel the *Shochet's* roof?" I always used to pick the early evening to go up on the roof, just before sundown, when I was supposed to be in the Synagogue saying *kaddish* for my father. That's the best time, when it's neither light nor dark. Lying on Mendel the *Shochet's* roof in the twilight I would look down on the orchard and I can swear to you that here was the true paradise. . . .

Early in the summer when the trees start budding and become covered with white fluff, you can start hoping that if not today, then tomorrow—any minute now—in the short prickly bushes, gooseberries will appear. This is the first fruit you wish you could taste. There are people who wait until the gooseberries are ripe. They are fools. May I have as many blessings how much better they are when they are still green. You will say that they are sour? That they set your teeth on edge? What of that? Sour things sharpen the appetite. And there is a remedy against having your teeth set on edge. The remedy is salt. You pour salt on your teeth and keep your mouth open for half an hour. Then you can start eating gooseberries again.

After the gooseberries come the currants. Bright red, tiny, with black muzzles, and yellow kernels, there are dozens of them growing on each sprig. If you pass one sprig between your lips you get a whole mouthful of currants—sweet, winy, delicious.

When currants are in season my mother buys me a small bag for a *groschen,* so that I can make the blessing over the first fruit of the season, and I eat them with bread. In Menashe's orchard there are two rows of currant bushes growing close to the ground, studded with currants. They glisten and twinkle in the sun and you long to pick one twig, or at least take one currant between your fingers and pop it into your mouth. Would you believe it, when I talk about green gooseberries and red currants my teeth are set on edge? Let's better talk about cherries.

Cherries don't stay green long. They ripen very quickly. I can swear to you by anything you wish that I myself saw, from Mendel the *Shochet's* roof, several cherries that were green as grass in the morning. I looked at them and marked in my mind the spot where they grew. During the day their cheeks reddened in the sun. That same evening they were as red as fire. My mother used to buy me cherries too. How many did she buy? Five cherries on a string. What can you do with five cherries? You fondle them and play with them until you don't know where they've disappeared to.

There are as many cherries in Menashe's orchard as there are stars in heaven. I once tried to count the cherries on one branch. I counted and counted and couldn't finish counting. Cherries cling very tightly to the branch. It's very seldom that a cherry will fall to the ground.

Before it falls it has to be over-ripe, and as black as a plum. But peaches are different. Peaches fall to the ground as soon as they turn yellow. Don't let me start talking about peaches. I love them more than any other fruit. In all my life I have eaten only one peach, and the taste still lingers in my mouth. That was several years ago, when I was not quite five years old and my father was still alive, and we still had the glass cabinet, the sofa, the books and all our beds. One day my father came home from the Synagogue and called me and my brother Elihu over to him. "Children," he said, "how would you like to taste a peach? I brought you two peaches, one peach for each of you."

He put his hand into his back pocket and brought out two large, round, yellow, fragrant pieces of fruit. My brother Elihu couldn't wait. He rushed through the words, "Blessed be the fruit of the earth . . ." and stuck the whole peach into his mouth at once. But I wasn't in such a hurry. I wanted to hold it in my hand awhile, to fondle it, smell it, play with it, and then when I was through playing, I began eating it, and that not in one gulp, but in little bites, a bite of peach and a bite of bread. Peaches taste very good with bread. Since that time I have never tasted another peach, but I have never forgotten the taste of that first one. Now a whole peach tree stands in front of me and I lie on Mendel's roof and watch the ripe peaches falling to the ground one by one. One ripe golden peach, streaked with pink, has split open and lies there with its fat kernel showing. What will Menashacha do with so many peaches? She will shake down the tree, gather them up, and make preserves. She will put the preserves on the back of the hearth and in winter she will take them down to the cellar. There they will stand until they become sugared over and are coated with mold.

After the peaches, the plums ripen. Not all the plums at once. I have two kinds of plum trees in Menashe's orchard. One tree bears plums called "chernitza." That's a hard, sweet, dark plum. The plums on the other tree are called "bucket plums" because they are sold by the bucket. They have thin skins and are slippery and sticky to the touch and they have a watery taste. Still, they are not as bad as you might think. I only wish I could have some of them. But Menashacha is not one of your generous givers. She would rather make plum jam for the winter. When in the world does she expect to eat up all this jam?

When I am through with the cherries, peaches and plums, then there begins for me a succession of apples. Apples, as you know, are not like pears. The best pears in the world, if they are not quite ripe, are absolutely no good. They are as dry as dust. Apples, though they are as green as grass and their seeds are still white, already taste like apples. You bury your teeth in a green apple and your whole mouth puckers up. And yet I wouldn't change half a green apple for two ripes ones. If you want your apples ripe you have to wait until late, late in the summer. But you can have green apples as soon as the tree has finished blooming. The difference is only in size. The longer an apple is left to ripen the larger it gets, just like a human being. But that doesn't mean that a large apple is the best. It often happens that a tiny apple tastes better than a big one. Take the little *Eretz-Isroel* apples for instance, they are tart but delicious. Or "kislitzas" or winesaps. Is there anything wrong with them, I ask you?

This will be a great year for apples. There will be so many apples that they will be carted around in wagonloads. I heard Menashacha herself tell it to Rueben the Appleman when the trees were still in bloom. Rueben the Appleman came to see her orchard, he wanted to buy the apples and pears "on the tree." Rueben knows all about apples and pears. He can glance at a tree out of the corner of his eye and tell you at once how much money the tree will bring. He won't be off by so much—unless the winds are unusually strong and the apples fall before their time, or worms get them or else the blight. All these are things a person can't foresee. A wind is sent by God and so is a blight. Though I can't understand what God wants with worms and blights. Unless it's to take the bread away from Rueben the Appleman. Rueben says that all he wants from a tree is a piece of bread. He has a wife and children and he has to find bread for them. Menashacha promises him not only a piece of bread, but bread with meat. "Are they ordinary trees?" she asks. "They are gold mines, not trees.

"You know yourself," says Menashacha," that I don't wish you any ill luck. May all the good fortune I wish to you come to me also."

"Amen," says Rueben with a smile on his kindly, red face that's peeling from the sun. "If you will sign a contract against winds, worms, and blights, I will give you even more than you asked for."

Menashacha gives him a peculiar look and says in her gruff, man's voice, "How about signing a contract that you will walk out of here and won't slip and break a leg?"

"No one is assured against falling and breaking a leg," says Rueben, looking at her with his kindly, smiling eyes. "That can happen to a rich man even quicker than to a poor man, for a rich man can afford it better."

"You are very smart," says Menashacha angrily. "But a man who wishes that another break his leg deserves to have his tongue shrink up in his mouth."

"Why not?" says Reuben, still with the same gentle smile. "A shrunken tongue isn't so bad either, as long as it doesn't happen to a poor man."

It's a great pity that the orchard doesn't belong to Rueben the Appleman. It would be much pleasanter for me. You've never seen such a witch as Menashacha. Let one little, wormy, dried-up apple, as wrinkled and shrunken as an old woman's face, fall to the ground and she will bend down, pick it up, hide it in her apron and carry it off. Where does she carry it off to? Either up into her attic or down into the cellar. I've heard it told that last year a whole cellarful of apples rotted on her. Now tell me, doesn't she deserve to have her apples picked by others? But how can you get to them? To steal into the orchard at night when everyone is asleep and fill your pockets would be one way. But there is that wild dog guarding it. And to make things worse the trees are loaded with apples this year. They beg you, they plead with you, to pick them. What to do? If only there were some charm, some magic words by which I could make them come to me of their own will. I think and I think and at last think up something.

What I have thought up is neither charms nor magic words, but an ordinary stick, a long stick with a nail at the end of it. If you reach the tree with the stick and catch the stem of the apple with the nail, and pull it gently toward yourself, the apple is yours. You just have to know how to hold the stick so that the apple won't fall to the ground. And if an apple does fall it isn't such a loss either. She will think the wind tore it off. But you must be careful not to touch the apple itself with the nail or you will bruise it. I promise you that I have never bruised an apple yet. And my apples don't fall to the ground either. I know how to operate the stick. The important thing is not to be caught at it. Just don't hurry. Take your time about it. Have you got an apple in your hands? Eat it quietly, rest a little, then start picking again. I give you my word not a soul will know. . . .

How could I have guessed that the witch Menashacha would know the exact number of apples on her trees? She must have counted them one day and counted them again the next day and found that some were missing. Then she hid herself in her attic and began spying to see if she could catch the thief. That's how I figured it out. For how else could she have found out that I lay on Mendel's roof and plied my stick in her orchard? If she had only caught me herself, without any witnesses, I might have begged off. After all, I am an orphan. She might have had pity on me. But she thought of a better way. She went to my mother and to our neighbor Pessie and to Mendel's wife, and took all three women up into our attic with her. (Only a witch could do a thing like that.) Crouching in the attic they could look through the window and see me operating the stick. . . .

"Well, and what have you got to say for your precious son? Do you believe me now?"

I recognized Menashacha's gruff voice and turned my head and saw the four women watching me. I didn't throw my stick away. It fell out of my hands. It was lucky that I didn't fall off the roof too. I couldn't look them in the face. If the dog weren't down there in the orchard I would have leaped to my death for very shame. Worst of all were my mother's tears. She began weeping and wailing and wringing her hands. "Woe is me, woe is me. That I should live to see this day. Here I am thinking that my orphan is at the Synagogue saying *kaddish* for his father, and instead he is lying on a roof—may thunder and lightning strike me—and picking apples from a stranger's orchard."

And Menashacha added in her deep, gruff voice, "He should be beaten, he should be whipped, the young apostate. Whipped till the blood comes. A boy should be taught not to be a th—"

My mother wouldn't let her finish the word "thief." "He is an orphan," she pleaded. "The poor child is an orphan." And she began kissing the witch's hands and begging her to forgive me, promising that it would never happen again. She swore with sacred oaths that this was the last time, the very last time, may she die if it wasn't, or else live to bury me. . . .

"I want him to swear that he will never even look into my orchard," demanded Menashacha ruthlessly, without a trace of pity for a poor orphan.

"Let my hand dry up," I swore. "Let my eyes drop out, before I touch another apple." Then I went home with my mother and had to listen to her scolding and weeping, and I began weeping lustily myself.

"What will become of you?" my mother asked with tears in her eyes. She told the story to my brother Elihu, and when my brother heard of the incident of the apples he went pale with rage. My mother saw this and whispered something into his ears. She whispered to him not to thrash me, I was an orphan.

"Who wants to touch him?" said my brother Elihu. "I would like to know just one thing. What will become of him? *What will become of him?"*

My brother gnashed his teeth and looked at me as though asking me if I knew what would become of me. How should I know? Do you know what will become of me?

Chava

"GIVE thanks unto the Lord, for He is good.—Whatever He ordains, His way is the best." It has to be the best, for if you had the wisdom of a Solomon could you improve on it? Look at me—I wanted to be clever, I turned and twisted, this way and that, and tried everything I knew, and then when I saw it was no use, I took my hand off my chest, as the saying is, and said to myself, "Tevye, you're a fool, you won't change the world. The Lord has given us the *'pain of bringing up children,'* which means that in raising children you have to accept the bad with the good and count them as one."

Take, for instance, my oldest daughter, Tzeitl, who went and fell in love with the tailor Motel Kamzoil. Have I got anything against him? True, he is a simple, unlettered fellow, who can't read the learned footnotes at the bottom of the page, but is that anything against him? Everybody in the world can't be a scholar. At least he is an honest man and a hard-working one. She's already borne him a whole brood of young ones; they have a houseful of hungry mouths to feed, and both of them, he and she, are struggling along *"in honor and in riches,"* as the saying is. And yet if you ask her, she will tell you that she is the happiest woman in the world, no one could be happier. There is only one tiny flaw—they don't have enough to eat. *"That's the end of the first round with the Torah.*—There's Number One for you."

About my second daughter, about Hodel, I don't have to tell you. You know about her already. With her I played and I lost. I lost her forever. God knows if my eyes will ever behold her again, unless it should be in the next world. To this day I can't bring myself to talk about her calmly. I mention her name and the old pain returns. Forget her, you say? How can you forget a living human being? And especially a child like Hodel! If you could only see the letters she writes me. . . . They are doing very well, she tells me. He sits in prison and she works for a living. She washes clothes all day, reads books in between, and goes to see him once a week. She lives in the hope that very soon the pot will boil over, as they say, the sun will rise and everything become bright. He will be set free along with many others like him, and then, she says, they will all roll up their sleeves and get to work to turn the world upside down. Well, what do you think of that? Sounds promising, doesn't it?

But what does the Lord do next? He is, after all, *"a gracious and merciful Lord,"* and He says to me, "Wait, Tevye, I will bring something to pass that will make you forget all your former troubles."

And so it was. It's a story worth hearing. I would not repeat it to anyone else, for while the pain is great, the disgrace is even greater. But how is it written? *"Shall I conceal it from Abraham?*—Can I keep any secrets from you?" Whatever is on my mind I shall tell you. But one thing I want to ask of you. Let it remain between you and me. For I repeat: the pain is great, but the disgrace—the disgrace is even greater.

How is it written in *Perek? "The Holy One, blessed be He, wished to grant merit to Israel—"* The Lord wanted to be good to Tevye, so He blessed him with seven female children, that is, seven daughters, each one of them a beauty, all of them good-looking and charming, clever and healthy and sweet-tempered—like young pine trees! Alas, if only they had been ill-tempered and ugly as scarecrows, it might have been better for them, and certainly healthier for me. For what use is a fine horse, I ask you, if you have to keep it locked up in a stable? What good are beautiful daughters if you are stuck away with them in a forsaken corner of the world, where you never see a live person except for Anton Poperilo, the village mayor, or the clerk Fyedka Galagan, a young fellow with a long mane of hair and tall peasant boots, or the Russian priest, may his name be blotted out?

CHAVA

I can't bear to hear that priest's name mentioned, not because I am a Jew and he is a priest. On the contrary, we've been on friendly terms for a number of years. By that I don't mean that we visit at each other's homes or dance at the same weddings. I only mean that when we happen to meet we greet each other civilly. "Good morning." "Good day. What's new in the world?"

I've never liked to enter into a discussion with him, for right away the talk would turn to this business of *your God* and *my God*. Before he could get started I would recite a proverb or quote him a passage from the Bible. To which he replied that he could quote me a passage from the Bible also, and perhaps better than I, and he began to recite the Scriptures to me, mimicking the sacred language like a Gentile: *"Berezhit bara alokim*—In the beginning the Lord created the Heavens. . . ." Then I told him that we had a folk tale, or a *medresh* to the effect that. . . . "A *medresh"* he interrupted me, "is the same as *Tal-mud,"* and he didn't like *Talmud,* "for *Tal-mud* is nothing but sheer trickery." Then I would get good and angry and give him what he had coming. Do you think that bothered him? Not in the least. He would only look at me, and laugh, and comb his long beard with his fingers. There is nothing in the world, I tell you, so maddening as a person who doesn't answer when you abuse him. You shout and you scold, you are ready to burst a gut, and he stands there and smiles. . . . At that time I didn't understand what that smile of his meant, but now I know what was behind it. . . .

Well, to return to my story. I arrived at home one day—it was toward evening—and whom should I see but the clerk Fyedka standing outside with my Chava, that's my third daughter, the one next to Hodel. When he caught sight of me, the young fellow spun around quickly, tipped his hat to me, and was off. I asked Chava, "What was Fyedka doing here?"

"Nothing," she said.

"What do you mean nothing?"

"We were just talking."

"What business have you got talking with Fyedka?" I asked.

"We've known each other for a long time," she said.

"Congratulations!" I said. "A fine friend you've picked for yourself."

"Do you know him at all?" she asked. "Do you know who he is?"

"No," I said, "I don't know who he is. I've never seen his family tree. But I am sure he must be descended from a long and honorable line. His father," I said, "must have been either a shepherd or a janitor, or else just a plain drunkard."

To this Chava answered, "Who his father was I don't know and I don't care to know. All people are the same to me. But Fyedka himself is not an ordinary person, of that I am sure."

"Tell me," I said, "what kind of person is he? I'd like to hear."

"I would tell you," she said, "but you wouldn't understand. Fyedka is a second Gorky."

"A second Gorky? And who, may I ask, was the first Gorky?"

"Gorky," she said, "is one of the greatest men living in the world today."

"Where does he live," I asked, "this sage of yours, what is his occupation and what words of wisdom has he spoken?"

"Gorky," she said, "is a famous author. He is a writer, that is, a man who writes books. He is fine and honest and true, a person to be honored. He also comes from plain people, he was not educated anywhere, he is self-taught . . . here is his portrait." Saying this, she took a small photograph from her pocket and handed it to me.

"So this is he," I said, "this sage of yours, Reb Gorky? I can swear I have seen him somewhere before, either at the baggage depot, carrying sacks, or in the woods hauling logs."

"Is it a crime then if a man works with his hands? Don't you yourself work with your hands? Don't all of us work?"

"Yes, yes," I said, "you are right. We have a certain proverb which says, *'When thou eatest the labor of thine own hands*—If you do not work, you shall not eat.' But I still don't understand what Fyedka is doing here. I would be much happier if you were friends at a distance. You mustn't forget *'Whence thou camest and whither thou goest*—Who you are and who he is.'"

"God created all men equal," she said.

"Yes, yes," I said, "God created Adam in his own image. But we mustn't forget that each man must seek his own kind, as it is written: *'From each according to his means . . .'*"

"Marvelous!" she cried. "Unbelievable! You have a quotation for everything. Maybe you also have a quotation that explains why men have divided themselves up into Jews and Gentiles, into lords and slaves, noblemen and beggars?"

"Now, now, my daughter, it seems to me you've strayed to the '*sixth millennium.*'" And I explained to her that this had been the way of the world since the first day of Creation.

"And why," she wanted to know, "should this be the way of the world?"

"Because that's the way God created the world."

"And why did God create the world this way?"

"If we started to ask why this, and wherefore that, '*there would be no end to it*—a tale without end.'"

"But that is why God gave us intellects," she said, "that we should ask questions."

"We have an old custom," I told her, "that when a hen begins to crow like a rooster, we take her away to be slaughtered. As we say in the morning blessing, '*Who gave the rooster the ability to discern between day and night. . . .*'"

"Maybe you've done enough jabbering out there," my wife Golde called out from inside the house. "The *borsht* has been standing on the table for an hour and he is still out there singing Sabbath hymns."

"Another province heard from! No wonder our sages have said, '*The fool hath seven qualities.*—A woman talks nine times as much as a man.' We are discussing important matters and she comes barging in with her cabbage *borsht.*"

"My cabbage *borsht,*" said Golde, "may be just as important as those 'important matters' of yours."

"*Mazl-tov!* We have a new philosopher here, straight from behind the oven. It isn't enough that Tevye's daughters have become enlightened, now his wife has to start flying through the chimney right up into the sky."

"Since you mention the sky," said Golde, "I might as well tell you that I hope you rot in the earth."

Tell me, Mr. Sholom Aleichem, what do you think of such crazy goings-on on an empty stomach?

Now let us, as they say in books, leave the prince and follow the fortunes of the princess. I am speaking of the priest, may his name and memory be blotted out. Once toward nightfall I was driving home with my empty milk cans—I was nearing the village—when whom should I see but the priest in his cast-iron *britzka* or carriage, approaching from the other direction. His honor was driving the horses himself, and his long flowing beard was whipped about by the wind.

"What a happy encounter!" I thought to myself. "May the bad luck fall on his head."

"Good evening," he said to me. "Didn't you recognize me, or what?"

"It's a sign that you will get rich soon," I said, lifted my cap and was about to drive on. But he wouldn't let me pass. "Wait a minute, Tevel, what's your hurry? I have a few words to say to you."

"Very well. If it's good news, then go ahead," I said. "But if not, leave it for some other time."

"What do you mean by some other time?" he asked.

"By some other time, I mean when the Messiah comes."

"The Messiah," said he, "has already come."

"That I have heard from you more than once," I said. "Tell me something new, little father."

"That's just what I want to tell you. I want to talk to you about yourself, that is, about your daughter."

At this my heart almost turned over. What concern could he have with my daughter? And I said to him, "My daughters are not the kind, God forbid, that need someone to do the talking for them. They can manage their own affairs."

"But this is the sort of thing she can't speak of herself. Someone else has to speak for her. It's a matter of utmost importance. Her fate is at stake."

"And who, may I ask, concerns himself with the fate of my child? It seems to me that I am still her father, am I not?"

"True," he said, "you are her father, but you are blind to her needs. Your child is reaching out for a different world, and you don't understand her, or else you don't wish to understand her."

"Whether I don't understand her, or don't wish to understand her, is besides the point. We can argue about that sometime if you like. But what has it got to do with you, little father?"

"It has quite a lot to do with me," he said, "for she is now under my protection."

"What do you mean she is under your 'protection'?"

"It means she is now in my care."

He looked me straight in the eye as he said this and stroked his long, flowing beard with his fingers.

"What!" I exclaimed. "My child is in your care? By what right?" I felt myself losing my temper.

He answered me very calmly, with a little smile, "Now don't start getting excited, Tevel. We can discuss this matter peaceably. You know that I am not, God forbid, your enemy, even though you are a Jew. As you know, I am very fond of the Jewish people, even though they are a stiff-necked race. And my heart aches for them because in their pride they refuse to admit that we mean everything for their own good."

"Don't speak to me of our own good, little father," I said, "for every word that comes from your lips is like a drop of poison to me—it's like a bullet fired straight at my heart. If you are really the friend you say you are, I ask only one thing of you—leave my daughter alone."

"You are a foolish person," he said to me. "No harm will come to your daughter. She is about to meet with a piece of great good luck. She is about to take a bridegroom—and such a bridegroom! I couldn't wish a better fate to one of my own."

"Amen," I said, forcing a laugh, though inside me burned all the fires of hell. "And who, may I ask, is this bridegroom, if I may have the honor of knowing?"

"You must be acquainted with him," he said. "He is a gallant young man, an honest fellow and quite well-educated, though he is self-taught. He is very much in love with your daughter and wants to marry her, but cannot, because he is not a Jew."

"Fyedka!" I thought to myself, and the blood rushed to my head, and a cold sweat broke out all over my body, so that I could barely sit upright in my cart. But show him how I felt? Never. Without replying I picked up the reins, whipped my horse, and *"departed like Moses."* I went off without as much as a fare-thee-well.

I arrived at home. What a scene greeted me! The children all lying with their faces buried in pillows, weeping; my Golde weaving around the house like a ghost. I looked for Chava. Where is Chava? She is nowhere to be found. I didn't ask where she was. I knew only too well. Then it was that I began to feel the tortures of a soul that is damned. I was full of rage and I didn't know against whom. I could have turned on myself with a whip. I began yelling at the children, I let out all my bitterness toward my wife. I couldn't rest in the house, so I went outside to the barn to feed my horse. I found him with one leg twisted around the block of wood. I took a stick and began laying it into him, as though I were going to strip off his skin and break his bones in half. "May you burn alive, you *shlimazl*. You can starve to death before I will give you as much as an oat. Tortures I will give you and anguish and all the ten plagues of Egypt. . . ."

But even as I shouted at him I knew that my horse did not deserve it; poor innocent creature, what did I have against him? I poured out some chopped straw for him, went back to the house and lay down. . . . My head was ready to split in two as I lay there thinking, figuring, arguing with myself back and forth. What could it all mean? What was the significance of all this? *"What was my sin and what my transgression?"* How did Tevye sin more than all the others that he should be punished thus above all the others? "*'Oh, Lord Almighty, what are we, and what is our life?'* What sort of cursed creature am I that you should constantly bear me in mind, never let any plague that comes along, any blight or affliction pass me by?"

As I lay there torturing myself with such thoughts, I heard my wife groaning and moaning beside me. "Golde," I said, "are you sleeping?"

"No," she said. "What is it?"

"Nothing," I said. "Things are bad with us, very bad. Maybe you can think of what's to be done."

"You ask me what's to be done. Woe is me, how should I know?

A child gets up in the morning, sound and fresh, gets dressed, and falls on my neck, kissing and hugging me, and weeping all the time, and she won't tell me why. I thought that, God forbid, she had lost her mind. I asked her, 'What's the matter with you, daughter?' She didn't say a word, but ran out for a while to see to the cows, and disappeared. I waited an hour, two hours, three hours. Where is Chava? There is no Chava. Then I said to the children, 'Run over and take a look at the priest's house. . . .'"

"How did you know, Golde, that she was at the priest's house?"

"How did I know? Woe is me. Don't I have eyes in my head? Am I not her mother?"

"If you do have eyes in your head, and if you are her mother, why did you keep it all to yourself? Why didn't you tell me?"

"Tell you? When are you at home that I can tell you anything? And if I do tell you something, do you listen to me? If a person says anything to you, you answer him with a quotation. You drum my head full of quotations and you've done your duty by your children."

After she finished I could hear her weeping in the dark. "She is partly right," I thought to myself, "for what can a woman understand of such matters?" My heart ached for her, I could not bear to listen to her moaning and groaning. "Look here, Golde," I said, "you are angry because I have a quotation for everything. I have to answer you even that with a quotation. It is written: *'As a father has mercy on his children.'* This means that a father loves his child. Why isn't it written: *'As a mother has mercy on her children'?* For a mother is not the same as a father. A father can speak differently with his child. You will see—tomorrow I will go and speak to her."

"I hope you will get to see her, and him also. He is not a bad man, even if he is a priest. He has compassion in his heart. You will plead with him, get down on your knees to him, maybe he will have pity on us."

"Whom are you talking about?" I said. "That priest? You want me to bow down to the priest? Are you crazy or out of your head? *'Do not give Satan an opening,'* it is said. My enemies will never live to see that day."

"What did I tell you?" she said. "There you go again."

"Did you think," I said, "that I would let a woman tell me what to do? You want me to live by your womanish brains?"

In such talk the whole night passed. At last I heard the first cock crow. I got up, said my morning prayers, took my whip with me, and went straight to the priest's house. A woman is nothing but a woman. But where else could I have gone? Into the grave?

Well, I arrived in the priest's yard and his dogs gave me a royal welcome. They leaped at me and tried to tear off my coat and sink their teeth into my calves to see if they liked the taste of a Jew's flesh. It was lucky that I had taken my whip along. I gave them this quotation to chew on—*"Not a dog shall bark."* Or, as they say in Russian: *"Nehai sobaka daram nie breshe."* Which means, "Don't let a dog bark for nothing."

Aroused by the barking and the commotion in the yard the priest came running out of his house and his wife after him. With some effort they drove off the happy throng that surrounded me, and invited me to come in. They received me like an honored guest and got ready to put on the samovar for me. I told the priest it wasn't necessary to put on the samovar, I had something I wanted to say to him in private. He caught on to what I meant and motioned to his spouse to please be so kind as to shut the door on the outside.

When we were alone I came straight to the point without any preambles, and asked him first of all to tell me if he believed in God. Then I asked him to tell me if he knew what it felt like to be parted from a child he loved. And then I asked him to tell me what, according to his interpretation, was right and what was wrong. And one more thing I wanted him to make clear for me. What did he think of a man who sneaked into another man's house, and began tearing it apart, turning beds, tables, and chairs—everything, upside down.

Naturally he was dumbfounded by all this, and he said to me, "Tevel, you are a clever man, it seems to me, and yet you put so many questions to me and you expect me to answer them all at one blow. Be patient and I shall answer them one at a time, the first question first and the last question last."

"No, dear little father," I said. "You will never answer my questions. Do you know why? Because I know all your answers beforehand. Just tell me this: is there any hope of my getting my child back, or not?"

He leaped up at this. "What do you mean getting her back? No harm will come to your daughter—just the opposite."

"I know," I said. "I know. You want to bring her a piece of great good luck. I am not speaking of that. I only want to know where my child is, and if I can see her."

"Everything, yes," he said, "but that, no."

"That's the way to talk," I said. "Come to the point. No mincing of words. And now good-bye. May God repay you in equal measure for everything you have done."

I came home and found Golde lying in bed all knotted up like a black ball of yarn. She had no more tears left to weep. I said to her, "Get up, my wife, take off your shoes, and let us sit down and mourn our child as God has commanded. '*The Lord hath given and the Lord hath taken away.*' We are neither the first nor the last. Let us imagine that we never had a daughter named Chava, or that like Hodel she went off to the ends of the earth. God is All-Merciful and All-Good. He knows what He does."

As I said this I felt the tears choking me, standing like a bone in my throat. But Tevye is not a woman. Tevye can restrain himself. Of course, you understand, that's only a way of speaking. First of all, think of the disgrace! And second, how can I restrain myself when I've lost my child, and especially a child like Chava. A child so precious to us, so deeply embedded in our hearts, both in her mother's and mine. I don't know why she had always seemed dearer to us than any of the other children. Maybe because as a baby she had been so sickly, and we had gone through so much with her. We used to stay up whole nights nursing her, and many a time we snatched her, literally snatched her, from the jaws of death, breathed life into her as you would into a tiny crushed chick. For if God wills it, He makes the dead come to life again, as we say in Hallel: *"I shall not die, but I will live.*—If you are not fated to die, you will not die." And maybe we loved her so because she had always been such a good child, so thoughtful and devoted, both to her mother and me. Now I ask you, how could she have done this thing to us?

Here is the answer: first of all, it is fate. I don't know about you, but as for me, I believe in Providence. Second, it was witchcraft. You may laugh at me, and I want to tell you that I am not so misguided as to believe in spirits, elves, *domovois* and such nonsense. But I do believe in witchcraft, in the evil eye. For what else could it have been? Wait, listen to the rest of the story, and you will agree with me.

Well, when the Holy Books say, *"Perforce you must live.*—Man does not take his own life—" they know what they are talking about. There is no wound so deep that it does not heal in time, there is no sorrow so great that you do not forget it eventually. That is, you do not forget, but what can you do about it? *"Man is likened to a beast.* —Man must work, man must till the earth in the sweat of his brow." And so we all went to work. My wife and children got busy with the pitchers of milk, and I took to my horse and wagon and *"the world continued in its course*—the world does not stand still." I told everyone at home to consider Chava as dead. There was no more Chava. Her name had been blotted out. Then I gathered up some dairy stuff—cheese and butter and such, all fresh merchandise—and set off for Boiberik to visit my customers in their *datchas.*

I arrived in Boiberik and I was met with great rejoicing. "How are you, Reb Tevye?" "Why don't we see you any more?" "How should I be?" I told them. "*'We renew our days as of old.*—I am the same *shlimazl* as always.' One of my cows just dropped dead." They appeared surprised. "Why do so many miracles happen to you, Reb Tevye?" And they began questioning me, wanting to know what kind of cow it was that had dropped dead, how much she had cost, and if I had many cows left. They laughed and joked and made merry over me as rich people will make merry over a poor man and his troubles, when they have just eaten their fill and are in a good mood, and the weather is perfect, sunny and warm and balmy, just the weather to drowse in. But Tevye is the sort of person who can take a joke even at his own expense. I would sooner die on the spot than let them know how I felt.

When I got through with my customers, I set out for home with my empty milk cans. As I rode through the woods I slackened the horse's reins, let him nibble at will, and crop a blade of grass now and then. I let my thoughts roam at will also. I thought about life and death, this world and the next, what the world is altogether about, what man has been created for, and other such things. Anything to drive my gloom away, to keep from thinking about Chava. But just as if to spite me she kept creeping in among my thoughts.

First she appeared before me in her own image, tall, lovely, blooming, like a young tree. Then I saw her as a little baby, sick and ailing, a frail little nestling, snuggled in my arms, her head drooping over my shoulder. "What do you want, Chaveleh? Something to suck on? A piece of candy?" And for the moment I forgot what she had done to me and my heart went out to her in longing. Then I remembered and a great anger seized me. I burned with anger against her and against him and against the whole world, but mostly against myself because I wasn't able to forget her, even for a minute. Why couldn't I forget her, why couldn't I tear her out of my heart completely? Didn't she deserve to be forgotten?

For this, I thought, Tevye had to be a Jew among Jews, to suffer all his life long, to keep his nose to the grindstone, bring children into the world—in order to have them torn from him by force, to have them fall like acorns from a tree and be carried away by wind and by smoke. I thought to myself, "It's like this: a tree grows in the forest, a mighty oak with outspread branches, and an ignorant lout comes along with an axe and chops off a branch, then another and another. What is a tree without branches, alas? Go ahead, lout, chop down the whole tree and let there be an end. . . . What good is a naked oak in the forest?"

In the midst of these thoughts I suddenly became aware that my horse had stopped. What's the matter? I lift up my eyes and look. It is she, Chava. The same as before, not changed at all, she is even wearing the same dress. My first impulse was to jump off the wagon and take her in my arms. But something held me back. "What are you, Tevye? A woman? A weakling?" I pulled in my horse's reins. "Giddap, *shlimazl.*" I tried to go to the right. I look—she is also going to the right. She beckons to me with her hand as though to say, "Stop a while, I have something to tell you."

Something tears at my insides, something tugs at my heart. I feel myself going weak all over. Any moment I will jump off the wagon. But I restrain myself, pull the horse's reins in and turn left. She also turns left. She is looking at me wildly, her face is deathly pale. What shall I do? Should I stop or go on? And before I know what's happened, she's got the horse by the bridle and is saying to me, "Father, I will sooner die on the spot before I let you move another step. I beg you, father, listen to me."

"So," I think to myself, "you want to take me by force. No, my dear, if that's what you are trying to do, I see that you don't know your father very well." And I begin whipping my horse with all my might. The horse obeys me, he leaps forward. But he keeps moving his ears and turning his head back. "Giddap," I tell him. "'*Judge not the vessel but its contents.*—Don't look where you aren't supposed to.'" But do you think that I myself wouldn't like to turn my head and look back at the place where I left her standing? But Tevye is not a woman. Tevye knows how to deal with Satan the Tempter.

Well, I don't want to drag my story out any longer. Your time is valuable. If I have been fated to suffer the punishments of the damned after death, I surely have expiated all my sins already. If you want to know about the tortures of hell that are described in our Holy Books, ask me. I can describe them all to you. All the rest of the way, as I drove, I thought I could hear her running after me, calling, "Listen, father, listen to me." A thought crossed my mind, "Tevye, you are taking too much upon yourself. Will it hurt you if you stop and listen to her? Maybe she has something to say that is worth hearing. Maybe—who can tell—she is regretting what she has done and wants to come back to you. Maybe she is being badly treated and wants you to save her from a living hell." Maybe and maybe and maybe . . . And I saw her as a little child once more and I was reminded of the passage: "*As a father has mercy on his children* . . ." To a father there is no such thing as a bad child. I blamed myself and I told myself, *"I do not deserve to be pitied*—I am not worthy of the earth I walk upon.

"What are you fuming and fretting for?" I asked myself. "Stubborn mule, turn your wagon around and go back and talk to her, she is your own child." And peculiar thoughts came into my mind. What is the meaning of Jew and non-Jew? Why did God create Jews and non-Jews? And since God did create Jews and non-Jews why should they be segregated from each other and hate each other, as though one were created by God and the other were not? I regretted that I wasn't as learned as some men so that I could arrive at an answer to this riddle. . . .

And in order to chase away these painful thoughts I began to chant the words of the evening prayer: *"Blessed are they who dwell in Thy house, and they shall continue to praise Thee. . . ."* But what good was this chanting when inside of me a different tune was playing? *Chava,* it went. *Cha-va.* The louder I recited the prayer, the plainer the word *Cha-va* sounded in my own ears. The harder I tried to forget her, the more vividly she appeared before me, and it seemed to me that I heard her voice calling, "Listen, father, listen to me." I covered my ears to keep from hearing her voice and I shut my eyes to keep from seeing her face, and I started saying *Shmin-esra,* and didn't know what I was saying. I beat my breast and cried out loud, *"For we have sinned,"* and I didn't know for what I was beating my breast.

I didn't know what I was saying or doing. My whole life was in a turmoil, and I myself was confused and unhappy. I didn't tell anyone of my meeting with Chava. I didn't speak about her to anyone and didn't ask anyone about her, though I knew quite well where they lived and what they were doing. But no one could tell from my actions. My enemies will never live to see the day when I complain to anyone. That's the kind of man Tevye is.

I wonder if all men are like me, or if I am the only crazy one. For instance, let us imagine—just suppose it should happen—if I tell you this, you won't laugh at me? I am afraid that you will laugh. But just let us suppose that one fine day I should put on my Sabbath gabardine and stroll over to the railway station as though I were going away on the train, going to see them. I walk up to the ticket window and ask for a ticket. The ticket seller asks me where I want to go. "To Yehupetz," I tell him. And he says, "There is no such place." And I say, "Well, it's not my fault then." And I turn myself around and go home again, take off my Sabbath clothes and go back to work, back to my cows and my horse and wagon. As it is written: *"Each man to his labor*—The tailor must stick to his shears and the shoemaker to his last."

I see that you are laughing at me. What did I tell you? I know what you're thinking. You're thinking that Tevye is a big imbecile. . . . That's why I say: *"Read to this part on the great Sabbath before Passover,"* meaning, it's enough for one day. Be well and happy and write me often. And don't forget what I asked you. Be silent as the grave concerning this. Don't put what I told you into a book. And if you should write, write about someone else, not about me. Forget about me. As it is written: *"And he was forgotten—"* No more Tevye the Dairyman!

The Joys of Parenthood

A RICH MAN, I am not. Far from it. But I am not complaining. I have a place of my own to live in. Though what do I get out of that? A headache. But there is one thing I can really boast of—more than the richest man in Kasrilevka—and that is my children. For instance, at the holidays, when all my children come together—my sons and daughters, daughters-in-law, and all the grandchildren—who can be compared to me?

For example, consider the *Purim sudah.* What satisfaction is there in a *sudah,* I ask you, if you sit down all alone with your wife and you eat? Well, picture it to yourself. So I've had my fish already, and noodle soup, *tzimmes,* this, that and the other. What satisfaction is there in that? None whatever. A horse can eat too. But a human being is not a horse. Especially a Jew. And on a holiday. And particularly a holiday like *Purim,* when there are so many good traditional dishes to feast on!

First of all—my children, long may they live. . . .

There are eight of them, may God protect them. All married. (There were twelve altogether, but four passed away.) Half are sons and half are daughters; four sons-in-law and four daughters-in-law. That makes a total of sixteen.

And then the grandchildren, Lord bless them!

I don't want to boast, but all my daughters and daughters-in-law are fruitful, they all bear children every year. One has eleven, one nine, another seven. Barren ones, that is, with no children at all, not one! Though with one son, the middle one, I had some difficulty. For a long time my daughter-in-law had no children at all. We wait and wait—not a sign of one. We tried everything. We went to doctors, rabbis. . . . We even tried a gypsy. Nothing helped.

Finally there was only one thing left to do. He had to divorce her. Well and good, he'll divorce her. But when it came down to getting the divorce . . . Who . . . What . . . She didn't want it.

"What do you mean, she doesn't want it?" I ask my son. And he tells me, "She loves me." "Fool!" I say. "Are you going to listen to that?" And he says, "But I love her too." Now what do you think of that smart boy? I tell him *children,* and he answers me *love.* What do you think of such an idiot?

To make a long story short, they didn't get divorced. But God had mercy on them; it's six years now since she started having them—a child every year. She showers me with grandchildren.

And you ought to see my grandchildren, all of them gifted and handsome, one better looking than the other. A joy to behold. I tell you—jewels!

And they're such good students, too. If you ask for a page of *Gamorah* they give you a page of *Gamorah* by heart. As for the Bible and all the commentaries, grammar, and all the modern nonsense they teach now, there's no use talking. They read and they write Yiddish, Russian, German, French, and anything you can think of. When I have a letter to be read or an address to be written, or anything else, a war starts: "Grandpa, I'll do it! Grandpa, let me."

What did you say? How do we all live? Never mind. God is all-powerful. He provides. Sometimes this way, sometimes that, sometimes better, sometimes worse. Naturally more often worse than better. We struggle along. We get through the year. We live. That's the important thing.

My oldest son was getting along pretty well for a long time. He lived in a village, in Zolodoievka, and made a pretty good living. But when the decrees of the Third of May were announced, he was politely asked to move on. Naturally he did everything he could to prove that he was not a newcomer, produced papers to show that he had lived there since the world was created, even appealed to the courts. Well, the Lord himself couldn't help him. He was driven out, and he hasn't recovered from it yet. So he lives with me, he and his wife and children. What else could we do?

My second son, poor fellow, just can't get along. No matter what he tries, he fails to make good. Everything falls, as they say, buttered side down. If he buys grain, the price drops; if he buys oxen, they die. If he tries wood, there is a warm winter. That's his luck. If he looked at the river, all the fish would die. So I thought it over and I said to him, "Do you know what? Pack up your things and move over with us."

My third son was getting along very well. But in the Great Fire, his house had to go and burn down, and he was left as naked as the day he was born. Besides that he had other troubles: a lawsuit, trouble with the record of his military service, various other things. Now he is living with me together with his whole family. Naturally!

But my youngest son is really doing well. What do I mean by that? He has nothing himself, but he has a rich father-in-law. That is, not really rich, but he makes a good living. A businessman, a conniver, a manipulator, may the Lord forgive him. He manipulates so long that he gets both himself and the other party all tangled up. But somehow he always squeezes out himself, the scoundrel. More than once he has gone through not only his own money but his children's as well. I tell him, "Why did you have to fool around with my son's money?" And he says, "Was any of it yours?" So I say, "My son is still my child." Says he, "And my daughter isn't mine?" "Huh," I say. "Bah" he says. "But after all," I say. "What do you want?" says he. And so one word leads to another. I called my boy aside and I said to him, "Go, spit on that father-in-law of yours, that conniver. Come, live with me. Whatever the Lord gives us, at least we'll be together."

But when it comes to sons-in-law, I have no luck at all. None whatever. That is, I have nothing against them either. I am not ashamed of them. For, believe me, I have such sons-in-law that the wealthiest man could envy me. Fine boys, from good families, handsome, brilliant, every one of them.

I have one son-in-law who comes from a very superior family. He is really something to brag about—a young man of refinement, talent, education, a great scholar. Day in and day out he sits and studies. I have been keeping him with us ever since the wedding, for if you knew him you would admit that it would be a sin to let him out into the world. What would ever become of him?

The next one is of not quite such a good family, but he's just as intelligent as the first. Whatever you think of, he can do. He can write, read, figure, sing, dance—everything. And what a chess player he is! And yet he is not a success. What does King Solomon say? "For the wise man there is often no bread." I have started him in every kind of business. He had a concession, he ran a store, he was a teacher, a matchmaker—he just couldn't make good. Now he and his family live with me. I can't throw my daughter out into the street, can I?

Then there is another son-in-law who is not a scholar like the others, but who still is not just a nobody. He has a good head, a fine handwriting, knows the *Gamorah,* can quote you Scriptures. It's a pleasure to listen to him.

He has only one drawback. He is too delicate, too spiritual—that is, he's none too healthy. He doesn't look so bad, but he sweats a great deal and he has a cough. He's had this cough, together with a wheeze, for quite a while now, and he has a hard time breathing. The doctors tell him to drink milk and to go to Boiberik for the summer. That's where all the sick people go. The pine trees, they say, are good for a cough. So I am planning to take him with me to Boiberik next summer, if God grants us life. In the meantime, until he gets well some day, he and his wife and children are naturally saddled on my shoulders. What choice do I have?

I have one more son-in-law. This one is very plain, but a hard-working fellow. Not, God forbid, an ordinary workingman, a tailor or a cobbler, but not a student either.

He is a fish peddler. He deals in fish. His father sells fish and his grandfather before him sold fish too. The whole family knows nothing but fish and fish and more fish. They're honest people, you understand, respectable people, but very common, ordinary people.

Maybe you will ask, how do I happen to have such a son-in-law? There must be a reason. What do they say? "In a river there are all kinds of carp." It must have been my daughter's luck to get a man like that.

Not that I have anything against him. My daughter is very happy with him, for he is a good man, a devoted husband, as kind to all of us as he can be. Whatever he earns he hands over to her and he helps my other sons-in-law and my sons also, as much as possible. I can even say that almost all the work he does is for us. He has great respect for us too. He understands well enough who he is and who we are. He is what he is and after all we are something else. You can't dismiss *that* with a shrug.

For whenever the rest of us get together with other people and my sons and other sons-in-law begin to talk over things—a sacred law or regulation passages from the *Talmud* or a passage in the *Gamorah,* he has to sit by himself, poor fellow, without opening his mouth. To him these things are all a deep mystery.

It's only right that he should be proud to have such brothers-in-law and he should be glad to labor in their behalf. Don't you agree?

And now that you know my family a little better, you can understand my pride in them and my enjoyment of their company, especially when the holidays come around. For instance, the *Purim sudah,* when all my children and grandchildren gather about the table and we make a blessing over the big shiny *Purim* loaf covered with saffron and studded with raisins, and my wife serves the good strong spicy fish with horseradish and the rich soup with the long yellow noodles in it. And we take a drop of something, if the Lord permits—a glass of port or cherry wine, if we have it, and if we don't, a sip of ordinary brandy is welcome too. And we sing in a chorus. I begin the song and the children come in on the refrain and the little ones, the grandchildren, pipe the second refrain in their high shrill voices. And then we get up and join in a dance. Who is equal to me then? What is Rothschild to me then? What is any other millionaire to me? I am a King. Look at me, a King—that's what I am.

A rich man, you understand, I am not. But one thing I can really boast of—my children! In that respect I am wealthier than the wealthiest man in Kasrilevka.

The Littlest of Kings

A LUCKY CHILD, ISAAC. The whole world loves him. He is everyone's darling; everyone fondles him, kisses him, showers him with endearments. If he were an only child, say the neighbors, his parents couldn't dote on him the way his two sisters, Sarah and Rebecca, dote on the boy. From morning till night it's Isaac and Isaac and Isaac. "Isaac, eat." "Isaac, drink." "Go to sleep, Isaac." "Isaac, here is some candy for you." "Isaac, we are making a new pair of pants for you for the holidays." "Isaac, we are going to send you to the baths before Passover." "Isaac, you will conduct the Passover ceremony this year." Isaac. Isaac. Isaac. A person gets sick and tired hearing that name from morning till night. "They have taken a child," say the neighbors, "a wonder child, a beautiful boy like Isaac, and between them they are spoiling him to death."

And yet these same neighbors who do the complaining are always calling Isaac over, slipping him a piece of candy, a slice of *shtrudel,* a baked chicken liver, a spoonful of jam. . . .

And they all do it because of pity. The whole world pities him, everyone feels sorry for the boy. For Isaac, the wonder child, the beautiful boy, is an orphan.

There was once a man named Raphael. He had been a poor man all his life and on top of that he was an asthmatic. Every time he drew a breath or let it out you heard strange music coming from his breast, as though a bow that hadn't been rubbed with rosin were drawn across some violin strings. And he was a most upright and honest man, but may God forgive me for saying this, also a very impractical man, in fact he was pretty much of a *shlimazl.* It was said about him in Kasrilevka that if he hadn't been so impractical, that is if he hadn't been such a *shlimazl,* he might have become a wealthy man.

And Raphael was in such sorry circumstances because all his life he had worked for Reb Simche Weiner as overseer in his wine distillery, and aside from his wages he could honestly say that he had never received a *groschen* from anyone. . . .

Reb Simche Weiner knew that he could depend on his overseer to the utmost. In return he treated him well, paid him regularly his six *rubles* a week, gave him an extra ten *rubles* before a holiday, wine for Passover and a bottle of Passover brandy besides. Why shouldn't he? Reb Simche was the sort of man who knew the value of an honest employee.

It is true that Raphael got rheumatism working in the damp wine cellar and later a heavy cold settled in his lungs and he began to cough and to wheeze. But who was to blame for that? Health—that is something that comes from God. The healthiest man can drop dead walking in the street. Our wise men have long ago said concerning this . . . but then you probably know what our wise men have said.

Well, our Raphael coughed and wheezed and sang like an untuned violin so long until one day—it was between the first and last days of Passover—he took to his bed, began to run a high fever, and never got up again.

Raphael died—and what a splendid funeral he had. Reb Simche outdid himself. He carried the body out of the house himself, put his own shoulder to the coffin, followed the hearse to the cemetery on his own two feet, saw to it personally that Raphael got a choice spot for his burial, himself supervised the digging of the grave, threw in the first shovelful of dirt with his own hands, and when he heard the boy Isaac repeat the first *kaddish* after the *shammes,* how Reb Simche wept!

"If only you knew . . . If you only knew," he told everyone he met separately, "what a loss this is to me. What a terrible loss!"

And to the widow he said, "Don't weep. You know that I won't forsake you and the orphans. Put your trust in God first, and then in me."

And Reb Simche kept his word as well as he was able. That is, for the first few weeks he paid the widow the same sum that Raphael used to receive from him. It is true she had to go after the money every week, and not once but several times, and she did not enjoy doing this. But I ask you, what did you expect? That he send the money to her house? It was enough that he should keep on paying a man's wages after the man was dead.

"You come to me for money," he said to her one day, "just as though I owed it to you, as though you had a share in my winery."

That day the widow wept more than she had wept when Raphael lay dead, and when her two daughters, Sarah and Rebecca, found out why their mother was weeping they made her swear that she would never go to him for money again.

"But what shall we do?" she asked.

"We'll do what others have done. We'll go into service, we'll wash clothes, we'll sew on a machine."

Sewing on machines had become quite an occupaion in Kasrilevka. You could earn as much as two *guldens* a day if you were willing to sit over a machine sixteen or seventeen hours a day. As for getting enough work, that was no problem. You got work. If you didn't get dresses, you got underwear; if you didn't get underwear, you got shirts; if not shirts then handkerchiefs to hem. The trouble was that they needed a machine, or, worse yet, two machines.

You could get a machine and pay for it in installments. But where to get enough money for the down payment?

"Go over to your *nogid,* your rich benefactor," the neighbor women advised the widow. "Tell him that you need money for a machine, that the girls will work and pay him back."

"Go to the *nogid.*" That was easier said than done. But what won't one do to earn a living? The widow went over to Reb Simche Weiner and found him in his most relaxed state, right after he had eaten. If you want to ask someone for a favor always lie in wait for him until he has eaten. After a meal the meanest man is more tender-hearted than before a meal. Before he has eaten, man is—a beast!

"And what good news do you bring today?" asked Reb Simche.

The widow made her request. She told him the whole story; in a word, she needed machines.

Reb Simche listened to her attentively the whole time. He picked his teeth, got red in the face, sweated a little, dozed a little. He didn't fall asleep—God forbid, no—he only dozed, looking at her with one eye shut, thinking meanwhile partly about business, and partly about his digestion. Reb Simche was somewhat lazy, somewhat too plump, and the doctors had told him to eat more meat and less starchy foods. But starchy foods were just what Reb Simche liked best—things such as bread, noodles, puddings, anything made of flour. He knew that they were bad for him, but he couldn't keep from eating when they were in front of him, and after he had eaten he had reason to be sorry.

"Well, and how are you getting along?" he said when the widow became silent. He looked at her now with one eye open and the other only half shut.

"How should I be getting along?" she said. "I've just told you how I am getting along. May my enemies get along as well. But if I had the money for a machine, better yet for two machines, or even for one machine . . ."

"What machines?" he asked, looking at her in astonishment, with both eyes open.

"I've just told you that my daughters want to take in sewing. They want to become seamstresses, to sew on machines. But we have no machines. They need two machines and they can get them on credit, they can pay for them in installments. . . ."

"That's a fine idea. A very proper thing . . . seamstresses. They will sew, they will earn money. Fine. Very good."

But while he was speaking to her he thought to himself, "Why does my stomach feel so loaded? It seems to me I didn't eat so much today." And one eye began to grow smaller. But because the widow became silent again he woke up and began talking to her.

"Well, well. That's fine. Sewing. *So be it.* Why not?"

"I wanted to ask you, Reb Simche, since you've already done so much for us, perhaps it might be possible that you . . ."

It suddenly dawned on Reb Simche that she was making a request of him, that this smelled of a loan, that she wanted money, and he at once became wide awake.

"What?" he said.

"That you lend us money for the first payment on the machines."

"Which machines?"

"Those I told you about. The two machines for my daughters. Or at least one machine."

"Where will I get machines? What kind of dealings do I have with machines?"

"Money," said the widow, "is what we need. They can get the machines themselves—on credit. For instance if I pay fifty *rubles* now and three months later I pay twenty-five *rubles,* and a little later . . ."

"I know, I know, you don't have to explain it to me. I am satisfied that they get along without machines. Machines all of a sudden!"

"How else can they sew? You can't get much sewing done by hand. All seamstresses have machines nowadays."

"So you want to make seamstresses out of your daughters? You've come to this! If your husband were to rise from the dead and hear that you were going to make seamstresses out of your daughters he would lie down and die all over again. Let me tell you, your Raphael was an honest, God-fearing man. There aren't many like him. He would never have stood for this seamstress business. He would have—God alone knows what he would have done."

Reb Simche spoke with feeling. He meant every word he said. And the more he talked the louder his voice grew.

"Seamstresses! Hah! A fine calling for Jewish girls. We know what it means to be a seamstress nowadays. Raphael's daughters, seamstresses. And what about me? Where am I? Do you know that I practically raised Raphael? I made him the man he was, first God, then I. And who married him off, if not I? And you expect me to permit such a thing. Never in this world. What am I? A stone? A bone? A block of wood?"

The widow left Reb Simche's house exactly as she had come, empty-handed.

She went home and made a vow with herself—she swore by everything holy that she would sooner not live to bring up her children than put a foot into Reb Simche's house again. She would go into service instead.

It is easy to say "go into service." But how could Raphael the Overseer's wife, a housewife like the other Kasrilevka housewives, become a servant? How could she stand at a stranger's oven, sit at a stranger's table? Rather than live like this it was better to die. And the widow wished for death to come.

And this time God, the great merciful God, father of orphans and protector of widows, took pity on the poor woman and did not allow her to linger long on this earth. He sent her an easy death, some sort of swelling inside. She suffered for three and a half months and then she died. And it so happened that aside from little children, no one had died in Kasrilevka during that time, so that the widow was buried next to her husband; their graves were almost side by side. Such a piece of luck must have been ordained from above.

From that time on, Isaac began to say *kaddish* for both his parents, his mother as well as his father. And he became the darling of all the neighbors and all the people who saw him standing on a bench in the Synagogue reciting in his high childish voice the words, *"Yisgadal v'yiskadash . . ."* Everyone who saw the small boy with his big brown eyes, his red cheeks, and the round cap on his head, standing on a bench in the Synagogue chanting the *kaddish,* was dazzled by the sight, and stood bemused, sighing deeply and thinking sad, sad thoughts. For every man may die and every man has young children who, God forbid, may become fatherless orphans. And this one gave the little orphan a *kopek,* that one slipped him an apple, partly out of pity, partly because "charity delivereth from death."

The truth was that Isaac was an unusual child, a child with a face one couldn't help loving. And he had a good head besides. He was the brightest boy in the Kasrilevka *Talmud Torah.* Reb Noah the *melamed* didn't have enough words to laud him. The whole town rang with his praises.

"Raphael's boy is very bright, they say."

"Isaac? They say he is going to be a great scholar some day."

"And where do you find such a treasure? Among the rich? Of course not. You find it among paupers on an ash heap."

"It's always this way. Who goes on living? Old Moishe Aaron, a cripple without hands or feet. And who has to die? Reb Simche's son-in-law, a young, healthy man, the head of a family, a man with money. He has to die."

"You talk about Reb Simche's son-in-law? What about Peisie the *Nogid's* daughter-in-law?"

"How is she getting along?"

"Getting along? They've had a specialist from Yehupetz for her, three times already."

"So? I wish I had at least half of what it will cost them."

"This is certainly a strange world!"

"A world with little worlds revolving around it."

This is how they talk in Kasrilevka, ceaselessly criticizing the works of the Almighty. They don't like the way He prolongs the life of some and cuts it short for others. They don't approve of the way He gives wealth to one, and nothing but bad luck to another. They can't understand why He blesses the poor with gifted children and punishes the wealthy with who-knows-what. No one ever stops to consider: How do these gifted children live? What do they eat? Who clothes them? Do they freeze during the long winter nights in their damp cellars? Will they not grow up crippled, hunchback, paupers from birth, unhappy and unwanted, a burden to humanity and themselves?

Luckily the two sisters, Sarah and Rebecca, scraped up enough for a sewing machine. They had to thank their neighbors for this, the three women who lived in the same house with them—Basha the Healer, Pessie the *Shammes'* Assistant, and Sossie the Second-hand Dealer. The three women each put in some money and raised enough for the first payment on the machine. The girls would pay the rest out of their work. What is so strange about that? A person has to live. And what else can two grown girls, with a small boy on their hands, do? They say even a snake looks out for its young. Can a human being do less?

The only drawback is that the machine makes such an infernal racket day and night. For there is plenty of work, God be thanked, and both sisters use the machine, which never stands idle. They take turns running it, "changing hands," so that while Sarah is sewing, Rebecca is making the fire in the oven or sweeping the floor. Or, while Sarah is cooking dinner, Rebecca is sewing on the machine. The machine never stops clattering and the neighbors grab their heads with both hands, stop up their ears, and mutter softly to themselves, "Rattle, rattle. There is a rattle for you."

But God is merciful. He sends a remedy for every disease. In this case the remedy was Isaac. There are times in every home when everything goes wrong, everyone's spirits are low, and life becomes dreary. Then a little creature is born and everything changes. At first the little one whines and screams, yells with colic, doesn't let anyone sleep nights. But soon *it* grows a little older, stops crying at night, opens its eyes and looks about. "See, he is looking around. He sees us." Then the creature opens its mouth, sticks out its tiny tongue and laughs, and everyone's heart grows lighter. "Look, the child is laughing." The gloom is dissolved, bad times are forgotten. A new soul has entered the house.

And that was how it was with our Isaac. He was the darling of the house. He was the creature that brought laughter and cheer with him. When Passover came they dressed him up like a king in a little coat and trousers with suspenders. His sisters had a pair of boots made for him and bought him a new cap. They promised to give him nuts to play with, and the neighboring women made him pans full of pancakes out of *matzo* meal. They stuffed him with pancakes and chicken fat until he got sick and almost died of overeating.

"Who asked you to feed him all this stuff?" the two sisters scolded the neighbors.

"Just listen to them. We give the child a pancake or two and they pounce on us like this."

Bashe the Healer used all the knowledge at her command and saved the boy's life. The day before Passover they gave Isaac a clean shirt and three *groschen* and sent him to the baths. When he came home they put his new clothes on him and he was a joy to behold.

"A royal child. A young prince," they nodded to each other.

"May no evil eye fall on him."

And Isaac took his small prayer book and went to the Synagogue. He said his *kaddish* and came home and greeted everyone with a cheery good *yom-tev*. The table was laid out for the *seder,* with *matzos,* a bottle of raisin wine, and bitter herbs and *charoses,* potatoes, and salt water. Everything was there except for one thing. There was no one to conduct the service. There was no king!

The three women were all widows; that is, two were widows and the third was divorced. They had no children; that is, they had children, but not at home. Their children were scattered far and wide over the whole world. This one was a workingman, that one had a store, others had emigrated to far-off America. Their various fortunes or perhaps misfortunes had drawn the three women together into one house, a house which belonged to Basha the Healer who was the wealthiest of the three.

The three lived under one roof, cooked at one oven, and set the dough for bread in one trough, but each kept her own table. For it is difficult for three women to live peacefully together at all times.

Out of the three hundred and sixty-five days in the year, the three women quarreled on about three hundred of them. But it depends on what you mean by quarreling. They never took anything from each other, they did not insult one another, never hurt one another's feelings. It was just that three different personalities had to disagree sometimes.

For instance Pessie the *Shammes'* Assistant liked to bank the fire in the stove and cover it with an oven lid. What harm was there in that? But Sossie the Second-hand Dealer had a habit of putting a pot of chicory on the hearth every morning. That wasn't so terrible either. She would never shove her pot of chicory in among the pots in which meat was cooking. But Pessie the *Shammes'* Assistant said it wasn't right that the bread in the oven should be ruined because of a mere pot of chicory. Sossie retorted to this, "May my enemies be ruined like this."

Said Pessie, "You must have quite a few enemies."

"I have enough, God be thanked," countered Sossie. "May they be planted in great numbers and fail to come up."

"Since when have you become such a shrew?" asked Pessie.

"Since I've come to live in this God-forsaken place."

At this Bashe the Healer, the owner of the house, who had been standing near by, rolling pin in hand, rolling out dough for noodles, spoke up.

"So it's a God-forsaken place to you? What makes it so? The high rent you are paying?"

Said Sossie the Second-hand Dealer, "You are the lucky one, you are so rich."

"What difference does it make how rich I am? Did I take it away from you?"

And Sossie replied, "What could you take from me? My bad luck? Go ahead, take it."

Said Bashe, "Keep it for yourself."

Pessie spoke up, "No one is guaranteed against bad luck. I've seen some people with homes of their own who have enough bad luck."

"Enough and to burn," added Sossie.

Bashe got angry and leaped at Sossie. Pessie the *Shammes'* Assistant took up for her. A hubbub arose among the three women; they began screaming and shouting all together: "Look at the defender she has." "How do you like the nerve of the woman?" "If you don't like it you don't have to marry me." "You are looking for scissors and the top of the mortar shows up." "Tavern talk!" "The rich lady—ruling over pokers and shovels." "Be still, loud-mouth, or I will throw a poker at you." "You'll get it first." "Here, take it then." "You take it." "Both of you take this."

Do you think it was blows they gave each other? God forbid. They shouted, gestured and threatened, thumbed noses at each other, and that was the end of it.

In spite of all the controversies and conflicts that took place among them, the three women harbored no enmity toward each other. For actually what did they have against each other? Had any of them taken away the other's livelihood? One moment they quarreled, the next they made up. And invariably when Passover came they declared peace by common consent, and all three became one in spirit, for all three baked their *matzos* on the same day, put up their beet juice in the same crock, dickered for and bought the same bargain, a sack of potatoes, and then sat down together at the same table to celebrate the Passover. They all sat at the table of the landlady, Bashe the Healer, ate together with her, followed the *Hagadah* softly after her word for word as she read it in Yiddish translation from a thick prayer book.

Some time ago, when Bashe the Healer's husband, Israel the Healer, had been alive, he had conducted the Passover service. After Israel's death the son of one of the other women officiated. Now that they were all scattered and gone to the four corners of the world and the only male person who remained in the house was little Isaac, there arose among the women some talk, the gist of which was that it might be a good idea to let Isaac lead the service. Isaac was already studying the Bible and he read Hebrew fluently. Why couldn't he be the man of the house, the king for one night?

"Isaac," they said to him, "would you like to be the king?"

"A king? Why not? Who would refuse a kingdom, even for one night?"

"Woe to the kingdom of which Isaac has to be king."

Nevertheless the three women and the two girls went to work and prepared a royal throne, well padded with pillows, for little Isaac. And when Isaac came home from the Synagogue with his cheery good *yom-tev,* he sat down on the throne and in his handsome new clothes, he looked like a real king.

There are three actions over which we have no control—yawning, laughing and weeping. Let anyone in the room begin to yawn or to laugh or to weep and everyone present will sooner or later be yawning or laughing or weeping.

And so it was during the *seder* we are describing. At the high point of the ceremony—after Isaac, the Littlest of Kings, had said, "Therefore we are bound to thank and praise Thee," and then "Halleluiah," and was lifting the second cup of wine to his lips and beginning to intone: "Behold I am about to observe the commandment of the second cup" —there arose on all sides of him such a weeping and wailing and sobbing you might have thought someone had just died in the house.

How it happened, which of the women started weeping first, is hard to say. When Isaac had finished the *kiddush* and began chanting, "For we were slaves," one of the sisters suddenly remembered that a year ago at this time they had also been sitting at a *seder*. But what a different *seder*. Their father and mother had both been alive, and the two girls had new dresses made for them for the holiday. Who would have dreamed then that this year they would be sitting at a strange table with three strange women and that little Isaac would be performing the Passover ceremony? She began to blink her eyes very fast and her lower lip trembled. Looking at her, the other sister began to blink also and tears fell from her eyes.

Glancing over at the girls, one of the women recalled her own sad plight. When her husband Nossi the *Shammes* was alive she had been as happy as anyone could be, that is, she had never been happy, but she had certainly been happier than she was now as assistant to the new *shammes* who had taken her husband's place. When her husband died his former assistant had been elevated to the rank of *shammes,* and his wife Gnessi put on such airs it was impossible to come near her. Thinking of her sorry lot, Pessie the *Shammes'* Assistant made such wry faces that Sossie the Second-hand Dealer, who sat by her, had to be stronger than iron to keep from tears.

Sossie remembered her own sad lot. The seventy-seven women who were so envious of her second-hand business, who dragged customers away from her, did everything they could to keep her from earning a *groschen,* tried to ruin her, ruin her completely. She thought of her oldest girl who had died long ago as a small child. Her name had been Rosie. If Rosie hadn't died she would be a grown woman by now, probably married and a mother herself. Then she thought of her husband who had been an unfortunate cripple, a good-for-nothing without a trade, and a sickly man besides. And Sossie the Second-hand Dealer, who had been softly repeating the words of the *Hagadah* after Bashe the Healer, swaying backwards and forwards in the same rhythm with her, was suddenly bathed in tears.

And Bashe the Healer did not hear the words of the *Hagadah* which flowed so easily from her lips, for she too was thinking of her troubles. She thought of her children who had gone off, far, far away to America. It is true, they wrote her pretty satisfactory letters, they assured her that they were making a living—that is, they worked hard and were as good as anybody. To demonstrate how well off they were they sent her photographs or as they called them "pictures." They promised her that if their affairs or as they called them "business" improved a little they would send her a few *rubles* or as they called them "dollars" and a ship's ticket so that she could come to this great and happy land where everyone made a living and where all men were free and equal. A person could lie down in the middle of the street and starve to death and no one would tell him he was in the way. But nothing could make Bashe move over there. She had children here too. They might not be so well off, but what of that? Their fate was in God's hands. Everything was in God's hands.

That is how Bashe the Healer thought and the words of the *Hagadah* kept pouring from her lips and she herself didn't notice that the tears were also pouring from her eyes. But when they reached the part in the ceremony when the Littlest of Kings stopped chanting and lifted the second cup of wine to his lips, the women stopped chanting also and looking around became frightened at their own noise. Bashe the Healer was the first to recover. She wiped her eyes on her apron, blew her nose and began scolding the others in a loud voice:

"What's all this yammering and yowling for? What is this? *Yom Kippur?* A fast day? Just look at them."

At this the women began to calm down. Sossie got up and handed the king a pitcher of water and a towel so that he could perform the washing-up ceremony, Pessie went to the oven and brought out the hot fish, Bashe put the horseradish on the table. The Littlest of Kings made the blessing over *matzos,* the women followed with a loud *Amen* and quietly, without any more talk, they began the Passover meal.

The Man from Buenos Aires

TRAVELING by train is not as dull as some people think. Not if you happen to run into congenial company. Sometimes you happen to be traveling with a merchant, a man who understands business. Then you don't know where the time goes. Or if not a merchant, then you run into some other man of experience, a witty fellow, shrewd and well-informed, a man who knows his way around. With such a person, it is a pleasure to travel. You can pick up a few choice tidbits from him. And sometimes the Lord sends you a fellow-passenger who is just good company, a lively, cheerful, talkative person. He talks and he talks and he talks. His mouth doesn't shut for a moment. And all he talks about is himself, nothing but himself.

I once had occasion to travel with such a man for quite a distance.

Our acquaintance began—how does an acquaintance in a railway car begin? With some such trifle, as, "Do you know what station this is?" Or, "Can you tell me the time?" Or, "Do you happen to have a match?" Very quickly we became friends, as though we had known each other for who knows how long. At the first station at which we happened to stop for a few minutes, he grabbed me by the arm, led me straight to the buffet and, without asking me whether I drank or not, he ordered two glasses of brandy. Right after that he motioned to me to pick up a fork and when we were through with the various snacks and appetizers that you find at a railway buffet, he ordered two mugs of beer, gave me a cigar, lit one for himself—and our friendship was as good as sealed.

THE MAN FROM BUENOS AIRES

"I want to tell you very frankly, without an ounce of flattery," said my new acquaintance when we were once more seated in the railway car, "that I took a liking to you, will you believe it or not, from the first moment I laid eyes on you. As soon as I saw you I said to myself, 'Here is a man you can talk to.' I don't like to sit by myself like a dummy. I like to talk to someone that's wide-awake. That's the reason I bought a third-class ticket, to have someone to talk to. Otherwise I would be traveling second class. And do you think I can't manage first class? I can swing that too. You may think I am boasting. Look!" And with these words my fellow-passenger reached into his back pants pocket, pulled out a fat wallet and showed it to me, stuffed full of banknotes. He slapped it with the palm of his hand as though it were a sofa cushion, then put it back into his pocket. "Don't worry," he said, "there is more where this came from."

I looked the fellow over curiously, but try as I might I couldn't figure out how old he was. You might say he was forty, and then again you might say he was a little over twenty. His face was smooth and round, and heavily tanned, without a sign of a beard or mustache. He had small, unctuous, laughing eyes. He was short, and round in build, sprightly and full of life and movement, dressed nattily from top to toe the way I like to see a man dress. He had on a snow-white shirt with gold buttons, a rich silk tie pierced by a showy tiepin, an elegant new suit made of real English broadcloth, and a pair of smartly shined shoes. On his finger, he wore a heavy gold ring with a diamond that blinked with a thousand facets in the sun. (The diamond, if it was real, must have been worth not less than four or five thousand *rubles*.)

To be well dressed is in my opinion the most important thing of all. I like to dress well myself and I like to see others well dressed. From the way a man is dressed I will tell you whether he is an upright person or not. True, there are those who maintain that this is no indication. A man can be most elegantly gotten up, they argue, and yet be a scoundrel. Then I will ask you this: Why is it that the whole world wants to dress well? Why does one man wear one kind of suit and another wear a different outfit? Why does one man buy himself a flowing tie of smooth satin, sea-green in color, and another insist on a bow tie, and a red one with white dots at that?

I could give you many more such examples, but there is no point to it. Why waste your time? Let us better return to our friend and listen to what he has to tell us.

"—and so you see, my friend, I can afford to travel second class, too. Do you think that I begrudge the expense? Expense is no object. But will you believe it or not—I like to travel third class. I am a plain person myself and I like plain people. I am, you understand, a democrat. I began my career at the bottom of the ladder, at the very bottom, like this." (My new acquaintance showed me with this hand to the ground how he had begun his career at the very bottom.) "And I came up higher and higher." (Here he reached with his hand to the ceiling to show me how high he had come up.) "Not all at once, mind you. But slowly, little by little, little by little. At the beginning I worked for others. I was just an employee. An 'employee' did I say?" (Here he laughed out loud.) "Believe me, before I attained the dignity of being called an 'employee,' much water flowed under the bridge.

"When I remind myself sometimes of what I was as a child, my hair—will you believe it or not—my hair, stands on end. I can't bear to remind myself of it, and what's more I don't want to. Do you think it's because I am ashamed of my past? Just the opposite. I tell everyone who I am. When people ask me, 'Where are you from?' I don't hesitate for a moment. I tell them right off that I come from that illustrious city, Somashken. Do you know where Somashken is? There is a tiny town in Kurland, not far from Mitau, that's called Somashken. The whole town is so big that I could easily buy it up today complete with all its assets. It is possible, of course, that the town has changed, that it has grown—I can't tell you, I don't know. But in my day the whole town of Somashken, will you believe it or not, owned exactly one orange, which traveled like a worn-out tune from one hostess to the next to be set before the guests every Saturday afternoon.

"In this very town of Somashken I was brought up on resounding slaps, ironclad kicks, and plain beatings. I saw stars in front of my eyes, wore black and blue marks on my body and nursed an empty stomach. There is nothing, I tell you, nothing, that I remember so well as hunger. I came into God's world hungry, I suffered hunger from the moment I became conscious of who I was. Painful, wracking hunger, the kind that knots up your belly and makes you retch with nausea . . . Wait! Have you ever heard of the sap of a pine tree? Musicians use it instead of rosin to rub on their fiddle strings. I lived on this sap, will you believe it or not, for one whole summer. That was the summer my stepfather, a snub-nosed tailor, dislocated my arm and drove me from my mother's house, the summer I ran away from Somashken to Mitau. This is the arm, see—there should still be a mark on it." And my new-found friend rolled up his sleeve and showed me a soft, healthy, plump arm. Then he went on talking.

"Wandering around, half-naked and hungry in Mitau, living in unbelievable filth, I at last with God's help landed a job. My first job. I became a companion to a blind old cantor. He had been a famous cantor at one time, but he had become blind in his old age and had to go begging from house to house. I was hired to lead him around. The job itself wouldn't have been so bad, but you had to be stronger than iron to put up with the old man's whims. He was never satisfied. Never. He was always grumbling at me, pinching me, tearing pieces of flesh out of me. He would complain that I didn't lead him where I was supposed to. To this day I don't know where I was supposed to lead him. He was certainly a cantankerous old man. Besides, he set me a fine example. He boasted in front of everyone, will you believe it or not, that my parents had turned Christian and had wanted to baptize me too, but he had rescued me with nobody knew how much trouble and anguish from the hands of the Christians. I had to listen to those lies and keep a straight face. More than that, he expected me to look woebegone when he told these wild tales. . . .

"I quickly saw that I wasn't going to live to a ripe old age in the service of my cantor, so I made a burnt offering of my 'job' and left Mitau for Libau. After I had wandered around in Libau for a while, homeless and hungry, I attached myself to a group of poor emigrants. These emigrants were getting ready to go by ship somewhere far off, all the way to Buenos Aires. I began to plead with them to take me along. It was impossible, they told me. It didn't depend on them, but on the

Committee. The Committee had the say-so. So I went to the Committee, wept and fell in a faint before them, implored them to have pity on me and finally they consented to take me to Buenos Aires.

"You ask me, why Buenos Aires? What drew me there, of all places? Nothing. Everybody was going to Buenos Aires, so I went too. Later I found out that Buenos Aires was only a point of departure and that actually we were going to be sent further out. And so it came to pass. No sooner had we arrived in Buenos Aires than our papers were taken away and we were reassigned to different places, such places as Adam himself had never seen in his wildest dreams. There they put us to work.

"No doubt you would like to know what kind of work. You'd better not ask. I am sure that our ancestors in Egypt never labored as we did. And the torments they endured as they are described in the *Hagadah* are not even a tenth as bad as what we had to endure. They tell us that our grandfathers kneaded clay with their hands, made bricks without straw and built the pyramids in that way. Do you call that an achievement? They should have tried, as we did, to plow, with their bare hands, the wild steppes overgrown with thistles, or drive tremendous oxen that could kill a man with one touch, or chase wild horses for a hundred miles with a lasso. They should have known for only one night what it felt like to be bitten by ferocious mosquitoes, or eaten dry biscuits that had the flavor of stones, or drunk stagnant worm-infested water. One day, will you believe it or not, I happened to look down into a river and I became frightened at my own image. My skin was all peeled off, my eyes were swollen shut, my arms were like sausages and my feet were bloody. I was covered with hair from top to toe.

" 'Is that you, Motek from Somashken?' I said to myself, and burst out laughing. That same day I spat at the huge oxen and the wild horses and the untamed steppes and the wormy water and went back on foot to Buenos Aires.

"It seems to me that the station we are stopping at now should have a large buffet. Look into your book. Don't you find it's time to get a bite to eat? It will give us strength to go on with the story."

After we had had a substantial "bite," and washed it down with some beer, we again lit cigars, fine aromatic cigars, genuine Havanas from Buenos Aires, and settled ourselves down in the railway car. My new acquaintance from Buenos Aires resumed his story.

"Buenos Aires is the sort of place, believe me, that since God created the world . . . Wait! Have you ever been in America? In the city of New York? Never? Or in London? No? In Madrid? Constantinople? Paris? Not there either? Well, then I can't explain to you what Buenos Aires is like. I can only tell you that it's an inferno. A *Gehenna.* A Hell and a Heaven rolled into one. That is, it's a hell for some and a heaven for others. If you just keep your eyes open and watch out for the main chance, you can make your fortune there. It's a place where, will you believe it or not, you will find gold lying in the streets. Bend down, stretch out your hand, pick up as much as you want. But you have to watch out that no one crushes you underfoot. The thing is—not to stop. Don't stop for anything. Don't stop to think, don't weigh one thing against another. Don't worry about what is proper and what isn't proper. Everything is proper. Is it a job waiting on tables in a restaurant? Good. Clerking in a store? Good. Washing bottles in a tavern? Good. Running through the streets shouting headlines in the papers? Good. Washing dogs? Good. Raising cats? Good. Catching rats? Also good. Skinning the rats? That too. In a word, everything is good. I have tried everything, and everywhere I have seen the same thing. Simply this, that it doesn't pay to work for someone else. It's a thousand times better to have someone else working for you.

"Can we help it if God created the world once and for all so that one man has to sweat brewing the beer and I can sit here and drink it? That another has to work at rolling the cigars and I can smoke them? That the engineer has to drive the locomotive, the stoker to stoke coal, the workman to oil the wheels, and you and I can sit here in the car and tell stories? There are those who don't like it? Then let them go ahead and change the world."

I looked at my companion and thought to myself, "What can the creature be? A man who has just struck it rich? A former tailor in

America who now has a ready-to-wear store? Maybe even a manufacturer? Or a landlord? Or just a capitalist living off interest?" But let him go on with the story. He tells it much better himself.

"This is a great world, I tell you, a sweet world and a lovely world, and it's a pleasure to be alive in this world. You just have to make sure that no one spits into your porridge. I have tried every occupation in the world. I have served, as they say, every kind of master. No work was too difficult for me, no occupation too mean. And if you want to know something, there is no such thing as an occupation that is too mean. All work is good, if you only deal honestly and keep your word. I know it from personal experience. I won't boast to you that I am as virtuous as the chief rabbi of Lemberg. But you can take my word of honor for it, that I am no thief either. And certainly not a robber. Nor am I a swindler. I swear to you by everything good, that I am an honest merchant. I carry on my business honorably. I don't cheat anyone. I sell only what I have to sell. I have no pig in the poke to sell. In short, do you want to know what I am? I am no more than a middleman, a jobber, or as you call it a '*podradchik*.' I supply the world with merchandise, something that everyone knows and nobody speaks of. Why? Because it's a cunning world and people are too shifty. They don't like it if you tell them that black is black and white is white. They would rather have you tell them that black is white and white is black. So what can you do with them?"

I looked at my friend from Buenos Aires and thought to myself, "Dear Lord, what is he anyway? What sort of goods does this jobber supply the whole world with? And what's all this strange talk about black and white and white and black?" I didn't like to interrupt and ask, "Uncle, what do you actually deal in?" So I let him go on.

"In short—where were we? At my present business in Buenos Aires. The business itself is actually not in Buenos Aires. My business, if you want to know, is everywhere, over the whole world. In Paris, in London, Budapest, Boston . . . but the main office is in Buenos Aires. It's too bad we are not in Buenos Aires right now. I would take you up to my place of business and show you my office and the people who work for me. My employees all live, will you believe it or not, like Rothschilds. Eight hours a day, that's all they work, not a minute more. The men who work for me are treated like human beings. Do you know why? Because I was an 'employee' once myself; I worked for my present partners. We are three partners now. At one time there were two partners and I worked for them. I was their right-hand man. The entire business, you might say, rested on my shoulders. I did all the buying and selling, the estimating, the sorting, everything. I have an eye for good merchandise, will you believe it or not; all I need is to take one look at a piece of goods and I will tell you right away how much it's worth and where it can go. But that alone is not enough. In our business you have to have a sense of smell too. You have to be able to smell out where something is hidden. And you need still another sense, to tell you where you can make a good transaction and where you can break your neck and sink into mire so deep that you won't talk your way out of it. . . .

"The trouble is that there are too many curious people in the world. Too many prying eyes. And in our business we fear the evil eye. . . . If you make one false step you won't wash yourself clean in a hundred waters. The least little thing and there is a hue and a cry and it's smeared all over the newspapers. That's all the papers need, you know. They are only too happy to publish the least little breath of a scandal, fan it into a huge conflagration and bring the police of the world down on us. Although I must tell you this in strict confidence, that the police of the whole world are in our pockets. If I were to mention the sums of money the police collect from us every year, you would just gape at me. But then to us, will you believe it or not, a sum like ten thousand, fifteen thousand, even twenty thousand, is a mere trifle. . . ."

Saying this, my friend waved his hand carelessly like a man who could afford to throw thousands around. The diamond on his finger flashed in the light and the man from Buenos Aires who threw thousands around so lightly looked at me briefly to see what impression he had made. Then he pushed forward with his story.

"And if it's necessary to put out a little more sometimes, do you think that stops us? On the other hand, we have complete confidence in each other, we three partners. No matter how many thousands we give the police, we trust each other implicitly. All our business is carried on in good faith. One of us wouldn't cheat the other by so much. Just let him try . . . he will live to regret it. We know each other very well, we know the place, and we know all that goes on in the world. Each of us has his own spies and agents. What do you expect? Business that is done on faith can't be carried on any other way. Don't you think it would be a good idea if we jumped off at this station and rinsed our throats a bit?" Saying this he took my hand and looked into my eyes.

Naturally I had nothing against his proposal and we jumped out at the next station and "rinsed our throats." The corks of the lemonade bottles popped one after the other. My friend drank with such evident enjoyment that it was a pleasure to watch him. But one thing still preyed on my mind. What sort of merchandise did he deal in, this man from Buenos Aires? How did he come to throw all those thousands around? And how could the police of the whole world be in his pockets? And what did he need agents and spies for? Did he deal in contraband goods? In false diamonds? Stolen merchandise? Or was he just a bluffer and a windbag, one of those creatures whose tongue wags at both ends and everything that rolls off is a hundred times more wonderful than life? We traveling salesmen have a name of our own for such a creature. We call him a "wholesaler," because everything he deals in is wholesale, on a large scale, blown up. In plain language he is nothing but a liar or a teller of tall tales.

Well, we lit fresh cigars, settled down in our seats again, and the man from Buenos Aires plunged on.

"Where were we? Oh, yes, I was talking about my partners. That is, my present partners. At one time they were my employers and I was, as I have already told you, their employee. I won't try to discredit them or to pretend that they treated me badly. How could they treat me badly when I was as faithful to them as a dog? Every cent of theirs was as precious to me as if it were my own. Over and over I made myself enemies for their sake, deadly enemies. There were times, will you believe me or not, when I came near being poisoned because of my faithfulness. Yes, poisoned. I can pride myself on the fact that I served them loyally, as loyally as a man could. True, I didn't forget about myself either. A person must never forget about himself. You have to remember you are only human, here today and gone tomorrow. And there is no point in slaving for someone else all your life. Why should I? Have I no hands? No feet? No tongue in my head? And especially since I knew that without me they couldn't get along for even one day. They couldn't and they shouldn't. There were too many secrets . . . as is natural in any business.

"One fine day I made up my mind and said to them, '*Adieu,* gentlemen.' They looked at me. 'What do you mean *adieu?*' '*Adieu* means good-bye,' I said. 'What's the matter?' they asked me. 'I've had enough,' I said, 'I am fed up.' They exchanged glances, and asked me how much capital I had. I told them whatever I had would be enough to start with and if it wasn't enough God was our Father and Buenos Aires was a city. They understood me at once. Why shouldn't they? Were their brains dried up? And that was how we became partners. Three partners, three bosses, all sharing equally in the business. There is no such thing among us as one getting more and the other getting less. Whatever God sends, we split three ways. And we don't quarrel among ourselves either. Why should we? We are doing quite well, God be thanked, and the business is growing. The world is getting bigger and our merchandise is getting dearer. Each of us takes out of the partnership as much as he needs for his personal expenses. And our expenses, I can tell you, are pretty large.

"I myself, will you believe it or not, without a wife and children to support, spend three times as much as another who has a wife and children. Some people would be glad to make what I give to charity alone each year. There isn't a thing in the world that doesn't cost me money—synagogues, hospitals, emigrant funds, concerts. Buenos Aires, God be praised, is a big city. And what about other places? Palestine alone, will you believe it or not, costs me a pretty penny. Not so long ago I received a letter from a *yeshiva* in Jerusalem. A handsome letter with a Star of David on top, with seals and signatures of rabbis. The letter was addressed to me personally in very impressive language: 'To our Master, the Renowned and Wealthy Reb Mordecai.'

" 'Oho,' I thought, 'since they address me in such respectful language and call me by my first name, I can't be small either. I have to send them a hundred at least.' These are only incidental donations. What about my native town, Somashken? Somashken costs me, will you believe it or not, a hatful of money as big as this, every year. I keep getting letters from there all the time. There is always a fresh catastrophe, one thing after another. Money for Passover—that goes without saying. Every Passover I send a hundred. That's become a rule. Right now I am on my way to Somashken and I know beforehand that I won't get by with less than a thousand. Why do I say a thousand? I hope I get by with two thousand. If not, I'll have to make it three thousand. Just think, I haven't been back home all these years, since childhood. And after all, Somashken is my *home*. I know beforehand what a commotion my coming will cause, how excited everybody will be to see me. The whole town will come running. 'Have you heard the news? Motek is here. Our Motek from Buenos Aires.' That's an occasion for them. Believe me, those poor souls are waiting for me as though I were the Messiah. From each station I send them a message that I am on the way. I send them a telegram every day. Just these words, 'I am coming. Motek.' And I myself, will you believe it or not, can't wait to get there. To see Somashken again, to kiss the earth of Somashken, the dust of Somashken. . . . Who cares about Buenos Aires? Or New York? Or London and Paris? Let them all perish. Somashken is my home town."

As he spoke his face was transformed. It seemed to grow younger, handsomer. His bright little eyes had a new light in them, a new glow of happiness and of love. Of genuine love. But there was one thing still troubling me. . . . I still didn't know what it was that he dealt in. But he didn't let me ponder long. He forged ahead with his story.

"Do you want to know the real reason for my going to Somashken? I am going there partly because I am lonesome for my home, and partly to visit the graves of my ancestors. My father and mother are buried there, and my brothers and sisters—my whole family. But the main reason is that I want to get married. How much longer can a man remain a bachelor? And when I marry, I want to marry a girl from Somashken, a girl from my own town, my own class, my own kind. I have already written about it to my friends in Somashken. I have asked them to look around, and find me something good . . .

They write me that if I only arrive safely, everything is bound to be for the best. That's the kind of crazy fool I am. . . . In Buenos Aires, will you believe it or not, the greatest beauties in the world have been offered to me in marriage. I could pick up something that the Sultan of Turkey doesn't boast of. But I've told myself once for all. No! I shall find myself a wife in Somashken. I want a girl of good family. A respectable Jewish girl. I don't care how poor she is. I will make her rich. I will shower her parents with gold, make her whole family wealthy.

"And the girl herself I will take to Buenos Aires with me and I will build her a palace fit for a princess. I won't let a speck of dust fall on her. She will be happy with me, believe me. She will be the happiest woman in the world. Nothing will touch her, she won't have to give a thought to a single thing, except her household and her husband and children. I will send my children to the best schools. My sons will all enter the professions. One will become a doctor, another a lawyer, another an engineer. . . . And my daughters I will send to private boarding schools. . . . Do you want to know where? In Frankfurt."

At this point the conductor came up to collect our tickets. The conductor (I have noticed this many times) always appears just when you least want him. A hubbub arose in the carriage, people began running back and forth, collecting their baggage, pushing and shoving. I reached for my luggage too. I had to get out and change to another train. The man from Buenos Aires helped me tie up my luggage, and in the meanwhile we carried on this conversation which I will transmit to you word for word.

Man from Buenos Aires: "Too bad you aren't going further. I won't have anybody to talk to."

I: "What can I do? Business is business."

Man from Buenos Aires: "Well said. Business is business. I am afraid I will have to pay the difference and move over to second class. I can swing first class too, thank God. When I travel . . ."

I: "Forgive me for interrupting you. We have only half a minute left. I wanted to ask you something."

Man from Buenos Aires: "For instance?"

I: "For instance, I wanted to ask you. . . . Oh, there goes the whistle. What, in short, is your business? What do you deal in?"

Man from Buenos Aires: "What do I deal in?" (He burst out laughing.) "Not in prayer books, my friend, not in prayer books . . ."

I was at the far end of the car now with my luggage, but I could still see the man from Buenos Aires with the smug look on his smooth round face and the fine aromatic cigar between his teeth and his laughter still rang in my ears. . . . "Not in prayer books, my friend, not in prayer books."

May God Have Mercy

ZAIDEL REB SHAYE'S was a young man who sat in his father-in-law's house and studied the *Torah*—never lifted a finger, only sat and studied, though he already has several children of his own. Why should he exert himself when he was the only son and his father-in-law, Reb Shaye, was a wealthy man and some day that wealth would pass on to him?

Reb Shaye's business was that of money-lender. His "capital" was scattered all over the town. There wasn't a single Kasrilevkite who didn't owe Reb Shaye money. His house was always full of people—some coming, others going, this one borrowing, that one paying back.

Reb Shaye had what might pass for an office or a bank—a bank, it is true, without highly polished desks and tables, without clerks in white coats, with curled mustaches and long fingernails, without grated windows and iron safes, without massive account books and ledgers heavy enough to knock a man down.

Reb Shaye had only a small table with an inkstand and sand-dispenser, and whenever he had to write something down he had to spit into the inkstand before it would produce any ink. Besides that, the table also had a drawer with two rings and a huge lock on it. In this drawer was locked up the account book with all the transactions which Reb Shaye kept according to his own peculiar bookkeeping system. This is how it went:

The book consisted of fifty-two pages; on each page were written out the days of the week, and each day was divided into two parts.

One side was headed *Received* and the other side, *Paid.* This is how the side labeled *Received* looked:

Rec'd from Gershon Pipik on the note of the weekly portion of *Genesis: 2 rubles.*

Received from Feivel Shmaye's on the note of the last portion of *Exodus: 5 rubles.*

Received from Simcha Lemeshke on the note of the Eleventh reading: 1 *ruble.*

Didn't receive from Gershon Pipik on the note of the second weekly reading of *Genesis:* 5 *rubles.*

And the *Paid* side:

Paid to Simcha Lemeshke on the note of the last week of *Exodus:* 13 *rubles.*

Paid again to Gershon Pipik: 7 *rubles.*

Didn't pay again to Feivel Shmaye's: 10 *rubles.* Bad debt.

I promised Reb Simcha to give him 11 *rubles.*

How Reb Shaye ever deciphered these jottings, God alone knew. And yet you may rest assured that there were never any protests, no quarrels, and no lawsuits. Everyone simply knew this: that if he stopped paying, he lost his credit, never to regain it.

And so it went, the borrowing and the paying back, smoothly, without a hitch for many years, until. . . .

Until Reb Shaye died.

When Reb Shaye died, Zaidel took over the business.

After the thirty-day period of mourning was over, Zaidel went to work on the accounts. He sat and labored over the account books for three weeks in a row, writing, jotting, figuring, computing. Finally he sent for the citizens of the town and said to them, "Gentlemen, I wish to announce to you that I have gone over your accounts carefully, and I have figured out that you don't owe me anything. You are all clear."

"What do you mean we don't owe you anything? What do you mean we are all clear?"

"Let me explain. According to algebra you have been paying interest and interest on top of interest until you've paid your debts seventeen times over. Here, take your I.O.U. notes."

When they heard this, the Kasrilevkites became furious. They thought he was playing a trick on them, trying to outwit them with clever words. They threw the notes back in his face and began yelling, "He is murdering us. Without a knife or gun he is killing us. Reb Shaye, may he enjoy everlasting glory, did business with us for so many years; his purse was always open to us, and this—this creature comes along and wants to make fools of us."

"Fools!" shouted Zaidel. "What kind of fools and imbeciles are you? I told you, you've paid your debts. I didn't make this up out of my own head. I worked it out according to algebra."

"What nonsense is this? What's this *albegra* he is blabbing about? Let's take our case to someone else. Let's go to the Rabbi."

"To the Rabbi! To the Rabbi!" they shouted in unison, and went straight to the Rabbi, Reb Yozifel.

Almost everybody in town had gathered at the Rabbi's house. There was a tumult and a shouting, loud enough to split the heavens. Zaidel let the others talk first; he allowed each one to say what was on his mind. Then when everyone had made his complaint and yelled to his heart's content, he asked that they all step out for a while, so that he could talk to the Rabbi alone.

What took place between Zaidel and the Rabbi, no one ever found out. They say that Zaidel and the Rabbi had a long discussion. Zaidel demonstrated to the Rabbi that it was wrong to take interest, for, according to the wise men, taking interest was the same as stealing. He who lives off unearned money is the lowest of the low. Everyone, he said, must labor in the sweat of his brow. There is no justice otherwise.

Reb Yozifel the Rabbi tried to discuss the point with him. He tried to prove that according to the Edict of *Mahram* of blessed memory the taking of interest was a necessary thing. He said that otherwise the world could not exist, and so on and so forth. But Zaidel answered him that this sort of "existence" was not to his taste. He didn't like the way the world was run. What sort of world was this? If a hungry man steals a *groschen's* worth of bread, that is considered a crime; but to rob a town full of widows and orphans, to take the last bite out of their mouths, was that righteousness? For cutting off a finger you got sent to hard labor in Siberia; but for killing off eighty-thousand men in South Africa as though they were oxen you got a medal for bravery.

"Is that justice?" he shouted, grabbing Reb Yozifel's lapels. "Is that righteousness? Here old Kruger, the governor of the Boers, is going around knocking on all the doors of the world, begging that we have pity on his poor country. All he wants is a court of justice, he wants impartial mediators to decide the rights of the matter. But this one says he doesn't want to interfere, that one says it won't look proper, this one says this, that one something else. In the meanwhile, blood is running like water.

"Where is justice? Where is humanity? You keep telling me about settlements, about customs, about the ways of the world. . . . A fine way I call it. A wonderful world."

He gave the Rabbi more such arguments, going off the subject into all sorts of speculations, denying the basic laws of what is "mine" and "yours" and "ours," making fun of everything sacred and proper.

Reb Yozifel finally refused to listen any further, stopped up his ears with both hands and shouted, "Enough. Enough. Enough."

When Zaidel had gone home, Reb Yozifel turned to the assembly and said with a deep sigh, "Poor fellow. Such a fine young man, so well-educated, so well-bred, and good-looking . . . but, may God have mercy on him."

Saying this the Rabbi touched his finger to his forehead, and everyone in the assembly understood what he meant.

Schprintze

I OWE you a greeting, a hearty greeting, Mr. Sholom Aleichem. It's a score of years since we've seen each other. My, my, how much water has flown under the bridge! How much agony we have lived through, you and I, and all of Israel, in these last few years! Oh, thou Father of the Universe, our dear God in Heaven! We have lived through a Kishinev and a Constitution, through pogroms and disasters of every kind. I am only surprised, if you will forgive me for saying this, that you haven't changed by a hair. May the evil eye spare you! But look at me: *"Behold, I look like a man of seventy.*—I am not sixty yet, and see how white Tevye has grown." It's the same old thing: *"the pain of bringing up children."* And who has suffered as much pain because of his children as I have? Since the last time I saw you a new misfortune happened to me, this time with my daughter Schprintze, something that put all my former troubles in the shade! And yet, as you see, I am still alive, still here. . . . As it is written: *"Perforce you must live."* Live, though you burst asunder singing this song:

> "The world doesn't please me and life isn't funny
> If I have no luck and I have no money."

In short what does it say in *Perek? "The Holy One, Blessed be He, wished to grant merit to Israel.*—God wanted to favor His chosen people." So a fresh calamity descended upon us, this time a Constitution. And such a panic overtook our rich people that they began leaving Yehupetz in droves, running off abroad, supposedly for their health, for mineral baths, salt water cures, nerves, and other such nonsense. And when Yehupetz is deserted then Boikerik with its fresh air, its pine woods, and its summer homes becomes a desert too. As we say in the morning prayer: *"Blessed be He who bestows mercy upon this earth."*

But that isn't all. We have a great God and a mighty God who watches over His poor and sees to it that they continue to struggle a little longer on this earth. What a summer we had! People began running to Boiberik from all over, from Odessa and Rostov, from Ekaterineslav and Mogilov, and Kishinev. There descended *"thousands upon thousands of rich men."* All the millionaires and plutocrats came to us. Apparently the Constitution was even worse for them than for us in Yehupetz, for they kept on coming, they didn't stop coming. The question is: Why should they run to us? And the answer is: Why do we run to them? It's become a custom with our people, God be praised, that as soon as there is a rumor of a pogrom we begin flying from one town to another, as it is written: *"They journeyed and they encamped, they encamped and they journeyed. . . ."* Which means, "You come to me and I will come to you."

Meanwhile you can imagine how crowded Boiberik became. It overflowed with people, it spilled over with women and children. And since children have to eat three times a day and they like to nibble besides, the demand for milk and butter and cheese kept growing. And from whom does one get milk and butter and cheese if not from Tevye? Overnight, Tevye became all the rage. From all sides you heard nothing but Tevye and Tevye and Tevye. "Reb Tevye, come to me." "Reb Tevye, you promised me." What more need I say? If God wills it, that's enough.

"And it came to pass—" Here is how it all began. Shortly before *Shevuos* I brought my wares to one of my new customers, a young widow and a rich one, from Ekaterineslav, who had just arrived with her son Aarontchik to spend the summer in Boiberik. And naturally the first person she became acquainted with in Boiberik was myself. "You've been recommended to me very highly," she says. "They tell me you have the best butter and cheese in these parts."

"How can it be otherwise?" I asked her. "Not in vain does King Solomon say that a good name can be heard like the sound of the *shofar* all over the world. And if you like," I added, "I can also tell you what a certain *medresh* has to say about that." She cut me short, however, saying that she was only a widow and inexperienced in such matters. She didn't even know what you ate it with. The important thing, she tells me, is that the butter should be fresh and the cheese taste good. There's a female for you.

Well, I began coming to the widow from Ekaterineslav twice a week, every Monday and Thursday, regularly, by the calendar. I brought her butter and cheese each time, without asking whether she needed it or not. I made myself at home in her house, took a friendly interest in the household, stuck my nose into the kitchen, told her a few times, whatever I saw fit to tell her, about the management of the house. The first time, as you might expect, I got a dressing-down from the servant who told me to mind my own business and not to stick my nose into strange pots. The second time, however, they stopped to listen, and the third time they asked my advice, because by then the widow had become aware of who Tevye was.

And so it went, until at last the widow disclosed to me her big problem, her secret sorrow, the thing that was eating away at her, and that was—Aarontchik! There he was, a young man, over twenty years old, and all he could think of was horseback riding, bicycling, fishing, and aside from that nothing! He wouldn't have anything to do with business, with the making of money. His father had left him a nice little fortune, almost a million *rubles,* but did he as much as look into it? All he cared about was spending money; his purse was wide open.

"Where is this young man?" I asked her. "Just turn him over to me. I'll have a good talk with him. I'll read him a lecture, quote him a passage or two, give him a *medresh*. . . ." She laughed at this. "A *medresh* did you say? A horse would be more like it."

Just at this moment *"the lad arrived."* Aarontchik himself walked in. He was a handsome young fellow, tall and husky, and bursting with good health. He wore a wide sash across his middle, with a watch stuck in the side, and his sleeves were rolled up above the elbows.

"Where have you been?" his mother asked him.

"I've been out in a boat," he said, "fishing."

"A fine occupation," I said, "for a young man like you. Over there in the city your inheritance is being frittered away, and you are out on the river catching fish."

I looked at the widow. She had turned as red as a beet. She must have thought her son would pick me up by the collar, *"and smite me as the Lord smote the Egyptians, with signs and symbols,"* that is, give me two slaps in the face, and throw me out of the house like a broken potsherd. Nonsense! Tevye is not afraid of such things. When I have something to say, I say it.

"And so it was." When the young man heard me, he stepped back, folded his arms over his chest, looked me over from head to foot, gave a long, low whistle, and then burst out laughing. We both thought he had lost his mind. And what shall I tell you? From that moment on we became like two comrades. And I must confess that the longer I knew him the better I got to like him, even though he was a rake and a spendthrift, much too free with his money, and something of a fool besides. For instance, who else but a fool would put his hand into his pocket when he met a beggar, and give him all he had without counting it? Or take a perfectly good coat off his back and give it away? Talk about folly.

I was honestly sorry for his mother. She wept and wailed and asked me what she should do. She begged me to have a talk with him. So I did her the favor. Why should I begrudge it to her? Did it cost me anything? I sat down with him, told him stories, cited examples, plied him with quotations and drummed proverbs into his ears, as only Tevye can do. And I must say that he seemed to enjoy listening to me. He kept asking me questions about how I lived and what my home was like. "You know what, Reb Tevye," he said, "I would like to come over and see you at home some day."

"That's easy," I said. "If you want to see me at home, just pick yourself up and drive over to my farm. It seems to me you have enough horses and bicycles. And if necessary, you can even pick up your two feet and walk over. It isn't far. You just have to cut through the woods."

"And when can I find you at home?" he asked me.

"You can find me at home only on Sabbaths and holidays. But hold on!" I said. "Do you know what? A week from Friday is *Shevuos*. If you want to come over to my house for *Shevuos*, my wife will treat you to such *blintzes* as your *'blessed ancestors never ate in Egypt.'"*

"What are you referring to?" he asked me. "You know that I'm weak in Biblical quotations."

"I know you are weak," I said. "If you had studied in *cheder* the way I did, you would have known not only what the rabbi, but also what the rebbitzen, the rabbi's wife, had to say."

He laughed at this. "Good," he said, "you can expect me on the first day of *Shevuos* along with a couple of friends. But see to it that the *blintzes* are good and hot."

"At white heat, inside and out," I said. "From the frying pan right into your mouth."

I came home and said to my wife, "Golde," I said, "we are going to have guests for *Shevuos."*

"Mazl-tov," she said. "And who are they?"

"That," I said, "you will find out later. Just get some eggs ready. We have plenty of butter and cheese, praise the Lord. I want you to make enough *blintzes* for three guests. And remember, they are the kind of people who believe in filling their stomachs; fine words mean nothing to them."

"I suppose you've picked up some starving wretches, some cronies of yours from Hungerland."

"You talk like a fool, Golde," I told her. "In the first place what harm would there be if we did feed some poor hungry wretch on *Shevuos?* In the second place, be thou informed, my dear spouse, my modest and pious wife, Madam Golde, that one of our guests is the widow's son, Aarontchik, the one I told you about."

"Oh," she said, "that's different."

Look at the power money has! Even my Golde, when she gets wind of money, becomes a different person. That's the way of the world. How is it written? *"Gold and silver, the work of man's hands—* Wealth is the undoing of man."

Well, *Shevuos* arrived. And how beautiful *Shevuos* in the country can be; how warm and sunny and fragrant, I don't have to tell you. The richest man in the city would envy us such a blue sky, such a green forest, such aromatic pine trees. Even the cows in the pasture keep chewing their cuds and look up at you as though to say, "Give us such grass all year round and we'll give you all the milk you want." You can tempt me all you like, you can offer me the richest livelihood in town, I wouldn't change places with you. Where can you get such a sky in town? How do we say it in Hallel: *"The heavens are the heavens of the Lord*—God's own sky." In town when you raise your head, what do you see? A brick wall, a roof, a chimney. Where will you find a tree? And if some scrubby little bush has crept in somewhere, you smother it with an overcoat.

Anyway, when my guests arrived, they couldn't find enough words to praise the beauty of the country. They came riding, three abreast, on horseback. You should have seen those horses, especially the one Aarontchik rode. An Arab steed. I figured that you couldn't buy him for three hundred *rubles.*

"Welcome, guests," I said to them. "I see that in honor of *Shevuos* you have come riding on horseback. Never mind. Tevye is not so pious either. And if you should be whipped for your sins in the next world, my back won't be sore. Golde," I called my wife, "get the *blintzes* ready and let's bring the table outdoors. I have nothing to show off to my guests inside."

Then I called my daughters, "Schprintze, Teibel, Beilke, where are you? Get a move on you." Soon the table was brought outside, and then benches, a tablecloth, plates, forks, salt. And right after that Golde appeared with the *blintzes* piled high on a platter, plump and juicy, and as *"sweet as the life-giving manna from heaven."* My guests ate and ate and couldn't praise them enough.

"What are you standing there for?" I said to Golde. "Repeat the same verse over again. Today is *Shevuos* and we have to say the same prayer twice." Golde didn't waste any time, but filled up the platter again, and Schprintze brought it to the table. I happened to look over at Aarontchik just then and saw him watching Schprintze. He couldn't take his eyes off her. What had he seen in her all of a sudden? "Go on and eat," I said to him. "Why aren't you eating?"

"What else am I doing if not eating?" he said. "You are looking at Schprintze," I told him. Everybody at the table burst out laughing, and Schprintze laughed too. Everybody was happy, everybody felt gay; it was a wonderful, happy *Shevuos*. How was I to know that from all this good cheer would come so much sorrow and misery? That God's punishment would descend on my head and blackest grief on my soul?

Man is a fool. If he was wise he would never let anything touch him too deeply. He would know that if things are a certain way that's the way they were intended to be. For if things were intended to be different, they wouldn't have been as they are. Don't we say in the Psalms: *"Put your trust in God?"*—Have faith in Him and He will see to it that you stagger under a load of trouble and keep on reciting: *"This too is for the best."* Listen to what can happen in this world, but listen carefully, for this is where my story really begins.

"It was evening and it was day." Once toward evening, I came home, worn out from the day's labors, from running all over Boiberik, delivering milk and cheese from *datcha* to *datcha*. When I approached my house I saw a familiar-looking horse hitched to my front door. I could have sworn it was Aarontchik's horse, the one I had valued at three hundred *rubles*. I went up to the horse, slapped him on the rump, scratched his throat and shook him by the mane. "Here, my fine fellow," I said to him, "what are you doing here?" He turned his engaging face toward me and gave me a look, as though to say, "Why ask me? Ask my master."

I went inside and asked my wife, "Tell me, Golde my treasure, what is Aarontchik doing here?"

"How should I know?" she said. "He is a friend of yours, isn't he?"

"Where is he now?" I asked.

"He went strolling in the woods with the children."

"What's all this strolling around for all of a sudden?" I said, and told my wife to give me supper. After I had eaten, I thought to myself,

"What are you getting so rattled about, Tevye? If someone comes to visit you, do you have to get so upset? You should be pleased."

As I tell myself this, I take a look outside and see my girls approaching with the young man, carrying bouquets of freshly picked flowers. The two younger girls, Teibel and Beilke, are walking together in front, and behind them are Schprintze and Aarontchik.

"Good evening."

"Good day."

Aarontchik stands at a side, stroking his horse, chewing at a blade of grass, and there is a strange look on his face. He says to me, "Reb Tevye, I want to do business with you. Let's exchange horses."

"You've found just the person to play a joke on," I said.

"No," he said, "I'm in earnest."

"So you're in earnest. And how much is your horse worth?"

"How much would you value him at?" he asks.

"I would value him at three hundred *rubles,* if not a shade more."

He burst out laughing at this and told me that the horse had cost him over three times as much. "Well, is it a deal then?"

I didn't find this kind of talk to my taste. What did he mean by wanting to change his expensive horse for my broken-down nag? I told him to put the deal off for some other time and I asked him jokingly if he had come all the way to my farm just to exchange horses. If so, I told him, he had wasted the train fare. . . .

He answered me quite seriously, "I came to see you, actually, in regard to something else. Shall we take a little stroll together, Reb Tevye?"

"What's he taken to strolling around for?" I thought to myself as I began walking with him in the direction of the wood. The sun had set some time ago and the little green wood was in darkness, the frogs were croaking in the marsh, and the grass was fragrant. Aarontchik walked and so did I. He was silent and so was I. All at once he stopped, cleared his throat and said to me, "Reb Tevye, what would you say if I told you that I am in love with your daughter Schprintze and that I want to marry her?"

"What would I say? I would say that a crazy man's name should be erased and yours put in his place."

He gave me an odd look and said, "What do you mean?"

"Just what I said."

"I don't understand you," he said.

"That shows that you are not very clever. As it is written: *'A wise man hath his eyes in his head.'* Which means that a smart man can understand a nod, but a fool needs a stick."

He said in a hurt tone of voice, "I ask you a plain question and you put me off with proverbs and quotations."

"Every cantor sings according to his ability and every orator speaks of what concerns him. If you want to know what kind of orator you are, talk it over with your mother. She will put you straight."

"I see that you take me for a child that has to run and ask his mother."

"Of course you have to ask your mother, and of course she will tell you that you are an imbecile, and what's more, she will be right."

"And she will be right?"

"Certainly she will be right. What sort of bridegroom would you make my Schprintze? And what kind of match is she for you? And most important of all, what kind of relative-by-marriage will I be to your mother?"

"If that's what's bothering you, Reb Tevye, you can rest easy. I am not a boy of eighteen and I am not looking for rich connections for my mother. I know who you are, and I know who your daughter is. She suits me and that's the way I want it, and that's the way it's going to be."

"Forgive me for interrupting you," I said to him. "I see that you are all done with one side. But have you settled it with the other side?"

"I don't know what you mean," he said.

"I mean my daughter Schprintze. Have you talked to her about all this? And what did she have to say?"

He pretended to look insulted, and then he said with a smile, "Of course I have talked with her, and more than once. I've talked to her many times. I've been coming here every day."

Did you hear that? He's been coming here every day and I knew nothing about it. "You're a donkey, not a man." I said to myself. "You should be given straw to chew on. Letting yourself be led by the nose like that. Your table and chairs could be sold out from under you and you wouldn't know it."

Thinking thus, I walked back to the house with Aarontchik. He took his leave of my family, jumped on his horse, and *"departed like Moses—"* He was off to Boiberik.

And now, it is time, as they say in books, to leave the hero, and follow the fortunes of the heroine, meaning in this case, Schprintze.

"Listen to me, my daughter," I said. "And listen well. Tell me, what did Aarontchik talk to you about behind my back?"

Does a tree answer when you speak to it? That's how she answered me. She blushed like a bride, lowered her eyes, and wouldn't utter a word.

I thought to myself, "If you won't talk now, you will later on. Tevye is not a woman. Tevye can wait." And I waited, as they say, till *"his day will come."* I watched for the moment when we should be alone. Then I said to her, "Schprintze, answer my question. Do you at least know this Aarontchik?"

She said, "Of course I know him."

"Do you know that he is nothing but a penny-whistle?"

"What is a penny-whistle?" she asked.

"It is an empty walnut-shell that whistles when you blow into it."

"You are mistaken," she said. "Arnold is a fine person."

"So he is Arnold to you, not Aarontchik—the charlatan!"

"Arnold is not a charlatan, father," she said. "Arnold has a kind heart. He is a man with principles. He is surrounded by a house full of vulgar people who think of nothing but money, money, and more money."

"So you've become an enlightened philosopher too, Schprintze?" I said to her. "And you've learned to despise money."

I could tell from this conversation that things had gone pretty far with them and that it was too late to undo them. For I know my daughters. Tevye's daughters, as I've told you before, when they fall in love with someone, it's with their hearts and souls and bodies. And I said to myself, "Fool, why do you try to outsmart the whole world?

Perhaps God has willed it that through this quiet little Schprintze you should be rewarded for all the pain and suffering you have undergone until now, and enjoy a pleasant and restful old age, and learn what life can really be like. Maybe it was fated that you should have one daughter, a millionairess. Why not? Won't the honor sit well on you? Where is it written that Tevye should be a pauper all his life, that he should always drag himself around with his horse and wagon, serving the rich people of Yehupetz who like to gorge themselves on butter and cheese? Who knows, maybe it has been inscribed above that I should become an important person in my old age, that I should dispense charity and entertain guests at my home, and sit together with the learned men and study the *Torah?"*

These and other such golden thoughts crowded through my head; as it is written in the morning prayer: *"Many thoughts are in man's heart."* Or, as they say in Russian, "An idea enriches a fool."

I came into the house, took my wife aside and said to her, "How would you like it if your Schprintze became a millionairess?"

"What is a millionairess?" she asks me.

"A millionairess is a millionaire's wife," I tell her.

"And what is a millionaire?" she wants to know.

"A millionaire is a man who has a million."

"How much is a million?" she asks.

"If you are so simple that you don't know how much a million is, how can I talk to you?"

"Who asked you to talk to me?" she says. And she was right.

A day passed, and I came home and asked, "Has Aarontchik been here?" "No, he hasn't." Another day passed. "Was the young man here today?" "No, he wasn't." To go to the widow and ask for an explanation didn't seem proper. I didn't want her to think that Tevye was running after the match. And besides I had a feeling that this whole affair was to her like *"a rose among thorns,"* or like a fifth wheel to a wagon. Though I couldn't understand why. Because I didn't have a million? So I was getting my daughter a mother-in-law who was a millionairess. And whom would her son get for a father-in-law? A pauper, a man who had nothing, a poor wretch called Tevye the Dairyman. Of the two, who had more to boast of? I'll tell you the honest truth, I began to be a little eager for the match myself. Not so much for the sake of the money as for the honor. The devil take those rich people of Yehupetz. It was time Tevye showed them a thing or two. All you had heard in Yehupetz till now was Brodsky and Brodsky and Brodsky. Just as though the rest of us weren't human beings.

This was how I reflected one day driving home from Boiberik. When I came into the house my wife met me with glad tidings. "A messenger has just been here from Boiberik. The widow wants to see you right away. Even if you come home after dark, she wants you to turn right around and go back to Boiberik. She must see you tonight."

"What's the hurry?" I asked. "Can't she wait?" I looked over at Schprintze. She didn't say a word, but her eyes spoke for her. How they spoke! No one could understand what was in her heart as well as I. I had been afraid all along that, who knows, the whole affair might come to nothing, and I wanted to save her heartache. I had said this and that against Aarontchik, belittled him in every way I knew. I might as well have talked to a stone wall. Schprintze was wasting away like a candle.

I harnessed my horse and wagon again and toward evening I set off for Boiberik. Riding along, I thought to myself, "Why should they want to see me so urgently? To arrange a betrothal? He could have come to me for that. After all, I am the girl's father." Then I laughed at the very thought. Who had ever heard of a rich man coming to a poor man? It would mean that the world was coming to an end, and the times of the Messiah had dawned, as some of those modern young people tried to tell me. The time will come, they said, when the rich will divide up everything with the poor, share and share alike—what's yours is mine and what's mine is yours, and everybody will be equal. It seems to me that it's a clever world we live in, and yet there are such fools in it!

I arrived at Boiberik and went straight to the widow's house. I stopped my horse and got off the wagon. Where is the widow? Nowhere in sight. Where is her son? I don't see him either. Then who sent for me? "I sent for you," said a short, round barrel of a man, with a sparse little beard and a heavy gold chain around his stomach.

"And who are you?" I asked.

"I am the widow's brother, Aarontchik's uncle," he said. "I was summoned from Ekaterineslav by telegram and I have just arrived."

"If so, *sholom aleichem* to you," I said, and sat down.

When he saw me sit down, he said, "Be seated."

"Thanks, I am already sitting," I said. "How are you, and how is the Constitution in your part of the country?"

He didn't even listen to me. Instead, he spread himself out in a rocking chair, with his hands in his pockets; and with his big stomach with the gold chain around it turned toward me and said, "I understand your name is Tevye."

"That's right. When I am summoned to read the *Torah,* that's the name they call me by. 'Arise, Reb Tevye, son of Reb Shneour Zalman.' "

"Listen to me, Reb Tevye," he said. "Why should we enter into a long discussion? Let's get right down to business."

"With pleasure. King Solomon said long ago, *'There is a time for eevrything.'* If you have to talk business, then talk business. I am a businessman myself."

"I can see you're a businessman. That's why I'm going to talk to you like one businessman to another. I want you to tell me, but tell me frankly, how much it will cost us all told. Remember now, speak frankly."

"Since you ask me to speak frankly," I said, "I must tell you that I don't know what you are talking about."

"Reb Tevye," he said once more, without taking his hands out of his pockets, "I am asking you how much this affair will cost us?"

"It depends on what kind of affair you mean. If you want an elaborate wedding, the sort of affair you're accustomed to, I'm not in a position to do it."

He looked at me as though I were out of my mind. "Either you are playing the oaf, or you really are one. Though I don't believe you are an oaf. If you were, you wouldn't have gotten my nephew into your clutches the way you did. Pretending to invite him to your house to eat *blintzes* on *Shevuos,* then putting a pretty girl in front of him—whether she is a daughter or not a daughter I won't go so far as to say. . . . But it's plain that she turned his head, made him take a fancy to her, and she took a fancy to him, that goes without saying. She may be a good girl and mean no harm, I won't go so far as to say. But you mustn't forget who *you* are and who *we* are. It seems to me you are a man with brains, how could you permit such a thing? That Tevye the Dairyman who delivers our cheese and milk should marry into our family! You will tell me that they made promises to each other? They can take them back. It's not a great catastrophe one way or the other. If it has to cost us something, we won't argue about it either. A girl is not a young man, whether a daughter or not a daughter, I won't go so far as to say. . . ."

"God in Heaven," I thought to myself, "what does the man want from me?" But he doesn't stop ranting. I needn't think, he tells me, that it will do any good to create a scandal, to spread the news that his nephew wanted to marry my daughter. And I should get it out of my head that his sister is a person who can be milked dry. If I don't make any trouble, well and good, I can get a few *rubles* from her. She will put it down to charity. After all, they are only human, they have to help another person once in a while.

Do you want to know how I answered him? *"May my tongue cleave to the roof of my mouth."* I didn't answer him at all. I had lost my powers of speech. I got up, turned my back on him, and went. I ran as from a fire, I escaped as from a dungeon. My head was humming, everything was going around in front of my eyes, in my ears buzzed bits of his conversation—"Speak frankly now . . ." "A daughter or not a daughter . . ." ". . . milking the widow dry." "Put it down to charity." I went up to my horse, buried my face in the wagon and—you won't laugh at me?—I burst into tears. When I had cried myself out, I got up on the driver's seat, and gave my horse as much as he could hold with the whip. Then I asked God, as Job had once asked Him, "What hast Thou seen in old Job, dear Lord, that Thou never leavest him be for a moment? Are there no other people in the world but him?"

I came home and found my family sitting around the supper table very cheerful, talking and laughing. Only Schprintze was missing.

"Where is Schprintze?" I asked.

"What happened?" they all wanted to know. "What did they want you for?"

"Where is Schprintze?" I asked again.

And again they asked me, "What happened? Tell us."

"Nothing," I said. "What should happen? Everything is quiet, thank God. There is no news of pogroms."

At these words Schprintze came in, looked into my eyes, then sat down at the table, without a word, as though this had nothing to do with her. There was no expression on her face and her silence was unnatural. I didn't like the way she sat there, sunk in thought, and the way she did everything we told her to do. When we told her to sit down, she sat. When we told her to eat, she ate. When we told her to go, she went. And when we called her name, she jumped. My heart ached at the sight of her and inside me burned a fire, against whom I didn't know. "O thou Heavenly Father, God Almighty, why do you punish me so? For whose sins?"

Well, do you want to hear the end of the story? I wouldn't wish such an end to my worst enemies. It would be wrong to wish it to any human being. For the curse of the children is the worst curse in the chapter of *Admonitions*. How do I know that someone didn't visit that curse on me? You don't believe in such things? What else could it be then? Tell me if you know, but what's the good of arguing about it? Better listen to the end of the story.

One evening I was driving home from Boiberik with a heavy heart. Just imagine the grief and the feeling of shame. And then, too, my heart ached for my child. You ask what happened to the widow and her son? They had gone, vanished without a trace. They left without so much as saying good-bye. I am almost ashamed to mention this, but they left owing me a small debt for butter and cheese. But I don't hold it against them, they must have forgotten. What hurt me most was that they went without saying good-bye. What my poor child went through no living person ever knew, except me. I am her father and a father's heart understands. Do you think she uttered a word to me? Or complained, or wept, even once? Then you don't know Tevye's daughters. She kept her grief to herself, but she wasted away, she flickered like a dying candle. Only once in a while she would let out a sigh, and that sigh was enough to tear out your heart.

Well, I was driving home that evening, sunk in meditation, asking questions of the Almighty and answering them myself. I wasn't worried about God so much, I could come to terms with Him, one way or another. What bothered me was people. Why should people be so cruel to each other, when they could be so kind? Why should human beings bring suffering to one another as well as to themselves, when they could all live together in peace and good will? Could it be that God had created man on this earth just to make him suffer? What satisfaction would He get out of that?

Thinking these thoughts, I drove into my farm and saw at a distance that over by the pond a big crowd had gathered, old people, young people, men, women, children, everybody in the village. What could it be? It was not a fire. Someone must have drowned. Someone had been bathing in the pond and had met his death. No one knows where the Angel of Death lurks for him, as we say on the Day of Atonement.

Suddenly I saw Golde running, her shawl flying, her arms outstretched, and in front of her the children, Teibel and Beilke, and all three of them screaming and weeping and wailing: "Daughter!" "Sister!" "Schprintze!" I jumped off the wagon so fast that I don't know to this day how I reached the ground in one piece. But when I got to the pond it was too late. . . .

There was something I meant to ask you. What was it? Oh, yes. Have you ever seen a drowned person? When someone dies he usually dies with his eyes closed. A drowned person's eyes are wide open. Do you know the reason for this? Forgive me for taking up so much of your time. I am not a free man either. I have to get back to my horse and wagon and start delivering milk and cheese. The world is still with us. You have to think of earning a living, and forget what has been. For what the earth has covered is better forgotten. There is no help for it, and we have to return to the old saying that as long as "*my soul abides within me*"—you have to keep going, Tevye. Be well, my friend, and if you think of me sometimes, don't think ill of me.

The Merrymakers

(Sketches of Disappearing Types)

CELEBRATING SIMCHAS TORAH

"THE CREW of Merrymakers," we call them in our town, or simply the "Merry Crew." Ordinarily they are timid, unpretentious folk, most of them quite poor, who have nothing to do with each other all year round. But when *Simchas Torah* comes they become jolly and full of life. They get together in one band, and go about the streets arm in arm, singing and dancing, as though they had planned it all out before. They visit every home in town, and wish one and all a merry good *yom-tev*. They invade the homes of the well-to-do householders and treat them to an elaborate *Simchas Torah kiddush,* the ceremonial blessing over wine. The unwilling hosts have no choice but to bring out the best brandy and wine and set the table with food. If they don't, the revelers will get it themselves. They know where everything is kept. They can find their way to the oven, they can drag the preserves out of the cupboard, they can go down to the cellar and bring up the cherry wines, the pickled melons and the cucumbers that the wealthy housewives have prepared for the winter. You wouldn't believe that God-fearing pious Jews would do such things, would you? But on *Simchas Torah* everything is possible.

But all that is nothing. In bygone days (ah, the bygone days!) they themselves would not only get as drunk as Lot, they would also get the mayor and the constables drunk, and all of them together would go dancing coatless and hatless over the roofs of the rich householders.

But times have changed and the mayor and constables have changed with the times. Now we are thankful if they permit us Jews to get drunk once a year and go freely from house to house singing holiday songs. For in some towns, they tell us, even this is forbidden.

Obviously the "Merry Crew" is getting smaller, is shrinking from year to year. Many of the revelers have died out and those who are left will soon go too. And so I hasten to set down their names and to describe each one separately with all his quirks and oddities. Let there be a memorial no matter how small, let there be a record of how Jews used to celebrate and make merry in their exile when *Simchas Torah* came. . . .

Aleck the Mechanic

He is not a mechanic at all, but a tailor, and a little bit of a tailor at that, a dwarf with short legs, tiny hands and a scrap of a beard. But his voice is that of a much bigger man, it's a deep resonant bass voice. Everyone marvels at how such a tiny man can have such a deep voice. But if you are in a mood to ask questions, you might also ask how such a small man can pour so much liquor into himself on *Simchas Torah.*

But it's only on *Simchas Torah.* All year round he drinks nothing, neither whisky nor wine. Not because he is averse to the bitter drop. Far from it. He doesn't drink for the simple reason that he can't afford to. He is a very poor man, almost a pauper. He has a houseful of children to support, but as for work, every year there is less and less. And it's all because of Lazer Ready-to-Wear, may the plague take him. Ever since he opened his Ready-to-Wear store it has become the fashion to buy ready-made clothes and on credit at that, and Aleck the Mechanic has been losing his customers one by one.

You might think that Lazer Ready-to-Wear might at least shove a little work his way, an alteration, a mending job. Not on your life. It all goes to an outsider from the city. Granted that this city tailor is more up-to-date in his work, does one have to go to him for some plain stitching, for making a lining or turning a garment inside out? Can't an ordinary tailor sew on a button, baste a ribbon, press a collar? It seems that he can't!

If this Lazer Ready-to-Wear were a merchant from the city at least! But no! He is one of our own people, a former tailor, a pious, "holier than thou" sort of fellow. He owns his home, he is on friendly terms with the mayor and the police; he travels abroad every summer and brings back all the latest styles and fashion plates. In the Synagogue, he has the best seat, right up front. He is always being called up to read the juiciest portions of the Law. He finds matches for his children among the best families. He has entirely forgotten that he was once a poor tailor himself, in fact the very word "tailor" is distasteful to him. He won't look at an ordinary workman. Poor people are chased from his door with sticks. And the good Lord sees it all and does nothing about it!

On the contrary. Each year Reb Lazer gets more prosperous. It's getting so that it's an honor to be a visitor in his house. You have to ring a bell to get in!

But there is one day in the year when you can get in without special intermediaries, without bells, and without announcements. That day is *Simchas Torah.*

Early in the morning when everyone else is still in the Synagogue, Aleck the Mechanic and the rest of the "Merry Crew," who have prayed and eaten and had something to drink before dawn, go up and down the streets arm in arm singing and making merry. They make the rounds of the houses to wish everyone a merry good *yom-tev,* and first of all they go to the house of the newly rich Reb Lazer Ready-to-Wear. (In honor of *Simchas Torah* the bell has been removed from the door.) Since early morning the table has been set with whisky and beer and a bottle of wine and all sorts of delicacies. Reb Lazer himself meets them at the door with a set smile on his face and asks Aleck to make the *kiddush.* Aleck obliges him by intoning the blessing in his deepest voice, chanting it in real holiday style, mimicking with his motions a cantor in the Synagogue. And the "Merry Crew" answers him like a choir: "A-a-a-men."

Lazer Ready-to-Wear goes into raptures over the *kiddush,* and his wife pretends to rejoice also, while inwardly she is trembling lest they spill wine on her best tablecloth or break one of her wineglasses.

They both consider themselves more than lucky if they escape without a scene. For when Aleck has had a few drinks and is somewhat tipsy he can tell Reb Lazer a few unpleasant truths.

He can take him by the hand and express himself thus, very delicately and subtly: "Listen to me, Brother Ready-to-Wear! Though you hate a poor Jew worse than a Jew hates pork, still because we are celebrating a holiday over the whole world today, and since you treated us to cake and wine, let us now drink each other's health and pray that we live until next *Simchas Torah* and remain as good Jews as we are now. Now let us kiss each other tenderly, and may the world never learn that you are a tailor and the son of a tailor as well as a scurvy knave and a low-down cur and an enemy of all Israel."

When they are through with Reb Lazer, the "Merry Crew" moves on to the next house. There they repeat the *kiddush* with the same flourishes and the same choral accompaniment. They even add a few choice bits to their performance. Aleck the Mechanic is a past master at this sort of thing. For instance, if you beg him very hard he will give you an imitation of a woman going into labor for the first time. Anything to divert the crowd, anything to make them lively and gay, for it's *Simchas Torah* and on *Simchas Torah* everyone must rejoice and make merry.

Kopel the Brain

That's what he is called, because he has a high, glistening forehead. "A forehead like a prime minister's," they say. But Kopel is not a prime minister. He is only a poor workman. He is a shoemaker.

Kopel is very gloomy by nature. He is always sad, worried, bedraggled-looking, unhappy and pessimistic.

What's the reason for this? Is it because he looks out at the world from a dark cellar? This cellar is his workshop; here is where he pounds on his last. This cellar is also his home; that's where he and his family live. For a shoemaker is not a tailor. A tailor must have light, while a shoemaker can get by in the dark. That is, if you stop to think about it, a shoemaker also has to see where to put his awl through and where to pound the pegs in. But a little window is enough for that, a quarter of a window with a greenish-yellow pane. A man who has sat for so many years on a round leather stool hammering away in the dark can't have a cheerful outlook on life.

And perhaps his melancholy stems from the fact that God has blessed him with such a terror of a wife who, aside from the fact that she makes life miserable for him, never stops talking; her mouth doesn't shut for a moment.

The neighbors call her "Sarah the Speechmaker" because she talks continually without pause and without rest. One thing leads to another, her voice goes on and on without end, its source never seems to run dry.

But we don't expect our reader to take our word for this. And so we present as proof a sample of the talk that Sarah the Speechmaker runs through of a fine morning, while Kopel is pounding on his last and his two apprentices are working alongside of him, one pulling a thread through with an awl, the other trimming a sole. Don't think that Sarah sits with her arms folded. She is doing three tasks at one time; she is peeling potatoes with her hands, she is rocking the cradle with her foot, and with her mouth she is talking away, talking to herself.

"What a day this has been . . . open the doors and gates and windows wide. . . . It's a madhouse, upstairs, downstairs, this one here, that one there. If this hammering would only stop—there he sits and hammers, may it hammer in his head. And she too, that sister of his, the way she claps her tongue, like a bell going ding-dong-ding. A wonderful piece of good luck has happened to her, she got a letter from her Doli, all the way from America. She is ready to lie down and die with gratitude, because he hasn't gone and married another woman out there, that fine husband of hers, may a plague take him, the way Chaya Kayla's husband did. May it sink into the ocean and never rise again—I mean that golden country, America. When they arrive there they forget they ever had a wife at home, they are as free as birds of passage. Shoo phoo, go away, chickens . . . may she sink into the earth. It's impossible to put up with her, with that poultry-woman, I mean, she and her fowls. She doesn't feed them a thing and expects them to get fat. Do you think they would do you a favor and lay an egg once in a while, just enough to brush the Sabbath loaf with? The way they charge for everything now, you can't touch a thing, neither an egg nor a potato nor an onion, though you run looking through the whole town. . . . May her face break out in a rash, may she get a sore in her insides—I mean that peasant, she is so smart she thinks she can swindle a Jew. 'Will you buy one of my chickens for the Sabbath?' It's a chicken just as you are a rabbi. 'And where is your chicken?' She shoves a pullet as big as a flea into your face. 'Is that a chicken?' She gets furious at that and begins teasing you: 'You have no money anyway.' And hides her fine chicken in her bosom. 'Give it to the cats.' As though it wasn't enough, now a tomcat has stolen in among the cats, the way Peisi Chaim has stolen into that stylish Riva Leah's graces, every morning and every night like a clock, sticking his nose into all the pots and kettles. 'Get out, scat! There is nothing left. It's all dried out.' May your intestines dry out and your brain and your . . ."

"Whom are your cursing?" Kopel asks her curiously, putting down his hammer and turning his high glistening brow toward his wife.

"You and your bastards, that's who," Sarah answers promptly and continues her three occupations—peeling potatoes, rocking the cradle, and talking as before—delighted to have found new material for her tongue to work over, her tongue that goes blabbing on and on, without pause and without rest. Her speech is as bottomless as the ocean, as long as the Jewish exile, as endless as Kopel's misery. Poor Kopel. How he would long to run away, if he weren't chained to his leather stool. But he has to finish a piece of work, or he wouldn't have money to provide for the Sabbath, and if he doesn't provide for the Sabbath he will get the sharp edge of Sarah's tongue.

Yes, Kopel the shoemaker is gloomy and sad, unhappy and depressed. But he doesn't utter a word of complaint. He bears his lot in silence; he carries his sorrow quietly within himself. A man has to be a philosopher to keep so much within himself. Kopel the Brain is a philosopher. A quiet philosopher and a gloomy one.

But if Kopel is gloomy all year round, there is one day when he is cheerful, and that day is *Simchas Torah*. Did I say cheerful? He is like a new-born soul, beside himself with joy, mad with happiness, literally mad. Just imagine Kopel the Brain among the crew of merry-makers, and the merriest one of them all. He has changed hats with Aleck the Mechanic. Since the one has a hat like a washbasin, and the other's hat is no bigger than a fig, you can split your sides laughing to watch them. But hold on, they wanted to change coats too, only Aleck's tiny coat didn't begin to cover Kopel's broad shoulders. It's comical to watch the two of them cavorting together, with their arms around each other, dancing in the streets. And though Kopel has a high thin voice, almost no voice at all you might say, still he summons all the strength he has in his lungs and sings along with Aleck like a faithful choir boy helping his cantor. And when Aleck starts intoning the holiday *kiddush,* Kopel helps him in that too, ending up with a "Bom." And when Aleck has ended the prayer with a drawn out *"M'kadesh Isroel"* and a beautifully warbled *"V'hasminim"* and starts to carry the glass to his lips, Kopel snatches the glass from his hand and before you know what's happened he has drained it and is ready to start dancing. Then Aleck begins to sing and the "Merry Crew" joins in, some singing, others clapping their hands. Here is the song they sing, half in Hebrew, half in Russian:

Thou has cho-o-osen us
Out of all the rest.
Of all the na-a-a-tions
Thou hast loved us best.

"Louder, men, louder," shouts Kopel the Brain, and his forehead runs with sweat. "Don't worry, brothers, the main thing is not to worry. Just keep on singing, keep on dancing, rejoice and make merry!"

Mendel the Tinman

"Tinsmith" would be more correct, for Mendel is a tinsmith by trade. But we call him the Tinman because he looks just as though he were made of tin. He is tall and thin and erect, and he wears a stiff narrow coat that looks like a tube made of tin. His face is the color of tin and his beard looks like a sheet of tin. Even his voice is tinny. His work is that of glazing samovars. But since samovars in our town are glazed only for Passover, that is the only time when Mendel is busy. The rest of the year he doesn't look a samovar in the face. With such a thriving business, Mendel the Tinman would starve to death if he didn't have more irons in the fire, other means of making a livelihood.

For instance, he knows how to doctor cows, how to make them give milk. You ask what this has to do with tinsmithing? Nothing whatever. But if a man has a talent for something else, what harm is there in using it? For instance, if a man also happens to know how to build ovens? Or to mend broken pots so that no one can recognize that they had ever been broken? And if you think he has no conception of the art of housepainting, then you are mistaken. When a man is talented there is no limit to what he can do.

But don't jump to conclusions. Out of all these trades and occupations Mendel barely gets enough to provide water for his *kasha.* And even for that his wife Reisel has to help him out.

Reisel is a midwife, but without a practice. It isn't that she is not a competent midwife, but there is a new fashion now of training licensed midwives. There is a name for them—*akusherka.* In recent years we have acquired these midwives, or *akusherkas,* in plenty. There isn't a home without its midwife. If a man has three daughters, two of them are *akusherkas,* and the third is studying to be one.

"A town full of midwives," shouts Mendel the Tinman going into a fine rage. "For every woman who gives birth there are two midwives—no, three, for the woman in labor is a midwife herself."

Mendel disapproves of the system. But then Mendel disapproves of everything. He is sharply critical of everything. There isn't a person in town with whom he doesn't find fault, no one of whom he will say a kind word. That's the sort of nature he has. He is a man whom nothing can satisfy and no one can please. For instance, if it's raining outside, he will never say it's a rain, it's always a downpour, a deluge. And on the other hand, if it isn't raining, that's bad too. Then you have a drought, the earth is parched, it's becoming a desert. The sun is never just warm, it's always blazing. Every snowfall is a blizzard. An ordinary frost is not enough for him. It's a "killing frost."

If anyone dies, then the whole town is dying out, people are dropping like flies. Whenever there is a funeral to attend, a condolence call to make, a sickbed to visit, Mendel is among the first. He offers comfort in these words, "It could have been worse." If you have a toothache, Mendel will say, "Do you call that a toothache? If you want to know what a toothache is, ask me." And he will tell you the agony he went through with a bad tooth, or will recount how a friend of his almost died from a sore tooth, he was barely, barely saved. . . .

Or try complaining of a cough. At once he will ask, "Are you spitting blood?" This is not because he wishes you ill or wants you to spit blood. It is just his temperament. He sees everything in the worst possible light; he likes to heap stones on everyone's head. He can't do otherwise. That is the way he was made.

Now would you ever believe that a misanthrope like Mendel the Tinman would be one of the crew of merrymakers on *Simchas Torah* —the greatest comedian, the biggest clown, the craziest buffoon of them all?

On *Simchas Torah,* Mendel becomes a "German." On that day he dresses up like a German and speaks no other language but German. He rolls up his long tube-like coat to look like a short jacket, he combs his earlocks behind his ears till there isn't a sign of hair on his face. And the hat he puts on his head—friends, where in the world does anyone find such a hat? From what ashheap did he rescue it? It is supposedly a "cylinder," a top-hat, but it's all bent out of shape, full of holes and as high as a chimney pot—it has no lid, only a hole on top, a regular factory chimney. And though this chimney pot is well known in town from last year and the year before and the year before that, he is greeted this year with the same joy and amazement with which he was greeted last year and the year before last and the year before that. The band of small boys gives him the same ovation: "Good *yom-tev,* German. Hurrah! Chimney! Hurrah, 'cylinder.'"

But Mendel the Tinman pays no attention to them. He won't have anything to do with the youngsters. Mendel the German has been created for the edification of grownups. The whole town has to enjoy his antics. Tables and chairs are dragged out of doors and Mendel the Tinman (now Mendel the "German") with the tall chimney pot on his head, one hand on his hip, and in the other a bottle, dances a German dance and sings a song in German:

We are Germans,
Free from sorrow.
If we have no money,
We go out and borrow.

And the rest of the crew joins in on the chorus:

Bim bom, bim bom
Bim bim, bim bom.

And Mendel sings further:

For we are Germans,
One, two, there and here,
If we can't get whisky
We'll drink beer.

And the chorus answers:

Bim bom, bim bom
Bim bim, bim bom.

And Mendel goes on:

For we are Germans
Known to great and small.
If you won't give us a little,
We'll take it all.

And the chorus picks it up from there:

Bim bom, bim bom
Bim bim, bim bom.

And so on. Suddenly Mendel stops. "Friends!" he shouts in a transport of joy. "I want to know, is there anything better than to be a Jew? I ask you one thing: What can be finer than to be a Jew on *Simchas Torah?*"

The crowd agrees with him that there is nothing better in the world than being a Jew on *Simchas Torah*. They become noisier and merrier all the time. They leap higher and higher, spin faster and faster. They take hands and make a big circle and go around and around, dancing and stamping their feet in wilder and wilder revelry.

An Easy Fast

AN EXPERIMENT which the famous Dr. Tanner was not able to perform was carried through successfully by a poor little Jew in poor little Kasrilevka. Dr. Tanner set out to prove that a man could fast for forty days, and he tortured himself for twenty-eight days and almost passed away. All through the experiment he was fed teaspoonfuls of water, given pieces of ice to swallow, attendants sat by him day and night watching his pulse. It was a great event.

While Chaim Chaikin showed that a man could fast much longer than forty days. Naturally, not consecutively, one day after another, but at least a hundred days through the year, if not more.

But real fasting!

Did anyone pour drops of water into his mouth? Was he given pieces of ice to swallow? No such thing. To him, fasting meant neither eating nor drinking for a day and a night, twenty-four hours in a row.

There were no doctors sitting at his side, no attendants counting his pulse. Nobody heard. Nobody knew. . . .

What's the story?

The story is that Chaim Chaikin is a poor man with a large family and it's his family that supports him.

His children are for the most part girls, and these girls work in a factory making cigarettes. This one earns a *gulden,* another half a *gulden* a day. And that, not every day. Sabbaths are not included. Nor holidays. Nor the days on which they are out on strike. For everywhere, God be thanked, and even here in Kasrilevka, we have learned how to strike.

And out of these earnings they have to pay rent for the damp corner of the cellar in which they all live.

And out of these earnings they have to buy dresses and shoes. Each girl has a dress of her own, but one pair of shoes has to serve two. And out of these earnings they have to eat. If you can call it eating. A piece of bread smeared with garlic, sometimes a barley soup, once in a while a piece of dried bloater that burns your gullet so that you have to drink all night long.

When the family sits down to eat, they have to divide up the bread and dole out a piece to each one as though it were cake.

"Eat. Eat. All they do is eat," complains Chaika, Chaim Chaikin's wife, a sickly woman who coughs all night long.

"May no harm come to them," observes Chaim Chaikin, and watches the children swallowing chunks of bread without chewing them. He himself would like to take a bite of bread too, but if he did, then the two little ones, Freidka and Beilka, would have to go without supper.

And so he divides his portion of the bread in half and calls over the two small children.

"Freidka, Beilka, here is another piece of bread for each of you. You'll have it for supper." Freidka and Beilka stretch out their thin, scrawny arms and look into their father's face not knowing whether to believe him or not. Could he be teasing them? They take the bread and play with it, stealing little bites out of it every now and then. Their mother sees them and begins scolding, "Always eating, always eating."

The father can't bear to listen to her scolding the children. He would like to say something, but he keeps his peace. He cannot speak, he must not speak. What is he anyway in this house but a broken reed? He is the meanest of the mean. Superfluous to everyone, superfluous to his family, and even superfluous to himself.

What else, alas, can he be, if he does no work? Absolutely none. Not because he doesn't want to, nor because he is too proud, but simply because there is no work for him. None whatever. The whole town complains that there is no work. The town is overflowing with Jews who have been driven there from other places. So many Jews gathered together in one spot. Something to rejoice about. Well, well.

"This too is for the best," reflects Chaim Chaikin. It's a lucky thing he has children who work, others don't even have that. But who likes to be dependent on his children?

For it isn't a good thing to be dependent on one's children. Not because they begrudge him the food. Not at all. It is just that he can't bear to accept it. He simply can't.

He knows how hard the children work all day long. He knows how they are being sweated. He knows it only too well.

Every bite of bread he takes is like a drop of blood to him. He is drinking his children's blood. Do you hear? He, Chaim Chaikin, is drinking his children's blood. And that is more than he can bear.

"Father, why don't you eat?" the children ask him.

"Today is a fast day," he says.

"Another fast day. How many fast days do you observe?"

"Less than there are days in the week."

Chaim Chaikin is not lying. He observes fast days frequently. But there are also days on which he eats.

But the days on which Chaim Chaikin fasts are for him the best days.

"First of all, fasting is an act of piety. With every fast I get closer to winning Eternal Life, my interest in the Hereafter keeps growing . . . my investment in Heaven gets bigger.

"In the second place, nothing is being spent on me, and I don't have to account to anyone. True, nobody asks for an accounting. But why should I owe anything when I can get by just as easily without it?

"And isn't it worth something to me that I feel a little superior to a dumb beast, a cow? A cow eats every day. I can get by, eating only every other day. A man has to rise above an animal."

If a man could only rise so high above an animal that he could get along without eating altogether! But his gizzard, the devil take it, won't let him. Being hungry, Chaim Chaikin begins to spin theories, to philosophize. It's all on account of this cursed gizzard, he thinks, all because of this wretched habit of eating, that most of the troubles of the world come about. It's all because of this habit of eating that I am a poor man and my children have to work and sweat and risk their very lives for a crust of bread.

"Just think, if a person only didn't have to eat, my children would all be home. There would be no more sweatshops. No more strikes. No factories. No factory owners. No rich. And no poor. No fanaticism and no hatred. We would then have a true paradise on earth."

Thus Chaim Chaikin reflects, and he grieves for this wretched world and it pains him. It pains him deeply that God created man so that he is not much better than a cow.

The days on which Chaim Chaikin fasts are, as I've told you, the happiest days for him. And the day of a real fast, the day of *Tish'abov* for instance is (he is almost ashamed to admit it) a real holiday.

Just figure it out for yourself. By not eating that day, he gains so much. He cannot be counted among the dumb beasts, nor does he profit from his children's sweated labor. He performs an act of piety, and he weeps, as a man is supposed to weep, for the destruction of the Temple.

For how can you weep when you are well fed? How can a man with a full belly feel honest grief? To feel real grief a man has to suffer hunger pangs first.

"Look at them, pampering their gizzards. They are afraid to fast, so they bribe the Lord with a *groschen.*" Thus Chaim Chaikin rages against those who in order to avoid fasting buy themselves out by putting a *kopek* in the charity box.

The most difficult of all fast days is *Tish'abov*. So the whole world says. Chaim Chaikin can't understand why. Because the day is longer? And the night shorter? Because it's hot outdoors? Who tells you to stroll around in the sun? Sit in the Synagogue and pray. There are enough prayers, God be thanked.

"And I tell you," insists Chaim Chaikin, "that *Tish'abov* is the easiest of all the fasts. For it's the best, the very best of them all. Take, for instance, *Yom Kippur.*—'Ye shall discipline yourselves,' it is written. Which means, 'You shall chastise your bodies.' For what purpose? To win for yourself a lucky number for the coming year. On *Tish'abov,* you are not required to fast, but you fast anyway. For how can you eat on the anniversary of the day the Temple was destroyed? When all the Jews—men, women and children—were slaughtered?

"It is not written that you must weep on *Tish'abov* and yet you weep. For how can you hold back the tears when you remember what we lost on that day?

"The pity of it is that there is only one *Tish'abov*. Only one *Yom Kippur*."

"And what about the Fast of the 17th day of *Tamuz?*" asks a bystander.

"Only one 17th day of *Tamuz*," says Chaim Chaikin with a deep sigh.

"And the Fast of Gedaliah? And the Fast of Queen Esther?" the other continues.

"Only one Fast of Gedaliah, only one Fast of Queen Esther," says Chaim Chaikin with another sigh.

"Why, Reb Chaim, you're a regular glutton for fasts."

"There are not enough fast days," repeats Chaim Chaikin. "Not enough fast days." And he undertakes to fast the day before *Tish'abov* too. He will fast two days in a row.

The only difficulty is with drinking. It's hard to go so long without a drink. Chaim Chaikin then resolves to fast a whole week, except for a glass of water every day.

Do you think this is idle talk? Not at all. Chaim Chaikin is a man who "saith and doeth." He does what he says.

For a whole week before *Tish'abov* he stopped eating, he lived on nothing but water.

Who is there to pay any attention to him? His wife, poor thing, is sick. The older children are at the factory, and the little ones are too young to understand. Freidka and Beilka only know that when they are hungry (and they are always hungry) their insides are all twisted up, and they crave food.

"Today you will get an extra piece of bread," their father tells them, and cuts his share in half, and Freidka and Beilka reach out their scrawny hands and grab the bread with delight.

"Father, why aren't you eating?" the older girls ask him. "Surely there is no fast today."

"Who said I was fasting?" he tells them, and he thinks to himself, "I fooled them and yet I didn't tell a falsehood. For what is a drink of water? It is neither fasting nor eating."

When *Tish'abov* Eve came, Chaim Chaikin felt free and happy. He was happier than he had ever been before. He had no desire for food. On the contrary, he felt that if he put a piece of solid food into his mouth it just wouldn't go down. It would simply stick in his throat.

That is to say, that actually he did feel some hunger pangs. His arms and legs trembled and he felt himself sinking, his strength was ebbing, his head was going around, and he was ready to faint. He thought, shame! To have fasted a whole week and then to give in on the very eve of *Tish'abov*. Unthinkable!

And Chaim Chaikin took his portion of bread and potatoes and called over the little girls, Freidka and Beilka, and told them in a low voice, "Children, take this and eat. But don't let your mother see you." The children took their father's share of bread and potatoes, looked up into his face, and saw that it was deathly pale and that his hands were trembling.

Chaim watched the children snatch the food, he watched them chew and swallow and he swallowed his saliva and shut his eyes. Then he got up, unable to wait any longer for the older girls to come home from the factory. He picked up his prayer book, took off his shoes as a sign of mourning, and went to the Synagogue, barely able to drag his feet.

At the Synagogue he was the first to arrive. He got himself the seat right next to the cantor's stand, on an upturned bench which lay against the wall of the pulpit. He provided himself with a bit of snuff which he stuck to the bench, stretched himself out with his head against the pulpit and began to read, "Mourn O Zion, weep O Zion, and all thy cities." He shut his eyes and saw "Zion" in front of him, in the shape of a tall woman dressed in black with a black veil over her face, weeping and lamenting and wringing her hands, mourning for her sons who fall every day on strange battlefields for strangers' sins.

"You ask O Zion for thy wretched sons
Who mourn thy fate upon a foreign shore.
I bring you news of the surviving ones,
The last sad remnant . . . the others are no more. . . ."

Opening his eyes he no longer saw "Zion" the beautiful woman in black. He saw instead, through the smoke-stained, dirty windowpane, a brilliant ray of the sun that was setting on the other side of the town. And though he shut his eyes again he still saw the rays of the sun, and not only the rays of the sun but the sun itself, the bright sun which no one else could behold and live. He, Chaim Chaikin, was looking straight at the sun and nothing happened to him. Why? Perhaps because he had shed the world and all its possessions. He was happy at last, he was light of heart, he knew that he could endure anything. He would have an easy fast, a very easy fast. . . .

And Chaim Chaikin kept his eyes closed and saw before him a strange world—many strange worlds—which he had never seen before. Angels floated in front of him and he looked at them and recognized the faces of his children, the older ones as well as the younger ones. He wanted to tell them something, but he couldn't speak. He wanted to ask their forgiveness, to explain that he wasn't to blame. Was it his fault that so many people had been herded together into one small spot, so that they were obliged to squeeze and shove and devour each other alive? Was it his fault that there were people who found it necessary to exploit others and suck their blood? Or that human beings hadn't yet attained such a high degree that they didn't have to drive others to work as they might drive a horse? That even a horse should be treated kindly? For he was one of God's creatures too.

Chaim Chaikin with his eyes shut saw the whole world and the world was clear and bright and he saw something rolling upwards like smoke. He felt something leaving his arms and legs, his bowels and his heart, and, pulling itself upward, separating itself from his body. He felt hollow and strangely light and he let out a deep sigh and a long, long groan. Then he felt nothing, absolutely nothing.

When Berel the *Shammes,* a little man with bushy red hair and puffy lips, came to the Synagogue in his stockinged feet with holes in the heels and saw Chaim Chaikin lying with his head against the pulpit, his eyes half open, he was very much annoyed. Thinking that Chaim was dozing, he began mumbling angrily and shaking his fist at him.

The impudence of the man. Spreading himself out like that. Count Pshagnitzky himself wouldn't dare. Probably had a big meal and came here to sleep it off. "Reb Chaim, get up. Reb Chaim, Say—Reb Cha-im."

The last ray of the setting sun burst through the Synagogue window and fell straight on Chaim Chaikin's peaceful face with its shiny, black, curly hair, its thick black eyebrows and its half-open fine dark eyes and it illumined his pale, waxen, starved features through and through. . . .

The Little Pot

RABBI, I want to ask your opinion. . . .

I don't know if you know me or not. I am Yenta—that's who I am—Yenta the Poultrywoman. I sell eggs and chickens and geese and ducks. I have my regular customers, two or three families that keep me going, may God grant them health and fortune. Because if I had to start paying interest, I wouldn't have enough bread to make a prayer over. But this way I borrow three *rubles* here, or three *rubles* there. I take from one and pay back the other, pay this one, borrow from that one—you twist and turn and keep going! Of course, you understand, if my husband were still alive—oh me, oh my! And yet to tell the truth, I wasn't exactly licking honey when he was alive either. He was never the bread-winner, may he forgive me for saying this, all he did was sit and study; he sat over his holy books all day long, and I did the work. I am used to hard work, I've worked all my life, even as a child I used to help my mother, Bashe her name was, Bashe the Candler. She used to buy tallow from the butchers and make candles, she twisted candles from tallow and sold them. That was long before anybody knew anything about gas or about lamps with chimneys that crack all the time—only last week I cracked a chimney and the week before I cracked another chimney. . . .

How did we get around to that? Oh, yes, you say about dying young . . . When he died, my Moses Ben-Zion, he was only twenty-six years old. What? Why do I say twenty-six? Because he was nineteen when we were married, and it's now eight years since he died, and nineteen and eight taken together make—twenty-three. Then how did I get twenty-six out of that? Because I forgot the seven years that he was sick. Actually, he was sick much longer than seven years, he was ailing all his life. That is, in some ways, he was healthy enough, but he coughed all the time, it was his cough that finished him. I shouldn't say that he coughed all the time, but once he got started he couldn't stop coughing—he coughed and coughed and coughed. The doctors said he had a kind of "spasm," this means that when he had to cough he coughed and when he didn't have to, he didn't cough. Doesn't that sound like nonsense? May goats know as much about jumping into strange gardens as these doctors know about curing the sick.

Take Reb Aaron the *Shochet's* boy, Yokel they call him. He had a very bad toothache, and they tried everything—prayers and potions, poultices, lotions. Nothing helped. Then he, that is Yokel himself, goes and puts a piece of garlic into his ear—they say that garlic is good for the toothache. The boy was in torture, he almost hit the ceiling, but he never said a word about the garlic. They call the doctor, and the doctor comes and feels his pulse. What are you feeling his pulse for, you idiot? If they hadn't taken the boy to Yehupetz right then—do you know where he would be resting now? In the same place where his poor sister Pearl is now, the one who passed away in childbirth.

How did we get around to that? Oh, yes, you said about widows . . . I was left a young widow with a small child and with half a house on Pauper's Row—next door to Lazer the Carpenter's, if you know where that is—it's not far from the bathhouse. You will ask me, why only half a house? It's because the other half isn't mine. It belongs to my brother-in-law Ezriel. You must know him, he is a Vaselikuter, he comes from a town called Vaselikut, and he deals in fish. He makes a good living too, depending on the river and the weather. If the weather is mild, the fish bite, and there's a good catch; and when there's a good catch, fish is cheap. But if it's windy, the catch is poor and fish is high. But it's better for everyone if the catch is good and fish is cheap. That's what he says, Ezriel, that is. "What's the sense of that?" I ask him. And he says it's very simple. "If the weather is mild, there's a good catch, and when there's a good catch, fish is cheap. But if the weather is rough, the catch is poor and fish is high. But it's better for everyone if the catch is good and fish is cheap." So I ask again, "Yes, but what's the sense of that?" And he repeats, "It's very simple. If the weather is mild there's a good catch and when there's a good catch fish is cheap. . . ." "Get out!" I tell him. How can you talk to a dummy like that?

Now how did we get around to that? Oh, yes, you say about owning one's home. . . . Naturally it's better to have a corner of your own than to rent from other people. How do you say it, "What's mine is mine and not another's." So I have my own half of a house, my inheritance or property, if you want to call it that. But I ask you, what does a widow with only one child need a whole half house for? If she has a place to rest her head, that's enough. Especially when the house needs a roof—it's been needing a roof for years. He keeps pestering me, that dear brother-in-law of mine, to have a roof put on. "It's time," he says, "we put on a roof." And I say, "Well, why don't we put on a roof then?" And he repeats, "Let's put on a roof." And I, "Come, let's put on a roof." Roof here, roof there—that's as far as it gets. Because if you're going to put on a roof, you need straw. I am not talking about shingles. Where would I get money for shingles?

So I rent out two rooms. In one lives Chaim-Choneh the Deaf, an old man in his dotage. His children pay me five *gulden* a week rent for his room, and he eats with them every other day, that is, one day he eats, and the next day he fasts, and the day that he eats he gets little enough. At least that's what he tells me, I mean Chaim-Choneh the Deaf. And maybe he is lying! Old folks like to grumble. No matter how much you give them, it isn't enough. No matter where you seat them, the place is no good. No matter where you let them sleep, the bed is too hard.

What were we talking about? Oh, yes, you say tenants and neighbors . . . May no good Jew ever have to put up with them. At least, that one, the deaf one, is deaf and he is a quiet old man. You neither see him nor hear him. But it was just my bad luck to rent the other room to a different sort, to a flour-dealer, Gnessi is her name and she has a small shop where she sells flour. What a harridan! At first she was as soft as honeycake. You should have heard her talk. She was all lovey-dovey. "My dear Yenta." "Yenta, my soul." She was going to do this and that for me. What did she need for herself? Nothing but a corner of the oven, just enough room for a small pot, an end of the wooden bench to salt her meat on once a week, an edge of the table to roll a sheet of dough on for noodles once in a blue moon.

"And the children?" I asked. "Where are you going to put those children of yours, Gnessi? You have a family of small children, may no harm come to them." "What are you talking about, Yenta, my life?" she says to me. "Do you have any idea what kind of children they are? They are jewels, they are diamonds—not children. In the summer they play outside all day, and when winter comes they climb up on the oven, quiet as lambs, you don't hear a peep out of them. The only trouble with them is that they eat so much, they have big appetites, God bless them, always chewing on something."

Well, well, if I had only known what I was getting into. Children are children—may God not punish me for my words. But you should see these children. Day and night, night and day, they deafen you with their noise, screaming, shouting, scrapping, fighting. It's a regular *Gehenna.* Did I say *Gehenna? Gehenna* is mild by comparison. But don't think that's the end. The children would be half a headache, because after all you can silence a child. You smack it or pinch it or shake it—it's only a child.

But God gave Gnessi a husband too. Ezer, his name is. You must know him, he is assistant *shammes* at the Basement Synagogue—an honest, pious man, poor fellow, and not such a fool either, it seems to me. But you should see the way she treats him, that Gnessi of his. "Ezer, do this." "Ezer, do that." Ezer here, Ezer there—Ezer—Ezer—Ezer. And Ezer? Either he answers with one of his quips—he is a quipster, he likes to make up jokes on top of everything else—or he pulls his cap down low over his eyes and runs out of the house.

How did we get around to that? Oh, yes, you say bad tenants . . . There are bad tenants and bad tenants. I hope God doesn't put me down as a back-biter—I shouldn't speak evil of Gnessi. What have I got against her? She is a woman who won't refuse a beggar a piece of bread. But when she's in a bad humor—may God have mercy! It's a shame to repeat things like that. I wouldn't say it to anyone else but you, and I know that you will keep it a secret. Sssh. She gives him a slap now and then, her husband I mean, when nobody is looking. "Gnessi, Gnessi," I say to her, "have you no fear of God at all?" But all she says is, "It's none of your business." And I say, "You can go—you know where." And she says, "Let him go there, who looks into other people's pots." And I say, "May his eyes fall out, who can't find a better place to look." And she says, "Let him become deaf who listens." Well, what do you think of such a foul-mouth?

What were we talking about? Oh, yes, you said a clean house . . . Why should I lie about it? I like a clean house, clean in every corner. Is there anything wrong with that? Maybe she can't stand it, I mean Gnessi, that my room is so clean and neat, so bright and sweet. And hers? You should see it—always dark and dingy, unswept, unkempt, with dirt and refuse as high as your neck and the water basin always full of slops—Ugh.

And when morning comes, you'd think the heavens were splitting open. Did I say they were children? They are devils, not children. Just compare them with my David. There is no comparison. My David, may he be strong and healthy, is in *cheder* all day; and when he comes home at night he gets to work again, saying his prayers, studying, or just reading a book. And her children? May God not punish me for these words—either they are eating or crying or pounding their heads against the wall. Is it my fault that God blessed her with such a crowd of hooligans and rewarded me with such a prize, such a jewel, may the Lord watch over him, he has cost me so many tears already.

And don't say it's because I am a woman. A man, if he was in my place, would never have lived through it all. I don't want to embarrass you, but there are men who are a thousand times worse than women. Let anything happen to them and they think the world is coming to an end. For example, how much proof do you need? Take Yossi, Moses Abraham's, as long as his Fruma-Necha was alive he was as good as anybody, but as soon as she died, he went to pieces completely. "Reb Yossi," I say to him, "God be with you. It's true that your wife died, but what can you do about it? It's God's work. 'He gives and He takes away.'" How is it written in the Holy Books? I don't have to tell you. You must know it better than I do.

Well, how did we get to talking about that? Oh, you were saying an only child . . . He is my only one, my Dovidl, how do we say it? The apple of my eye. Don't you know him? He is named after my father-in-law, David Hersch. If you could only see him, he is just like his father, just likes Moses Ben-Zion, the same build, the same face, just like my husband's, yellow, lean, drawn—skin and bones—and weak, so weak, all worn out from *cheder,* tired out from his studies. I say to him, "That's enough, Dovidl. Enough, my son, rest up a little. Just look at yourself. See how pale you look. Take something to eat," I say. "Eat something, drink something. Here, take a glass of chicory, take it." "Chicory?" he says. "You'd better drink it yourself, mother. You are working beyond your strength. I wish I could help you. Let me carry your basket from the marketplace."

"What an idea!" I say. "What are you saying? Do you know what you are talking about? What do you mean—you will carry baskets? My enemies will never live to see the day. And I have enough enemies. I want you to study, just sit there and study." And I look at him, at my David, sitting there, just like his father. Exactly like him, even to his cough. Every time he coughs, part of my heart is torn loose. Oh, if you knew what I went through before I lived to see him grow up. When he was a baby, you understand, nobody believed he would survive at all. Every sickness, every ailment, every malady you ever heard of—he had it. Was it measles? He had the measles. Smallpox? He had smallpox. Diphtheria also, and scarlet fever and stomachaches and toothaches. All the nights that I sat up with him—may God Himself not count them. But with all my prayers and tears, and a little grace from Heaven, I lived to see him *Bar Mitzvah* at last.

But do you think that was the end of my troubles? Then just listen to this. He is on his way from *cheder* one night, it's the middle of winter, and he sees someone coming his way draped in pure white and slapping his hands together at every step. The poor child is scared out of his wits, he falls in a faint right into the snow, and they bring him home half-dead. We barely revive him, and when he comes to, he runs up a fever and he lies there on fire for six whole weeks.

How I ever lived through those six weeks, I don't know. It must have been a miracle from heaven. What didn't I do to save him? I made vows, I sold him and bought him back again, I gave him an extra name—Chaim-David-Hersch—I did all the customary things. And then my tears, who could count the tears I poured out over him? "Dear God," I pleaded with the Eternal One, "do you want to punish me? Punish me then in any way you like, but don't take my child from me." And God heard me, He granted my wish, the boy became well again, and when he sat up he said to me, "Do you know what, mother? I have a message to you from father. He came to see me." When I heard that my soul almost leaped out of my body and my heart began pounding. "That's a good omen," I told him. "It's a sign that you will get well and live to a ripe old age." But my heart kept on pounding inside of me.

It was much later that I found out what this thing in white had been that scared him so. Can you guess, Rabbi? Well, it was Reb Lippa, that's who it was, Lippa the Water-Carrier. Just that day he had bought himself a coat of white fur, and because it was so bitterly cold outside, he was trying to get warm by slapping his hands together. Have you ever heard anything like it? A man has to go dress himself up in a white fur coat all of a sudden!

How did we get around to that? Oh, yes, you were saying, good health . . . Good health, that's the main thing in life. That's what the doctor says, and he warns me to take good care of my David. "Give him soup," he says. "Make him a soup every day out of at least a quarter of a chicken, if you can manage it." He says to feed him on milk and butter and chocolate, provided I can manage it. Did you ever hear anything like it? *Provided,* he says, that I can manage it. As if there was anything in the world I couldn't manage for my David's sake. For instance, if I were told, "Go, Yenta, dig in the earth, chop wood, carry water, knead clay, rob a church!" If it were for my David's sake, I would do it all, even in the middle of the night and in a bitter frost.

For instance—this was last summer—he decides that he needs certain books. I don't know anything about books and I have no such books. But he says that when I go to the homes of my rich customers I can borrow these books, and he writes the names down on a piece of paper. So I go to them and show them the paper and ask for the books—I ask once, twice, three times. They laugh at me. "What do you need these books for, Yenta? Do you feed them to your chickens and ducks and geese?" "Laugh, laugh, if you like," I think to myself, "just so my Dovidl gets his books." Night after night, all night long, he reads these books, and then asks me to bring him others. Am I going to begrudge him a few books? So I take these back, and bring him others. And now along comes this clever doctor and asks me if I can manage to make soup out of a quarter of a chicken. And if he told me to make it out of three-quarters of a chicken, would that stop me? Tell me, where do they get such smart doctors? Where do they grow them? On what kind of yeast do they raise them and in what oven do they bake them?

How did we get to that? Oh, yes, you were saying, chicken soup . . . So every day I make him a chicken soup out of a quarter of a chicken, and every night when he comes home from *cheder* he eats it. And I sit across the table from him with some work in my hands and rejoice at the sight. I pray to God that He should help me so that tomorrow I should be able to make him another soup out of another quarter of a chicken. "Mother," he asks me, "why don't you eat with me?" "Eat," I say, "eat all you want. I ate already." "What did you eat?" "What did I eat? What difference does it make what I ate, as long as I ate?" And when he is through reading or studying, I take a couple of baked potatoes out of the oven, or rub a slice of bread with onion and make myself a feast. And I swear to you by all that is holy, that I get more enjoyment and satisfaction out of that onion than I would out of the finest roast or the richest soup, because I remember that my Dovidl, may the evil eye spare him, had some chicken soup and that tomorrow he will have chicken soup again.

But still he doesn't stop coughing, he coughs all the time—cough—cough—cough. I beg the doctor to give him some medicine for that cough and he says to me, "How old was your husband when he died, and what did he die of?" "What should he die of?" I say. "Death came to him. His time ran out and he died. What's that got to do with my Dovidl?" "I have to know," he says. "I have examined your boy, he's a good boy and a gifted boy. . . ." "Thank you," I tell him. "That's very kind of you, but I know that myself. What I want is medicine for his cough, something to make him stop coughing." "That I can't give you," he tells me. "But you have to watch him, don't let him study too much." "What then should he do?" "He should eat a lot and go for a walk every day, and the most important thing of all—don't let him sit up nights over those books. If he is fated to be a doctor, tell him he'll become a doctor a few years later." "What kind of nightmare is that? What foolish dream?" I ask myself. "The man is talking out of his head. What does he mean that my Dovidl should become a doctor? Why not a governor? What's wrong with being a governor?"

So I go home and tell David what the doctor said. He becomes red as fire and says to me, "Do you know what, mother? Don't go to the doctor any more—don't even talk to him." "I don't want to see his face," I tell him. "I can see that he's a fool, with that ridiculous habit he has of asking questions of sick people, wanting to know how they live, and where they live and what they live off. What difference does it make to him? Do we begrudge him the half-*ruble* fee? Let him write a prescription, that's what we came for!"

How did we get around to that? Oh, yes, you say I am always hustling and bustling. But who wouldn't hustle and run her legs off with a basketful of eggs and chickens and geese and ducks, and the customers always on my neck, each one wanting to be the first, each one afraid that the others will pick out the largest eggs and the best fowl? Tell me yourself, when do I have the time to cook a chicken soup if I am never home? But how do you say it—a clever person finds a way.

So early in the morning, before it's time to go to market, I light the oven and salt a piece of chicken. Then I run to the marketplace, and later in the morning I run back home, rinse off the chicken, and put the pot on the stove. I ask my tenant Gnessi to watch the pot for me; when the soup comes to a boil, I ask her to put the cover on and bank the pot with ashes and let the soup simmer. Is that too much to expect of a neighbor? Many is the time I have cooked a whole supper for her. After all, we are human beings, we live among people, not off in the woods somewhere. Then at night when I come from work I blow the ashes away, and get the blaze started again, and heat the pot and he has a fresh bowl of soup to eat.

Sounds simple, doesn't it? But then that tenant of mine is a great big—— I won't say the word. Just this morning of all mornings she decides to cook a meal for her children, buckwheat dumplings with milk. With milk, mind you. Now what kind of delicacy are buckwheat dumplings with milk? And why of all times does she have to make them on Friday—the day before the Sabbath? She is a peculiar woman, that Gnessi. With her it's either everything or nothing. For a whole week she won't even light the oven, and then suddenly something gets into her and she has to stir up a whole panful of millet or barley soup, though you'd have to put on a pair of glasses to see a grain of barley in the soup—or else she puts on a pot of fish-and-potatoes with so much onion in it that you can smell it a mile away, and so strongly seasoned with pepper that they go around for a day after with their mouths open and their tongues hanging out trying to cool off. . . .

What were we talking about? Oh, yes, you say a *shlimazl* . . . So my tenant decides to stir up some buckwheat batter, and she puts a pitcher of milk in the oven to boil, and her children start dancing with joy, you'd think they had never seen milk before. . . . And actually, how much milk do you think there was in the pitcher? Not more than two spoonfuls, and the rest water. But to paupers like them, even that's something.

In the meantime some ill wind brings her husband the *shammes* along. It seems that over there in the Synagogue he smelled a feast cooking at home. And he comes flying in with one of his quips, "Good *yom-tev.*" "A miserable good *yom-tev* to you," she snarls at him. "What brings you home so early?" "I was afraid I might miss a few blessings," he says. "What are you cooking over there?" "A little pot full of misery, and all for you," she says. "Why not a bigger pot, so there'd be enough for both of us?" he says. "To the devil with you and your jokes," she says and reaches for the milk and upsets the pitcher. The pitcher turns over and splash!—the milk gushes all over the oven.

Then hell breaks loose. Gnessi curses her husband with the deadliest curses. Lucky for him that he took himself off just in time. The children climb off the top of the oven and begin crying and wailing just as though both of their parents had been murdered. "Your dumplings are a small loss," I say, "but my Dovidl's soup is ruined, and I am afraid that my pot has become *treif* in the bargain." "The devil take your pot and your soup," she cries. "My dumplings are just as important to me as all your pots and all the soups that you cook for your pride and joy are to you." "Do you want to know something?" I tell her. "The whole lot of you aren't worth my Dovidl's tiniest fingernail." "You can't say that," she screams. "What's so great about him? He is only one." What do you think of the slut? Doesn't she deserve to be smacked across the face with a wet towel?

How did we get around to that? Oh, yes, you say no good can come of cooking milk and meat at the same time. Well, her pitcher of milk had turned over and the milk splashed over the whole oven. And if a drop of the milk touched my soup pot, then I am lost! Even though you might ask, how could a drop of milk touch it if my pot is banked with ashes and stands far in back of the oven? Still, how can I be sure? Who can tell? It's just my miserable luck. To tell you the truth, I am not worrying so much about the soup. Of course it's something of a heartache, for what will my Dovidl eat tonight? But I will probably think of something. Just yesterday I had some geese killed, and cut up the portions to sell for the Sabbath, and I left a few odds and ends for myself, heads, entrails, this, that—you can make a meal out of those things. But the trouble is I have no pot to cook it in. If you decide that my pot is *treif,* then I am left without a pot, and being without a pot is like being without a hand, because all I have is this one pot to cook meat in.

I had three pots to begin with, but Gnessi borrowed one from me, a brand-new pot, and brought back one that was all scratched and chipped. "What kind of pot is that?" I asked her. And she says, "It's your pot." And I say, "What do you mean by bringing me this broken old pot when I gave you a clean new pot?" "Don't yell like that," she says. "You are not doing me any favors. In the first place, I brought back a fine, clean pot. In the second place, when I got the pot from you it was all scratched and chipped, and, in the third place, I never borrowed a pot from you at all, I have my own pot. So go away and leave me alone." A slut like that!

How did we get to talking about that? Oh yes, you say a housewife can't have too many pots. So I was left with two pots, the chipped one and two good ones, that is, only two pots. But how can a pauper have two good pots? So it has to happen that I come home from the market one day with some chickens, and one chicken gets loose and is frightened by the cat. Maybe you will ask, how did the cat get to be there? It's those children of hers again. They have to go and find a kitten somewhere and bring it home and torture it. "Poor little thing," says my David. "A living creature . . ." But how can you talk to such hoodlums, such loafers? They keep torturing the cat. They tie something to its tail and the cat starts jumping and clawing; the chicken gets frightened and flies to the top shelf and crash!—goes a pot to the ground. And maybe you think it was the chipped one? Of course not. If it had to break, it had to be a good one. That's the way it's always been since the world was created. I want to know, why does it have to be this way? For instance, two men are walking down the street—one walking this way, the other walking the other way—one of them an only child, his mother's darling, and the other one . . .

Rabbi! What's the matter? What's happened to you? Rebbitzen! Rebbitzen! Where are you? Come here, quick. The Rabbi looks sick, he's fainting. Help! Water! Water!

Two Shalachmones

or

A *Purim* Scandal

KASRILEVKA had not seen such a warm, mild *Purim* for a long time. The ice had melted early this year, and the snow had turned into mud that stood as high as a man's waist. The sun was shining. A lazy breeze was blowing. A foolish calf sniffing spring in the air lifted up his tail, lowered his head and let out a short me-e. In the streets, snakelike rivulets wound downhill carrying with them anything they came across—splinters, bits of straw, scraps of paper. A lucky thing that almost nobody in town had money for *matzos* yet, or you might have thought it was Passover and not *Purim*.

Right in the middle of town where the mud was deepest, two girls met. Both of them were named Nechama. One was dark-haired and stocky, with thick, dark eyebrows and a pug nose; the other was pale and scrawny with red hair and a pointed nose. The dark-haired girl's short, stocky legs were bare and she wore no shoes. The other girl had on shoes whose mouths gaped open as though begging for something to eat. As she sloshed along in the mud, one of the soles dragged behind making now a slapping, now a squeaking, sound. When she took them off they weighed a ton. Each of the girls was holding aloft in both hands a plate of *Shalachmones* covered with a white napkin. When they saw each other they stopped.

"Hello, Nechama."

"Hi, Nechama."

"Where are you going, Nechama?"

"What do you mean where am I going? I am carrying *Shalachmones.*"

"Where are you carrying it?"

"To your house. And where are you going?"

"What do you mean where am I going? Can't you see that I am carrying *Shalachmones?*"

"Where are you carrying the *Shalachmones?*"

"What do you think? Right to your house."

"That's a good joke."

"A regular farce."

"Come on, Nechama, let's see your *Shalachmones.*"

"You show me yours first."

Both girls looked around for a dry spot where they could sit down. The Lord sent them such a spot. They saw a block of wood in front of a doorway, lifted their feet out of the clayey mud, and sat down on the block. They put their plates on their laps, lifted up their napkins and examined the *Shalachmones.*

First Red Nechama uncovered her *Shalachmones.* She worked for Zelda, the wife of Reb Yossie. She was paid four and a half *rubles* for the winter season and was provided with shoes and clothes besides. But such shoes and such clothes! The dress she wore was covered with patches, still, it was a dress. But her shoes! She wore men's shoes that had belonged to Zelda's son Menashe who had tremendous feet and the habit of turning his heels in. Elegant shoes.

The *Shalachmones* which Red Nechama carried consisted of a large *hamantash* filled with poppyseed, two cushion cakes—one open-faced and filled with *farfel,* the other round and handsomely decorated on both sides—a sugar cooky with a plump raisin stuck right in the middle of it, a large square of *torte,* a big slice of nut-bread, two small cherub cakes, and a large piece of spice cake which had turned out better than any that Zelda had ever made. Whether the flour was exceptionally good this year or the honey purer, or whether the cake had baked just long enough, or she had beaten it more than usual, it doesn't matter. It was light and puffy as a feather cushion.

After she had examined Red Nechama's *Shalachmones,* Black Nechama lifted the napkin off her plate. She worked for Zlata, the wife of Reb Isaac, and got six *rubles* a season, without shoes or clothing. That was why she went barefoot; and Zlata scolded her continually, "How the devil can a big wench like you go around barefoot all winter? You'll catch your death."

But Nechama paid no attention to her. She was saving up her money for Passover. Then she would get herself button shoes with high heels and a new dress. Let Kopel the Shoemaker who was courting her drop dead in his tracks when he saw her.

The *Shalachmones* that Black Nechama carried consisted of a fine slice of *shtrudel,* two big sugar cookies, a large honey *teigl,* two cushion cakes stamped with a fish on both sides and filled with tiny sweet *farfel,* and two large slabs of a poppyseed confection, black and glistening, mixed with ground nuts and glazed with honey. Besides all this, there lay on the plate, smiling up at them, a round, golden sweet-smelling orange that wafted its delicious odor right into their nostrils.

"Listen, Nechama, do you know what? I think that your *Shalachmones* is better than mine," said Red Nechama to Black Nechama, graciously, giving her a compliment.

"Your *Shalachmones* isn't bad either," Black Nechama answered her, returning the compliment. As she spoke she touched her *hamantash* with the tip of her finger.

"What a *hamantash!*" said Black Nechama, licking her lips. "That's what I call a real *hamantash.* I'll tell you the truth, I begrudge my mistress such a delicious *hamantash.* The Lord knows she deserves to get a boil on her face instead. I haven't had a thing to eat all day. I ought to get at least a bite of this *hamantash.*"

"What about me? Do you think I had anything to eat today? If only they got as little to eat the rest of their lives!" Red Nechama looked about her cautiously. "Go on, Nechama, listen to me, take the *hamantash* and break it in half, we'll both have a bite. There is no rule that says that there must be a *hamantash.* See, you haven't any."

"God knows you are right," said Black Nechama, breaking the *hamantash* in half and sharing it with Red Nechama.

"M-m-m. It's perfectly delicious. Too bad there isn't any more. Now that you have given me some *hamantash* I owe you a piece of cake. The way they've been tipping me, they can have a piece of cake less. Just think, I've been running around since early this morning, and guess how much I've made so far. Barely one *gulden* and two *groschen*. And the two *groschen* has a hole in it. How much did you make, my dear?"

"I didn't even make that much, a plague on them," said Red Nechama, taking big bites of cake and swallowing them whole like a goose. "I'll be lucky if I get a *gulden* for the day's work."

"Generous, aren't they, those rich women? I hope they die and get buried," said Black Nechama, licking the crumbs from her fingers. "I came to Chiena the Haberdasher's wife with my *Shalachmones*. She takes it and begins scratching around in her pocket, then tells me to come back later. May the Angel of Death come to her instead."

"That's what I got from Keilah Reb Aaron's," said Red Nechama. "I came to her with my *Shalachmones* and she offers me a cooky. May God offer her a new soul."

"And throw the old one to the dogs," Black Nechama finished for her, and took one of Zlata's big sugar cookies and broke it in half. "Here, eat this, my dear. May the worms eat them. If your mistress has one cooky less, it won't hurt me any."

"Oh, my goodness!" Red Nechama jumped up suddenly and began wringing her hands. "Look at what's left of my *Shalachmones*."

"They will never find out," Black Nechama comforted her. "Don't be frightened, foolish girl. They are so busy with their *Shalachmones* today, they won't notice anything."

And the two girls covered up their *Shalachmones* with their napkins and went off through the mud, one this way, and one that way, as though nothing had happened.

Zelda, Reb Yossie's wife, a round-faced, rather good-looking woman in a red silk apron with white dots, stood at her table arranging and distributing the *Shalachmones* she had received and that which she had to send out. Reb Yossie Milksop (that was the nickname he was known by in Kasrilevka) lay on the sofa snoring, and Menashe, her eighteen-year-old son, a large boy with red cheeks and a shiny long coat, hung around his mother snatching now a piece of honeycake, now two poppyseed bars, now a cooky. He had stuffed himself so full of these good things that his teeth and lips were black and his stomach was beginning to rumble.

"Menashe, when will you stop eating? Menashe, haven't you had enough?" Zelda kept saying to him.

"Enough, enough," he mimicked her, and stuffed another chunk of cake into his mouth, "the very last one" this time, and licked his lips with his tongue.

"Good *yom-tev,* my mistress sent you *Shalachmones,*" said Black Nechama, walking in and handing her the covered plate.

"Whom do you work for?" said Zelda, smiling graciously and taking the plate from her.

"I work for Zlata, Reb Isaac's-May-his-tribe-increase," said Black Nechama, and waited for Zelda to take the *Shalachmones* and return the plate to her.

Zelda put one hand into her pocket to give the girl a *kopek* for the trip and with the other she uncovered the plate. She took one look and stood there as if turned to stone.

"What is this? Menashe, just take a look."

Menashe took one look at the *Shalachmones,* grabbed himself around the middle and doubled over with laughter. He laughed so hard that Reb Yossie Milksop almost rolled off his couch in fright.

"Ha?" he cried. "What is it? What's happened? Who's there?"

"Look at this *Shalachmones,*" said Zelda, folding her arms over her stomach. Menashe kept on laughing, and Reb Yossie spat in disgust, turned himself around to the wall and went back to sleep.

Zelda threw the plate with the napkin back at Nechama and said to her, "Tell your mistress that I hope she lives until next year and isn't able to afford a better *Shalachmones* than this."

"Amen, the same to you," said Black Nechama, taking the plate.

"To the devil with you," said Zelda angrily. "The insolence of the wench! Did you ever see the like of it, Menashe?"

TWO SHALACHMONES

Zlata, Reb Isaac's wife, a woman who gives birth to a child every year and is always doctoring in between, was so worn out from receiving and sending *Shalachmones* that she had to sit down on a chair and order her husband Isaac around. (He was known as Isaac-May-his-tribe-increase because of the fact that his wife presented him with a child every year.)

"Isaac, take this piece of *torte* there and put it right here. And take that piece of nut-bread and those two poppyseed bars from over there and put them here. Isaac, hand me that cushion cake—not that one, this one. Get a move on you, Isaac. Look at the way I have to show him how to do the least little thing, like a baby. And take that cake there, the bigger one, and put it here, like this. And cut that piece of *torte* in half, this piece is too large. Isaac! Get out of here, you brats. Get!"

These last words were addressed to a swarm of half-naked youngsters who stood around her watching the sweets with greedy eyes and drooling mouths. Though she chased them away, the children kept stealing back to the table, trying to lift a cooky or a sweet from the pile. The mother would catch them at it, and give them now a slap, now a shove, now a cuff on the nape of the neck.

"Good *yom-tev,* my mistress sends you *Shalachmones,*" said Red Nechama, bringing in the covered plate of *Shalachmones.*

"Whom do you work for?" asked Zlata, smiling sweetly and taking the plate out of her hands.

"I work for Zelda, Reb Yossie Milksop's," said Red Rechama, and waited for her plate to be returned to her.

Zlata reached one hand into her pocket to tip the girl and with the other she uncovered the plate, and almost fainted on the spot.

"Of all the black, miserable, ugly nightmares that anybody ever had. Of all the bad luck that I wish to my enemies. Look at this *Shalachmones.* She's insulting me, the slut.

"Here, give this back to your mistress," and Zlata flung the plate with the napkin with the *Shalachmones* straight into Red Nechama's face.

Reb Yossie Milksop and Reb Isaac-May-his-tribe-increase are both shopkeepers in Kasrilevka. Their stores are right next door to each other. Though they are competitors and don't hesitate to drag customers away from each other, still they are good friends and neighbors. They borrow money from each other, go to each other's homes for *kiddush* during the holidays, help each other celebrate family events such as weddings and circumcisions. In summer they sit together all day playing dominoes, and in winter they run in to warm themselves at each other's stoves. Their wives are close friends also. They gossip together about the whole world, borrow flour and sugar from each other, entrust each other with their deepest secrets. They seldom quarrel, and if they do fall out over some trifle, they make up very quickly. In short, they live together as peacefully as doves in a dovecote.

The day after *Purim* when Reb Isaac-May-his-tribe-increase went to open his shop, Reb Yossie Milksop already stood in front of his shop all puffed up like a turkey cock waiting for Reb Isaac to come up and tell him good morning so that he could snub him. Reb Isaac, who had been well-primed by his wife also, unlocked the door and stood waiting for Reb Yossie to come up to him first so that he could snub him. And so they stood there, opposite each other, like two angry cocks, and they would have stood there all day if their wives hadn't appeared just then from the marketplace with angry faces and eyes flashing fire.

"Isaac, why don't you thank him for the wonderful *Shalachmones* that his wife sent me?" said Zlata to her husband.

"Yossie, why don't you say something about the *Shalachmones* we got?" Zelda demanded of her husband.

"Isaac, did you hear that? Isaac, she is picking on us. Why don't you speak to him, Isaac?"

"How can I talk to a milksop like him?" said Reb Isaac, speaking loudly enough for Reb Yossie to hear.

"I am afraid to start anything with a fellow with such a fine name as Isaac-May-his-tribe-increase."

What's so terrible in the words "May his tribe increase?" It seems to me it's a harmless enough blessing, but Reb Isaac could put up with anything in the world better than with being called Isaac-May-his-tribe-increase. He would rather be cursed with the blackest curses, and he would gladly tear the person apart who called him by that nickname.

It was the same with Reb Yossie. He would rather get a slap in the face than be called a milksop.

People came running from all over the marketplace, and tried to separate the two men. They couldn't understand how two such close friends and neighbors had suddenly become tangled in each other's beards. But Reb Isaac and Reb Yossie, Zelda and Zlata were all talking together, one trying to outshout the other, and making such a racket that all that anyone could make out was the word *Shalachmones* repeated over and over. Which *Shalachmones?* What about the *Shalachmones?* It was impossible to get to the bottom of it.

"If you don't report the Milksop to the Magistrate, you might as well put an end to your life," Zlata screamed at her husband.

And Reb Yossie appealed to the gathering.

"Good people, you are witnesses here that the slut called me 'Milksop.' I am going to report her to the Magistrate, and her husband, Isaac-May-his-tribe-increase."

"Friends," called out Reb Isaac, "I ask you to be witnesses before the Magistrate that this—this—this—I don't want to call him by his elegant name—just called me Isaac-May-his-tribe-increase."

Within the hour both parties went to Zaidel the Clerk, each of them bringing his own witnesses, and drew up a complaint to the Magistrate.

The Kasrilevka Magistrate, Pan Milinewsky, a portly squire with a long beard and a high forehead, had been magistrate for so long that he was acquainted with the whole town, was on good terms with everyone, and especially with the Jews of Kasrilevka. He knew each one's weaknesses and peculiarities thoroughly and spoke Yiddish as well as any of them. "He has a real Jewish head on his shoulders," they used to say about him in Kasrilevka.

In autumn, around the time of the high holidays, he was deluged with written complaints, all of them from Jews. They were not, God forbid, reports of thefts or robberies or serious crimes. No! They were all concerned with petty quarrels, and fights over precedence in the Synagogue and interpretations of the Law over the privilege of closing and reopening the reading of the *Torah*. Pan Milinewsky didn't stand on ceremony with the Jews of Kasrilevka. He didn't like to enter into long disputes with them and never let them talk much, because he knew that once started they would never stop. If they were willing to make peace, good. He was all for making peace. If not, he put on his chain and laid down the judgment, *"Po ukazu na osnowanie, takoio-to i takoio*. I hereby pronounce that Hershko may read for three days and Yankel may read the next three." As you see, he made no exceptions and he had no favorites.

Exactly two weeks before Passover the case of the *Shalachmones* came up. The Magistrate's office was crowded with people, most of whom were witnesses for either one or the other party. They were wedged in so tightly there wasn't room for a pin to squeeze through among them.

"Izak, Yosek, Zlata, Zelda," Pan Milinewsky called out, and from the front row stepped out Reb Yossie Milksop, Reb Isaac-May-his-tribe-increase and their wives. Before the Magistrate could say a word, all four began talking at once, and of course the women outtalked the men.

"Gospodin Mirovoi," said Zelda, pushing her husband aside and pointing at Zlata. "This here slut sent me this *Purim* a *Shalachmones* that made me a laughing stock before the town. A wretched little piece of *shtrudel* and one cooky. It's an insult, a disgrace." And she spat.

"Oh, oh, I can't stand it, I can't," shouted Zlata, beating her breast. "May God give me such a piece of gold . . ."

"Amen," said Zelda.

"Shut up, you loud-mouth. Two cushion cakes, *Gospodin Mirovoi*, as I live, and one nut-bread, and a cake, may God punish her, and macaroons. May the plagues descend on her. And a *hamantash*. Woe is me."

"What *hamantash*? There was no *hamantash*. She is lying."

The Magistrate tried to calm down the women, first gently and then with force, ringing his bell for them to be quiet. When he saw that he was getting nowhere and that it was impossible to shut them up, he chased them out of the room so that he could hear himself talk and he advised the men to go to the Rabbi.

"Do rabina," he told them. "Go to the Rabbi with your *hamantash*."

And the crowd all went off to the Rabbi.

Reb Yozifel, the Rabbi, as our readers know, is a man who can bear up under anything. He is willing to hear everyone out to the end. Reb Yozifel goes according to the theory that every person, no matter how long he talks, must finally stop; for a man, he says, is not a machine. The only trouble was that this time all four of the litigants talked at once and even the bystanders each tried to get a word in.

But what did it matter? Everything in the world must come to an end; and when everyone had talked himself out, and it grew quiet again, Reb Yozifel addressed himself to both sides, speaking calmly and pleasantly as was his custom. He gave a sigh, and began:

"Ah, my children, we are now approaching a holiday, a blessed holiday, Passover. Does it mean anything to you? Reflect, my children. Our ancestors escaped from Egypt, they came to a sea and the sea divided itself and they crossed upon dry ground. They wandered in the desert for forty years. Think of it, forty years. They received the Holy *Torah* on Mt. Sinai. The *Torah* in which it is written *'V'ahavta*—and thou shalt love—*l'reachta*—thy neighbor—*kamocha*—as thyself.' And now it has come to this, that we quarrel and bicker among ourselves 'because of our many sins'; we tear each other's beards out, and over what? Over foolishness, mere childishness. It's a disgrace, I tell you, a disgrace and a reproach. At a time like this we should be thinking instead of providing the poor with *matzos* for Passover. There are many people in our town who will be without *matzos*. Of eggs and chicken fat and other things, I do not even speak. But *matzos*, God in Heaven, we must provide them with *matzos*. Reflect, my children. Our ancestors escaped from Egypt, they came to the sea and the waters divided themselves and they crossed upon dry ground. They wandered in the desert for forty years. They received the blessed *Torah* on Mt. Sinai. Take my advice, my children, you are all children of Israel, ask each other's forgiveness, make peace with each other and go home and bear in mind the blessed holiday that is approaching. . . ."

Slowly, one by one, one by one, the people began slipping out of the Rabbi's house. They made a jest about Reb Yozifel's verdict, in typical Kasrilevka fashion—"It's not a sentence, but a discourse." But each one felt deep in his own heart that Reb Yozifel was right and they were ashamed to talk further about the *Shalachmones.*

On the first day of Passover, after the services at the Synagogue, Reb Yossie Milksop (he was the younger of the two) went to the home of Reb Isaac-May-his-tribe-increase, for *kiddush.* He praised the Passover wine which had turned out exceptionally well this year and licked his fingers after Zlata's *falirchiks.* On the second day of Passover, after the services, Reb Isaac (he was the older of the two) went to Reb Yossie's house, praised the raisin wine to the skies and smacked his lips over Zelda's *falirchiks.*

And that afternoon, after dinner, when the two women got together and talked over the *Shalachmones,* the truth rose like oil on the waters and both girls, Red Nechama and Black Nechama, got their just deserts. Right after Passover they were both sent packing.

Tevye Goes to Palestine

WELL, well, look who's here! Reb Sholom Aleichem, how are you? You're almost a stranger. I never dreamed of this pleasure. Greetings! Here I've been wondering over and over, why we haven't seen him all this time, either in Boiberik, or in Yehupetz. Who can tell? Maybe he had packed up and left us altogether—gone off yonder where people don't even know the taste of radishes and chicken fat. But then I thought: Why should *he* do such a foolish thing? A man of wisdom and learning like *him?* Well, thank God, we meet again in good health. How does the passage go? *"A wall cannot meet a wall*—Man meets man. . . ."

You are looking at me, sir, as though you didn't recognize me. It's me, your faithful old friend, Tevye. *"Look not at the pitcher but at its contents."* Don't let my new coat fool you; it's still the same *shlimazl* who's wearing it, the same as always. It's just that when a man puts on his Sabbath clothes, right away he begins to look like somebody—as though he were trying to pass for a rich man. But when you go forth among strangers you can't do otherwise, especially if you are setting out on a long journey like this, all the way to Palestine. . . .

You look at me as if you're thinking: How does it happen that a plain little man like Tevye, who spent all his life delivering milk and butter, should suddenly get a notion like this into his head—something that only a millionaire like Brodsky could allow himself in his old age? Believe me, Mr. Sholom Aleichem, *"it is altogether questionable. . . .*" The Bible is right every time. Just move your suitcase over this way, if you will be so good, and I will sit down across from you and tell you the whole story. And then you'll know what the Lord can do. . . .

But first of all, before I go on, I must tell you that I have been a widower for some time. My Golde, may she rest in peace, is dead. She was a plain woman, without learning, without pretensions, but extremely pious. May she intercede for her children in the other world; they caused her enough suffering in this one, perhaps even brought on her untimely death. She couldn't bear it any longer, seeing them scatter and disappear the way they did, some one way, some another. "Heavens above!" she used to say. "What have I left to live for, all alone without kith or kin? Why, even a cow," she would say, "is lonesome when you wean her calf away from her."

That's the way she spoke, and she wept bitterly. I could see the poor woman wasting away, day by day, going out like a candle, right before my eyes. And I said to her with my heart full of pity, "Ah, Golde, my dear, there is a text in the Holy Book: *'Im k'vonim im k'vodim—Whether we're like children or like slaves,'* which means that you can live just as well with children as without them. We have," I told her, "a great Lord and a good Lord and a mighty Lord, but just the same I'd like to be blessed for every time He puts one of His tricks over on us."

But she was, may she forgive me for saying this, only a female. So she says to me, "It's a sin to speak this way, you mustn't sin, Tevye." "There you go," said I. "Did I speak any evil? Did I do anything contrary to the Lord's will? All I meant was that if He went ahead and did such a fine job of creating this world of His so that children are not children, and parents are no better than mud under one's feet, no doubt He knew what He was doing."

But she didn't understand me. Her mind was wandering. "I am dying, Tevye," she said. "And who will cook your supper?" She barely whispered the words and the look in her eyes was enough to melt a stone. But Tevye is not a weakling; so I answered her with a quip and a quotation and a homily. "Golde," I said to her, "you have been faithful to me these many years, you won't make a fool of me in my old age." I looked at her and became frightened. "What's the matter with you, Golde?" "Nothing," she whispered, barely able to speak. Then I saw that the game was lost. I jumped into my wagon and went off to town and came back with a doctor, the best doctor I could find. When I come home, what do I see? My Golde is laid out on the ground with a candle at her head, looking just like a little mound of earth that had been raked together and covered with a black cloth. I stand there and think to myself: "*'Is that all that man is?* —Is this the end of man?' Oh, Lord, the things you have done to your Tevye. What will I do now in my old age, forsaken and alone?" And I threw myself on the ground.

But what good is shouting and weeping? Listen to me and I will tell you something. When a person sees death in front of him he becomes a cynic. He can't help thinking, "*What are we and what is our life?*—What is this world altogether with its wheels that turn, its trains that run wildly in all directions, with all its tumult and confusion, noise and bustle?" And even the rich men with all their possessions and their wealth—in the end they come to nothing too.

Well, I hired a *kaddish* for her, for my wife Golde, and paid him for the whole year in advance. What else could I do if God had denied us sons to pray for us when we were dead, and given us only daughters, nothing but daughters one after another? I don't know if everybody else has as much trouble with his daughters, or if I'm the only *shlimazl,* but I've had no luck with any of my daughters. As far as the girls themselves are concerned, I have nothing to complain about. And as for luck—that's in God's hands. I wish I had half the happiness my girls wish me to have. If anything, they are too loyal, too faithful—and too much of even the best is superfluous. Take my youngest, for instance—Beilke we call her. Do you have any idea of the kind of girl she is? You have known me long enough to know that I am not the kind of father who will praise his children just for the sake of talking. But since I've mentioned Beilke I'll have to tell you this much: Since God first began making Beilkes, He never created another like this Beilke of mine. I won't even talk about her looks. Tevye's daughters are all famous for their great beauty, but this one, this Beilke, puts all the others in the shade. But beauty alone is nothing. When you speak of Beilke, you really have to use the words of the Proverbs regarding *"a woman of valor."* Charms are deceitful. I am speaking of character now. She is pure goodness all the way through. She had always been devoted to me, but since Golde died I became the apple of her eye. She wouldn't let a speck of dust fall on me. I said to myself, as we say on the High Holy Days: *"The Lord precedes anger with mercy.*—God always sends a remedy for the disease." Only sometimes it's hard to tell which is worse, the remedy or the disease.

For instance, how could I have foreseen that on my account Beilke would go and sell herself for money and send her old father in his declining years to Palestine? Of course that's only a way of speaking. She is as much to blame for this as you are. It was all his fault, her chosen one. I don't want to wish him ill, may an armory collapse on him. And yet if we look at this more closely, if we dig beneath the surface, we might find out that I am to blame as much as anyone, as it says in the *Gamorah: "Man is obligated . . ."* But imagine my telling *you* what the *Gamorah* says.

But I don't want to bore you with too long a tale. One year passed, then another. My Beilke grew up and became a presentable young woman. Tevye kept on with his horse and wagon, delivering his milk and butter as usual, to Boiberik in the summer, to Yehupetz in the winter—may a deluge overtake that town, as it did Sodom. I can't bear to look at that place any more, and not so much the place as the people in it, and not so much the people as one man, Ephraim the *Shadchan,* the matchmaker, may the devil take him and his father both. Let me tell you what a man, a *shadchan,* can do.

"And it came to pass," that one time, in the middle of September, I arrived in Yehupetz with my little load. I looked up—and behold! *"Haman approacheth. . . ."* There goes Ephraim the *Shadchan.* I think I've told you about him before. He is like a burr; once he attaches himself to you, you can't get rid of him. But when you see him you have to stop—that's the power he has in him.

"Whoa, there, my sage!" I called out to my little horse. "Hold on a minute and I'll give you something to chew on." And I stop to greet the *shadchan* and start a conversation with him. "How are things going in your profession?" With a deep sigh he answers, "It's tough, very tough." "In what way?" I ask.

"There's nothing doing."

"Nothing at all?"

"Not a thing."

"What's the matter?"

"The matter is," says he, "that people don't marry off their children at home any more."

"Where do they marry them off?"

"Out of town, out of the country in fact."

"Then what can a man like me do," I say, "who has never been away from home and whose grandmother's grandmother has never been away either?"

He offers me a pinch of snuff. "For you, Reb Tevye," he says, "I have a piece of merchandise right here on the spot."

"For instance?"

"A widow without children, and with a hundred and fifty *rubles* besides. She used to be a cook in the very best families."

I give him a look. "Reb Ephraim, for whom is this match intended?"

"For whom do you suppose? For you."

"Of all the crazy fantastic ideas anybody ever had, you've dreamed up the worst." And I whipped my horse and was ready to start off. But Ephraim stopped me. "Don't be offended, Reb Tevye, I didn't want to hurt your feelings. Tell me, whom did *you* have in mind?"

"Whom should I have in mind? My youngest daughter, of course."

At this he sprang back and slapped his forehead. "Wait!" he cried. "It's a good thing you mentioned it! God bless you and preserve you, Reb Tevye."

"The same to you," I said. "Amen. May you live until the Messiah comes. But what makes you so joyful all of a sudden?"

"It's wonderful! It's excellent! In fact, it's so good, it couldn't possibly be any better."

"What's so wonderful?" I ask him.

"I have just the thing for your daughter. A plum, a prize, the pick of the lot. He's a winner, a goldspinner, a rich man, a millionaire. He is a contractor and his name is Padhatzur."

"Hmm. Padhatzur? It sounds familiar, like a name in the Bible."

"What Bible? What's the Bible got to do with it? He is a contractor, this Padhatzur, he builds houses and factories and bridges. He was in Japan during the war and made a fortune. He rides in a carriage drawn by fiery steeds, he has a lackey at the door, a bathtub right in his own house, furniture from Paris, and a diamond ring on his finger. He's not such an old man either and he's never been married. He is a bachelor, a first-class article. And he's looking for a pretty girl; it makes no difference who she is or whether she has a stitch to her back, as long as she is good-looking."

"Whoa, there! You are going too fast. If you don't stop to graze your horses we'll land in Hotzenplotz. Besides, if I'm not mistaken you once tried to arrange a match for this same man with my older daughter, Hodel."

When he heard this, the *shadchan* began laughing so hard I was afraid the man would get a stroke. "Oh-ho, now you're talking about something that happened when my grandmother was delivered of her firstborn. That one went bankrupt before the war and ran off to America."

"*'When you speak of a holy man, bless him. . . .'* Maybe this one will run off too."

He was outraged at this. "How can you say such a thing, Reb Tevye? The other fellow was a fraud, a charlatan, a spendthrift. This one is a contractor, with business connections, with an office, with clerks, everything."

Well, what shall I tell you—the matchmaker became so excited that he pulled me off the wagon and grabbed me by the lapels, and shook me so hard that a policeman came up and wanted to send us both to the police station. It was lucky that I remembered what the passage says: "*You may take interest from a stranger.*—You have to know how to deal with policemen."

Well, why should I drag this out? Padhatzur became engaged to my daughter Beilke. "*The days were not long.*" It was quite a while before they were married. Why do I say it was quite a while? Because Beilke was no more eager to marry him than she was to lie down and die. The more he showered her with gifts, with gold watches and rings and diamonds, the more distasteful he became to her. I am not a child when it comes to such matters. I could tell from the look on her face and from her eyes red with weeping how she felt. So one day I decided to speak to her about it. I said to her as if I had just this minute thought of it, "I am afraid, Beilke, that this groom of yours is as dear and sweet to you as he is to me."

She flared up at this. "Who told you?"

"If not," I said, "why do you cry nights?"

"Have I been crying?"

"No, you haven't been crying, you've just been bawling. Do you think if you hide your head in your pillow you can keep your tears from me? Do you think that your father is a little child, or that he is in his dotage and doesn't understand that you are doing it on his account? That you want to provide for him in his old age, so he will have a place to lay his head and won't have to go begging from house to house? If that's what you have in mind, then you are a big fool. We have an all-powerful God, and Tevye is not one of those loafers who will fold his hands and live on the bread of charity. *'Money is worthless,'* as the Bible says. If you want proof, look at your sister Hodel, who is practically a pauper; but look at what she writes from the ends of the earth, how happy she is with her Feferl." Well, do you know what she said to this? Try and make a guess.

"Don't compare me to Hodel," she said. "Hodel grew up in a time when the whole world rocked on its foundations, when it was ready at any moment to turn upside down. In those days people were concerned about the world and forgot about themselves. Now that the world is back to where it was, people think about themselves and forget about the world." That's how she answered, and how was I to know what she meant?

Well. You know what Tevye's daughters are like. But you should have seen my Beilke at her wedding. A princess, no less. All I could do was stand and gaze at her, and I thought to myself, "Is this Beilke, a daughter of Tevye? Where did she learn to stand like this, to walk like this, to hold her head like this, and to wear her clothes so that she looked as though she'd been poured into them?"

But I wasn't allowed to gaze at her very long, for that same day at about half past six in the evening the young couple arose and departed. —They went off, the Lord knows where, to Nitaly somewhere, as is the custom with the rich nowadays, and they didn't come back until around *Hannukah.* And when they came back I got a message from them *to be sure* to come to see them in Yehupetz at once, *without fail.*

What could it mean? If they just wanted me to come, they would simply have asked me to come. But why *be sure to come* and *without fail?* Something must be up. But the question was, what? All sorts of thoughts, both good and bad, crowded through my head. Could the couple have had a fight already and be ready for a divorce? I called myself a fool at once. Why did I always expect the worst? "Maybe they are lonesome for you and want to see you? Or maybe Beilke wants her father close to her? Or perhaps Padhatzur wants to give you a job, take you into the business with him, make you the manager of his enterprises?" Whatever it is, I had to go. And I got into my wagon, and *"went forth to Heron."* On to Yehupetz!

As I rode along, my imagination carried me away. I dreamed that I had given up the farm, sold my cows, my horse and wagon and everything else, and had moved into town. I had become first a foreman for my son-in-law, then a paymaster, then a factotum, the general manager of all his enterprises, and finally a partner in his business, share and share alike, and rode along with him behind the prancing steeds, one dun-colored and the other chestnut. And I couldn't help marveling, *"What is this and what is it all for?"* How does it happen that a quiet, unassuming man like me should have suddenly become so great? And what do I need all this excitement and confusion for, all the hurry and flurry, day and night, night and day? How do you say it? *"To seat them with the mighty*—hobnobbing with all the millionaires?" Leave me be, I beg of you. All I want is peace and quiet in my old age, enough leisure so that I can look into a learned tome now and then, read a chapter of the Psalms. A person has to think once in a while of the next world too. How does

King Solomon put it? Man is a fool—he forgets that no matter how long he lives he has to die sometime.

It was with thoughts like these running through my head that I arrived in Yehupetz and came to the house of Padhatzur. What's the good of boasting? Shall I describe to you his *"abundance of wealth"?* His house and grounds? I have never had the honor of visiting Brodsky's house, but I can hardly believe that it could be more splendid than my son-in-law's. You might gather what sort of place it was from the fact that the man who stood guard at the door, a fellow resplendent in a uniform with huge silver buttons, wouldn't let me in under any consideration. What kind of business was this? The door was of glass and I could see the lackey standing there brushing clothes, may his name and memory be blotted out. I wink at him, I signal to him in sign language, show him with my hands that he should let me in because the master's wife is my own flesh and blood, my daughter. But he doesn't seem to understand me at all, the pig-headed lout, and motions to me also in sign language to go to the devil, to get out of there.

What do you think of that? I have to have special influence to get to my own daughter. "Woe unto your gray hairs," I told myself. "So this is what you have come to." I looked through the glass door again and saw a girl moving about. A chambermaid, I decided, noticing her shifty eyes. All chambermaids have shifty eyes. I am at home in rich houses and I know what the maids who work there are like.

I wink at her. "Open up, little kitty." She obeys me, opens the door and says to me in Yiddish, "Whom do you want?" And I say, "Does Padhatzur live here?" And she says, louder this time, "Whom do you want?" And I say still louder, "Answer my question first. 'Does Padhatzur live here?' " "Yes," she says. "If so," I tell her, "we can talk the same language. Tell Madame Padhatzur that she has a visitor. Her father Tevye has come to see her and has been standing outside for quite some time like a beggar at the door, for he did not have the good fortune to find favor in the eyes of this barbarian with the silver buttons whom I wouldn't exchange for your littlest finger."

After she heard me out, the girl laughed impudently, slammed the door in my face, ran into the house and up the stairs, then ran down again, opened the door and led me into a palace the like of which my father and grandfather had never seen, even in a dream. Silk and velvet and gold and crystal, and as you walked across the room you couldn't hear your own step, for your sinner's feet were sinking into the softest carpets, as soft as newly fallen snow. And clocks. Clocks everywhere. Clocks on the walls, clocks on the tables. Clocks all over the place. Dear Lord, what more can you have in store? What does a person need that many clocks for? And I keep going, with my hands clasped behind my back. I look up—several Tevyes at once are cutting across toward me from all directions. One Tevye comes this way, another Tevye that way; one is coming toward me, another away from me. How do you like that? On all sides—mirrors. Only a bird like him, that contractor of mine, could afford to surround himself with all those mirrors and clocks.

And he appeared in my mind's eyes the way he had looked the first day he came to my house—a round, fat little man with a loud voice and a sniggering laugh. He arrived in a carriage drawn by fiery steeds and proceeded to make himself at home as though he were in his own father's vineyard. He saw my Beilke, talked to her, and then called me off to one side and whispered a secret into my ear—so loud you could have heard it on the other side of Yehupetz. What was the secret? Only this—that my daughter had found favor in his eyes, and one-two-three he wanted to get married. As for my daughter's finding favor in his eyes, that was easy enough to understand, but when it came to the other part, the one-two-three—that was *"like a double edged sword to me"*—it sank like a dull knife into my heart.

What did he mean—one-two-three and get married? Where did I come into the picture? And what about Beilke? Oh, how I longed to drum some texts into his ears, and to give him a proverb or two to remember me by. But thinking it over, I decided: "Why should I come between these young people? A lot you accomplished, Tevye, when you tried to arrange the marriages of your older daughters. You talked and you talked. You poured out all your wisdom and learning. And who was made a fool of in the end? Tevye, of course."

Now let us forsake the hero, as they say in books, and follow the fortunes of the heroine. I had done what they asked me to do, I had come to Yehupetz. They greeted me effusively: *"Sholom Aleichem." "Aleichem sholom."* "How are *you?"* "And how are things with you?" "Please be seated." "Thank you, I am quite comfortable." And so on, with the usual courtesies. I was wondering whether I should speak up and ask why they had sent for me—*"Today of all days"*—but it didn't seem proper. Tevye is not a woman, he can wait.

Meanwhile, a man-servant with huge white gloves appeared and announced that supper was on the table, and the three of us got up and went into a room that was entirely furnished in oak. The table was of oak, the chairs of oak, the walls panelled in oak and the ceiling of oak, and all of it was elaborately carved and painted and curlicued and bedizened. A kingly feast was set on the table. There was coffee and tea and hot chocolate, all sorts of pastries and the best of cognacs, appetizers and other good things, as well as every kind of fruit. I am ashamed to admit it, but I am afraid that in her father's house, Beilke had never seen such delicacies.

Well, they poured me a glass, and then another glass and I drank their health. I looked over at my Beilke and thought to myself, "You have really done well by yourself, my daughter. As they say in Hallel: *'Who raiseth up the poor out of the dust . . .'* When God has been kind to a poor man, *'and lifteth up the needy out of the dunghill,'* you can't recognize him any longer." She is the same Beilke as before and yet not the same. And I thought of the Beilke that used to be and compared her to this one and my heart ached. It was as though I had made a bad bargain—let us say I had exchanged my hard-working little horse for a strange colt that might turn out to be a real horse or nothing but a dummy.

"Ah Beilke," I thought, "look at what's become of you. Remember how once you used to sit at night by a smoking lamp, sewing and singing to yourself? Or how you could milk two cows in the blink of an eye. Or roll up your sleeves and cook a good old-fashioned *borsht,* or a dish of beans or dumplings with cheese, or bake a batch of poppyseed cakes. 'Father,' you would call, 'wash up, supper is ready.' And that was the finest song of all to my ears."

And now she sits there with her Padhatzur, like a queen, and two men run back and forth waiting on the table with a great clatter of dishes. And she? Does she utter a single word? But let me tell you, her Padhatzur isn't silent. He talks enough for two. His mouth doesn't shut for a moment. In all my life I had never seen a man who could jabber so endlessly and say so little, interspersing all his talk with that sniggering laugh of his. We have a saying for this: "He makes up his own jokes and laughs at them himself."

Besides us three, there was another guest at the table—a fellow with bulging red cheeks. I don't know who or what he was, but he seemed to be a glutton of no mean proportions. All the time Padhatzur was talking and laughing, he went on stuffing himself. As it is written: *"Three who have eaten*—he ate enough for three." This one guzzled and the other one talked, such foolish empty talk—I couldn't understand a word of it. It was all about contracts, government pronouncements, banks, money, Japan.

The only thing that interested me was his mention of Japan, for I too had had dealings with that country. During the war, as you know, horses *"commanded the highest prices*—they went looking for them with a candle." Well, they finally found me too, and took my horse with them. My little horse was measured with a yardstick, put through his paces, driven back and forth, and in the end he was given a white card—an honorable discharge. I could have told them all along that their trouble was for nothing. *"The righteous man knoweth the soul of his animal."* No horse of Tevye's will ever go to war. But forgive me, Mr. Sholom Aleichem, for straying away from my subject. Let's get back to the story.

Well, we had eaten and drunk our fill, as the Lord had bade us do, and when we got up from the table, Padhatzur took my arm and led me into an office that was ornately furnished, with guns and swords hanging on the walls, and miniature cannon on the table. He sat me down on a sort of divan that was as soft as butter, and took out of a gold box two long, fat, aromatic cigars, lit one for himself and one for me. He then sat down opposite me, stretched out his legs and said, "Do you know why I have sent for you?"

"Aha," I thought, "Now he is getting down to business." But I played dumb and said, "*'Am I my brother's keeper?'*—How should I know?"

So he said, "I wanted to talk to you, and it's you yourself I want to talk about."

"If it's good news," I replied, 'go ahead, let's hear it."

He took the cigar out from between his teeth, and began a long lecture. "You are a man of sense, I believe, not a fool, and you will forgive me for speaking frankly with you. You must know already that I am doing business on a very big scale, and when a man does business on such a tremendous scale . . ."

"Now he is getting there," I thought to myself, and interrupted him in the middle of his speech. "As the *Gamorah* says in the Sabbath portion: *'The more business the more worries . . .'* Do you happen to be familiar with that passage in the *Gamorah?*"

He answered me quite frankly. "I will tell you the honest truth, I have never studied the *Gamorah* and I wouldn't recognize it if I saw it." And he laughed that irritating laugh of his. What do you think of a man like that? It seems to me that if God has chastised you by making you illiterate, at least keep it under your hat instead of boasting about it. But all I said was, "I gathered that you had no knowledge of these things, but let me hear what you have to say further."

"Further I want to tell you, that it isn't fitting, considering the scale of my enterprises, and the repute in which my name is held, as well as my station in life, that you should be known as Tevye the Dairyman. I'll have you know that I am personally acquainted with the Governor, and that it is very likely that one of these days Brodsky might come to my house or Poliakov or maybe even Rothschild, whomever the devil sends."

He finished speaking, and I sat there and looked at his shiny bald spot and thought to myself, "It may be true that you are personally acquainted with the Governor, and that Rothschild might even come to your house some day, but just the same you talk like a common cur."

And I said, not without a touch of resentment in my voice, "Well, and what shall we do about it, if Rothschild does happen to drop in on you?"

Do you suppose that he understood the dig? Not a bit of it. As we say: *"There was neither bear nor woods."*

"I would like you to give up the dairy business," he said, "and go into something else."

"And what," said I, "would you suggest that I go into?"

"Anything you like. Aren't there enough different kinds of business in the world? I'll help you with money, you can have whatever you need, as long as you quit being Tevye the Dairyman. Or, look here, do you know what? Maybe you'd like to pick yourself up one-two-three and go to America?"

Having delivered himself of this, he put the cigar back between his teeth, looked me straight in the eye, and his bald head glistened.

Well, what would you say to such a vulgar person?

At first impulse I thought, "What are you sitting there for like a graven image? Get up, kiss the *mazuza,* slam the door in his face, and —*'he went to his eternal rest'*—get out without as much as a good-bye." I was as stirred up as all that. The colossal nerve of this contractor. Telling me to give up an honest, respectable livelihood and go off to America. Just because it might come to pass that on some far-off day Rothschild might condescend to enter his house, Tevye the Dairyman had to run off to the ends of the earth.

I was boiling inside and some of my anger was directed at her, at Beilke herself. How could she sit there like a queen among a hundred clocks and a thousand mirrors while her father Tevye was being tortured, was running the gauntlet? "May I have as many blessings," I thought to myself, "how much better your sister Hodel has made out than you. I grant you this, she doesn't have a house with so many fancy gew-gaws in it, but she has a husband who is a human being who can call his soul his own, even if his body is in prison. And besides that he has a head on his shoulders, has Feferl, and not a pot with a shiny cover on it. And when he talks there is something to listen to. When you quote him a passage from the Bible he comes back at you with three more in exchange. Wait, my contractor, I will drum a quotation into your ears that will make your head swim."

And I addressed myself to him thus: "That the *Gamorah* is a closed book to you, I can easily understand. When a man lives in Yehupetz and his name is Padhatzur and his business is that of contractor, the *Gamorah* can very well hide itself in the attic as far as he is concerned. But even a peasant in wooden sandals can understand a simple text. You know what the *Targum* says about Laban the Arameian?" And I gave him a quotation in mixed Hebrew and Russian. When I finished he threw an angry look at me and said, "What does *that* mean?"

"It means this—that out of a pig's tail you cannot fashion a fur hat."

"And what, may I ask, are you referring to?"

"I am referring to the way you are packing me off to America."

At this he laughed that snickering laugh of his and said, "Well, if not America, then how would you like to go to Palestine? Old Jews are always eager to go to Palestine."

Something about his last words struck a chord in my heart. "Hold on, Tevye," I thought. "Maybe this isn't such a bad idea after all. Maybe this is the way out for you. Rather than to stay here and suffer such treatment at the hands of your children, Palestine would be better. What have you got to lose? Your Golde is dead anyway, and you are in such misery you might as well be buried six feet underground yourself. How much longer do you expect to pound this earth?" And I might as well confess, Mr. Sholom Aleichem, that I've been drawn for a long time toward the Holy Land. I would like to stand by the Wailing Wall, to see the tombs of the Patriarchs, Mother Rachel's grave, and I would like to look with my own eyes at the River Jordan, at Mt. Sinai and the Red Sea, at the great cities Pithom and Raamses. In my thoughts I am already in the Land of Canaan—*"the land flowing with milk and honey"*—when Padhatzur breaks in on me impatiently: "Why waste all this time thinking about it? Make it one-two-three and decide."

"With you, thank the Lord, a trip to Palestine is one-two-three like a simple text in the Bible. But for me it's a difficult passage to interpret. To pack up and go off to Palestine one has to have the means."

He laughs scornfully at this, gets up and goes over to a desk, opens a drawer, takes out a purse, and counts out some money—not a trifling sum, you understand—and hands it to me. I take the wad of paper he has handed to me—the power of money!—and lower it into my pocket. I would like to treat him to a few learned quotations, a *medresh* or two, that would explain everything to him, but he won't listen to me.

"This will be enough for your trip," says he, "and more than enough. And when you arrive and find that you need more money, write me a letter, and I will send it to you—one-two-three. I hope I won't have to remind you again about going, for, after all, you are a man of honor, a man with a conscience."

And he laughed again that sniggering laugh of his that penetrated to my very soul. I was tempted to fling the money into his face and to let him know that you couldn't buy Tevye for money and that you didn't speak to Tevye of "honor" and "conscience." But before I had time to open my mouth, he rang the bell, called Beilke in, and said to her, "Do you know what, my love! Your father is leaving us, he is selling everything he owns and going one-two-three to Palestine."

"*'I dreamed a dream but I do not understand it,'* as Pharaoh said to Joseph. What sort of nightmare is this?" I think to myself, and I look over at Beilke. Do you think she as much as frowned? She stood there rooted to the ground, pale and without expression on her face, looking from one to the other of us, not uttering a word. I couldn't speak either, and so we both stood there looking at each other, as the Psalm says: *"May my tongue cleave to the roof of my mouth."* We had both lost our powers of speech.

My head was whirling and my pulse beating as though I had been breathing in charcoal fumes. I wondered why I felt so dizzy. Could it be that expensive cigar he had given me? But he was still smoking his and talking away. His mouth didn't shut for a moment, though his eyelids were drooping as though he were ready to fall asleep.

"You have to go to Odessa by train first," he said. "And from Odessa by sea all the way to Jaffa, and the best time for a sea voyage is right now, for later on the winds and the snows and the hurricanes begin and then and then. . . ." His words were getting jumbled, he was asleep on his feet, but he didn't stop jabbering. "And when you are ready to start let us know and we'll both come to see you off at the station, for when can we hope to see you again?" He finished at last, with a huge yawn, and said to Beilke, "Why don't you stay here awhile, my soul? I am going to lie down for a little bit."

"That's the best thing you have said so far," I thought to myself. "Now I will have a chance to pour my heart out to her." I was ready to spill out all the wrath that had been accumulating in my breast all morning. But instead Beilke fell on my neck and started weeping. You should have heard her weep! My daughters are all alike in this respect. They can be very brave and manly up to a point—then all of a sudden, when it comes to something, they break down and weep like willow trees. Take my older girl Hodel. How she carried on at the last moment when she was telling me good-bye and went to join her Feferl in his exile. But how can I compare the two? This one isn't worthy of lighting the oven for the other. . . .

I will tell you the honest truth. I myself, as you well know, am not a man who is given to tears. I wept once in my life when my Golde lay stretched out on the ground with the candles at her head, and once when Hodel went off to join her husband and I was left standing alone at the station with my horse and wagon. There may have been one or two other occasions on which I weakened, I don't remember. I am not given to weeping. But Beilke's tears wrung my heart so that I couldn't hold myself in. I didn't have the heart to scold her. You don't have to explain things to me. I am Tevye. I understood her tears. She was weeping for *"the sin I have sinned before thee"*—because she hadn't listened to her father. Instead of scolding her and voicing my anger against Padhatzur, I began to comfort her with this story and that proverb as only Tevye can do.

But she interrupted me, "No, father, that isn't why I am crying. It's only because you are leaving on my account and there is nothing I can do to stop it, that's what hurts me."

"You talk like a child," I told her. "Remember we have a merciful God and your father is still in possession of all his faculties. It's a small matter for him to take a trip to Palestine and back again. As it is written: *'They journeyed and they encamped—Tuda i nazad*—I will go and I will return.' "

As though she had guessed my thoughts, she said, "No, father, that's the way you comfort a little child, you give it a toy or a doll and tell it a story about a little white goat. If you want a story, let me tell you one instead. But the story I will tell you is more sad than beautiful."

And she began telling me a long and curious tale, a story out of the thousand and one nights, all about Padhatzur, how he came up from obscure beginnings, worked himself up by his own wits to his present station in life, rose from the lowest to the highest rank. Now that he was rich he wanted the honor of entertaining important people in his home, and to that end he was pouring out thousands of *rubles,* handing out charity in all directions. But money, it seems, isn't everything. You have to have family and background, as well. He was willing to go to any length to prove that he wasn't a nobody, he boasted that he was descended from the great Padhatzurs, that his father was a celebrated contractor too. "Though he knows," she said, "quite well, and he knows that I know, that his father was only a poor fiddler. And on top of that he keeps telling everyone that his wife's father is a millionaire."

"Whom does he mean? Me? Who knows, maybe I *was* destined at one time to be a millionaire. But I'll have to let this suffice me."

"If you only knew how I suffer when he introduces me to his friends and tells them what an important man my father is, and who my uncles were and the rest of my family. How I blush at the lies he makes up. But I have to bear it all in silence for he is very eccentric in those matters."

"You call it being an 'eccentric.' To me he sounds like a plain liar or else a rascal."

"No, father, you don't understand him. He is not as evil as you think. He is a man whose moods change very frequently. He is really very kind-hearted and generous. If you happen to come to him when he is in one of his good moods he will give you anything you ask for. And nothing is too good for me. He would reach down and hand me the moon and the stars on a platter if I expressed a wish for them. Do you suppose I have no influence over him at all? Just recently I persuaded him to get Hodel and her husband out of exile. He promised to spend as much money as necessary on only one condition —that they go from there straight to Japan."

"Why to Japan?" I asked. "Why not to India, or to Persia to visit the Queen of Sheba?"

"Because he has business in Japan. He has business all over the world. What he spends on telegrams alone in one day would keep us all alive for a half year." Then her voice dropped. "But what good is all this to me? I am not myself any more."

"It is said," I quoted, "*'If I am not for myself who will be for me?—* I am not I and you are not you!' "

I tried to distract her with jokes and quotations and all the time my heart was torn into pieces to see my child pining away—how do we say it—*"in riches and in honor."*

"Your sister Hodel," I told her, "would have done differently."

"I've told you before not to compare me to Hodel. Hodel lived in Hodel's time and Beilke is living in Beilke's time. The distance between the two is as great as from here to Japan." Can you figure out the meaning of such crazy talk?

I see that you are in a hurry, but be patient for just a minute and there will be an end to all my stories. Well, after having supped well on the grief of my youngest child, I left the house *"in mourning and with bowed head,"* completely crushed and beaten. I threw the vile cigar he had given me into the street and shouted, "To the devil with you."

"Whom are you cursing, Reb Tevye?" I heard a voice behind my back. I turned around and looked. It was he, Ephraim the *Shadchan,* may no good come to him.

"God bless you, And what are you doing here?" I asked.

"What are *you* doing here?"

"I've been visiting my children."

"And how are they getting along?"

"How should they be getting along? May you and I be as lucky."

"Then I see you are satisfied with my merchandise."

"Satisfied, did you say? May God bless you doubly and trebly for what you have done."

"Thank you for the blessings. Now if you could only add to them something more substantial."

"Didn't you get your matchmaker's fee?"

"May your Padhatzur have no more than I got."

"What's the matter? Was the fee too small?"

"It isn't the size of the fee so much as the manner of giving it."

"What's the trouble then?"

"The trouble is," said he, "that there isn't a *groschen* of it left."

"Where did it disappear to?"

"I married off my daughter."

"Congratulations. Good luck to the couple and may you live to rejoice in their happiness."

"I am rejoicing in it right now. My son-in-law turned out to be a crook. He beat up my daughter, took the few *guldens* away and ran off to America."

"Why did you let him run off so far?"

"How could I stop him?"

"You could have sprinkled salt on his tail."

"I see you are feeling pretty chipper today, Reb Tevye."

"May you feel half as good as I feel."

"Is that so? And I thought you were fixed for life. If that's the case, here is a pinch of snuff."

I got rid of the matchmaker with a pinch of snuff, and went on home. I began selling out my household goods. It wasn't easy, I can tell you, to get rid of all the things that had accumulated through the years. Every old pot, every broken kettle wrenched my heart. One thing reminded me of Golde, another of the children. But nothing hurt me so much as parting with my old horse. I felt as though I owed him something. Hadn't we labored together all these years, suffered and hungered together, known good luck and bad luck together? And here I was up and selling him to a stranger. I had to dispose of him to a water-carrier, for what do you get from a teamster? Nothing but insults. Here is how the teamsters greeted me when I brought my horse to them.

"God be with you, Reb Tevye. Do you call this a horse?"

"What is it, then, a chandelier?"

"If it isn't a chandelier then it's one of the thirty-six saints who hold up the world."

"What do you mean by that?"

"We mean an old creature thirty-six years old without any teeth, with a gray lip, that shivers and shakes like an old woman saying her prayers on a frosty night."

That's teamsters' talk for you. I could swear that my little horse understood every word, as it is written: *"An ox knows his master.*— An animal knows when you are offering him for sale." I was sure he understood, for when I closed the deal with the water-carrier and wished him luck, my horse turned his patient face to me and gave me a look as though to say: *"This is my portion for all my efforts.*— Is this how you reward me for my years of faithful service?"

I looked back at him for the last time as the water-carrier led him away and I was left standing all alone. I thought, "Almighty, how cleverly You have fashioned Your world. You have created Tevye and You have created his horse and to both You have given the same fate. A man can at least talk, he can complain out loud, he can unburden his soul to another, but a horse? He is nothing but a dumb beast, as it is said: *'The advantage of man over animal.'* "

You wonder at the tears in my eyes, Mr. Sholom Aleichem. You are probably thinking that I am weeping for my horse. Why only for my horse? I am weeping for everybody and everything. For I shall miss everybody and everything. I shall miss my horse and the farm, and I shall miss the mayor and the police sergeant, the summer people of Boiberik, the rich people of Yehupetz, and I shall miss Ephraim the Matchmaker, may a plague take him, for when all is said and done, if you think the whole matter over, what is he but a poor man trying to make a living?

When God brings me safely to the place where I am going, I do not know what will finally become of me, but one thing is clear in my mind—that first of all I shall visit the grave of Mother Rachel. There I will offer a prayer for my children whom I shall probably never see again and at the same time I will keep in mind Ephraim the Matchmaker, as well as yourself and all of Israel. Let us shake hands on that, and go your way in good health and give my blessings to everyone and bid everyone a kind farewell for me. And may all go well with you.

Gy-Ma-Na-Si-A

LISTEN to me, your worst enemy can't do to you what you can do to yourself, especially if a woman—I mean a wife—interferes.

Why do I say this? I'm thinking of my own experience. Look at me, for instance. Well, what do you see? A man, you'd say—just an average man. You can't tell from my face whether I have money or not. It is possible that once I may have had some money, and not only money—for what is money?—but a decent livelihood, an honorable position, without rush and bustle and noise. No, the way I look at it, the quiet, unassuming way is best. I've always operated in a quiet, unspectacular way. In a quiet unspectacular way, I've gone broke twice. Quietly, and without fuss, I settled with my creditors and started all over again. . . .

But there is a God who rules over all of us, and through my own wife, He chastened me. She isn't here, so we can talk freely. To look at her you might say she is a wife like all wives. A pretty decent woman as women go. A big woman, God be praised, twice as big as I am, and not bad-looking. Really handsome, you might say, and not a fool either. She is smart—very smart, you might say—in fact, a woman with a masculine brain. And that's just the trouble. It's not so good when a woman has brains like a man. It doesn't matter how smart she is—after all, the good Lord created Adam first, and Eve after him! But try to point that out to her, and she answers, "If the Highest One wanted to create you first and then us—that's His affair.

But if He saw fit to put more brains into my little toe than into your whole head, I'm not to blame for that either."

"How did we come around to that?" I ask.

"Very simply," says she. "Whenever there is a decision to be made around here, I am the one who has to rack her brains. Even when our boy has to be sent to the *Gymnasia,* I have to do the planning."

"Where is it written?" I ask, "that he has to go to the *Gymnasia?* I'll be just as happy if he studies the *Torah* right here at home."

And she says, "I've told you a thousand times already that you won't succeed in setting me against the whole world. Nowadays the whole world sends its children to the *Gymnasia.*"

"To my way of thinking," I say to her, "the whole world is crazy."

"And I suppose you are the only sane one," says she. "The world would come to a pretty pass if everybody did what you wanted."

And I tell her, "Everybody acts according to his way of thinking."

"May all my enemies and my friends' enemies," says my wife, "have in their pockets, in their chests, and in their cupboards as much as you have in your head! They'd starve to death."

"Pity the poor man," says I, "who has to listen to a woman's advice."

And she says, "Pity the poor woman who has a husband who needs her advice."

Well, try to argue with a woman. If you say this, she says that. If you say one word she gives you back twelve. And if you stop talking altogether she bursts into tears or better still falls in a faint. To make a long story short, she had her way. For let's not fool ourselves: if a woman makes up her mind, is there anything we can do?

Well, what shall I tell you? *Gy-ma-na-si-a!*

First of all we had to start getting him ready to enter the *Mladshi Prigotovitelnie,* the junior preparatory school. "What's there to worry about?" I said with a shrug. "A trifle like that—*Mladshi Prigotovitelnie.* It seems to me that any little schoolboy among us can put them all in the shade. Especially a child like ours!" If you travel the length and breadth of the Empire, you won't find another like him. I'm his own father and I may be prejudiced, but you can't get away from it—the child has a head on him. He's the talk of the province. . . .

Well, why should I make a long story out of it? He made his application, went for his examination, took his examination, and—he didn't pass! What happened? He failed in arithmetic. He's a little weak, they tell me, in figuring. In math-e-ma-tics, they call it. How do you like that? Here's a boy with such a head—he's the talk of a province—you can travel the length and breadth of the Empire . . . And they tell me: math-e-ma-tics. At any rate, he failed. That made me good and mad. If he took that examination, he should have passed it. But after all, I'm a man, not a woman. So I thought it over: the devil take it! We Jews are used to such treatment. Let's forget the whole thing.

But try to convince *her* once she'd got that crazy idea into her head! She's made up her mind once for all—*Gy-ma-na-si-a!* So I plead with her. "Tell me," I say, "my dear wife, what does he need it for? Will it keep him out of the army? For that, the Lord has already provided. He's an only son. What then? To help him make a living? I can get along without it. What do I care if he becomes a storekeeper like me, or some other kind of businessman? And if it's his luck to become a millionaire or a banker, I'll bear up under that too." Thus I plead with her. But does it do any good?

"It's just as well," she tells me, "that he didn't get into the *Mladshi Prigotovitelnie* after all."

"Why?" I ask.

She says, "He might just as well go right into the *Starshi Prigotovitelnie,* the advanced preparatory school." "Well," I think, "why not? After all, with a head like that . . . you can travel the length and breadth . . ."

But what happened? When it came to the final test, he failed again! Not in math-e-ma-tics this time. Something new. His spelling is not what it might be. That is, he spells the words all right, but there is one letter on which he is a little weak. The letter *yati.* He puts it in all right, but the trouble is that he doesn't put it where it belongs. So I'm heart-broken! I don't know how I'll ever be able to go to Poltava or to Lodz for the fairs, if he doesn't learn to put the letter *yati* where they want him to. . . .

Anyway, when they told us the glad tidings, *she* almost had a fit. She rushed right off to the director and insisted that the boy could do it; he knew how to spell. Just let them try him out again right from the beginning. Naturally, they paid no attention to her. They gave him a *two*—the failing grade—and what kind of a *two? A two minus!* And go do something about it. Help! Murder! He failed again. So I say to her, "What do you want us to do? Commit suicide? We're Jews. We're used to such treatment."

At this, she flares up at me and starts to yell and to curse as only a woman can do. That doesn't bother me. The only one I feel sorry for is my boy, poor child. Think of it. All the other boys will be wearing uniforms with silver buttons and he won't. So I plead with him. "You dummy!" I say. "You fool! Is it a law that everybody has to go to *Gymnasia?* Silly child, somebody has to stay home, doesn't he? And besides . . ."

But she doesn't let me finish. "Such comfort he offers! Who asked for your sympathy? What you can do instead is to go and find a good teacher for him, a tutor, a Russian tutor to teach him *gra-ma-ti-ka,* grammar."

Listen to her. She wants two tutors. One tutor and one *melamed* for Hebrew isn't enough for her. Well, we argued back and forth, but in the end she won the point. Because when she makes up her mind, is there anything I can do?

Well, what shall I say? We hired another tutor, a real Russian this time, because the examination in Grammar for First Class is a tough proposition. It's strong medicine to take, as strong as horse-radish. You can't trifle with *gra-ma-ti-ka* with the *bukva yati,* the letter *yati.* And what kind of tutor does the good Lord send us? I am ashamed to talk about it. He made life unbearable for us. He belittled us and made fun of us right to our faces. May he burn in hell! For instance, he couldn't find another word to practice on than garlic—*Tchasnok! Tchasnok, tchasnoka, tchasnoku, tchasnokoi* . . . If it hadn't been for *her,* I'd have taken him by the collar and thrown him out together with his grammar. But to her it was worth going through. Why? Because the boy was going to know where to put a *yati* and where not to put it. Think of it! All winter we tortured him and it was not until late spring that he had to go to the slaughter. And when the time came, he made his application, took his examination, and this time he didn't fail. He got the best marks, a four and a five. Hurrah! Let's celebrate! *Mazl-tov!* Congratulations! But wait! Don't be in such a hurry. We don't know yet if he'll be admitted. We won't know till August. Why not? Go ask them. What can we do about it? It's *their* world. A Jew is used to such treatment. . . .

Comes August, my wife can't rest. She rushes around, from the director to the inspector, from the inspector to the director. "Why do you keep running, like a poisoned rat, from one hole to the next?" I ask her.

"What do you mean—why do I keep running?" she says to me. "Are you a stranger around here? Don't you know what goes on these days? Haven't you heard about quotas?"

And what finally happened? He *didn't* get in. Why not? Because he didn't get two *fives*. If he had gotten two fives, they told us, then *maybe* he would have got in. How do you like that? *Maybe*. Well, I'd just as soon forget what I got from her that day. But the one I felt sorry for was *him*. The poor boy. He lay there with his head in the pillow and wouldn't stop crying. So there was nothing else to do; we had to get another tutor, a student at the *Gymnasia,* and we started grooming him all over again, this time for second class. And that was a real task, because to get into the second class you had to know not only math-e-ma-tics and grammar, but geography and penmanship and I don't know what else besides. Though, if you ask me, for three *groschen,* you can have it all. Any Bible text our boys have to learn in *cheder* is harder than all their studies and much more to the point. But what can we do about it? A Jew is used to such treatment. . . .

There followed a round of lessons. We lived on lessons. When we got up in the morning—lessons. After we had finished the morning prayer and eaten—lessons. All day long—lessons and more lessons. Until late at night we could hear him reciting: "Nominative, genitive, dative, accusative . . ." It rang in my ears, it pounded in my head. I couldn't eat. I couldn't sleep. "Look," I said, "you take an innocent creature and you torture him. It's a crime. The poor child will get sick."

And she exclaims, "Bite your tongue for these words!"

And once more he went to the slaughter, and this time he brought home nothing but *fives!* But, then, did you expect anything different? A head like his—you can travel the length and breadth of the Empire and you won't find another like it! It sounds good, doesn't it? Well, listen to this then. When they posted the names of the boys who were accepted, and we looked—ours wasn't there. Help! Murder! It's a disgrace, a crime! He had perfect marks. Watch her go! Watch her run! She'll show them. Well, she went, she showed them—and all they told her was to stop annoying them. In plain language, they showed her the door. And she came rushing into the house with a roar that could be heard in heaven.

"You!" she yelled. "A fine father you are! If you were a real father like other fathers, if you had an ounce of love for your child, you'd find some way. You'd see people. You'd do something. You'd use your influence, with the director, the inspector, somebody. . . ."

What do you think of that? There's a woman for you! "Is that all I have to do? Isn't it enough that I have to carry on my mind all the seasons, the markets, the fairs, and notes and receipts and checks and drafts, and I don't know how many more things? Maybe you want me to go bankrupt on account of your *Gy-ma-na-si-a* and your classes? You know what I think of them! You know where you can put them!"

After all, I'm only human and there is a limit to what a person can stand. So I let her have it. But it was she who had her way, not I. Because when she makes up her mind . . .

And what did I do then? I began trying to use influence. I humbled myself, I underwent all sorts of humiliations; because everyone I came to asked me the same questions and everyone of them was correct. "Here you are, Reb Aaron," they said, " a person of some consequence, with an only son. What possesses you to go sticking your head where you're not wanted?"

Go tell them the whole story—that I have a wife—may she live to be a hundred and twenty years old—who has one obsession: *Gy-ma-*

na-si-a and *Gy-ma-na-si-a* and *Gy-ma-na-si-a!* But I'm not such a half-wit either. With God's help I worked my way in where I wanted to be, right into the office of the director himself, and I sat down to talk it over with him. After all, thank the Lord, I know how to talk too. No one has to show me how.

"Tchto was ugodno?" he says to me. "What is your wish?" And he asks me to sit down.

I come close and whisper into his ear, *"Gospodin* Director," I say, *"mi ludi ne bogati,* we are not rich people, but we have a boy, an only child who," I say, "wants to study, and I want him to study too, and my wife," I say, "wants very much . . ."

So he says to me again, *"Tchto was ugodno?*—What is your wish?"

So I come a little closer and say to him, "Your honor, we are not rich people, but we have a boy, an only child, who" I say, "wants to study, and my wife," I say, "wants *very much* . . ." And I stretch out the *ve-ry* so he'll understand. But he's thick-headed and slow. He doesn't seem to know what I'm talking about. He repeats angrily, *"Tak tchtozhe was ugodno*—once and for all, what is your wish?"

So slowly, cautiously I put my hand into my pocket. Slowly, cautiously I pull it out again, and slowly and cautiously I say, "I beg your pardon, *Gospodin* Director, *mi ludi ne bogati*—we are not rich people, but we have a boy"—and I pause—"an only child"—and I pause again—"who wants to study." And I look meaningfully at the director. "And my wife," I almost whisper, "wants *very, very* much to have him study." And this time I stretch out the *ve-e-ry* even longer than before, and I put my hand into his. . . .

All at once he knew what I meant. He took a little book out of his drawer, and asked me what my name was, and what my boy's name was, and which class I wanted him to enter. I thought to myself, "That's the way to talk!" And I told him that my name was Katz, Aaron Katz, and my boy was named Moishe or Moshka, and I wanted him to enter third class. So he told me that seeing that my name was Katz, and my boy's name was Moishe or Moshka, and he wanted to enter the third class, I should bring him back in January and then he'd surely get in. You understand. An entirely different language. Apparently if you grease the axle the wheels will turn. The only trouble was that we still had to wait. But what could we do about it? They told us to wait, so we waited. A Jew is used to such treatment. . . .

Came January, and again a tumult, a clamor, a rushing around. Any day now a meeting would be held, a *soviet,* they called it. The director and the inspector and all the teachers of the *Gymnasia* were going to come together, and when the meeting was over we'd know if they were going to take him in. The day came; my wife wasn't home. There was no dinner, no samovar, not a thing in the house to eat. Where was she? She was at the *Gymnasia.* That is, not at the *Gymnasia* itself, but in front of it. All day long she trudged back and forth in the deep snow, back and forth, waiting for them to come out of the meeting. It's a bitter frost, the wind is sharp, it cuts your breath off. And she walks back and forth outside, waiting. What for? She must know that a promise is sacred . . . and specially since . . . you understand? But try to tell that to a woman!

Well, she waited an hour, she waited two, three, four hours. All the boys have gone home already, and still she waits. At last the door opens and one of the teachers comes out. She jumps at him and grabs him by the arm. Does he know how the meeting—the *soviet*—came out? So he says, why shouldn't he know? They decided to admit, all in all, eighty-five boys. Eighty-three Christians and two Jews. So she asks, who were the Jews? And he tells her a Shepselson and a Katz. When she hears the name Katz, she turns around and comes running home all out of breath, falls into the house in ecstasy. *"Mazl-tov,"* she cries. "Oh, I thank Thee, Heavenly Father, I thank Thee! They've accepted him! They've accepted him!" And tears stand in her eyes. Naturally, I am pleased too, but do I have to start dancing to show my joy? After all, I'm a man, not a woman.

"It looks to me," my wife says, "as if you're not too excited about all this."

"What makes you think so?" I ask her.

"Oh," she says, "you're a cold, heartless person. If you only saw how eager the child is, you wouldn't be sitting there so calmly. You would have been on your way long ago to buy him a uniform, a cap, and a satchel for his books. And you'd be doing something about a celebration for our friends."

"Why a celebration all of a sudden?" I ask her. "Is the boy being confirmed, or getting married?" So she gets angry and stops talking to me altogether. And when a woman stops talking it's a thousand times worse than when she's cursing, because if she is cursing you, at least you hear a human voice. But this way it's like talking to a brick wall. Well, who do you think won out? She or I? Naturally, she did, because if she makes up her mind, is there anything I can do?

And so we had a celebration. We invited all our friends and relatives and we dressed the boy up from head to foot in a handsome uniform with shiny buttons and a cadet's cap with a metal gadget in front—just like a general. You should have seen him. He was a different lad altogether, with a new soul, a new life. He shone, like the sun in July! The guests drank toasts to him, wished that he might study in the best of health and go on and on to higher studies.

"That," I said "is not so important. We can get along without that. Just let him go through the first few years of the *Gymnasia,*" I said, "and with God's help I'll get him married off."

My wife smiles at the guests and gives me a funny look. "You can tell him that he's very much mistaken," she says. "He has old-fashioned ideas."

"And you can tell her," I say, "that I wish I had a hundred blessings for every way in which the old-fashioned ideas are better than the new-fangled ones."

And she says, "You can tell *him* that he is a . . ."

At this everybody starts laughing. "Oh, Reb Aaron, Reb Aaron," they cry, "have you got a wife, God bless her! A Cossack, not a wife!"

On the strength of that everybody took another drink, somebody struck up a tune, the crowd made a ring with the two of us and our boy in the middle, and we lifted our feet and danced. We danced until dawn. As soon as it was light outside we took the boy and went straight to the *Gymnasia.* When we got there it was still early, the door was locked, there wasn't even a cur in sight. . . . We stood there until we were frozen stiff, and when the door was finally opened we went in and began to thaw out. Before long the youngsters began coming, with knapsacks full of books on their shoulders. Soon the place was full of them, talking, laughing, joking, shouting—like a circus. In the midst of all this a man comes up to us, obviously one of the teachers, with a sheet of paper in his hands.

"What are you here for?" he asks me.

So I point to the boy and tell him that I had just brought him to start *cheder* here, that is, the *Gymnasia.* So he asks me what class he's in and I say the third. He's just been admitted.

So he asks, "What's his name?"

And I tell him, "Katz. Moishe Katz. That is, Moshka Katz."

So he says, "Moshka Katz? There is no Moshka Katz in the third class. There *is* a Katz in the class" he says, "but not Moshka. Morduch. That's the only one. Morduch Katz."

So I say, "What do you mean—Morduch? Not Morduch—Moshka."

He says, "Morduch!" And he waves the paper in front of my face.

I say "Moshka!" He says "Morduch!" Well, what shall I tell you? Moshka—Morduch, Morduch—Moshka. We Moshka'd and Morduch'ed until at last we found out what had happened. Would you believe it? They did take in a boy named Katz. But they made a mistake and took in a different Katz. There were two Katzes in our town.

Well, what shall I tell you? You should have seen the boy's face when we told him to take that gadget off his cap. A bride doesn't shed as many tears when she is led to the canopy as my boy did that day. I begged him to stop, I threatened him. It didn't help. "Look!" I said to my wife. "See, what you've done to him! Didn't I tell you that this *Gy-ma-na-si-a* of yours would be the death of him yet? May God help us," I said. "I only hope we don't have more trouble on account of this. I hope he doesn't get sick."

"Let my enemies get sick, if they like," says she, "but my child *must* get into the *Gymnasia!* If he didn't get in now, he'll get in a year from now. If he didn't get in here, he'll get in somewhere else. But," she says, "he must get in—unless I die first and you bury me."

Did you ever hear the like of that? And who do you think won out? Let's not fool ourselves. If she makes up her mind, can I do anything?"

Well, I won't take up much more of your time. We traveled from one end of the country to the other. Wherever there is a city, wherever there is a *Gymnasia,* there we went. We registered him, he took his examinations, he passed his examinations, he passed with top grades—and he *didn't* get in. Why not? Because of the quota. Always the quota.

I began to think that I had really gone crazy. "Fool!" I said to myself. "What is this? What are you flying around for, from one city to the next? What good will it ever do you? What do you need it for? And if he does get in, so what?" Well, you can say what you want, ambition is a great thing. It finally got me too. I became stubborn. I wouldn't give up. At last the Almighty had pity on me and sent across my path, in Poland somewhere, a certain *Gymnasia,* a *komertcheska,* they called it, a business school, where for every Christian they were willing to take in one Jew—a quota of fifty percent, that is. But here was the catch. Every Jew who wanted to have his son admitted had to bring along with him a Christian boy, and if he passed the examination, this Christian, that is, and if all his fees and expenses were paid, then there was a chance! In other words, you had not one headache, but two. It was bad enough to have my own son to worry about, but now I had to eat my heart out over somebody else's son too. For—woe is me!—if Esau fails to make the grade, then Jacob lies in the dust together with him.

So I set out to find a Christian youth, and what I went through before I found one! He was a shoemaker's boy, a shoemaker named Holiava. And then what do you think happened? The shoemaker's boy failed in his examinations. And in what? In religion. And my boy had to sit down and drill him in religion! You ask, how does my boy come to know religion? You don't have to ask. After all, with a head like his! As I told you, you can travel the length and breadth of the Empire. . . .

Well, in spite of that, at last God came to our aid. The lucky day arrived. They both got in. But do you think we're through? No. When it came to paying the fees, I look around; my man has vanished. What's the matter? He doesn't want his son to go to school with so many Jews. You can't budge him. He says, "What good is it to me? Aren't all schools open to me anyway? Can't my boy go to any school he wants to?" And can I contradict him?

"What do you want, *Panie* Holiava?" I say. And he says,

"Nothing." I try this, I try that. I went to see some friends of his, drinking companions, we went into a tavern together, had a glass or two, maybe three. Well, before I lived to see him enrolled, my hair almost turned gray. But anyway, praise the Lord, my work was done.

When I came home I found a new headache. What now? My wife has made up her mind. After all, he is an only child, the apple of her eye. . . . Was it right to leave him out there all by himself?

"What," I ask, "are you driving at now?"

"What am I driving at?" she asks. "Don't you know what I'm driving at? I want to be with him."

"Oh," says I. "And the house?"

"The house," says she, "is nothing but a house."

And what do you think she did? She packed up and went over there to be with him, and I remained all alone at home. You can imagine what it must have been like. May my enemies live like that! My life was no life any more, my business was no business. Everything went wrong. And we kept writing letters to each other. I write to her. She answers. Letters go back and forth. "To my beloved and cherished wife—peace!" "Peace to my dear husband."

"In the name of God," I write to her, "what will be the outcome of all this? I am only human. And what's a house without a mistress? Listen to reason, my wife."

Well, she paid as much heed to my pleas as she might to the snows of last year. She won her point, not I. For if she makes up her mind—is there anything I can do?

Well, I'm coming to the end of my story. I was ruined. I went broke. I lost everything. My business disappeared, my last few remnants were sold. I was left penniless. I had no choice. I had to swallow my pride and move over there with them. There, I had to start all over again. I looked around, sniffed here and there and tried to figure out where I was in the world. At last I found something. I went into partnership with a merchant from Warsaw, a man of some means, a householder, a president of a synagogue, but at bottom a manipulator, a swindler, a pickpocket! He just about ruined me all over again. I couldn't hold up my head any more.

In the meanwhile, I come home one day and my boy opens the door for me. He has a strange look on his face. He is blushing and I see that the fancy gadget, the insignia, is gone from his cap. I say to him, "Look, Moishe, my boy, what happened to the gadget?"

He says to me, "What gadget?"

I say, "The insignia, the thing-a-ma-jig."

The boy turns redder still and says, "I tore it off."

"What do you mean, you tore it off?"

And he says, "I am free."

"What do you mean—you are free?"

And he tells me, "We're through. We are not going back to school any more."

So I say, "What do you mean *you're* not going any more?"

And he says, "We're all free. We didn't like the way they treated us. So we went out on strike. We all agreed not to go back."

"What do you mean—strike?" I shout. "What do you mean—agreed? Was it for this that I gave up my home and my business? Was it for this that I sacrificed myself? So that you could go out on strike? Woe is me. And woe is you. May God protect us. Who will suffer for it? We Jews."

That's the way I talk to him, warn him, lecture him, the way a father naturally does to a child. But I also have a wife, God bless her. She comes running in and lays down the law to me. I'm slightly backward, she tells me. I don't know what's going on in the world. We're living in a new era, she tells me. A better life, a newer life has come into existence, she tells me, where all are equal. There are no rich, no poor; no master, no slave; no lamb, no shears; no cats, no mice. . . .

"Tut-tut, my dear," I say to her. "Where did you learn all this funny talk? It sounds like a new language to me. By the same token, maybe you want to open up the chicken coops and let out all the chickens? Here, chickie-chickie! Shoo, chickie! You're free."

At this, she flares up at me. It's just as if I had poured a bucket full of boiling water at her. She went after me. . . . I had to listen to a whole sermon, from beginning to end. The only trouble is, there was no end. "Just a second," I beg. "Listen to me. Just a minute." And I beat my breast with my fist, as we do on *Yom Kippur:* "I have sinned I have subverted, I have transgressed. Now let's call a halt."

But she pays no attention to me. "No," she says. And she wants to know "why" and "how" and "besides" and "for Heaven's sake," and "what do I mean," and "how does it happen" and "who says so"? And then a second time and a third time, and once again for good measure. I was lucky to escape alive. . . .

Tell me, I beg you. Who ever invented wives?

The Purim Feast

"I DON'T know what's to become of the child, what he's going to grow up into. He's like a dripping dishrag, a soggy handkerchief, like a professional mourner. . . . A child that can't stop crying."

This was my mother talking to herself as she dressed me in my holiday clothes. As she spoke she gave me now a shove, now a push, now a cuff over the head; she grabbed me by the hair or pulled my ear, pinched me, and slapped me—and with all that she expected me to be laughing instead of crying! She buttoned me up from top to toe in my best coat which was much too tight for me. I could barely breathe and my eyes almost popped out of my head. The sleeves were so short that my bluish red wrists stuck out of my cuffs as though they were swollen. This was more than my mother could bear.

"Look at that pair of hands!" And she slapped me smartly across my wrists to make me drop them. "When you sit at Uncle Hertz's table remember to keep your hands down, do you hear me? And don't let your face get as red as Yadwocha the peasant girl's. And don't roll your eyes like a tomcat. Do you hear what I'm telling you? And sit up like a human being. And the main thing—is your nose. Oh, that nose of yours. Come here, let me put your nose in order."

Alas for my poor nose when my mother decides to "put it in order." I don't know what my nose has done to deserve such a fate. It seems to me that it's a nose like all noses, short and blunt, slightly turned up at the end, pinkish in color, and usually dripping. But is that a reason for such cruel treatment? Believe me, there have been times when I have begged the Almighty to take my nose away altogether, to cause it to fall off and end my misery once for all. I used to imagine that I would wake up one fine morning without a nose. I would come up to my mother after breakfast and she would grab hold of me and cry out in a terrible voice, "Woe is me, where is your nose?"

"Which nose?" I would say innocently, passing my hand over my face. I would look at my mother's horror-stricken face and taste the joys of revenge. "Serves her right. Now she can see what her son looks like without a nose."

Childish dreams! Foolish imaginings! God didn't hear my prayer. My nose kept on growing, my mother kept on "putting it in order" and I went on suffering. My nose had to take the worst punishment when a holiday approached, for instance before *Purim* when we were getting ready to go to Uncle Hertz's for the *Purim* Feast.

Uncle Hertz was not only the rich uncle in the family, he was also the foremost citizen in our town, and in all the surrounding towns you heard nothing but Hertz and Hertz and Hertz. Of course he had a pair of high-spirited horses and a carriage of his own, and when he rode out in his carriage the wheels made such a clatter that the whole town ran outside to see Uncle Hertz riding by. There he sat, high up in his carriage, with his handsome, round, copper-colored beard and his fierce gray eyes, rocking himself back and forth and looking down at everyone through his silver-rimmed spectacles, as though to say, "How can you worms compare yourselves to me? I am Hertz the *Nogid* and I ride in a carriage, while you poor Kasriliks, you paupers, you crawl in the mud."

I don't know how the rest of the world felt about him, but I detested Uncle Hertz so that I couldn't bear to look at his fat, red face, his copper-colored beard and his silver-rimmed spectacles. I hated his big paunch and the massive gold chain that rode around his paunch, the round silk skullcap that he wore on his head, and above all I hated his little cough. He had a peculiar little cough which went along with a shrug of the shoulders, a toss of the head, and pout of the lips, as though he were saying, "Show respect. It was I, Hertz, who coughed, not because, God forbid, I have caught cold, but just because I wanted to cough."

I can't understand my family at all. What's the matter with them that they are so excited over going to Uncle Hertz's for *Purim?* It seems to me that they all love him as they love a toothache, and even my mother who is his own sister is not too crazy about him either, for when the older children are not at home (she apparently isn't embarrassed by my presence) she showers strange blessings on his head. She hopes that next year, "he will be in her circumstances." But let anyone else try to say a word against him, and she will scratch his eyes out. I happened to be by one day when my father let something fall. Do you think it was something disrespectful? Not at all. He only remarked to my mother, "Well, what's the news? Has your Hertz arrived yet, or not?" And she gave him such a fare-thee-well that my poor father didn't know whether to stand up or to sit down.

"What do you mean by *my* Hertz? What kind of talk is that? What sort of expression? What do you mean he is mine?"

"Whose is he if not yours? Is he mine?" said my father trying to give battle. But he didn't advance far. My mother attacked him on all sides at once.

"Well, if he is mine, what of it? He is mine, then. You don't like it? His ancestry isn't good enough for you? You had to divide your father's inheritance with him? Is that it? You never got any favors from him? Is that it?"

"Who says I didn't?" my father offered in a milder tone, ready to surrender himself. But it didn't do any good. My mother wasn't ready to make a truce yet.

"You have better brothers than I have? Is that it? Finer men, more important, more prosperous, more respectable ones, is that it?"

"Quiet now. Let there be an end to this. Leave me alone," said my father, pulling his cap over his eyes and running out of the house. My father lost the battle and my mother remained the victor. She is always the victor. She wins every battle, not because she wears the pants in the family, but because of Uncle Hertz. Uncle Hertz is our rich uncle and we are his "poor relations."

What is Uncle Hertz to us? Do we live off him? Or have we received so many favors from him? I cannot tell you, because I don't know. I only know that everyone in our house, from the oldest to the youngest, lives in fear and trembling of Uncle Hertz. *Purim* is two weeks off and we are already getting ready for the Feast at Uncle Hertz's. My older brother, Moses Abraham, a boy with pale, sunken cheeks and sad dark eyes, strokes his earlocks whenever you mention the *Purim* Feast at Uncle Hertz's. As for my two big sisters, Miriam Reizel and Hannah Rachel, it goes without saying that they have been getting ready for a long time. They are having new dresses made in the latest fashion just for the occasion, and they have bought combs and ribbons to put in their hair. They wanted to have their shoes mended too, but my mother put that off for Passover, though it cost her plenty of heartache. She is especially concerned about Miriam Reizel, because Miriam Reizel is engaged, and suppose her young man sees her torn shoes! She has enough trouble with that young man as it is. To begin with, he is a common fellow, a "bookkeeper" he calls himself, because he is a clerk in a store. As though that weren't bad enough, he likes to put on airs, and he expects his betrothed to go around dressed in the latest fashion, like a princess.

Every Saturday afternoon this young man comes to our house and he sits by the window with my two sisters and all they talk about is new clothes, stylish costumes, patent leather shoes, galoshes, hats with feathers, pointed parasols. They also talk about embroidered pillow cases, red pillowslips, white sheets, and fine quilts, fluffy and warm, so that it's a pleasure to get under them on a cold winter night. As he talks, I look over at my sister Miriam Reizel and see her go red as a beet. She has a habit of blushing very easily. She hides her feet under the chair, so that her young man won't see the run-down heels and shabby toes if he should look at them.

"Well, are you prepared for the Feast?" my mother asks my father the day after the reading of the *Megilah*.

"Prepared?" says my father. "With what?" And he puts on his Sabbath gabardine. "Where are the children?"

"The children are almost ready," says my mother, though she knows quite well that the children, meaning my two sisters, are far from ready. They are still washing their hair, putting almond oil on it, braiding it for each other, primping, and putting on their new dresses. They have smeared their shoes with fat to make them sparkle like new. But what good is this sparkle when the heels are almost off, and the toes show through in front? How can they keep Miriam Reizel's young man from seeing her shoes? Just then, as if some ill wind blew him in, the young man himself appears, in a new suit with a stiffly starched collar and a bright green tie. From his starched white cuffs dangle his big red hands with the black-rimmed nails. He has just had a haircut and his short hair stands on end. Out of his back pocket he pulls a huge white, starched handkerchief, redolent of spices. The strong scent of cloves and spice is wafted to my nostrils and makes me sneeze suddenly, so that I burst two buttons off my coat. My mother lets fly at me. "Look at the scamp. He can't keep a button on. May you not burst apart altogether." She picks up a needle and thread and sews the buttons back on. Now everyone is ready and we start out all together for Uncle Hertz's house.

In front of the procession walks my father, the skirts of his coat lifted high from the mud. Behind him walks my mother in high men's boots. After her come my sisters tripping daintily with parasols in their hands. (Why anyone needs a parasol at this time of year is beyond me.) After them my older brother Moses Abraham leaps through the mud, holding me by the hand and trying to find a dry spot, but landing each time in the deepest mud and jumping back as though he had been scalded. Alongside of us walks my sister's young man in his new tall galoshes. He is the only one of us who has galoshes and he calls out in a loud voice for everyone to hear, "I hope I don't get my galoshes full of mud."

Though it is still broad daylight, many candles are burning at Uncle Hertz's house. All the lamps have been lighted and sconces burn on the walls. The table has been set. A monstrous *Purim* loaf, as big as the legendary ox reserved for the pious when the Messiah comes, takes up half of the table. All around the table are gathered our relatives, all the uncles and aunts and cousins, poor people all of them, one poorer than the next. They are standing around, whispering among themselves as though they were at a circumcision ceremony waiting for the godparents to bring in the child. Uncle Hertz is nowhere to be seen, and my Aunt, a woman with a string of huge pearls around her neck and a set of false teeth, is bustling around, putting plates on the table, counting us with the left hand, apparently not afraid of the evil eye. . . .

And now the door opens and Uncle Hertz himself appears, dressed in holiday clothes, a shiny black silk coat with wide sleeves, and a fur hat on his head, which he wears only for the *Purim* Feast and the Passover *Seder*. The whole family bows to him and the men smile nervously, rubbing their hands together, and the women wish him a loud good *yom-tev*. We children stand around stiffly, not knowing what to do with our hands. Uncle Hertz gives us all a sweeping glance out of his fierce gray eyes, over the tops of his glasses, coughs and waves his hand at us. "Well, why don't you sit down? Sit down, everybody, here are the chairs."

The whole family sits down. Each one is sitting on the edge of his chair, afraid to touch anything on the table. A terrible silence reigns in the big room. You can hear the candles guttering, everything swims in front of our eyes, and our hearts are heavy. We are hungry, but nobody feels like eating. Our appetites have been taken away as if by magic.

"Why is everybody so quiet? Speak! Let's hear you tell us something," says Uncle Hertz, and he coughs his little cough, shrugs his shoulders, tosses his head and pouts with his lips.

The family is silent. No one dares to utter a word at Uncle Hertz's table. The men smile stupidly as though they would like to speak and don't know what to say. The women exchange frightened glances. We youngsters burn as if in a fever. Miriam Reizel looks over at Hannah Rachel and Hannah Rachel looks back at Miriam Reizel, as though they had never seen each other before. My brother Moses Abraham looks out at the world with a pale scared face. Nobody, nobody dares utter a word at Uncle Hertz's table. Only one person feels at home here, as he does everywhere, and at all times. That is Miriam Reizel's young man, the bookkeeper. He pulls out his huge, starched and strongly perfumed handkerchief from his back pocket, blows his nose with relish, and says, "Did anybody ever see such deep mud at this time of year? I thought sure my galoshes would be filled up."

"Who is this young man?" asks Uncle Hertz, lifting up his silver-rimmed spectacles and giving his little cough.

"He is—my Miriam Reizel's—betrothed," says my father in a low voice like a man confessing to a murder. All of us sit as though turned to stone. And Miriam Reizel, poor Miriam Reizel—her face flames like a straw roof on fire.

Uncle Hertz looks the family over once more with his fierce gray eyes, offers us another cough and a shrug, another toss of his head and pout of his lips and says, "Well, why don't you go and wash? Go on and wash your hands, the water is right here."

After we had washed our hands and said the proper prayer over the little ceremony, we sat down around the table and waited for Uncle Hertz to say grace and to cut the huge *Purim* loaf. We were getting hungry now and would have liked to start eating, but just as if to spite us Uncle Hertz took his time over the grace and the cutting up of the huge ox, prolonging the ceremony and drawing it out as though he were a rabbi in front of his congregation. At last we saw the ox slaughtered and pieces of the loaf were passed to us, but before we had swallowed the first bite Uncle Hertz looked us over with his fierce gray eyes and said, "Well, why don't you sing? Sing somebody. Let's hear a tune in honor of the Feast. The whole world is celebrating today."

The family began exchanging glances among themselves, whispering and arguing and nudging each other. "You sing." "No, you sing." "Why should I? Why not you?" This went on for some time until one of the relations, my young cousin Abraham, Uncle Itzy's son, burst into song. He was a beardless youth with a squeaky voice and blinking eyes and he fancied himself as a singer. What it was that my cousin Abraham wanted to sing, I don't know. He started in his high squeaky voice on a falsetto note that broke in the middle, and the tune was so mournful and the look on his face was so tragic and so comic at once that you had to be God himself or one of His angels to keep from laughing out loud. And especially since right opposite me sat all the boys making faces.

The first burst of laughter came from me, and it was I who caught the first slap from my mother. But the slap did not cool me off. It brought a burst of laughter from the other children, and from me as well. This burst of laughter brought another slap and the slap brought fresh laughter and the laughter another slap and this went on until I was led out of the dining room into the kitchen and from the kitchen outdoors, and then I was brought home, beaten black and blue and drowning in tears.

That night I cursed my own bones and I cursed *Purim* and the *Purim* Feast and my cousin Abraham and more than anyone else I cursed Uncle Hertz, may he forgive me, for he has long since passed on to his reward. On his grave stands a tombstone, the most imposing tombstone in the whole cemetery, and on it in gold letters are engraved the virtues in which he excelled during his life: "Here lies an honest man, kind-hearted, lovable, generous, charitable, good-tempered, devoted and faithful." And so on and so on. . . . "May he rest in peace."

From Passover to Succos

or

THE CHESS PLAYER'S STORY

IT WAS late one winter's night—long past midnight. The guests had finished a late supper and the remains on the table bore witness to the fact that they had done well by themselves. The green card tables were covered with chalk marks and scattered piles of cards from which aces and kings peeped out in profusion as though to say, "Now we are here." The guests would have loved nothing better than to sit down to a game of preference or whist, but somehow it didn't seem proper. It was much too late. So they just sat around, smoked, drank black coffee, and gossiped. The conversation was dying out when someone threw in a word about chess. Another picked it up, then another, and another. It was plain that they were trying to draw out a certain ardent chess player by the name of Rubinstein.

Rubinstein was a rabid chess fiend. He was willing to travel ten miles on foot, to go without food or drink or sleep for a game of chess. It was a passion with him. Many stories made the rounds about his chess playing. It was said: 1. That he played chess with himself all night long. 2. That he had divorced his wife three times already because of chess. 3. That he had once disappeared for three years because of a chess game. In a word, wherever you found Rubinstein, there you found chess. And wherever there was chess, there was Rubinstein.

And Rubinstein loved to talk about chess as a confirmed drunkard loves to talk about liquor.

When you looked at Rubinstein, you were struck first of all by his enormous forehead—it was high and broad, and rounded like a bay window. His eyes also were enormous. They were round and black, but without expression, like two lumps of coal. He was thin and bony in build, but he had a voice like a bell, deep and sonorous. When Rubinstein was among a group of people you heard only Rubinstein and no one else.

When he heard the guests mention chess, Rubinstein wrinkled his already deeply wrinkled forehead, squinted with one eye at the coffee he was drinking as though to determine whether it smelled of soap or of dishwater, and spoke to everyone in general and to no one in particular. His voice rang out like a cathedral bell. "Ladies and gentlemen! If you want to hear a story about a chess player, sit down, all of you, right here near me, and I will tell you a story that happened long ago."

"A story about a chess player? A story of long ago?" The hostess who had been afraid that the gathering was about to break up caught up his words eagerly. "Wonderful! Excellent! Tell Felitchka to shut the piano, and will you please lock the doors and bring in two-three more chairs? Sit down, everybody, please sit down. Mr. Rubinstein is going to tell us a story about a chess player, a story of long ago."

Rubinstein examined the cigar his host had just handed him, from all sides, as though to determine how much it had cost, then he made a grimace and furrowed his enormous brow as though to say, "Maybe it looks like a cigar, but it tastes more like a broom." And he began his story:

"I don't have to explain to you that I am a devoted chess player, ladies and gentlemen, and that our whole family are chess players by nature. The name of Rubinstein is known all over the world. In fact, I would like to have you show me a Rubinstein who is *not* a chess player."

"Why, I know a fellow named Rubinstein who is an insurance salesman. He comes in to see me every week. Aside from life insurance, he knows absolutelv nothing. A regular dolt."

This remark was thrown in by one of the guests, a young man with a narrow, pointed head, and gold-rimmed glasses, who considered himself quite a wit. But Rubinstein remained calm. He looked the young man over with his coal-black frigid glance and said in his deep sonorous voice, "He can't be one of our Rubinsteins. A true Rubinstein has to be a chess player. That is as natural as it is natural for a buffoon to crack jokes. My grandfather, Rubin Rubinstein, was a true Rubinstein, for he was, ladies and gentlemen, a born chess player. The world could turn upside down and he wouldn't notice it when he was in the middle of a chess game. People came to play chess with him from all over the world—noblemen, counts, princes. By trade he was only a watchmaker, a poor workingman, but a real craftsman, an artist at his trade. But since the only thing that really mattered in his life was chess, he had difficulty in making a living, and earned barely enough to feed his family.

"And it came to pass, ladies and gentlemen, that one day there rode up to my grandfather's hut a splendid equipage drawn by two pairs of fiery steeds, and a nobleman leaped out of this equipage followed by two men-servants in livery. The nobleman was covered with medals and orders from head to foot, like royalty. He walked into the hut and asked, 'Where is the Jew, Rubin Rubinstein?' At first my grandfather was a little frightened, but he recovered quickly and spoke up, 'I am the Jew, Rubin Rubinstein. How can I be of service to you, your Highness?' The nobleman was pleased with this answer and said to my grandfather, 'If you are the Jew, Rubin Rubinstein, then I am very happy to know you. Have the samovar put on to boil, and bring out your chessboard. I'll play you a game. I've heard it said that you are a very fine chess player and that so far no one has ever checkmated you.'

"Saying this the nobleman sat down (apparently he was a lover of chess) and began playing with my grandfather. They played on and on, one game after another, one game after another. Meanwhile the samovar boiled and tea was served in proper style, on a large tray with preserves and pastries of all sorts. My grandmother saw to that, though she hadn't a *groschen* in her purse. . . .

"Meanwhile a crowd had gathered around the carriage outside my grandfather's door. Everyone was curious to know who it was that had come to see Rubin the Watchmaker. All kinds of rumors flew around the village. It was rumored that the nobleman had come from the capital of the province to carry out an investigation—something about counterfeit money—that it was the work of an informer, a plot of some sort that had been cooked up against Rubinstein. No one dared to walk in and see for himself what was going on. For who would have dreamed that the nobleman and my grandfather were only playing chess?

"And what shall I tell you, ladies and gentlemen? Though the nobleman was a good chess player, a very good chess player indeed, he was checkmated by my grandfather over and over again, and the more he played the more excited he became, and the more excited he became the worse he played. As for my grandfather, do you think he as much as winked an eyelash? Not he. He might as well have been playing with—I don't know whom—for all the emotion he showed. The nobleman must have been pretty much put out by all this. No one likes to be beaten, and to be beaten by whom? By a Jew! But what could he say, when the other was obviously the better player? Ability cannot be denied. And besides, I will have you know, ladies and gentlemen, that a real chess player is more interested in playing the game than in winning or losing. To a real chess player the opponent is nothing, only the game itself counts. I don't know if you will understand this or not."

"We can't swim either, but we understand what swimming is," broke in the witty fellow with the gold-rimmed glasses. Rubinstein the chess player measured him with his chilly glance and said, "Yes, we can see that you know all about swimming." He took a puff of his cigar and went on:

"And since everything in this world must come to an end, ladies and gentlemen, their chess game came to an end too. The nobleman arose, buttoned up the gold buttons on his coat, extended two fingers to my grandfather, and said, 'Listen to me, Rubin Rubinstein, you have beaten me, and I concede that you are the finest chess player not only in my province, but in the whole country, and perhaps in the whole world. I consider myself fortunate to have had the honor and the pleasure of playing with the finest chess player in the whole world. Rest assured that your name will become even more famous than it has been. I shall convey this to the king's ministers. I shall report it in Court.'

"When he heard him mention the king's ministers and reports to the Court, my grandfather asked, 'And who are you, your Highness?'

"The nobleman burst out laughing, puffed out his beribboned and bemedaled chest and said to my grandfather, 'I am the Governor of the Province.'

"My grandfather's heart sank at this. If he had only known with whom he was playing he might have played differently. But it was too late. What was done couldn't be undone. The Governor made his farewells in the friendliest possible manner, went out to his carriage, got in, and rode off.

"It was then that the whole village came flocking around my grandfather wanting to know who the nobleman had been. When they found out that it was the Governor himself, they went on to ask, 'And what did the Governor want with you?' When my grandfather informed them that the Governor had come for a game of chess they spat three times to ward off the evil eye, and each one went on his way. They talked about the affair and talked about it among themselves, but in time it was forgotten. My grandfather forgot about it also. His head was filled with new chess problems and incidentally with the lesser problem of making a living.

"And it came to pass, ladies and gentlemen, a long time after, how long I do not know myself—I only know that it was Passover Eve and my grandfather had nothing with which to celebrate the holiday, not even a piece of *matzo*. He had a houseful of children and this one needed a shirt, that one a pair of shoes. Things were bad. My grandfather, poor soul, was sitting doubled up, a magnifying glass screwed into his eyes, tinkering with a watch that had stopped running and refused to start again, and thinking to himself, 'From whence shall come my help?'

"Suddenly the door opened and in walked two gendarmes and made straight for my grandfather. '*Pazhaluista*,' they said to him, 'If you please.' A thought flashed through my grandfather's head (my grandfather was a man given to strange thoughts), 'Perhaps they have come from the Governor.' Who could tell? Maybe the Governor wanted to reward him, make him wealthy? Hadn't it happened before that through some chance happening, through some little incident, a nobleman had taken a poor Jew and showered him with gold, and endowed his children and his children's children forever and ever?

But it turned out, ladies and gentlemen, to be nothing of the sort. They were only asking him to be so kind as to pick himself up and set out at once, for—guess where—Petersburg! Why, they themselves didn't know. They had just received a paper from Petersburg on which was written: '*Niemedlannia dostavit yevreya Rubina Rubinsteina v Sankt Peterburg.*' This meant that they must this instant deliver the Jew Rubin Rubinstein to St. Petersburg. There must be a reason for this. 'Confess, fellow, what have you done?' My grandfather swore that he was innocent, in all his life he hadn't as much as hurt a fly on the wall. The whole town could vouch for him. They paid no attention to him, but ordered him to come along with them and join the convoy. The order had said to *deliver* the Jew Rubinstein, and what else could that mean except to bring him by convoy and in chains? And *this instant.* Which meant the quicker the better.

"Without wasting any more time, ladies and gentlemen, on unnecessary ceremonies, they took my grandfather, bound chains around his hands and feet, and led him away in a convoy with all the thieves and criminals. And what it meant in those days to 'go by convoy,' I don't have to explain to you. You know yourselves that an ordinary person who was led by convoy seldom reached his destination. There were no trains, no highways. People fell like flies by the roadside. More than half of them died on the way and the rest arrived worn out, sick, and crippled for life.

"But as luck would have it, my grandfather was of the same physical make-up as I am, thin and bony, but with a strong constitution. Besides he was a thinking man, a man with a philosophy of his own. 'A man,' he said, 'dies once, not twice, and if it is fated that he should continue to live, no one can take his life away.' Why did he speak thus of life and death? For it was apparent that this smacked of exile, of Siberia, or maybe even worse. He not only bade his wife and children and the whole village good-bye, he asked for the book of the dying and the dead, and wanted to make his last confession. The whole town turned out to see him off, as though it were his funeral. They mourned for him already as though he were dead, and tears poured like a deluge. . . .

"To describe to you, ladies and gentlemen, what my grandfather went through on his journey, I would have to spend not one night with you, but three nights in a row. And that would be a pity. The time could be much better spent in playing chess. Briefly I can tell you that the journey lasted the whole summer, from Passover to *Succos*. The convoy, ladies and gentlemen, was divided into stations, and at each station the prisoners had to wait a week, or two weeks, or sometimes longer, until new groups of thieves and brigands were assembled. Then they were driven further.

"And when finally after many trials and tribulations they arrived in the great and glorious city of St. Petersburg, do you think that they were through with him? If you think so, you are greatly mistaken. For here at the end of the journey they took my grandfather and locked him up in a stone cell, a tiny dark room in which he could neither sit nor lie, nor move nor even stand upright. . . ."

"Just the place for a game of chess!" broke in the witty young man with the gold-rimmed glasses.

"Or for telling rotten jokes," added Rubinstein the chess player, and went on with his story.

"Here in this stone cell my grandfather prepared himself in earnest for death. He recited the last prayer, beheld the Angel of Death in front of his eyes, and felt his soul leaving his body before sentence could even be passed on him. And to tell the truth, he now wished for death to come. He had only one flicker of hope left. . . . He was certain that his townspeople would intercede for him. There would be mediators, people of good will who would use their influence to set him free. They would go to the various officials, offer bribes if necessary, do everything in order to deliver an innocent man who had been the victim of an ugly frame-up.

"And my grandfather was not wrong, ladies and gentlemen. From the day he had been led away, the town had busied itself about his case. The townspeople consulted lawyers, sought influence in high places, gave money wherever they could. But nothing helped.

"Their money was accepted, but no promises were made. It was impossible, said the officials, to do anything for my grandfather, and here is how they explained it. It is easy to buy the freedom of a thief or a common criminal. Why so? For the simple reason that you knew the thief had stolen a couple of horses, or the criminal had set fire to a house. But a fellow like this Rubinstein who had neither stolen horses nor set anything on fire—who could tell what sort of offender he was? Maybe he was even a 'political'? In those days a 'political' was worse than a murderer who had slaughtered a whole province. To intercede for a 'political' was very dangerous. The very word '*politichesky*' couldn't be spoken out loud, only whispered in the dark. But what did Rubin Rubinstein the Watchmaker have to do with politics? Still, who could tell? Wasn't he a brainy man, a chess player, a philosopher?

"But, ladies and gentlemen, as I have said before, all things come to an end. The day arrived when the doors of the prison opened, and two gendarmes, armed from head to foot, came in, dragged my grandfather out, more dead than alive, put him into a carriage and drove off. Where to? He didn't ask. To the judgment? Let it be to the judgment. To the scaffold? Let it be to the scaffold. Anything to put an end to this. He saw himself standing in front of the Court. 'Rubin Rubinstein,' they said to him. 'Confess your guilt.' And he answered, 'I confess that I am a Jew and a poor watchmaker, and I live by the work of my hands. I have never stolen anything, never swindled anyone, nor insulted anyone. God is my witness. If you want to torture me, do so, but first take away my immortal soul. It is in your hands.'

"As my grandfather argued with the Court in this vein, the carriage drove up to a large building and my grandfather was told to get out. He obeyed. They took him into a room, then into a corridor, then into another room, and told him to take off all his clothes down to his undershirt. He couldn't figure out what this meant, but when an armed gendarme tells you to take off your clothes, you can't very well be impolite and disobey. Then they told him—and I wish to beg your pardon a thousand times for mentioning such a thing, ladies and gentlemen—to take off his undershirt, too. He took off his undershirt, too. Then they took him stark naked into a bathroom and proceeded to give him a bath. And what a bath. They scrubbed him and rubbed him, they scoured him and polished him, rinsed him and dried him. Then they let him get dressed, took him out once more, and drove off. They drove and they drove and they drove. And my grandfather thought to himself, 'Dear Lord, what will become of me now?' He tried to recall all the stories he had ever read of the Spanish Inquisition and he couldn't recall ever having read of a single instance where a condemned man was given a bath before being led to the gallows.

"As he was musing thus, ladies and gentlemen, the carriage drove up to a courtyard surrounded by an iron picket fence; each picket was tipped with gold and on each tip was an eagle. He was led through rows of generals decorated with golden epaulettes and with medals on their chests. He was told that he must not be frightened, he was going to be presented to the King. He was instructed to look straight in front of him, not to say anything unnecessary, not to complain about anything, and only answer the questions put to him with 'yes' or 'no.'

"Before my grandfather could get his bearings he found himself in a magnificent hall hung with paintings and filled with golden furniture. Opposite him stood a tall man with sideburns. The man with the sideburns (it was Tzar Nicholas I) looked my grandfather over and the following conversation took place between them:

The King: What is your name?

Grandfather Rubinstein: Rubin Sholemov Rubinstein.

The King: How old are you?

Grandfather Rubinstein: Fifty-seven.

The King: Where did you learn to play chess?

Grandfather Rubinstein: The knowledge is passed on in my family from father to son.

The King: They tell me that you are the foremost chess player in my kingdom.

"To this my grandfather wanted to say, 'Would that I were not the foremost chess player in your kingdom.' Then the King would surely have asked, 'Why do you say this?' Then my grandfather would have let him know that this was no way to treat an eminent chess player with whom the King wanted to have an audience. Grandfather Rubinstein would have known what to tell the Tzar, you may be sure of that!

"But at this moment the King waved his hand, the generals leaped forward, and the same gendarmes who had brought him in led my grandfather out into the courtyard. There they set him free and ordered him to leave the city instantly, for a Jew had no right to be there. Don't ask how he finally got home. It's enough that he got there alive. He had left home before Passover and he arrived just in time to celebrate *Succos*. Ladies and gentlemen, I have finished. . . ."

Get Thee Out

GREETINGS to you, Mr. Sholom Aleichem, heartiest greetings. I've been expecting you for a long time and wondering why I didn't see you any more. I kept asking, *"Where are you?"* as God once asked of Adam, and I was told that you have been traveling all over the world, visiting faraway countries—*"the one hundred and twenty-seven provinces of Ahasheurus,"* as we say in the *Megilah*.

But you are looking at me strangely. You seem to be hesitating and wondering, "Is it he, or isn't it he?" It is he, Mr. Sholom Aleichem, it is he, your old friend Tevye in person. Tevye the Dairyman, the very same as before, but not a dairyman any longer. Just an ordinary, everyday Jew, and greatly aged, as you can see. And yet I am not so old in years. As we say in the *Hagadah: "I look like a man of seventy.* —I am still far from seventy." Then why should my hair be so white? Believe me, dear friend, it's not from joy. My own sorrows are partly to blame and partly the sorrows of all Israel. For these are difficult times for us Jews—hard, bitter times to live in.

But that isn't what's troubling you, I can see. The shoe pinches on the other foot. You must have remembered that I told you good-bye once, as I was about to leave for Palestine. Now you are thinking, "Here is Tevye, just back from the Holy Land," and you are eager to know what's going on in Palestine—you want to hear about my visit to Mother Rachel's Tomb, to the Cave of Machpelah, and the other holy places. Wait, I will set your mind at rest; I will tell you everything, if you have the time and would like to hear a strange and curious tale. Then listen carefully, as it is written: *"Hear ye!"* And when you have heard me out, you yourself will admit that man is nothing but a fool and that we have a mighty God who rules the Universe.

Well, what portion of the Bible are *you* studying this week in the Synagogue? *Vaikro?* The first portion of Leviticus? I am on a different portion entirely—on *Lech-lecho* or *Get thee out.* I have been told, *"Get thee out*—get a move on you, Tevye—*out of thy country*—leave your own land—*and from thy father's house*—the village where you were born and spent all the years of your life—*to the land which I will show thee*—wherever your two eyes lead you." That's the lesson I am on now. And when was I given this lesson to study? Now that I am old and feeble and all alone in the world, as we say on *Rosh Hashono: "Do not cast me off in my old age."*

But I am getting ahead of my story. I haven't told you about the Holy Land yet. What should I tell you, dear friend? It is indeed a *"land flowing with milk and honey,"* as the Bible tells us. The only trouble is that the Holy Land is over there and I am still here—*"outside of the Promised Land."* He who wrote the *Megilah* or Book of Esther must have had Tevye in mind when he had Esther say, *"If I perish, I perish."* I have always been a *shlimazl* and a *shlimazl* I will die. There I stood, as you remember, with one foot practically in the Holy Land. All I had to do was to buy a ticket, get on a ship, and I'm off. But that isn't the way God deals with Tevye. He had something different in store for me. Wait and you will hear.

You may remember my oldest son-in-law Motel Kamzoil the tailor from Anatevka. Well, our Motel goes to sleep one night in the best of health, and never gets up. Though I shouldn't have said he was in the *best* of health. How could he be, a poor workingman, alas, sitting day and night *"absorbed in study and worship of God,"* meaning that he sat in a dark cellar day and night bent over a needle and thread, patching trousers. He did this so long that he got the coughing sickness, and he coughed and coughed until he coughed out his last piece of lung. Doctors couldn't help him, medicines didn't do any good, nor goats' milk nor honey and chocolate. . . . He was a fine boy, the salt of the earth; it's true, he had no learning, but he was an honest fellow, unassuming, and without any false pretensions. He loved my daughter with all his heart, sacrificed himself for the children—and he thought the world of me!

And so we conclude the text with: *"Moses passed away."* In other words, Motel died, and he left me with a millstone around my neck. Who could begin to think about the Holy Land now? I had a Holy Land right here at home. How could I leave my daughter, a widow with small children, and without any means of support? Though if you stop to think, what could I do for her, an old man like me, a sack full of holes? I couldn't bring her husband back to life or return the children's father to them. And besides, I am only human myself. I would like to rest my bones in my old age, take life easy, find out what it feels like to be a human being. I've done enough hustling and bustling in my lifetime. Enough striving after the things of this world. It's time to begin thinking about the next world. I had gotten rid of most of my goods and chattels, sold my cows and let my horse go quite some time ago. And all of a sudden in my old age I have to become a protector of orphans, and provide for a family of small children. But that isn't all. Wait. More is coming. For when troubles descend on Tevye, they never come singly. The first one always brings others trailing after it. For instance, once when a cow of mine died, didn't another one lie down and die the very next day? That's how God created the world and that's how it will remain. There is no help for it.

Do you remember the story of my youngest daughter Beilke and her great good fortune? How she caught the biggest fish in the pond, the contractor Padhatzur who had made a fortune in the war and was looking for a beautiful young bride—how he sent Ephraim the Matchmaker to me, how he met my daughter and fell in love with her, how he begged for her on his knees, threatened to kill himself if he couldn't have her, how he was ready to take her just as she was, without any dowry, and showered her with gifts from head to foot, with gold and diamonds and jewels? It sounds like a fairy tale, doesn't it? The wealthy prince, the poor maiden, the great palace. But what was the end of this beautiful tale? The end was a sorry one. May God have pity on us all! For if God wills it, the wheel of fortune can turn backwards and then everything begins to fall buttered side down as we say in Hallel: *"Who raiseth up the poor out of the dust."* And before you can turn around—Crash! *"That looketh down low upon heaven and upon the earth*—everything is shattered into little pieces."

Thus God likes to play with us human beings. That's how he played with Tevye many times, raising him up, and casting him down, like Jacob ascending and descending the ladder. And that is what happened to Padhatzur. You remember his great riches, his airs and pretensions, the splendor of his mansion in Yehupetz with its dozen servants and thousand clocks and mirrors. What do you think was the outcome of all this? The outcome was that he not only lost everything, and had to sell all his clocks and mirrors and his wife's jewels, but went bankrupt in the bargain, and made such a sorry mess of everything that he had to flee the country and become a fugitive. . . . He went to where the holy Sabbath goes. In other words, he ran off to America. That's where all the unhappy souls go, and that's where they went.

They had a hard time of it in America at first. They used up what little cash they had brought with them, and when there was nothing more to chew on, they had to go to work, both he and she, doing all kinds of back-breaking labor, like our ancestors in Egypt. Now, she writes me, they are doing quite well, God be thanked. Both of them are working in a stocking factory, and they manage to "scrape up a living," as they say in America. Here we call it being one jump ahead of the poorhouse. It's lucky for them, she tells me, that there are just the two of them—they have neither chick nor child. *"That too is for the best."*

And now, I ask you, doesn't he deserve to be cursed with the deadliest curses, I mean Ephraim the Matchmaker, for arranging this happy match? Would she have been any worse off if she had married an honest workingman the way Tzeitl did, or a teacher, like Hodel? You might argue that their luck didn't hold out either, that one was left a young widow, and the other had to go into exile with her husband? But these things are in God's hands. Man cannot provide against everything. If you want to know the truth, the only wise one among us was my wife Golde. She looked about her in good time and decided to leave this miserable world forever. For tell me yourself, rather than to suffer the *"pain of bringing up children,"* the way I have suffered, isn't it better to lie in the earth and be eaten by worms? But how is it said: *"Perforce thou must live.*—Man doesn't take his own life, and if he does, he gets rapped on the knuckles for it." But in the meanwhile we have strayed off the path. *"Let us return to our original subject."*

Where were we? At section *Lech-lecho* or *Get thee out*. But before we go on with section *Lech-lecho* I shall ask you to stop with me for a moment at section *Balak*. It has always been a custom since the world began to study *Lech-lecho* or *Get thee out* first, and *Balak* or the lesson of revenge later, but with me the custom was reversed and I was taught the lesson of *Balak* first and *Lech-lecho* afterward. And I was drilled in *Balak* so thoroughly that I want you to hear about it. The lesson may come in handy some day.

This happened some time ago, right after the war, during the troubles over the Constitution when we were undergoing *"salvations and consolations,"* that is, when reprisals were being carried out against Jews. The pogroms began in the big cities, then spread to the small towns and villages, but they didn't reach me, and I was sure that they never would reach me. Why? Simply for this reason: that I had lived in the village for so many years and had always been on such friendly terms with the peasants. I had become a *"Friend of the Soul and Father of Mercy"* to them—"Brother Tevel" was their best friend. Did they want advice? It was, "do as brother Tevel says." Did one of them need a remedy for fever? It was, "Go to Tevel." A special favor? Also to Tevel. Tell me, why should I worry about pogroms and such nonsense when the peasants themselves had assured me many times that I had nothing to be afraid of? They would never permit such a thing, they told me. *"But it came to pass."*—Listen to my story.

I arrived home from Boiberik one evening. I was still in my prime then—how do you say it?—in high feather. I was still Tevye the Dairyman who sold milk and cheese and butter. I unhitched my horse, threw him some oats and hay and before I had time to wash my hands and say a prayer before eating, I take a look outside and see the yard is full of peasants. The whole village has turned out to see me, from the Mayor, Ivan Poperilo, down to Trochin the Shepherd, and all of them looking stiff and strange in their holiday clothes. My heart turned over at the sight. What holiday was this? Or had they come like Balaam to curse me? But at once I thought, "Shame on you, Tevye, to be so suspicious of these people after all these years you have lived among them as a friend." And I went outside and greeted them warmly, "Welcome, friends, what have you come for? And what good news do you bring?" Then Ivan Poperilo the Mayor stepped forward and said, right out, without any apologies, "We came here, Tevel, because we want to beat you up."

What do you think of such talk? Tactful, wasn't it? It's the same as speaking of a blind man as *sagi nohor* or having too much light. You can imagine how I felt when I heard it. But to show my feelings? Never. That isn't Tevye's way. *"Mazl-tov,"* I said, "why did you get around to it at this late date? In other places they've almost forgotten all about it." Then Ivan said very earnestly, "It's like this, Tevel, all this time we've been trying to decide whether to beat you up or not. Everywhere else your people are being massacred, then why should we let you go? So the Village Council decided to punish you too. But we haven't decided what to do to you. We don't know whether to break a few of your windowpanes and rip your featherbeds, or to set fire to your house and barn and entire homestead."

When I heard this, my spirits really sank low. I looked at my guests standing there, leaning on their sticks and whispering among themselves. They looked as though they really meant business. "If so," I said to myself, "it's as David said in the psalm, *'For the waters are come in even into the soul.'* You are in bad trouble, Tevye. *'Do not give Satan an opening.*—You cannot trifle with the Angel of Death.' Something has to be done."

Well, why should I spin out the story any longer? A miracle took place. God sent me courage and I spoke up boldly. "Listen to me, gentlemen. Hear me out, dear friends. Since the Village Council has decreed that I must be punished, so be it. You know best what you do, and perhaps Tevye has merited such treatment at your hands.

But do you know, my friends, that there is a Power even higher than your Village Council? Do you know that there is a God in Heaven? I am not speaking now of *your* God or *my* God, I am speaking of the God who rules over all of us, who looks down from Heaven and sees all the vileness that goes on below. It may be that He has singled me out to be punished through you, my best friends. And it may be just the opposite, that He doesn't want Tevye to be hurt under any circumstances. Who is there among us who knows what God has decreed? Is there one among you who will undertake to find out?"

They must have seen by then that they couldn't get the best of Tevye in an argument. And so the Mayor, Ivan Poperilo, spoke up. "It's like this, Tevel, we have nothing against you yourself. It's true that you are a Jew, but you are not a bad person. But one thing has nothing to do with the other. You have to be punished. The Village Council has decided. We at least have to smash a few of your windowpanes. We don't dare not to. Suppose an official passed through the village and saw that your house hadn't been touched. We would surely have to suffer for it."

That is just what he said, as God is my witness. Now I ask you, Mr. Sholom Aleichem, you are a man who has traveled all over the world. Is Tevye right when he says that we have a great and merciful God?

Well, that's the end of section *Balak*. They came to curse and remained to bless. Now let us turn to section *Lech-lecho* or *Get thee out*. This lesson was taught to me not so long ago and in real earnest. This time fine speeches didn't help me, orations didn't avail me. This is exactly the way it happened. Let me tell it to you in detail, the way you like to have a story told. . . .

It was in the days of Mendel Beiliss, when Mendel Beiliss became our scapegoat and was made to suffer the punishments of the damned. I was sitting on my doorstep one day sunk in thought. It was the middle of summer. The sun was blazing and my head was splitting. "Lord, Lord," I thought, "what times these are! What is the world coming to? And where is God, the ancient God of Israel? Why is He silent? Wherefore does He permit such things to happen?" Wherefore and why and wherefore once more? And when you ask questions of

God you begin to ponder about the universe and go on asking: What is this world? And the next world? And why doesn't the Messiah come? Wouldn't it be clever of him to appear at this very moment riding on his white horse? That would be a master stroke! It seems to me that he has never been so badly needed by our people as now. I don't know about the rich Jews, the Brodskys in Yehupetz for instance, or the Rothschilds in Paris. It may be that they never even give him a thought. But we poor Jews of Kasrilevka and Mazapevka and Zolodoievka, and even of Yehupetz and Odessa, watch and wait and pray for him daily. Our eyes are strained from watching. He is our only hope. All we can do is hope and pray for this miracle—that the Messiah will come.

And while I am sitting there deep in such thoughts, I look up and see someone approaching, riding on a white horse. He comes riding up to my door, gets off, ties the horse to the post, and comes straight up to me. *"Zdrastoi,* Tevel," he says—"Greetings, Tevye." "Greetings to you, your honor," I answer him with a smile, though in my heart I am thinking, *"Haman approacheth.*—When you're waiting for the Messiah, the village constable comes riding." I stand up and say to him, "Welcome, your honor, what goes on in the world? And what good news do you bring?" And all this time I am quaking inside, waiting to hear what he has to say. But he takes his time. First he lights a cigarette, then he blows out the smoke, spits on the ground, and at last he speaks up. "How much time do you need, Tevel," he says, "to sell your house and all your household goods?"

I look at him in astonishment. "Why should I sell my house? In whose way is it?"

"It isn't in anybody's way," he says, "but I came to tell you that you will have to leave the village."

"Is that all?" I asked. "And how did I come to deserve such an honor?"

"I can't tell you," he says, "I am not the one who's sending you away. It's the provincial government."

"And what has the government against me?"

"Against you? Nothing. You aren't the only one. Your people are being driven out of all the villages, out of Zolodoievka and Rabilevka, and Kostolomevka, and all the others. Even Anatevka, which up to now has been a town, has become a village and your people are being driven from there too."

"Even Lazer-Wolf the Butcher?" I asked. "And Naphtali-Gershon the Lame, and the *Shochet* of Anatevka? And the Rabbi?

"Everybody, everybody." And he made a motion with his hand as though he were cutting with a scythe. I felt a little easier at this. How do we say it? *"The troubles of the many are a half-consolation."* But anger at this injustice still burned inside of me. I said to him, "Is your honor aware of the fact that I have lived in this village much longer than you have? Do you know that in this corner of the world lived my father before me, and my grandfather and grandmother before him?" And I began naming all the different members of my family, telling him where each one had lived and where each one died. The Constable heard me out, and when I had finished he said, "You are a clever Jew and you certainly know how to talk, but what good are these tales of your grandfather and grandmother to me? Let them enjoy their rest in Paradise. And you, Tevel, pack up your things and go, go to Berdichev."

That made me good and angry. It wasn't enough that you brought me this glad tidings, you Esau, you have to poke fun at me besides? "Pack up and go, go to Berdichev," he tells me. I couldn't let that pass. I had to tell him a thing or two. "Your honor," I said, "in all the years you have been Constable here, have you ever heard the villagers complaining of Tevye, has anyone ever accused Tevye of stealing from him, or robbing him, or cheating him in any way? Ask any of the peasants if I didn't live alongside them like the best of neighbors? How many times did I come to you yourself, your excellency, to plead in their behalf, to ask you not to ill-treat them?"

I could see that this was not to his taste. He got up, crushed his cigarette between his fingers, threw it away, and said to me, "I have no time to waste on idle chatter. I received a paper and that's all I know. Here, sign right here. They give you three days to sell your household goods and get out of the village."

When I heard this, I said, "You give me three days to get out, do you? For this may you live three years longer *'in honor and in riches.'*

May the Almighty repay you many times over for the good news you brought me today." And I went on, laying it on thick, as only Tevye can do. After all, I thought to myself, what did I have to lose? If I had been twenty years younger and if my Golde had still been alive, if I were the same Tevye the Dairyman as in ancient days, I would have fought to the last drop for my rights. But *"what are we and what is our life?"* What am I today? Only half of my former self, a broken reed, a shattered vessel. "Ah, dear God, our Father," I thought, "why do You always have to pick on Tevye to do Thy will? Why don't You make sport of someone else for a change? A Brodsky, for instance, or a Rothschild? Why don't You expound to them the lesson *Lech-lecho*—Get thee out? It seems to me that it would do them more good than me. In the first place they would find out what it means to be a Jew. In the second place, they would learn that we have a great and mighty God."

But this is all empty talk. You don't argue with God, you don't give Him advice on how to run the world. When He says, *"Mine is the heaven and mine is the earth,"* it means that He is the master and we have to obey Him.

I went into the house and said to my daughter, "Tzeitl," I said, "we are going away. We are moving to town. We've lived in the country long enough. *'He who changes his place changes his luck.'* Start packing right away, get together the pillows and featherbeds, the samovar and the rest. . . . I am going out, to see about selling the house. An order came for us to get out of here in three days and not leave a trace behind us."

When she heard this, my daughter burst into tears. The children took one look at her and burst out crying too. What shall I tell you? There was weeping and wailing and lamentation, just like on *Tishabov,* the day on which we mourn the destruction of the Temple. I lost my temper and began scolding. I let out all the bitterness that was in my heart to my daughter. "What have you got against me?" I said. "Why did you have to start blubbering all of a sudden like an old cantor at the first *Slichos?* What do you think I am—God's favorite son? Am I the only one chosen for this honor? Aren't other Jews being driven out of the villages too? You should have heard what the Constable had to say. Even your Anatevka which has been a town since the world began has, with God's help, become a village too, all for the sake of the few Jews who live there. Are we any worse off than all the others?"

That is how I tried to comfort her. But after all she is only a woman. She says to me, "Where will we turn, father? Where will we go looking for towns?" "You talk like a fool," I said to her. "When God appeared to our great-great-great-grandfather Abraham and said to him, 'Get thee out of this country,' did Abraham question Him? Did he ask, 'Where shall I turn?' God told him, 'Go unto the land which I will show thee.' Which means, '. . . into the four corners of the earth.' And we too will go wherever our eyes lead us, where all the other Jews are going. Whatever happens to all the children of Israel, that will happen to this son of Israel. And why should you consider yourself luckier than your sister Beilke who was once a millionairess? If 'scraping up a living' in America with her Padhatzur is good enough for her, this is good enough for you. Thank God that we at least have the means with which to go. We have a little saved up from before, a little from the sale of the cows, and I will get something from the house. A dot and a dot make a full pot. *'That too is for the best.'* And even if we had nothing at all, we would still be better off than Mendel Beiliss."

And so I persuaded her that we had to go. I gave her to understand that when the Constable brings you a notice to leave, you can't be hoggish and refuse to go. Then I went off to the village to dispose of my house. I went straight to Ivan Poperilo the Mayor because I knew that he'd had his eye on my house for a long time. I didn't give him any reasons or explanations, I am too smart for that. All I said was, "I want you to know, Ivan, my friend, that I am leaving the village." He asked me why. I told him that I was moving to town because I wanted to live among Jews. "I am not so young any more," I said. "Who knows—I might die suddenly." Says Ivan to me, "Why can't you die right here? Who is preventing you?" I thanked him kindly and said, "You'd better do the dying here, instead of me. I will go and die among my own people. I want you to buy my house and land. I wouldn't sell it to anyone else, but to you I will."

"How much do you want for your house?" he asked me. "How much will you give me?" I said. Again he asked, "How much do you want?" And I countered with, "How much will you give?" We bargained and dickered thus until at last we agreed on a price, and I took a substantial down payment from him then and there, so that he wouldn't change his mind. I am too smart for that. And that was how in one day I sold out all my belongings, turning everything into good money, and went off to hire a wagon to move the few odds and ends that were left. And now something else happened to me, something that can happen only to Tevye. Be patient a little longer and I will tell it to you in a few words.

Well, I arrived at home, and found not a house, but a ruin—the walls bare, stripped of everything, almost weeping in their nakedness. The floor was piled with bundles and bundles and bundles. On the empty hearth sat the cat, looking as lonely and forsaken as an orphan. My heart was squeezed tight and tears stood in my eyes. If I weren't ashamed before my daughter, I would have wept. After all, this was my homestead. This village was the nearest thing to a fatherland that I could ever have. Here I had grown up, here I had struggled all my days, and now all of a sudden in my old age, I am told, "Get thee out." Say what you will, it's a heartache. But Tevye is not a weakling. I restrained myself and called out in a cheerful voice, "Tzeitl, where are you, come here." And Tzeitl came out of the other room, her eyes red and her nose swollen with weeping. "Aha," I thought, "my daughter has started wailing again like an old woman on the Day of Atonement. That's women for you—crying at the least excuse. Tears must come cheap to them." "Fool," I told her, "why are you crying again? Aren't you being silly? Just stop and consider the difference between you and Mendel Beiliss." But she wouldn't listen to me. "Father," she said, "you don't know why I'm crying."

"I know very well why you're crying," I told her. "Why shouldn't I know? You are crying because you will miss your home. You were born in this house, this is where you grew up, and your heart aches at having to leave it. Believe me, if I were someone else and not

Tevye, I'd be kissing these bare walls myself and embracing these empty shelves. . . . I would be down on my knees on this earth. For I shall miss every particle of it as much as you. Foolish child! Look, do you see the cat sitting there like an orphan on the hearth? She is nothing but an animal, a dumb creature, and yet she too is to be pitied, left alone and forsaken without a master."

"I want to tell you that there is someone who is more to be pitied," said Tzeitl.

"For instance?" I asked.

"For instance, we are going away and leaving a human being behind us, alone and forsaken."

"What are you talking about?" I said to her. "What's all this gibberish? Which human being? Whom are we forsaking?"

"Father," she said, "I am not talking gibberish. I am speaking of Chava."

When she uttered that name it was just as if she had thrown a red-hot poker at me, or hit me over the head with a club. I began yelling at her, "Why bring Chava up all of a sudden? How many times have I told you that she is dead?"

Do you think she was taken aback by this outburst? Not in the least. Tevye's daughters are made of sterner stuff. "Father," she said, "don't be angry with me. Remember what you yourself told me many times, that it is written that one human being must have pity on another the way a father has pity on his child."

Did you ever hear anything like this before? I grew even more furious with her. "Don't speak to me of pity," I shouted. "Where was her pity when I lay like a dog in front of the priest while she was probably in the next room and no doubt heard every word? Where was her pity when her mother lay covered with black in this very room? Where was she then? And all the sleepless nights I spent? And the heartache I suffered and that I suffer to this day when I remember what she did to me and for whom she forsook me? Where is her pity for me?" My throat went dry, my heart began to hammer, and I couldn't speak any more.

Do you think that Tevye's daughter didn't find an answer to this too? "You yourself have said, father, that God forgives him who repents."

"You speak of repentance, do you? It's too late for that. The limb which has been torn from the tree must wither. The leaf which has fallen to the ground must rot. Don't say another word to me about it. *'Here ends the lesson for the great Sabbath before Passover.'* "

When she saw that she was getting nowhere with talk, and that Tevye was not the person to be won over with words, she fell on my neck and began kissing my hands and pleading with me, "May I suffer some evil, may I die here on the spot, if I let you cast her off as you cast her off that time in the forest when she came to plead with you and you turned your horse around and fled."

"What are you hanging around my neck for? What do you want from me? What have you got against me?" I cried.

But she wouldn't let me go. She clasped my hands in hers and went on, "May I meet with some misfortune, may I drop dead, if you don't forgive her, for she is your daughter the same as I am."

"Let me go. She is not my daughter. My daughter died long ago."

"No, father, she didn't die, and she is your daughter still. The moment she found out that we were being sent away she swore to herself that if we were driven out, she would go too. That's what she told me herself. Our fate is her fate, our exile is her exile. You have the proof right here. This bundle on the floor is hers," said Tzeitl, all in one breath the way we recite the names of the ten sons of Haman in the *Megilah,* and pointed to a bundle tied in a red kerchief. Then she opened the door to the next room and called out, "Chava."

And what shall I tell you, dear friend? There she stood in the doorway, Chava herself in the flesh, tall and beautiful, just as I remembered her, except that her face looked a little drawn and her eyes were somewhat clouded. . . . But she held her head up proudly and looked straight at me. I looked back at her, and then she stretched out both arms to me and said one word—"Father."

Forgive me if tears come to my eyes when I recall these things. But don't think that Tevye weakened and wept in front of his daughters. I have my pride to consider. But you understand that in my heart I felt differently. You are a father yourself and you know how you feel, when a child of yours, no matter how it has erred, looks into your eyes and says, "Father." But then again I remembered the trick she had played on me, running off with that peasant Fyedka Galagan. I remembered the priest, may his name and memory be blotted out, and poor Golde lying dead on the ground. . . . How can you forget such things? How can you forget?

And yet she was still my child. The same old saying came to me: *"A father has mercy on his children."* How could I be so heartless and drive her away when God Himself has said, *"I am a long-suffering God and slow to anger"*? And especially since she had repented and wanted to return to her father and to her God? Tell me yourself, Mr. Sholom Aleichem, you are a wise man who writes books and gives advice to the whole world. What should Tevye have done? Should he have embraced her and kissed her and said as we do on *Yom Kippur* at *Kol Nidre: "I have forgiven thee in accordance with thy prayers.*—Come to me, my child?" Or should I have turned my back on her as I did once before and said, "Get thee out. Go back where you came from"? Try to put yourself in my place and tell me truthfully what would you have done? And if you don't want to tell me right away, I will give you time to think it over. Meanwhile I must go—my grandchildren are waiting for me. And grandchildren, you must know, are a thousand times dearer and more precious than one's own children. *Children and grandchildren*—that's something to reckon with!

Farewell, my friend, and forgive me if I have talked too much. You will have something to write about now. And if God wills it, we shall meet again. For since they taught me the lesson—*Lech-lecho,* Get thee out—I have been wandering about constantly. I have never been able to say to myself, "Here, Tevye, you shall remain." Tevye asks no questions. When he is told to go, he goes. Today you and I meet here on this train, tomorrow we might see each other in Yehupetz, next year I might be swept along to Odessa or to Warsaw or maybe even to America. Unless the Almighty, the Ancient God of Israel, should look about him suddenly and say to us, "Do you know what, my children? I shall send the Messiah down to you." Wouldn't that be a clever trick? In the meanwhile, good-bye, go in good health, and give my greetings to all our friends and tell them not to worry. Our ancient God still lives!

The Passover Expropriation

KASRILEVKA has always been known to ape Odessa. But since the recent disturbances began, Kasrilevka hasn't deviated from Odessa by a hair's breadth. Is there a strike in Odessa? Then there is a strike in Kasrilevka. A Constitution in Odessa? Then there is a Constitution in Kasrilevka. A pogrom in Odessa? Then there is a pogrom in Kasrilevka. Once a certain wag broadcast the news that in Odessa people were beginning to cut off their noses. Right away the people of Kasrilevka began sharpening their knives. Luckily, in Kasrilevka itself, one person apes another, so that each one waited for the next person to cut off his nose first. And they are waiting to this day.

After such an introduction, you won't be surprised to hear that hardly a day passes that you don't read in the papers of some fresh catastrophe taking place in Kasrilevka. You read, for instance, of how a gang of hoodlums broke into a bakery and expropriated all the twists and *beigels*. Or of how a shoemaker who had just finished a pair of shoes—he had only to add the soles and heels—was attacked in broad daylight, told "to lift up his hands and bless the Lord" and the shoes were carried off! Or again of how a poor man was going from house to house begging—this took place on a Thursday—when he was held up in a dark side street, a pistol was stuck in front of his face, and he was cleaned out of everything he had on him. Or listen to the story a woman tells. . . . But a woman's tale is not to be trusted. Women have notoriously weak nerves, the times are unsettled, and she might have mistaken a stunted cow for a man. I don't want to be responsible for spreading idle tales.

Suffice it to say that a whole series of expropriations took place in Kasrilevka, one more terrible than the next. It got so that people trembled for their very lives. Everyone longed for the good old bygone days when a single police official, who took a bribe now and then, held the whole town in his grasp. They began to offer up prayers to God: "Have pity on us, Almighty God, permit us to go backwards, dear loving Father, renew our days as of old."

But this is still the introduction. The real story begins now.

Benjamin Lastechka is the richest man in Kasrilevka and the most important. The extent of his wealth—and of his importance—is hard to estimate. In the first place, he has rich relatives all over the world. These relatives, it is true, are not as rich as they once were. What can you expect in these times, with failures and bankruptcies taking place every day? The wonder is that people still manage to exist, and especially the people of Kasrilevka who are packed together like herring in a barrel, in one small spot, devouring each other alive. It is a lucky thing that there is an America which every year drains off almost twice as many people as are killed in pogroms or die of starvation.

And yet you see that in spite of all this, if God wills it, there is still a rich man left in Kasrilevka, a man by the name of Benjamin Lastechka, whom everyone envies because he doesn't have to ask help of anyone except his rich relatives. Asking help of rich relatives is not the easiest way in the world of earning one's bread, either, for the majority of rich relatives, if you will pardon my saying so, are notoriously hoggish by nature. And yet the fact remains that Benjamin Lastechka is still the richest man in Kasrilevka. When you need a favor, to whom do you go? To Benjamin Lastechka, of course. And Benjamin Lastechka listens to your troubles, helps out sometimes with a piece of advice, sometimes with a word of encouragement, and once in a while with a groan of sympathy. These are good too, for without them would it be any better? You'd still have the same pack of troubles.

THE PASSOVER EXPROPRIATION

What is the difference between a rich man of Kasrilevka and, let us say, a rich man of Yehupetz? The rich people of Yehupetz have such tender hearts that they can't bear to look on at the plight of a poor man. They keep their doors locked and a lackey stationed outside to turn away anyone who is not respectably dressed. And when summer comes, they rise up like swallows and fly off abroad. Just try and follow them. But let a Kasrilevka *nogid* attempt such a thing—he won't get far, I promise you. Whether he likes it or not, Benjamin Lastechka has the honor of being the foremost citizen in our community. In all matters of charity, he has to be the first. He has to be the first not only in giving a donation, but the first to pick up his walking stick and go from door to door collecting charity from the poor to give to the poor.

And especially when it comes to collecting "wheat tithes" or money for *matzos* for the poor before Passover. Then you should see Benjamin Lastechka. I doubt if the greatest welfare worker on earth laboring in the most important cause, has ever sweated as much as Benjamin Lastechka sweats those four weeks before Passover. He swears that between *Purim* and Passover he sleeps every night with his clothes on. We might as well take his word for it, for what does he get for his pains? You might say that he does it for glory. And why not? Everyone likes a little glory, even a king doesn't scorn it. That's only human nature.

The custom of collecting "wheat tithes" before Passover is a very old one. It is an old-fashioned form of philanthropy, and yet I don't think it's as terrible a custom as people nowadays try to make you believe. They tell you that philanthropy is the ruin of Society. I don't care to enter into a philosophical discussion on the subject. I only want to say that according to my lights there is a far worse custom than this—and that is that the rich people aren't willing to give. And a thousand times worse than that is the fact that these noble souls who refuse to give anything try to make you believe that it's a matter of "principle" with them. I advise you to run from such people. They are as dry as a dried fish, and as lonely as a cat. . . .

Thank God that in Kasrilevka "principles" haven't become fashionable as yet. Those who don't give anything, don't give for the simple reason that they have nothing to give. But when it comes to raising "wheat tithes" for Passover, even that is no excuse. There is a common saying in Kasrilevka: "Every man must either give charity for Passover or he must receive it."

Strange people, these Kasrilevkites. Thousands of years have passed since their great-great-great-grandfathers freed themselves from their Egyptian bondage, and they still can't wean themselves away from the habit of eating *matzos* eight days in a row every year. I am afraid that this cardboard-like delicacy won't go out of fashion for a long, long time to come. All year long a Kasrilevkite is allowed to swell up from hunger, but when Passover comes—let the world stand on its head—he must be provided with *matzos.*

And so it has never yet happened in Kasrilevka that a person has died of hunger during Passover. And if by chance such a thing did happen it should have been marked elsewhere on the calendar. For obviously he did not die because he had no *matzos* to eat during the eight days of Passover, but because he had no bread during the remaining three hundred and fifty-seven days of the year. There is, you will admit, quite a difference between the two.

However, there is no rule to which you won't find an exception. The year in which my story takes place was such an exception, something happened that had been unheard of in the annals of Kasrilevka. It turned out that there were more people asking for help than there were people giving it. If it hadn't been for a feeling of pride, almost everyone in Kasrilevka would have applied for aid. It was truly pitiful to watch our *nogid,* Benjamin Lastechka, sitting in the Committee room the day before Passover, turning away people right and left, saying over and over, "There is no more money. It's all gone. I am very sorry."

"May you live until next year," they answered, and muttered under their noses, "and come to us for charity."

One after another the people came out of the Committee room with empty hands and flushed faces, as though they were coming out of a steam bath, and cursed the rich people with every curse known to them.

The last to enter was a band of young fellows, workingmen, who had been going around all winter without a stitch of work. They were banded together like a commune. They had sold everything they had to sell, and shared the proceeds. One of them had just pawned a silver watch and bought cigarettes which they were all smoking to still their hunger pangs.

When they arrived before the Committee, the workingmen put forward as their spokesman a ladies' tailor, by the name of Samuel Abba Fingerhut. But they didn't let Samuel talk alone. They all helped him present their case, talking, pleading, explaining that they were starving, that they were ready to fall down on their faces and pass out any minute. The Chairman of the Committee, Benjamin Lastechka, let them have their say, and when they were through, he spoke to them:

"I am very sorry, but you are all wasting your breath. First of all, none of you is married, and we give money only to married men. Second, you are healthy young men, well able to work and earn money for Passover. Third, we have a plentiful supply of poor people this year, a bumper crop in fact, more takers than givers. Fourth, we are ashamed to admit it, but since early morning we haven't had a crooked *kopek* in the safe. If you don't believe me, just take a look."

Saying this, the Chairman of the Committee turned all his pockets inside out for everyone to see how empty they were. The young men stood gaping, unable to speak. Only their leader Samuel Fingerhut wasn't overawed. He had a tongue in his head, that one, you didn't have to coach him. He addressed himself to the Chairman, half in Yiddish, half in Russian:

"It's a pity that you didn't start at the end, you would have saved yourself gunpowder. But I can give you an answer to all your arguments. In the first place, that we are single. That's to your advantage—you have that many less poor to provide for. In the second place, that we are able to work. *Zdelatie odolzhenie*—do us a favor: Give us work and we will turn the world upside down for you. Third, you speak of the numbers of poor people. Capitalism is to blame for that, *z'odnoi storoni*—on one side—, and the exploitation of the proletariat, *z'drugoi storoni*—on the other side. Fourth, as for your turning your pockets inside out for us, that's no *dokozhatelstvo*—it doesn't prove a thing. I have no doubt, *naprimer*—for instance—that at home your cupboards are bursting with *matzos,* eggs, onions, goose fat, *i tomu podobnoie*—and other such things—as well as wine for the *Seder*. All of you on the Committee are nothing but bourgeois exploiters and men without conscience, and *bolshe nitchevo*—nothing else—*Tovarishchi,* come, let's go!"

I must report that Kasrilevka, which imitates Odessa and other big towns, has not sufficiently progressed to the extent that an exploiter like our *nogid,* Benjamin Lastechka, should throw open his cupboards, divide the *matzos,* eggs, onions, potatoes, goose fat, and wine among the poor, and leave nothing for himself and his family. But I am convinced as surely as two times two makes four that our Kasrilevka exploiters will do it only if Odessa and Yehupetz and other big cities set the example. Kasrilevka, my friends, is not obliged to be the first at the Fair.

With a clear conscience, bathed, and dressed in holiday clothes, Benjamin Lastechka sat down to the *Seder* with his wife and children the first night of Passover. He felt tranquil and at ease, like a monarch who is secure in his kingdom. On his right hand sat his Queen, his wife, Sara-Leah, also dressed in her holiday best, with a new silk kerchief on her head from the folds of which peeped two dangling earrings of genuine 84-carat silver. All around the table sat the children, the princes and princesses, a whole bouquet of newly washed heads, rosy cheeks, and sparkling eyes. Even Zlatka the servant girl, who all year long labors like a donkey harnessed to a yoke, had washed her hair, bathed with perfumed soap, and put on a new cotton dress, fancy boots, and a wide red ribbon on her black hair. They all felt happy, free and unfettered as though they themselves had just escaped from bondage. The youngest boy had just rattled off the four questions with great aplomb, and his father the King, Benjamin Lastechka, was just beginning to deliver in a slow, solemn chant, at the top of his voice, the age-old response: "Because we were slaves unto Pharaoh in Egypt and the Eternal brought us forth with a mighty hand and with many wonders. And he punished Pharaoh with ten plagues. . . ." Benjamin was just beginning to enumerate the plagues when suddenly . . .

Suddenly there was a knock on the door, then another and then two more knocks. Who could it be? To open or not to open? They decided to open, since the knocking was getting louder and more insistent. The King and Queen and the Princes and Princesses all sat very still while Zlatka the maid opened the door and the band of young fellows entered with their leader, Samuel Abba Fingerhut, in front, and greeted the assembled company with a broad, good *yom-tev.* Our *nogid,* Benjamin Lastechka, though his spirits had sunk far down into his boots at the sight, put on a cheerful face and said, "Good *yom-tev.* Good day. Look who's here! And what good news do you bring?"

Samuel Fingerhut, the spokesman, stepped out from the rest of the group and began a speech in mingled Russian and Yiddish as was his custom:

"Here you sit, all of you, in a bright, warm room with the wine glasses in front of you, observing the holy *Seder,* while we poor proletarians are perishing of hunger outside. I consider this a great injustice. I hereby command you to have the dinner served to us instead. And if anyone of you lets out as much as a peep or opens a window, or dares call the police or—*tomu podobniu*—it will be the worse for you. *Tovarisch* Moishe—where is the bomb?"

The last words were enough to turn the family into graven images right where they sat. But when *Tovarisch* Moishe, a swarthy shoemaker with a black shock of hair falling over his eyes and grimy fingers, approached the table and placed on it a tall, rounded object, covered with a rag, the whole household became as Lot's wife when she turned to see what had become of the cities of Sodom and Gomorrah.

And then Zlatka, the servant girl, her teeth chattering with fright, brought to the table, first the hot, spicy fish, then the soup with dumplings, then the pancakes and other holiday dishes—and the guests went after the food and wine with such appetite you could see they had not eaten for many days. They pledged themselves not to leave a crumb of food or a drop of wine. They even ate up the symbolical foods—the egg and shank-bone, the parsley and the bitter herbs. When they were done, nothing remained of the *Seder* except the prayer books. And while they were eating, the tailor Samuel Fingerhut mocked his host Benjamin Lastechka in these words:

"Every year we recite the *Hagadah* and you eat the dumplings. *Wnastojatcheie wremie*—this time—you recited the *Hagadah* and for once we are eating the dumplings." He raised his wineglass. *"L'chaim* —long life to you—my bourgeois friend, may God grant that you become a proletarian like the rest of us. Next year may we celebrate the Constitution!"

It was long past midnight and the poor *nogid,* Benjamin Lastechka, and all his family still sat around the table. In front of them stood the fearful unknown—the tall, rounded object covered with a rag. The young workingmen had warned them before leaving to remain sitting in their places for two hours—or there would be trouble. That night not one of them slept. They thanked God that they had escaped alive.

Well, and what happened to the tall, rounded object that stood on the table covered with a rag, the anxious reader asks. We are happy to reassure him. A tin container, which once held shoewax, now filled with *matzo* meal is not dangerous. It can stand for a thousand years and it won't blow up anything, except, God forbid—a good *yom-tev.*

The German

I AM as I've told you a Drazhner, that is I come from Drazhne, a tiny, a very tiny town in the Province of Podolia. Nowadays Drazhne has, so to speak, become a big town, with a railway station, a baggage room, a depot. When Drazhne first became a railway town, the whole world envied us. They all thought our fortunes were made. We would be shoveling up money in the streets. The town would become a gold mine. And people began pouring in from the surrounding villages into town. The townspeople began remodeling their houses, putting up new stores. The tax on meat was raised, there was talk of hiring another *shochet,* of building a new synagogue, of buying more land and enlarging the old cemetery. In short, there was great rejoicing. Just think of it. A station, a baggage room, a depot! It's true the town's teamsters rebelled a little, they didn't like the turn of events. But who listened to them? Rails were laid, railway cars brought down, a depot was built, a bell was hung, and a board was nailed up with the words *Stancya Drazhna.* And the deed was done!

When the train began running, my wife said to me, "What do you think you'll be doing now, Jonah?" (That's my name—Jonah.) "What should I be doing? The same thing everybody else is doing. All the citizens of Drazhne are hanging around the train. I'll hang around too." I took my walking stick, strolled over to the depot, and became, with God's help, a station agent—a *pravitel.* What does a station agent do? Well, if a man buys a wagonload of wheat he has to have someone load it on a car and send it off. A *pravitel* does that for him.

But since nearly everybody in Drazhne became a *pravitel,* business was not good. You spent most of your time hanging around, waiting for something to turn up. Sometimes you bought a sack of wheat from a peasant and sold it. You either made a profit on it or you took a loss. Sometimes you picked up a little commission on the side, you tried this, that and the other, anything that came along. But most of the time things were bad. There was nothing to do. You will say that we had nothing to do before either? Yes, but at least we had no railway station then. Now we had a station, with a depot, with a baggage room, with a bell, with trains coming and going, with noise and smoke and confusion—and we weren't any better off!

One day it happened that I was standing at the station in a rather dejected mood seeing off the Potchevo Express. The third bell had sounded, the locomotive had whistled, smoke was pouring out of the chimney. I take a good look, and there on the platform stands a tall, lean individual, an aristocratic-looking fellow in checkered trousers and a tall hat, surrounded by a pile of luggage. He stands there with his long neck stretched out, turning it this way and that way looking for something. "His lordship seems to be in want of something," I think to myself and it's as though something shoved me from behind. "Go up and ask him what he wants." Just as I start out toward him, if he doesn't move right toward me and lift off his tall hat and say to me in German in a sing-song accent, *"Gutt mo-yen, Mein Herr."*

"Good day to you," I answer him, partly in German, partly in Yiddish and the rest with my hands.

I ask him where he hails from. And he asks me if I know of a good inn, that is, a lodging place near by.

"Certainly," I tell him. "Why not?" And to myself I think, "What a pity that I don't own an inn. If only I had an inn I could take him to it myself. He is a fine-looking German, he looks as though he is able to pay." And then a thought flits through my head. "Fool! Is it written on your forehead that you don't own an inn? Just imagine to yourself that you do." And I address myself to him, partly in German, partly in Yiddish and the rest with my hands. "If *Mein Harr* wishes, let *Mein Harr* have me summon a driver and I will lead him, that is, conduct him, to the finest inn, that is, lodging place, immediately."

When he hears this the German is overjoyed and says pointing to his mouth, *"Haben sie vass essen? Shpeizen?"*

"The very best *shpeizen,"* I assure him. "You will feast like a Lord, *Harr* German. For my spouse, that is, my *frau,* is an excellent housekeeper, that is *hausfrau.* Her cooking and her baking are famous in this part of the country. The fish she makes may be eaten by royalty, by Ahasheurus himself."

"Ja wohl," he says joyfully, and his eyes sparkle and his whole face shines like the sun.

"A clever man, this German," I think to myself, and without wasting any more time I hire a wagon and take him straight to my house.

When we arrive I pass the whole story on to my wife—how God has sent me a guest, a German of a very superior sort. But does a woman understand such things? She begins abusing me because I have arrived at the wrong moment, right in the middle of housecleaning. "What's this guest you have there? What's the idea of bringing unexpected guests all of a sudden?"

"Woman," I tell her, "don't converse in our language. This gentleman understands German."

But does she listen to me? She goes on with her cleaning, sweeping her broom right in our faces, muttering angrily. All this time, the German and I are standing in the doorway not knowing whether to back out or to come forward.

At last I convinced her that this was no ordinary guest I was bringing. This guest would pay and pay well for his food and lodging. And we could make something extra from the deal too, lick a bone, as they say. Is that good enough for you? But no, when I finally convinced her, she turns around and says to me, "And where do you want me to put him, in the ground?"

"Be quiet, stupid woman. I told you not to talk, he understands what we are saying."

At last she caught on to what I meant. We showed him to our room, and in no time at all my wife was blowing up the coals under the samovar and getting ready to make supper.

When the German took a look at our room he turned up his nose, as though to say, "It could have been better." But what does a German understand? As soon as the samovar was brought in and tea was brewed, he took out a bottle of rum, poured himself a stiff drink, gave me a little drink too, and all was well. He spread out his suitcases, made himself at home as though he were in his father's vineyard, and we sat down together like old friends.

After we had finished our tea I began a conversation, about this, that and the other. What was he doing in Drazhne? Perhaps he wanted to sell something? Or buy something? It turned out that he was neither buying nor selling. He was expecting some machinery to pass through—some foolishness or other—and in the meanwhile he kept stealing looks into the oven and asking every minute or so when the meal would be ready.

"Apparently, *Mein Harr,*" said I, "you believe in taking nourishment." He didn't answer me. But then how can you expect a German to understand when a person is trying to make a joke?

At last the table was set, and supper was brought in—a hot delicious chicken soup with dumplings, a whole chicken with grits and carrots and parsnips and all the other trimmings. (When my wife wants to she knows how!) "A good appetite to you," I said, but he didn't answer. He was going after that chicken as though he'd just been through a fast. "Enjoy your food in good health," I tell him, and he keeps on guzzling the hot soup. Do you think he even said "thank you" to this? Not a word or a nod. "He has no manners and he is a glutton besides," I think to myself.

Well, he finished eating, lit his pipe and sat smoking and smiling to himself. I could see my German friend looking all about him, he was looking for a place to rest his head, his eyes were shutting, and he wanted to go to sleep.

I beckoned to my wife. "Where can we put him to sleep?"

"What do you mean?" she says. "In my bed, of course."

Without any more ado she goes up to the bed and begins getting it ready for him, beating up the featherbed, beating and fluffing up the pillows. (When my wife wants to she knows how!) I look over at the German—he doesn't look very happy, he is probably displeased because feathers are flying. He wrinkles his nose and begins to sneeze violently.

I tell him, *"Gesundheit, Mein Harr,* long may you live." Do you think he says "thank you" to this? "He has no manners," I think to myself. "He isn't even civilized." Well, my wife made up the bed in good style, with featherbeds and pillows as high as the ceiling. A king might rest in such a bed. We wished him a very good night, and then we all turned in.

After I had gone to bed I heard the German snoring in his room, puffing like a locomotive, then gurgling and whistling like a slain ox. Suddenly he wakes up and begins to moan and groan and to scratch himself, to spit and to mutter. Then he turns over on the other side, begins to snore and to puff and to whistle for a while again, and then wakes up once more with a groaning and a moaning and a scratching and a spitting and mumbling. This happened several times over, until I heard him leap out of bed and begin tossing the bedding to the floor, one pillow after another with terrible fury, uttering strange oaths all the time such as, "A thousand devils! Sacramento! *Donner-wetter!"* I ran up and looked through a crack in the door. There stood my German, stark naked, in the middle of the floor, throwing the pillows one after another off the bed and spitting and cursing fearfully in his own language.

"What seems to be the trouble, *Mein Harr?"* I asked, opening the door. When he saw me, he fell on me in a great fury, hitting out with his fists as though he were going to murder me, then he grabbed my hand and led me to the window. He showed me his body, how it had been bitten all over, then chased me out and shut the door behind me.

"That German is crazy," I told my wife. "And much too finicky besides. He imagines he's been bitten by something and you should hear him. It's the end of the world."

"I can't understand it," my wife said. "What could be biting him? I just cleaned all the bedding for Passover, and doused it in kerosene."

The next morning I thought the German would be so insulted that he would run off to where the pepper trees grow. But nothing doing. He greeted us with a cheerful *"gutt mo-yen,"* again puffed on his pipe, again smiled, and again ordered food to be prepared. He wanted soft-boiled eggs with his tea. And how many do you think? Not less than ten eggs. With his meal, he poured himself a stiff drink, poured me a little drink too, and all was well.

Night came and the same thing happened all over again. At first he snored, whistled, puffed and gurgled, then he moaned, groaned, scratched himself and mumbled, leaped out of bed, threw all the bedding on the floor, spat and cursed in his own language: "To the devil! Sacramento! *Donner-wetter!*" And he got up in the morning, again said *"gutt mo-yen,"* again puffed on his pipe and smiled and ate and poured himself a drink and gave me a little drink too. This went on for several days in a row, until the appointed day came, his machines went through, and it was time for him to leave.

When it was time for him to leave, he began to pack his things, and he asked me to figure what he owed me. "What is there to figure?" I said, "It's a short account. *Harr* German, you owe me exactly twenty-five *rubles.*"

He opened his eyes wide as though to say, "I don't understand." So I said to him in my best German, *"Mein Harr,* you will pay me if you please the sum of twenty-five *rubles,* that is five and twenty *rubles."* And I showed him with my fingers, ten and ten, and then five more. Do you think he appeared shocked at this? Not at all. He merely smiled and puffed on his pipe and then took out a pencil and paper and handed them to me saying that he wanted me to list each item separately.

"You are a clever German," I thought to myself, "but I am cleverer than you. I have more brains in my left heel than you in your whole head."

"Write down, *Harr German,* if you please—For the room, that is for six days' lodging, six times a *ruble* and a half, which makes nine *rubles.* Six times two is twelve samovars, which is twelve *guldens* or ninety *kopeks.* Six times ten eggs in the morning and ten at night is one hundred and twenty eggs, or twice threescore eggs, at a *ruble* a threescore—is two *rubles.* Six chickens at five *guldens* a chicken—aside from the grits and dumplings, the carrots and all the rest—is an even six *rubles.* Six nights—six lamps is sixty *kopeks.* You drank your own schnapps—two *rubles.* You had no sugar or tea—one *ruble,* which makes three *rubles* altogether. You had no wine—one *ruble,* which makes four *rubles* in all. There was no beer—seventy *kopeks.* Five *rubles* altogether. But to make it an even sum, put down five-fifty. Well, Reb German, doesn't that add up to twenty-five *rubles?"* I said this to him in all seriousness, and do you think he disagreed with me? God forbid. He kept on puffing at his pipe and smiling, then he took out a twenty-five *ruble* note and threw it at me the way you might throw a copper coin. We made our farewells, in a most friendly manner, and he went off on the train.

"What do you think of this kind of German, my wife?" said I.

"If God sent us this kind of German every week," she said, "it wouldn't be so bad."

The German left town. Scarcely three days had passed before the mail carrier came and handed me a letter, but first he told me to pay him fourteen *kopeks.* Why fourteen *kopeks?* The sender, he said, forgot to put a stamp on the letter. I paid him fourteen *kopeks* and opened the letter—it's written in German. I can't read a word of it. I began carrying the letter around with me from one end of the town to the other, trying this one and that one. Nobody knew how to read German. What's to be done? I searched the whole town through and at last found one man—the pharmacist at the drugstore—who could read German. He read the letter, then translated it for me. A German was writing to me to thank me for the comfortable and restful lodging he had at my house and for our hospitality and our kind-heartedness which he would never forget.

"Be it so," I think to myself. "If you are happy, I am satisfied." And to my wife I said, "What do you think of our German? Not a little bit of a fool, eh?"

"If God sent us such fools every week," she said, "it wouldn't be so bad."

Another week passed. I come home one day from the railway station and my wife hands me a letter and tells me the mailcarrier told her to pay twenty-eight *kopeks.* "Why twenty-eight *kopeks?"* "Because he wouldn't have it otherwise."

I opened the letter—it's again in German. I ran straight to my pharmacist and asked him to read it to me. The same German, he read, had just crossed the border and since he was on his way to his

Fatherland he wanted to thank me again for the comfortable and restful lodging I had given him and for our hospitality and kind-heartedness which he would never, never forget.

"Let my troubles fall on his head," I thought to myself. When I came home and my wife asked me, "What was in the letter?" I told her, "It's from the German again. He can't forget the favor we did him, the crazy fellow."

"If God sent us crazy fellows like him every week," she said, "it wouldn't be so bad."

Two more weeks passed and a large envelope arrived by mail and I was asked to pay fifty-six *kopeks.* I wouldn't pay it. The mail carrier said, "As you like," and took the letter back. But I had a pang of regret. I was curious to know where the letter was from—maybe it was something important. I paid him the fifty-six *kopeks* and opened the letter. I looked—it's again in German. I went right to my pharmacist and asked him to forgive me for annoying him so often. What else could I do? I was an accursed creature, I couldn't read German. The pharmacist took the letter and read me a long legend. It was the German once more. Since he had just arrived at home, he wrote, and had seen his beloved family, his *"frau"* and his *"kinder,"* he told them the whole story of how he had come to Drazhne, and how he had met me at the station, how I took him to my house, and gave him a most comfortable and restful lodging. Therefore he thanked us over and over for our hospitality and our kind-heartedness which he would never, never forget as long as he lived.

"To the devil with him," I said, wishing him every kind of ill luck. I wouldn't even tell my wife about this letter. I acted as though nothing had happened.

Three more weeks passed and I get a notice from the Post Office for a *ruble* and twelve *kopeks.* "What is this *ruble* and twelve *kopeks?"* my wife asks.

"I haven't the least notion," I told her. "May I know as little of evil." I made straight for the Post Office and began to inquire where I was getting this *ruble* and twelve *kopeks* from. I wasn't getting a *ruble* and twelve *kopeks,* they told me. On the contrary, I had to pay it. "For what?" I asked. "For a letter." "What letter? Maybe it's from the German."

They wouldn't tell me a thing. Would arguing with them have helped? I paid the *ruble* and twelve *kopeks* and got the letter—a large packet this time. I opened it up—it's again in German. I go to my pharmacist. "Forgive me sir, for bothering you again. I have a fresh affliction, a German letter." The pharmacist, not too bright a fellow either, you understand, left all his work in the middle and began reading me another long tale. It was from the same German, may his name be blotted out. What did he write? He wrote that this being a *"Firetag,"* that is a holiday in his country, he had invited all his friends and relatives to his house and when they were all gathered together he told them the whole story from a to z. How he had come to the small town of Drazhne, how he was stranded at the railway station, all alone in a foreign land, unable to speak or understand the language, how he met me and how I took him to my house, in what friendly manner my wife and I received him, gave him a comfortable and restful lodging, let him have the finest room in the house, the best of food and drink and treated him altogether with such honesty and decency, that he couldn't refrain from writing again to thank me for our hospitality and kind-heartedness which he would never, never in the world forget.

"A practical joker, that German," I thought. "I'll never accept another letter, not even if it's stamped with gold."

Another month passed—two months. No more letters. Finished. I was almost beginning to forget about the German. Suddenly there arrives a notice from the railway station that there is a package for me worth twenty-five *rubles*. What kind of package could this be for twenty-five *rubles?* I racked my brain. My wife sat and racked her brain also, and we could think of nothing. Then something occurred to me. We have friends in America—it must be a present from them, a ship's ticket, a lottery ticket, something of the sort. I didn't waste any more time, but went straight to the railway station and asked for my package. They told me to be so kind and please pay two *rubles* and twenty-four *kopeks* first. What could I do—I had to get the two *rubles* and twenty-four *kopeks* and pay it in to get my package.

I got the package—a very handsome little box, carefully wrapped—and ran home with it. I began to unpack the box and what should fall out of it but a portrait? We take a good look. What sort of nightmare or evil visitation is this? The portrait is of him, the *shlimazl,* the German himself with his long scrawny neck, and his tall hat and a pipe in his mouth. With the photograph was a short note written in German, probably the same thing again; he was thanking us for the lodging and our hospitality and our kind-heartedness which he would never, never forget. What a thorn in the flesh this German was getting to be! You can imagine what we both wished him at that moment.

Several more months passed. It's the end. No more German. Thank God we were rid of this affliction. He was as good as buried. My mind was at ease again. I was a happy man. But do you think we were through at last? Listen—it was not the end.

One night without warning there arrived a telegram for me telling me to go to Odessa without fail and to find a certain merchant named Gorgelshtein. This merchant was stopping at the Hotel Victoria and had to see me on very important business. Odessa? Gorgelshtein? Hotel Victoria? Business? "What can it all mean?" I asked my wife. She at once began to urge me to go, for who knows, it might be something important. Maybe a commission, maybe something to do with wheat.

But it's easy to say—go to Odessa. A trip to Odessa costs money. But lack of money is no excuse, when it comes to an important business matter. I borrowed a few *rubles,* got on the train and went off to Odessa. I arrived in Odessa and began inquiring everywhere for the Hotel Victoria. I found the Hotel Victoria, went in, and asked, "Do you have a man here by the name of Gorgelshtein?"

"We have a man by the name of Gorgelshtein," they told me.

"Where is he?"

"He is not in his room right now. Could you please return at ten o'clock in the evening?"

I returned at ten o'clock in the evening. Gorgelshtein was not in. "If you come back at ten in the morning you will find him in."

I came back at ten in the morning. Where was Gorgelshtein? Gorgelshtein had just been there and had left. Before leaving, he had asked them very particularly that if a man from Drazhne should come to see him, they should tell him to be so kind as to return either at three in the afternoon or at ten in the evening.

I returned at three in the afternoon and again at ten in the evening. No Gorgelshtein at either hour.

What more shall I tell you? I wandered around Odessa like a lost soul for six days and six night. I neither ate nor slept. I suffered tortures of body and mind until I finally succeeded in meeting Gorgelshtein.

Gorgelshtein turned out to be a dignified-looking man with a handsome black beard. He greeted me cordially, invited me to be seated.

"You are," he said, half in German, half in Yiddish, "the man from Drazhne."

"I am," I said to him, "the man from Drazhne. What about it?"

"Last winter," he continued, "a certain German lodged at your house."

"Yes," I said. "He did. What about it?"

"Nothing," he said. "This German is a partner of mine in the machinery business." He combed his black beard with his fingers and leaned back in his chair. "I have a letter from him from London. He writes me that when you come to see me in Odessa I must be sure to convey to you his kindest greetings, and to thank you for the comfortable and restful lodging he had at your house and for your hospitality and kind-heartedness. He is indebted to you for your honest and decent treatment of him which he can't possibly forget forever and ever, as long as he lives."

That's the affliction I have to bear. I am planning, with God's help, after the holidays, if God grants me life, to move from Drazhne to some other town. I will run wherever my eyes lead me, wherever my feet carry me, I don't care where, just to get rid of this *shlimazl,* this German, may his name be blotted out from memory forever and ever.

Third Class

THIS, dear reader, is not a story. It is just a few words at parting, a little advice from a good friend.

Before I leave you for good, I should like—out of gratitude for the patience with which you have listened to my tales—to be of some use to you, to leave you with a few last cordial words of advice from a practical person, a traveling salesman. Pay attention to what I tell you and remember it.

If you ever plan to take a trip of any distance at all, and you want to feel that you are really traveling, that is, if you want to get some pleasure out of your trip, don't under any circumstances travel first class or second class.

As far as first class is concerned, there isn't much to say. May Heaven protect you from that! I don't mean the first-class carriage itself. That's comfortable enough. The seats are soft and roomy and rich, with every convenience you can ask for. That much, I'll admit. What I'm talking about is the passengers, the people you have to travel with. The first-class carriage is usually empty, and what's the pleasure in riding all by yourself with no one to talk to? You might even forget *how* to talk. And if once in fifty years you are lucky enough to find another person in the car with you, it turns out to be either a fat aristocrat with puffed-out cheeks like a trombone player blowing on his instrument, or a haughty dame that reminds you of your mother-in-law, or a foreigner in checkered trousers who sits glued to the window so that you couldn't tear him away even if the train caught on fire. If you have to ride with people like that, all sorts of gloomy thoughts begin to crowd into your head, and pretty soon, against your own will, you find yourself thinking about death. And what's the sense of that?

And do you think that second class is any better? Here you sit surrounded by people, people who may look no different from yourself, people with the same desires and the same temptations as yours. They would like to speak to you, they may be dying to know who you are, where you come from and where you're going. But they sit facing each other like dummies in a store window. They have filled their mouths with water and are afraid to open them up. You don't get a word out of them.

Across the aisle from you sits a fashionable gentleman, with long fingernails and a waxed mustache, who looks familiar. You'd swear that you had seen him somewhere before, but you can't remember where. You have a feeling that his pedigree is like yours; his grandfather may have been a count, but much more likely he was a *shammes*. But what can you do when he won't say a word? He twirls his mustache, looks out of the window, and whistles.

If you want to annoy this kind of person, or better still if you want to kill him outright so that he won't even get up on the Day of Resurrection, speak to him in any language you like, but preferably in Russian so that the gentlemen—and even more, the ladies—in the carriage will hear every word: *"Yesli ja nie oshabaius*—if I am not mistaken—didn't I once have the pleasure of meeting you in Berdichev?"

That is a thousand times worse than spitting on his father's grave.

Or if you happen to be somewhere in Poland, you can start talking to him in Polish: *"Pszepraszam pana*—I beg your pardon, sir—but if I am not in error, I think I once had the honor of meeting your father not far from Yarmelinetz. He was a tenant, if I remember correctly, of Count Potocki."

You might argue that this is not such a great insult, but tell me—what does Yarmelinetz and a tenant of Count Potocki smack of? You might as well have come right out and told the whole carriage that this elegant young man is a Jew. But wait! I will tell you something that I actually witnessed and you will see what I mean.

I was traveling in an express train and there was no third-class carriage, so that I had no choice, I had to ride second class. Across the aisle from me sat a young gentleman who might have been either Jewish or Gentile, but he seemed to be more Jewish than Gentile. Still, how could you tell? He was a good-looking young fellow, well-dressed, clean shaven, from all appearances a sportsman, with a black belt on his white trousers, and quite obviously a ladies' man, a gay young blade. Why do I say a blade? Because throughout the trip he was most attentive to a certain young lady, a *fraulein* with an elaborate *chignon* and a pince-nez stuck on a small up-turned nose. They had become acquainted on the train, but they were carrying on like old friends. She offered him chocolates and he, in turn, kept her amused first with Armenian and then with Jewish anecdotes, after which they both rolled with laughter. Especially the Jewish stories, which he told with great gusto, and without paying any attention to the fact that I who sat across from them was a Jew and might feel insulted. . . .

In short, the romance was rolling along, the wheels were well-greased. Before long he was sitting in the same seat with her (at first he had sat across from her) looking deep into her eyes, and she was toying with the chain of his watch. Suddenly at some little station—I have forgotten its name—a man got on, a lame, sallow-faced, perspiring little man with an umbrella. He advanced toward our sportsman, with outstretched hand, and said in a loud voice, in plain, clear Yiddish, "Well, well, how are you? I recognized you through the window. I can give you regards from your uncle Zalman from Menastishtch."

I don't have to tell you that before the train started again our sportsman had disappeared and the young lady was left alone. But that is not the end of the story. A few stations further on the young lady began to get her things together too. Though I sat near her, she didn't even look in my direction. I might as well have not been there. But when she got off, who should meet her on the platform but a fine, patriarchal-looking Jew with a long beard like Father Abraham himself, and a stout woman in a peruke, with diamond earrings. They fell or her neck with tears in their eyes. "Riveleh," they cried, "Riveleh, my daughter."

I don't have to point out the moral of this story. I only wanted to show you the kind of people you meet when you travel second class, and to urge you not to travel that way, because when you travel second class you are bound to feel like a stranger, you're a stranger among your own people.

But if you travel third class, then you're completely at home. If anything, you may feel yourself just a little too much at home. It's true that you won't be as comfortable. If you want a place to sit, you have to fight for it. All around you there is noise and confusion, crowding and pushing. You don't know just where you are and who your neighbors are. But it doesn't take you long to become acquainted with each other. Soon everybody knows who you are, where you are going and what your business is. And you in turn know who they are, where they are going, and what their business is. At night you don't have to worry about sleeping. There is always someone to talk to. And if you don't happen to feel like talking, the others will and you won't get any sleep anyway. But why should anybody want to sleep in a train? There is too much going on all the time. If you talk long enough, you will arrive at something. I have seen perfect strangers close important business deals, find matches for their children, become friends for life in the course of a trip. At the very least you are bound to learn something that will come in handy sometime.

For instance, the conversation will get around to doctors, influenza, toothache, nerves, rest cures, Karlsbad and such things. Sounds like a waste of time, doesn't it? Nevertheless, I once had an experience. . . . I was traveling with a group of men and the talk got around to doctors and medicines and what not. I was suffering at that time from stomach-trouble. One of the men, a salesman from Kamenitz, recommended a powder to me. He had gotten it, not from a doctor of medicine, but from a dentist. It was an excellent remedy, he said, a sort of yellow powder. That is, the powder itself was white like most powders, but it came in a yellow paper. He swore—this salesman from Kamenitz—by his own good health and by his wife and children that if he was still alive today it was due entirely to this yellow powder. If it hadn't been for this powder he would have been eaten by worms long ago!

I wouldn't need many of these powders, he told me. Only two or three and I would be a new man. No more indigestion, no more doctors; bloodsuckers, liars and quacks, every one of them. I could tell them all to go to the devil.

"If you like," he said, "I will give you a few of my powders and you will have something to thank me for the rest of your life."

Well, he gave me the powders. I came home, took one powder, then another, then a third. I went to sleep, and about midnight I woke up in such pain I thought my soul was passing out. I was sure that I was dying. They called a doctor, they called two doctors—they barely saved my life. And now I know from experience that if a Kamenitzer salesman offers you a yellow powder that is a sure cure for anything, you can tell *him* to go to the devil. You see, every bit of knowledge has its price.

If you are traveling third class and the time comes for morning prayers and you don't have a *tallis,* a prayer shawl, and *tfillin,* or phylacteries, with you, don't worry. Someone will see to it that you get both *tallis* and *tfillin,* and anything else you need. In return, however, when you are through with your prayers, be so kind please as to open your suitcase and pass around whatever food you have brought. Whisky is good, cakes are fine, eggs are always welcome, chicken or fish are excellent. If you have only an apple or an orange or a piece of *shtrudel,* don't be ashamed, pass it around. We'll take whatever you have to offer, nobody will refuse. On the road and in company, appetites are lively.

If you have a bottle of whisky or wine with you, you will certainly get plenty of customers. Everyone will taste your wine and give you his expert opinion of it. One will tell you that it's Bessarabian Muskat, another that it's imported Akerman. A third will get up and try to shout them both down: "What do you mean—Akerman? Muskat? It's a Kovashener Bordeaux." At this, another man will appear from the farthest corner and with a knowing smile will take the glass out of your hands as if to say, "Listen to me, friends, when it comes to wine, ask a real expert." He takes a few sips, his cheeks begin to flame and he becomes as jolly as a wedding guest. He lifts the glass and announces, "Gentlemen, do you know what this is? I can see quite clearly that you don't. It's plain—simple—pure—clean—kosher home-made Berdichev port."

And everyone agrees with him, that's just what it is, Berdichev port, the kind we make in our own cellars. And everyone takes a few more sips, and everyone's tongue becomes loosened, and he tells you all about himself, and listens while you tell about yourself. We talk, joke, exchange stories, like good friends and comrades. It's a wonderful feeling.

If you are traveling third class to a town you're not familiar with and if you don't know where to stop, ask anyone in the carriage. You will get as many suggestions as there are people. One will tell you that the only place to consider is the Frankfurt Hotel. The Frankfurt, he will tell you, is bright and clean, and warm and cheap. "Frankfurt?" another will break in. "God help you. It's dark and dingy and cold and dear, they'll rob you. If you want to be comfortable, go to the Hotel New Yorker." At this a third man interrupts, "What for? Is he lonesome for bedbugs? Don't listen to them. Frankfurt, New Yorker, bah. You come with me, let me take your suitcase and we'll go to the only good hotel in town, the Rossya. That's where real Jews go."

But be careful about letting him take your suitcase, or you may never see it again. But I ask you, is there any place nowadays in this land of ours where you can be sure that you won't be robbed? After all, being robbed or not being robbed, if you want to know the truth, is no more than a matter of destiny. If it is your fate to be robbed, it will happen to you in broad daylight on the public highway. Police won't save you, neither will a bodyguard. And neither will prayers. If you come out alive, you can bless your lucky stars!

So you might as well travel third class. Take the advice of a good friend and a practical man, a traveling salesman.

Adieu. . . .

Glossary

Bar Mitzvah: A thirteen-year-old Jewish boy who is confirmed; the confirmation ceremony itself.

beigel: Hard circular roll with hole in center like a doughnut.

blintzes: Cheese or *kasha* rolled in thin dough and fried.

borsht: A beet or cabbage soup, of Russian origin.

cheder: Old-style orthodox Hebrew school.

charoses: A mixture of nuts and apples to symbolize the clay which the children of Israel worked into bricks as slaves in Egypt. Eaten at the *Seder* services on Passover.

datcha: Summer cottage in the country.

farfel: Doughy preparation cut into small pieces.

Gamorah: The Aramaic name for the *Talmud*. (See *Talmud*.)

Gehenna: Hell.

groschen: Small German silver coin whose old value was about two cents.

gulden: Austrian silver florin worth about forty-eight cents.

Gymnasia: A secondary school preparing for the university.

Hagadah: The book containing the Passover home service, consisting in large part of the narrative of the Jewish exodus from Egypt.

hamantash: A triangular pocket of dough filled with poppyseed or prunes, and eaten on Purim.

Hannukah: Described variously as "The Festival of Lights," "The Feast of Dedication," and "The Feast of the Maccabees." It is celebrated for eight days from the 25th day of *Kislev* (December). It was instituted by Judas Maccabeus and the elders of Israel in 165 B.C. to commemorate the rout of the invader, Antiochus Ephinanes, and the purification of the Temple sanctuary.

Hashono Rabo: The seventh day of *Succos* (Feast of Booths).

kaddish: The mourner's prayer recited in synagogue twice daily for one year by the immediate male relatives, above thirteen years of age, of the deceased; a son who recites the *kaddish* for a parent.

kasha: Groats.

kiddush: Ceremonial blessing said before Sabbath and other holiday meals.

knishes: Potato or *kasha* dumpling, fried or baked.

Kol Nidre: The opening prayer of the synagogue liturgy on the eve of *Yom Kippur.*

kopek: Small copper coin; there are about 100 *kopeks* in a *ruble.*

kreplach: Small pockets of dough filled with chopped meat, usually boiled and eaten with chicken soup.

luftmensch: Literally "air man," but refers to a person who has neither trade, calling, nor income and is forced to live by improvisation, drawing his livelihood "from the air" as it were.

mah nishtano: Literally, "What is the difference?" The first words in the opening "Four Questions" of the Passover *Hagadah,* traditionally asked by the youngest child in the household at the *Seder* service.

matzos: Unleavened bread eaten exclusively during Passover to recall the Jewish Exodus from Egypt.

mazl-tov: Good luck.

mazuza: Small rectangular piece of parchment inscribed with the passages Deut. VI. 4-9 and XI. 13-21, and written in twenty-two lines. The parchment is rolled up and inserted in a wooden or metal case and nailed in a slanting position to the right-hand doorpost of every orthodox Jewish residence as a talisman against evil.

Megilah: Literally "a roll," referring to the Book of Esther which is read aloud in the synagogue on *Purim.*

medresh: A citation from the *Midrash,* a body of exegetical literature, devotional and ethical in character, which attempts to illuminate the literal text of the Bible with its inner meanings. The *Midrash* is constantly cited by pious and learned Jews in Scriptural and *Talmudic* disputation.

melamed: Old-style orthodox Hebrew teacher.

nogid (pl. *negidim*)*:* A rich man, the leading secular citizen of a community.

Purim: Festival of Lots, celebrating the deliverance of the Jews from

Haman's plot to exterminate them, as recounted in the Book of Esther. It is celebrated on the 14th and 15th of *Adar,* the twelfth Jewish lunar month (March).

Reb: Mister.

rebbitzen: The rabbi's wife.

Rosh Hashono: The Jewish New Year, celebrated on the 1st of *Tishri* (in September); the most solemn day next to *Yom Kippur.*

Seder: The home service performed on the first two nights of Passover.

shadchan: A matchmaker; a marriage broker.

Shalachmones: A friendly offering of food or drinks on *Purim.*

shammes: A synagogue sexton.

Shevuos: Variously known as "The Festival of Weeks" and "Pentecost." It originally was a harvest festival and is celebrated seven weeks after Passover.

shlimazl: One who has perpetual bad luck. Everything happens to him.

Shma Yisroel: The first words in the confession of the Jewish faith: "Hear, O Israel: the Lord our God the Lord is One!"

Shmin-esra: Eighteen (actually nineteen) benedictions, forming the most important part of the daily prayers, recited silently, standing up, by the worshipper.

shochet: Ritual slaughterer.

shofar: Ram's horn blown in the synagogue at services on *Rosh Hashono.*

Sholom aleichem: Peace be unto you! Equivalent to the more prosaic greeting "Hello!"

Simchas Torah: "Rejoicing over the *Torah,*" the last day of *Succos* (Feast of Tabernacles), celebrating the completion of the reading of the *Torah.*

Slichos: Penitential prayers.

succah: A booth made of fresh green branches in which pious Jews celebrate the Feast of Tabernacles. This is done symbolically to recall the forty years of wandering—"that your generation may know that I made the children of Israel to dwell in booths, when I brought them out of the land of Egypt."

Succos: The Feast of Tabernacles, survival of the ancient festival on which male Jews were required to go on a pilgrimage to the Temple in Jerusalem. Lasts nine days and begins on the 15th day of the seventh lunar month of *Tishri* (September-October).

sudah: A feast.

tallis: Prayer shawl.

Talmud: The Corpus Juris of the Jews. A compilation of the religious, ethical and legal teachings and decisions interpreting the Bible; completed circa A.D. 500.

Talmud Torah: Hebrew school for children.

teigl: A confection.

tfillin: Phylacteries.

Tish'abov: Ninth day of the month of *Ab* (August) set aside by Jewish tradition for fasting and mourning to commemorate the destruction of Jerusalem and the Temple, by Nebuchadnezzar in 586 B.C. and by Titus in A.D. 70.

Torah: "Doctrine" or "law"; the name is applied to the five books of Moses (Pentateuch), and in a wider sense to all sacred Jewish literature.

treif: Food forbidden by dietary laws or not prepared according to their regulations.

tzimmes: Dessert made of sweetened carrots or noodles.

vertutin: Cheese or cooked cherries rolled in dough.

yeshiva: Talmudic college.

Yom Kippur: Day of Atonement. The most important Jewish religious holiday; a fast day, spent in solemn prayer, self-searching of heart and confession of sins by the individual in direct communion with God. Takes place on the 10th day of *Tishri,* eight days after *Rosh Hashono.*

yom-tev: Holiday.